"A beautiful and haunting book. Not only does Mr. Dunning offer us a terrific plot and intriguing characters, he also re-creates a whole bygone era and provides an insider's view of the workings of a small wartime radio station. Fascinating stuff."

—Peter Robinson, author of *In a Dry Season*

BOOKED TO DIE

"A joy to read for its wealth of inside knowledge about the antiquarian book business and its eccentric traders. . . . A soundly plotted, evenly executed whodunit in the classic mode. . . . Cliff Janeway makes a honey of a debut."

—*The New York Times Book Review*

"I am . . . an unabashed admirer of John Dunning's *Booked to Die*. No one . . . can fail to be delighted by the sort of folkloric advice Janeway carries with him."

—*Boston Sunday Globe*

THE BOOKMAN'S WAKE

"Dunning weirdly and wonderfully intersperses publishing arcana with fisticuffs, gunplay, and an impossibly dense plot, until he has you believing the unspeakable things his obsessional cast would do for a single precious book."

—*Kirkus Reviews*

"The author immerses the reader in this intriguing, little-known milieu without losing sight of the page-turning yarn he's spinning. In the end you may be disappointed that the last plot twist has finally played out."

—*People*

TWO O'CLOCK, EASTERN WARTIME

A NOVEL

JOHN DUNNING

$(\ (\ (\ \bullet\ )\ )\ )$

POCKET BOOKS

NEW YORK LONDON TORONTO SYDNEY SINGAPORE

This book is a work of fiction. Names, characters, places, and
incidents are products of the author's imagination or are used
fictitiously. Any resemblance to actual events or locales or persons,
living or dead, is entirely coincidental.

 POCKET BOOKS, a division of Simon & Schuster, Inc.
1230 Avenue of the Americas, New York, NY 10020

Copyright © 2001 by John Dunning

Originally published in hardcover in 2001 by Scribner

All rights reserved, including the right to reproduce
this book or portions thereof in any form whatsoever.
For information address Scribner, 1230 Avenue of the
Americas, New York, NY 10020

ISBN: 0-7434-0615-X

Pocket Books printing January 2002

10 9 8 7 6 5 4 3 2 1

POCKET and colophon are registered trademarks of
Simon & Schuster, Inc.

For information regarding special discounts for bulk purchases,
please contact Simon & Schuster Special Sales at 1-800-456-6798
or business@simonandschuster.com

Cover design by Rod Hernandez; front cover illustration by Brian Bailey

Printed in the U.S.A.

TWO O'CLOCK, EASTERN WARTIME

The Face
from
the Past

(((1)))

DULANEY dreamed there was no war. A thousand years had passed and he had come to the end of an endless journey, closing an infinite circle in time and space. But when he opened his eyes it was still Sunday, May 3, 1942.

He had slept less than two hours. The sky outside his window had just gone dark but the moon was up, shrinking his world to a small silver square on the floor, this eight-by-ten room with bars. His eyes probed the shadows beyond his cell—the dark hallway, the line of light on the far side of the bullpen where the office was. He had come awake thinking of Holly.

His peace had been shaken. The steadiness born in his soul now drained away, leaving a growing sense of unease. He heard the radio droning in the outer office. Charlie McCarthy had given way to Walter Winchell with no loss of comedy, but even when the jailer laughed at something Winchell had said, even with the sound of another human voice in close proximity, Dulaney felt isolated, alone on an alien planet in a time he barely knew.

Winchell had a name for Hitler's gang. The Ratzis had struck again. Exeter had been bombed in retaliation for RAF raids on Lübeck and Rostock. There was an almost imperceptible lull as Winchell hit a word beyond his grade-school vocabulary. Baedeker raids, Dulaney thought as if coaching. They were called Baedeker raids because they were aimed at the guidebook towns that symbolized British antiquity.

Winchell blew the word, but by then Dulaney was only half listening. He was thinking about Holly and the last time he had seen her, almost two years ago in New York. He had collected his pay and gone back to his apartment to clear out his stuff, and there she was waiting for him. She had been sitting on the floor all night, in the hallway outside his door. They walked through Central Park and the air was clear and cold, the trees stripped bare in the third week of autumn and the leaves rustling under their feet. The skyline loomed over the trees and at last she made the effort to say her piece. She looped her arm in his and drew him close. "These things happen, Jack. It's nobody's fault, least of all yours." But he wouldn't let her get into it any deeper than that, and it was the only time they had touched even the edges of what they both knew had always been between them.

She understood then the hopelessness of it. They walked out of the park and stood self-consciously outside the apartment house that in another hour would be his former address. Dulaney offered coffee but she said no, she'd rather just say good-bye here on the street. She took his hand. "It's all right, Jack. Everything's fine."

Just before she walked away she said one last thing to him. "You told me something once and I can't get it out of my mind. A man needs something that's bigger than life, something he'd die for. I've been thinking about that all night."

"That sounds like me. Sounds a little silly now, doesn't it?"

She shook her head, impatient at his attempt to belittle it. "Good-bye, Jack. I wish only good things for you. I hope you find whatever life holds that makes you feel that way."

But he had already found it. He knew it then, in New York; knew it now, sitting alone in a California jail cell. This thought sank into silence. Then, from the darkness beyond the bullpen, he heard Winchell's announcer, recapturing the moment for the makers of Jergens lotion.

(((**2**)))

TODAY, if she should by some trick materialize in the jail beside him, he could do a better job explaining it to her. It began with the fact that his lifelong pal had seen her first. He would always think of them as a couple, even if the stars weren't working and they never actually married. She knew this, of course, but there are shades of truth. He and Tom had been closer than brothers.

Most people would say that didn't matter now. Tom Rooney was at the bottom of Pearl Harbor, but even after his death she was still, in Dulaney's mind, Tom's woman. He would not come slithering upon her like some carpetbagger, wearing the shoes of a summer soldier. Tom would come calling, like Marley in chains.

But she was always on his mind as he worked his way across the land, and he'd thought about little else since yesterday noon. It had begun with the clang of the jailhouse door, the deputy waking him from a light sleep. "You got comp'ny, Dulaney. Fella says he's your lawyer."

Dulaney didn't have a lawyer. It had to be Kendall: nobody else would know or care where he might possibly be. The deputy opened the cell and motioned Dulaney ahead of him, along a dimly lit hallway to a little room at the end. The window was barred and the room was empty except for a battered wooden table and two rickety chairs.

Kendall was sitting in one of the chairs. He didn't look like a lawyer. His clothes, like Dulaney's, were those of a workingman. His shoes were scuffed and coming out at the toes. He looked like what he was, an out-of-work radio actor who had seen better days.

They shook hands and Dulaney sat at the table. The deputy stayed in the room, at the edge of earshot.

"How'd you find me, Marty?"

Kendall smiled sadly. "You weren't at the hotel, so I tried the café. I got there just as the paddy wagon was pulling out."

"I'm a little amazed they let you in here."

Kendall lowered his voice, cutting his eyes at the deputy. "I keep telling you, Jack, I was a damn good actor in my day. So what happened?"

Dulaney smiled. "Just a little mayhem. Resisting arrest. Assault on a police officer. Kid stuff."

Kendall stifled the urge to laugh. Dulaney noticed streaks of gray in his mustache and in the curly hair around his ears.

He had always thought of Kendall as around forty but now he thought fifty was closer.

He told Kendall how the trouble had started. He had gone out to get something to eat. Some sailors and some girls started razzing him about being in the home guard. "I guess I was the only fellow in the place out of uniform. This is nothing new. In the Civil War women would see a man out of uniform and they'd shame him in public."

Kendall said nothing. "They probably don't bother you," Dulaney said. "You're a bit older than me. And most of the time I don't let it bother me. But this one gal wouldn't leave it alone. She had the waiter bring me some squash. That's supposed to be the last word in insults. You feed squash to the home guard so the color'll stay bright in their backbones."

"So what did you do?"

"Hell, I like squash. Figured I might as well eat it." Dulaney leaned forward. "I've been hungry enough times that I'm not about to let good food get chucked just because some silly female wasn't raised right. What happened next is probably in the arrest report."

"They say you took on the whole café."

"One thing led to another. I finally told those boys they'd end up in the clap shack if they didn't quit messing with whores. I didn't have to say that, but there we were. The sailors had to stand up and they came up short. If those are the best fighting men we've got in this war, we may be in trouble."

The deputy cleared his throat. "You boys start winding it up."

"It didn't last long. The gendarmes came, four big cops with their billies out." Dulaney touched his head, a tender place the size of a peach.

"I wish you hadn't taken on the cops, Jack."

"I've got nothing against cops as a rule, but the sight of a billy club gets my back up. I've known too many good people who got their heads busted open just because they were down on their luck. So here I am."

"I hear judges get real mean when you start fighting with cops."

"The guard says he'll give me six months, unless I've got the money for the fine. That seems to be automatic for a first offense. If I volunteer to go to the work camp he'll cut my time in half."

"What are you talking about, a chain gang?"

"They don't call it that and they don't chain you together. I get the feeling it's not official and maybe that's why we get to choose. The word comes back to the prisoners through the guards—if you work, they'll cut your time; if you don't, you go to jail and serve it all."

"Man, that stinks. Goddamn judge is probably getting paid off."

"Maybe so, but I'm going to take it. I'll use it in a book."

Kendall didn't say anything but again Dulaney felt a strain in the room between them. He couldn't put his finger on it, what it was about Kendall that had bothered him from the start. He thought there was a lie somewhere, that some part of Kendall's old life had been omitted or fabricated, and Kendall couldn't lie without turning away. Kendall had been an accomplished radio actor who could live a dozen lies a week on the air, but in real life he was like Dulaney: he couldn't lie to a friend.

"What's the matter with you, Marty? Something's been eating you since the day we met."

The deputy's voice cut across the room. "You boys about done?"

"Give us one more minute," Dulaney said.

He leaned over, and softly, so the guard wouldn't hear, said, "Are you in trouble with the law?"

"Hell no. I've never even been inside a jail before today. Christ, why would you even think of something like that?"

"I've been around enough men on the lam to know another one when I see him. Something's been on your mind, right from the start."

Kendall shook his head, a slight movement, barely perceptible. "That doesn't make any sense. How could I be running from the law and still trying to get back into radio?"

Dulaney waited but Kendall did not enlighten him. The guard made a time's-up motion with his hands. Dulaney said,

"Look, I'd appreciate it if you'd check me out of that hotel. Pick up my papers and my notes. There's a half-finished story I'm working on: make sure you get that. Put it in a box and stash it in the trunk of the car."

"Consider it done."

"You've been a good friend, Marty. Even if I'm not always sure I know you."

"Let's go, boys," the deputy said.

But then at the last moment Kendall said, "Just one more thing. Do you know a woman named Holly Carnahan?"

Dulaney tensed. "Yes, I know Holly."

"There's a letter for you at the hotel. It just came today. It's three months old."

"Go back to the hotel right now," Dulaney said. "Open it and read it, then come here tomorrow and tell me what it says."

$$((3))$$

HE thought about Holly all afternoon and occasionally he thought about Kendall. He still thought Kendall had done something somewhere. Maybe it hadn't been illegal but it had shamed him and kept him looking over his shoulder. Kendall had suddenly appeared at Santa Anita last November, a fellow down on his luck who'd drifted into racetrack life hoping to find some contentment there. It was a lean life. A man could walk horses six hours and make $3. He could sleep free on an army cot in the tack room, and $3 was good money when all he needed was food and an occasional pair of dungarees. Dulaney knew men who had done this all their lives.

A camaraderie forms between men who cook for one another on tack room hot plates and take their suppers together in racetrack kitchens: who pick up one another's mail, sleep in the same small room, and shower in the same open bathhouse. But the race meet never got under way that winter.

Pearl Harbor got bombed and the whole West Coast was a military zone, the racetrack put under control of the army. "There's a rumor that we're closed for the duration," Kendall said one night. "They're going to turn it into a camp for American Japs."

Until they did, the horses had to be walked. In one sense it didn't matter: Kendall and Dulaney each had a greater purpose in life. Dulaney had a book to write and Kendall kept talking about returning to big-time radio. Kendall had been one of New York's busiest radio actors. In his best year, 1938, he had worked fifteen shows a week, hopping across networks and using the full range of his talent on the soap serials of Frank and Anne Hummert. He was an elderly shopkeeper on *John's Other Wife* and a high-strung concert pianist on *Just Plain Bill*. He carried a torch for Young Widder Brown, helped Stella Dallas find her lost daughter, Laurel, and plotted against Lord Henry Brinthrope on *Our Gal Sunday*. Kendall spoke of these melodramas so often that Dulaney could almost hear them in his mind, though he seldom listened to the radio. To Kendall it was part of a glorious past, lost to alcohol. The Hummerts gave no second chances: Kendall had missed a rehearsal and was fired from six continuing daytime roles. Word spread through the trade: Kendall was on the bottle. Within a year he was finished.

Dulaney had told Kendall little of his life. Kendall knew he was writing a book, but Dulaney had not revealed what he wrote or how long it might take him to finish it. Dulaney had made himself a promise: he would finally get serious about his new novel, which would be dedicated to his dead friend Tom. He rented a room offtrack, where he worked from noon, when the last horse was walked cool and put away, until the creative spark burned out, around seven o'clock at night. Then he'd walk back to the track, across the endless parking lot to the stable area, where he'd eat supper with Kendall and turn in by nine. In the morning it would begin again. They divvied up the chores and Kendall always picked up the mail for both of them. Kendall had a thing about the mail: he was always there when the mail room opened in the morning, and his pursuit of the mail now struck Dulaney as curious. Dulaney never got any mail. He had drifted after Tom's death, moving from one racetrack to another, seldom bothering with changes of address until Kendall met him at Santa Anita.

On days when his novel bogged down he wrote short stories about racetrackers. His agent had begun placing them in magazines, and one day Kendall saw one of the magazines and asked if he might read what Dulaney had written. It was a sad tale about a man who had bought a cheap and gimpy claiming horse, saving it from the killers: how he'd done this with money he'd put away for his daughter's education, how he'd nursed the horse back to health, but an unscrupulous trainer, posing as a friend, had stolen the horse through the claiming process just as it was ready to win again. Kendall chased him down with a wild, excited look in his eyes. He followed Dulaney around the tow ring, gushing over the lyrical truth of what Dulaney had written.

Dulaney had published six of the racetracker stories and now Kendall read them all. And in Dulaney's small success Kendall saw the chance of his own salvation. "Jack, these would make fantastic radio plays. If you can put 'em in script, I *know* I could get a national client interested. Once you've got a client, the networks fight over you."

Dulaney was intrigued in spite of himself and Kendall was on fire with it. "Man, I'm talking about real radio, not the junk I did for the Hummerts. I'm talking about something so new and exciting that nobody knows how good it can be."

Dulaney led his horse off under the trees for a roll in the sand. Kendall persisted, following at his heels. "You've got a gift, Jack, and I'm gonna be your calling card straight to the big time. I know everybody in New York radio. I'll be your agent."

"I've got an agent, Marty. His name's Harold Ober."

"Get rid of him. He can't do what I can do for you."

"I was a long time getting this agent. He represents William Faulkner and some other writers I admire." Dulaney didn't like saying this. It made him feel like a cheap name-dropper. But when Kendall still wasn't impressed, he said, "Maybe you've heard of Scott Fitzgerald. Ober was his agent, so if I seem a little too proud of myself, that's the reason why."

Kendall smiled sadly, like a man losing an argument he should by all rights be winning. "Goddammit, Dulaney, you could be another Norman Corwin. Do you understand what I'm telling you?"

Even Dulaney had heard of Corwin, resident genius on the Columbia Network, who was said to be producing the first real literature of the air. Dulaney had always wanted to hear one of Corwin's programs but had never been next to a radio when they came on.

They stood in the Santa Anita mail room filling out change-of-address forms, and he told Kendall he'd think about it. Maybe he'd write and ask Ober about it when they got up to Tanforan.

The next night Kendall had a radio playing in the tack room. On Monday they heard *A Tale of Two Cities* with Ronald Colman playing his role from the movie. Dulaney knew Dickens well and he figured they'd caught the heart of it, dressed it up with music and sound, and made it play in his mind, all in sixty minutes, less gab time for Lux soap. He stood in the shedrow and filled his water cup as the guillotine fell, and he looked off to the Hollywood hills, fifteen miles away, where they were doing it at that exact moment, and he was touched by the miracle of it.

They pooled their money, $75, and bought a car: a bright red Essex twelve years old with a radio that played. On a warm Sunday night they drove north looking for work. They listened to a mangy love drama, then an all-girl orchestra that reached across the country from Cincinnati. It was WLW, Kendall said: "Greatest signal in the universe. You can't flush your crapper in Dayton without WLW comes out of the pipes."

What amazed Dulaney was the versatility, the scope. You heard something great, then something so bad it almost hurt your ears to listen. Bad or good, it never stopped. Radio consumed material like a runaway fire. It burned words like tinder.

They arrived at Tanforan, just south of Frisco, but again the horses had been moved out and Japanese families were living in the stalls. A cop had replaced the guard at the stable gate and the place had the air of a concentration camp. Dulaney walked around the compound and watched the processing through the high wire fence. New arrivals were unloaded from a truck while a fat man in uniform called their names. "Mr. Ben Doi," the man said, and Mr. Doi stepped forward and his eyes found Dulaney's through the wire. The woman who was probably his wife looked at no one. Their children faced the terrors of the camp with brave, dry eyes. The little girl saw Dulaney watching and waved shyly, and suddenly he felt a streak of indignation. What had these Japs done to be yanked out of their homes and locked in a barn still reeking of horse turds? I will write about this, he thought.

It looked like racing was finished on the coast. They heard that Bay Meadows might still have a meet, and Longacres might open if a man wanted to go to Seattle on the chance of it. But there was plenty of work; the depression was over and they had no trouble finding jobs. Kendall had their mail routed to general delivery and they slipped into new lives away from the horses. They were working half days in a labor pool, giving Dulaney five good hours to write. At night Kendall would come and dole out what mail there was; they'd eat supper together and perhaps later they'd listen to the radio and talk about heading east. Soon there'd be a summer lull on the air as the big-time comedians and the established crime shows took their eight-week vacations. This was the time to try something new.

It was a daunting prospect to a high school dropout who had never seen the inside of a broadcast station. He put off writing to Ober and started another racetracker story. Then he got arrested, and now it would be a while before Ober heard from him about anything.

((4))

In the morning he was taken to the same room, where Kendall was already waiting at the same table. Kendall looked pale, like a man who'd slept with a goblin. Or a bottle. Dulaney felt heartsick in the face of news that was sure to be bad, but when Kendall spoke, it was not about Holly at all. "What's going on with you, Jack?"

"What's going on how? What are you talkin' about?"

"Yesterday you asked me what's going on with me. Now I'm asking you the same question. There's something you haven't told me about."

Dulaney fought back his impatience. "That could be anything. There's a lot two fellows won't know about each other when they haven't been together six months yet. Hell, Marty, you know I'm not the confessor type."

"I'm not talking about your love life." Kendall's eyes were red and watery.

Again Dulaney wondered if he'd dropped off the wagon and he decided to ask straight-out. "Are you drinking again?"

"Not a drop, Jack. I swear, I haven't had a drink the whole year."

"Then what's wrong with you?"

"I just need to tell you something. I've been thinking about it for some time now, but I don't know how to get at it."

Kendall was sitting half turned in the chair, looking at Dulaney in profile. He's in pain, Dulaney thought: somebody worked him over.

"What happened to you, Marty? You look like you can barely sit up."

"I took a fall, that's all." But as their eyes met, the truth came out: Kendall shrugged and said, "I got mugged last night."

Dulaney started to speak but Kendall cut him off. "That guard's not gonna give us all day." But again as Dulaney waited the seconds ticked away.

Finally Kendall said, "The road does funny things to two guys. After a while you grow on each other. You know what I'm saying?"

Dulaney nodded, but warily.

"So what do you think, Jack? Am I your friend, or just some goombah you're killing time with?"

Kendall was looking straight into his eyes now and Dulaney understood what he wanted. Acquaintances came and went; a friend was for life, and Dulaney had never made friends easily. You never knew about each other until you had passed some test of fire together.

The question hung in the air and now Dulaney had to grope for an answer. What he said was half-assed but the best he could do. "I think we've got the start of a good friendship. There's no telling where something like that can go."

Kendall gave a dry little laugh.

"These things take time, Marty. But I do believe we'll be friends."

Kendall looked at his feet. "Well, I've come to think of you as my friend, even if you don't quite feel that way. But maybe it's time I moved on."

"If that's how it is, I can understand that."

"There's nothing I can do for you here. I'd just be marking time. Maybe later, if you wanted to look me up."

Dulaney just watched him. Something was eating him, you could see it working on him. The lie, Dulaney thought: he's trying to get rid of all the stuff he's been lying about.

"I want you to remember this," Kendall said. "What I told you about radio is God's truth. You could set that world on its ass. You already know how to make words live. And you've got one other thing. You make people want to do their best for you. I hear Corwin's got that. Maybe that's why he directs his own stuff so well. People give him every-thing they've got. This is all gospel now, straight from the heart."

"I never doubted that. At least I know you believe it."

"Hang on to that thought because now I've got to tell you something that hurts. You've already guessed it, I haven't been square with you. We didn't just meet by accident. I was sent to find you."

Dulaney glared across the table. "You found me months ago. Why am I just hearing about it now? And who the hell is this who's taken such an interest in my habits?"

Kendall shook his head. "I've got some more thinking to do before I decide to tell you that."

"Did somebody rough you up on my account?"

Kendall said nothing but his silence said much.

"Who beat you up, Marty?"

"Just a thug. Some goddamn mulligan. I don't know who he was."

"But you know why he did it. Don't deny that, I can see it in your face. Somebody sent him to work you over. Something about me."

Dulaney thought about old enemies, but none he could remember would have gone to such trouble. Suddenly the guard stirred and Dulaney was aware of the time. "What about Holly?"

"I don't know. She seems to be the cause of it."

Dulaney absorbed this in a long moment. "This is hard for me to imagine. In all these months you never once mentioned her name."

"You weren't supposed to know."

"Know what, for Christ's sake?" Dulaney's anger was so strong now that Kendall could barely look at him.

"I'm sorry, Jack. It was just an acting job to me. That's how it started. Then we got to know each other."

"You son of a bitch."

"I did it because I needed the money. I didn't know you or this woman." Kendall tried to look away but Dulaney gripped his arm.

"Tell me about the letter."

"She . . . said she needed something. Something you've been holding for her. She had . . . gotten herself in some kind of jam. Butted heads with somebody, made herself a powerful enemy."

This sounded unreal. It sounded calmly terrifying. It grew like a virus, gripping him tighter with every heartbeat.

"What was it she wanted?"

"Don't you know that?"

"How the hell would I know? When was this letter mailed?"

"Postmark was February."

Three months ago. She had been in trouble three months ago and had written him for help.

"Where was it mailed?"

"Someplace called Sadler, Pennsylvania."

Her hometown. The weight of it grew as he sat thinking. "This changes everything," he whispered.

Kendall didn't seem to hear, or understand what he meant. "Listen, Jack, if you want my strong advice, I say send her what she wants. Tell me where it is and I'll take care of it for you today. Maybe it's some little thing her father sent."

Again this startled him. "How do you know about her father?"

"That's not important now. We're gonna run out of time."

Dulaney nodded at the guard, hoping to buy a few extra minutes. "I haven't got anything of Holly's," he said. "Her father never sent me anything."

Kendall leaned toward him, his face flushed. "Jack, listen to me. Whatever it is, let's give it up. These people aren't fooling around. Man, I think that gorilla cracked one of my ribs."

"Who are these bastards? . . . You called the tough one a mulligan. In my lingo that's an Irish hood."

"He's Irish, all right." Kendall swallowed hard and Dulaney could see the pain in his face. "He doesn't matter. He's just a thug."

Dulaney sat still, listening to time run down in his head. Three months ago she had been in trouble. Three months.

"Time's up, boys."

Dulaney said, "Just a minute, please," and suddenly he had a hundred questions and no time for any of them.

"Did you get my stuff out of the hotel?"

"It's in the car. But listen, Jack—"

Dulaney held up his hand. "I'm coming out of here."

"How, for Christ's sake?"

"You can always run from a road gang if you're willing to risk taking some buckshot."

Kendall closed his eyes and shuddered. "Are you crazy?"

"You can help me, or not. Either way I'm coming out."

Suddenly the thing took another twist. Kendall leaned close and his voice was a trembly whisper. "You're going to get yourself killed for nothing. Listen to me now, Jack. Listen! . . . There is no letter."

"Now what are you saying?"

"There is no letter. There never was any letter. I was told to say that. I'm telling you the truth now, Jack. It's all a ruse."

The deputy coughed. "Come on, boys, let's wind it up."

Dulaney smiled and made a plea with his hands. "I'm coming out, Marty," he whispered. "It's up to you whether you want to help me or not."

"What do you want from me?"

"Find out where the work camp is. Play that lawyer role you do so well, see if they'll tell you where they took us. If you can leave the car on the nearest road east of the camp, do that. If you can't, I'm out of luck and on my own."

Dulaney cocked his head. "This is going to be damned hit-or-miss but it's the only chance I've got. I'll run east in the morning, just as the sun comes up."

He stared into Kendall's eyes. "This means you'll be on foot. It's a risk I'm asking you to take, but I'll be in prison clothes and I'm gonna need that car."

He reached across the table and gripped Kendall's hand. This was their test of fire.

Kendall smiled, wary and pale. "That's what I meant about you, Jack. You always make people do their best for you. Hope it doesn't get you killed."

((5))

By the time he got to the county court it had all been reduced to a formality. He pleaded guilty and that afternoon a bus with barred windows came for the new prisoners and took them into the hills east of Oakland.

Their destination was Camp Bob Howser, a cluster of barrackslike buildings surrounded by a wire fence with squat guard posts at two corners. He was given an issue of clothes, gingham gray, and made to wear a duck-billed cap. He never learned who Bob Howser was. Nobody seemed to care.

The warden, a thin bald-headed man named Murf Ladson, was exactly what Dulaney expected. He walked in front of the ragged men cradling a shotgun and looking into each gaunt face. He stopped and looked at Dulaney and the look was as old as time, coming up through all the endless wars between authority and defiance. This one I'll have trouble with, the warden thought, and Dulaney could see the thought in his face. The warden leaned close enough to share the last sour memory of his meat loaf and ketchup dinner. "Mess with me, big man, and you'll wish to Christ you hadn't."

So we are slaves here, Dulaney thought: sold down the river to the same mean-hearted overseer Uncle Tom knew. In another time it might not bother him. Now he'd kiss the devil's ass for a greater gain tomorrow, but a primal loathing lingered between them.

At the end of the line the warden turned to face the sorry crew the county had sent him. "The only thing that matters here is the schedule. We're clearing land for a state road going through. If the state says get it cleared by July, I want it done by the middle of June. I always beat the schedule. Now, you boys get your asses on that truck. You got five good working hours left in the day."

They were taken into the hills. There were stumps to be cut out of the earth and burned, rocks to be broken and dug up. The men were watched by guards in plain clothes and the guards carried shotguns but there were no shackles. The men were mostly vagrants and drunks, not violent criminals. Few would ever muster the grit to make a break for it. Kendall was probably right: it was a little pocket of county corruption, with the judge getting kickbacks for free labor.

The country was on wartime. The Daylight Savings Act had been passed in February, giving them an extra hour of daylight for the duration. This meant they could work till eight, and as the summer came on, the workday could be pushed back even later. The men were quiet and grim. Dulaney worked steady and hard and tried to make the guards forget he existed.

That night there was a blackout. The truck had shades over its headlights that were supposed to make it invisible from the air if the Japs were flying over. The whole West Coast was nervous and Jap-happy. As Kendall and Dulaney had come north from Los Angeles they heard rumors of a Japanese invasion coming out of every crack and doorway.

At Camp Bob Howser the guard was doubled on blackout nights. It was Monday: the men would change clothes on Wednesday, and again on Saturday when they took their weekly gang shower. They ate in a smoky room with blackout curtains, a mix of flour and beans and ground meat ladled out of a pot by a Mexican cook. In their bunks the men lay soaked in sweat, staring into blackness.

Somewhere in the night came the hum of airplanes.

"Hey, Billy," said a voice across the way. "Them sound like Uncle Sugar's planes to you?"

"Sure they do, sure they do, why the hell wouldn't they be?"

"I heard the Nip planes got a different sound to 'em."

"Shaddap, Mac," said a third voice. "Keep it to yourself."

Dulaney closed his eyes.

He dreamed of Holly. And there was Tom, alive again.

((**6**))

THEY were sitting on the steps of his old apartment house, listening to the Yanks play the Red Sox. DiMaggio homered in the sixth and Tom went to get some beer. But then he'd met some fellows who had a crap game going, and time got away from him.

Holly and Jack talked into the evening and something happened. The air between them was charged with it. At seven o'clock Holly said, "I think we've been abandoned. Let's go get something to eat."

Over supper in the neighborhood cookhouse he learned about her life. She lived on Keeler Avenue in a Pennsylvania coal-mining town, where her father had taught school for years. But classes were consolidated and the school closed when the depression came; their savings vanished, and with $900 remaining on the house, Holly learned about the threat of foreclosure.

Her father went on the road looking for work. It was 1932, the cruelest year, the year of the hobo whore, when thousands of young girls sold themselves in hallways and sent the money home. Families broke apart but not theirs. Carnahan wrote them every week: sometimes he sent money, but there were days when all he could manage was the penny postcard. He sent that without fail, no matter how hard his life was.

Holly was sixteen. Her mother was an invalid and their survival was largely up to her. She washed and mended for the miners; cooked and carried food to the mines. Corn bread, rice, and black-eyed peas. Hot bean soup dished up from a steaming iron kettle off the tailgate of her daddy's old pickup. She could sit with the miners and put it away with most of them. A few years after her father left home, a photographer from *Life* came through and took her picture for a "Faces of a Depressed America" layout. She sat on the running board with her mud-

streaked skirt pushed down between her legs, her hair limp
from the rain and a steaming cup of soup in her hands. She
didn't know if they had ever put it in the magazine. It cost ten
cents a week to find out, and that seemed pretty damned extrav-
agant under the circumstances.

They were survivors, though. Whenever something
threatened the house, a miracle seemed to happen: Holly
would get work downtown, money would come from her
father—something would happen so she could get up the
mortgage. A few times her father had come home. He looked
around Sadler and talked of how things were getting better:
how maybe in another year or two he could come home for
good. But he never did.

Her mother died in 1937. Carnahan arrived too late for
the funeral. He hung around for a week, stayed away from
old friends, and left again when he saw that Holly could take
care of herself. But she always got her penny postcard. It came
every Monday, year in and year out.

Tom had met her on a train: her first trip east, to visit her
father in New York. She was twenty-two then, in the summer
of 1938. Jack had never known anyone that young who bristled with intelligence and wit and had the manners to go with
it. But she never showed off: he loved that about her from the
start. She dismissed her abilities as trivial and counted her
understanding of the world as her father's accomplishment.
"That's my dad talking," she would say. "He made sure I
knew what to read, from the time I was able to crawl down
from the high chair."

She didn't know where life was taking her. She had always
wanted to sing with a big band but the only singing she'd ever
done was in the Sadler Presbyterian Church. Her voice was
full at fifteen, and sometimes she thought she could lift the
roof off that little wooden building with nothing more than
the power in her lungs.

"So that's me," she said, blushing slightly. "What about
you?"

Dulaney was born in Charleston, and he too was formed
by his father. For years Jack's father had lived in sin with

Tom's mother, Megan Rooney, and the boys were raised as brothers. Aunt Meg was a lifelong Catholic and could not get a divorce from her old husband, wherever he was.

His schooling ended with his father's death but his education had never stopped. He read hundreds of books before he was twenty and remembered much of what he had read. He and Tom were big strapping kids and had found work even in the worst years of the depression. In their late teens they went on the road together, working their way across the country and through the cities of the East and Midwest. For a time Jack had bounced drunks in a Manhattan speakeasy. He had walked horses at Belmont and had loaded hundred-pound sacks of cocoa beans on the Brooklyn waterfront. He took up boxing and had once sparred with Jack Sharkey. In one furious round Sharkey had busted his ear and made him disqualify ever after for the military. He had uncorked a powerhouse right and dropped Sharkey flat on his ass, but he didn't tell her that. It would seem too much like bragging.

His love affair with words continued and he began to write, supporting himself with odd jobs. He and Tom drifted through the Midwest, doing terrible grunt work on an Oklahoma pipeline. There he met a writer, Jim Thompson, and in Oklahoma City, Thompson took him to a few meetings of communists. He didn't like the politics and soon stopped going. But Thompson liked him, and when Thompson became head of the WPA Federal Writers Project in Oklahoma, he hired Dulaney as a writer at $65 a month. They were putting out a road-by-road guide to the state, and Dulaney's job was to travel the back roads and write what he saw.

Its lasting impact was what he learned from Thompson. Dulaney had always been a careful, plodding writer. He believed in the powers of the unconscious mind and the importance of dreams, and he was trying to teach himself to meditate immediately after sleep, to call up those hidden visions for his use as a writer before they slipped away forever. The mind worked while the body slept, but Thompson taught him another kind of writing. How to get it said fast, because if you wanted to make a living you had to deal with magazines that paid half a cent a word. You couldn't be Hemingway at rates like that.

Holly was thrilled that he had written a novel. Alfred A. Knopf had published it in the spring of 1937, billing it as a story of the proletariat. Sales had been nil, but it had a short second life when Senator Bilbo of Mississippi denounced it as dangerously communistic and untruthfully sympathetic to the Negro. But Dulaney had lived it. It was neither untruthful nor pro-communist, and he wore the condemnation of rednecks easily and well.

She had never been to New York and she wanted to see it all. Not the tourist traps: she wanted to see the neighborhoods. She waved off the Statue and the Empire State in favor of a day on the Lower East Side. Walking where people lived and worked was what she liked best: browsing in their shops, listening to accents still mired in Old Europe. She had a nose for finding the city's most authentic eating places and she would eat anything; she had an iron constitution, she never got sick.

At night she was off to dinner with her father, and Tom made his first shivery confession. "I never felt like this before, Jack. Man, I feel like I've been hit by a truck." On Friday and Saturday her dad had to work overtime and Tom took her to a Harlem hot spot. The next night they insisted that Jack come along and the three of them wound up in Yorkville. "I've heard it's like some neighborhood right out of Munich," she said. "We can get a close-up look at what the Nazis are up to." Their cabdriver was a beefy Irish pug who lectured as he drove. "This used to be a great neighborhood. All kinds of people before the heinies took it over. There's still an Irish section on Eightieth between Fifth and Lexington but it's going to hell south of there. Lots of coloreds on Seventy-ninth, nothing but spics on Ninetieth. But this is what you came for. This is what it is today."

He turned into Eighty-sixth, awash with Bavarian glitter. "They call this street Hitler's Broadway."

She wanted to walk. She was charmed by the European flavor as accordion music followed them down the block:

lighthearted polkas from the dance halls and heartrending torch songs from the cabarets. They passed an open-air restaurant with yodeling waiters, doormen decked out in high socks and brief leather pants, suspenders, and Tyrolean hats. The neighborhood rippled with nightlife and almost everything seemed to be open.

"This would be lovely," Holly said, "if only you could separate it from Hitler."

They saw Nazi newspapers for sale everywhere. There were Nazi magazine stands, tiny film houses with movies of Nazi content, and in the windows of souvenir shops were brown shirts and swastikas. The young German woman stood in the doorway, smoking a cigarette and smiling blondly as they looked in her window. "Good evening . . . Can I interest you in some flagks from Chermany?"

Holly stepped inside. "I have some lovely things here," the woman said. "A scarf, perhaps, from Berlin. I just got these last week."

The scarf was a scenic cloth with subtle black lines separating its panels. But on closer look the lines became hundreds of tiny swastikas. "I was thinking of something more, um, you know, German American," Holly said, and the German woman looked away and her smile faded to nothing. "You are in the wrong part of town for merchandise like that. Surely you must know where you are." Holly smiled and said, "Aren't I in America?" The woman came along behind her, straightening her scarves with exaggerated patience. "You want to go down to Times Square, you'll find what you want there. Lots of American flagks, maybe even some British. You like the British?"

The woman went away but they could hear her in the back room, talking German on the telephone. Almost at once a group of young men gathered on the sidewalk outside the store. Holly came out and they continued their leisurely stroll with a pack of wolves on their trail. Tom draped an arm over Holly's shoulder and whistled "The Star-Spangled Banner" in short phrases as they walked. They went into a place called the Konditorei and sat at a table in a corner. The waiter brought them pastries and coffee and was pleasant until the brownshirts gathered in his doorway. "No trouble in here," he said. "You'll have to leave now."

"We're not done eating yet," Tom said.

The boys came in. None of them was older than eighteen. They took seats in an intimidating semicircle a few feet away. Their leader spoke: "So. Who are you people?"

Tom leaned forward and said, "So, who are you people?"

"We're the Hitler Youth Movement. We're here to save America from the Jews."

"Lucky America. So what do I look like, a Jew?"

The boy pointed at Holly. "*She* was rude to Frau Hessin. She should go back and apologize."

"Maybe it's just a cultural misunderstanding. In this country it's not polite to point at someone when the lady's sitting right here in front of you."

The boy cocked an eyebrow. "Yes?"

"Absolutely. This is Miss Carnahan. And if you point your finger at her again I'll break it off and shove it up your nose. Then you can go see Miss Gretchenweiler and tell her about it yourself."

"You are insulting. You'd better pay attention. There are six of us here."

"Seven. I guess they don't teach you to count that high in the Hitler Youth Movement."

"So, seven of us. Two of you."

"Which almost makes it even. Maybe you'd like to call for help."

The boy flushed red.

"Take your time," Tom said. "We'll wait."

"You think the big man there scares us?"

"He does if you're smart. He doesn't talk, he just kills."

The boy pushed back his chair. "He's an idiot, he doesn't scare us. I'd get out of Yorkville if I were you."

They sauntered out the door and Holly let out a long breath. Tom said, "Finish your strudel stuff," but she had lost her appetite for it. Now when they walked back up the street faces watched them from storefronts. People looked down from second-story windows and eyes followed them from across the street.

That was Tom. Afraid of nothing, impudent and brash. But he was nervous when he met her father, on her last day in town.

"I don't think he liked me much," he told Jack that night. "He was way too polite, and I don't think I ever got to first base with him."

She came over to say good-bye and Tom did everything but beg her to stay. "Come live in New York if you love it so much. What the hell are you doing back in that little town?"

She never answered that. She had a job there but it wasn't important. Her mother was gone, her father hadn't lived there in years, and she seemed to have no close friendships to hold her there. "She's got nothing back there," Tom said in disbelief, after she'd gone. "Can you imagine a great girl like her with no friends at all? And she still won't give up that half-assed town."

They wrote each other and in August Tom went to Pennsylvania for a visit. She came east again in the fall and they went club hopping on Fifty-second Street. Jack got a date for himself, a woman he had met a few months earlier. Her name was Bonnie and she was pretty and full of fun. But he couldn't keep his eyes away from Holly. A dozen times he found himself staring, and when it finally happened that she looked at him, what he saw was what he felt, and he looked away quickly.

Her voice came out of the predawn darkness at Camp Bob Howser, toasting them all that Thanksgiving three years ago. A special toast for her father. "To you, Dad, you wonderful old cuss. You made me think. You made me learn. You gave me hope."

Carnahan might have been his own father: a man of fifty-something who shared what he knew with reluctance and tact. If Jack had expected a scholar, he was surprised to meet a workingman like himself. A man in dungarees and a flannel shirt, wearing a battered fedora.

That was the beginning of his strange relationship with Carnahan: strange because it largely excluded Holly, who was the reason for it, and Tom, who was Jack's best friend and Carnahan's certain son-in-law-to-be. Sometimes on a Saturday he'd meet Carnahan downtown and they'd kill an afternoon prowling through the secondhand-book stores on Fourth Avenue. In the evenings they'd meet in a neighborhood bar, where they'd sit and talk philosophy or their own short brushes with communism. Carnahan too had been to a few meetings in his day. "I was really taken with Marx when I first went out on the road. I was ready to buy the whole package. You see so damned much greed in this country, and the system seems to reward it again and again. But eventually you see the holes in that communistic ideal and you know that's never gonna work."

They talked literature and Carnahan read his book. "A damn good and honest work," he said. In a Brooklyn pool hall he showed Jack how to make a cushion shot. He looked up from his beer and finally, in that quiet but direct way of his, said the unthinkable.

"This thing between Holly and Tom. It's not right."

Jack froze over his stick.

"What's more, you know *why* it's not right."

Jack held up his hands, as if he could push the words away. "I don't think we should talk like this."

Carnahan leaned his stick against the wall. "Tom's always wondering why she won't move to New York. Listen, Jack, and know the truth. She won't come here because of you. That child has seen more trouble and heartache than a dozen others her age. She can't stand thinking that someday she might be the cause of you and Tom falling out."

"She won't be."

"Maybe she should be, if it's a lie that holds you together."

"I really can't get into this."

Carnahan circled the table. "Well, somebody'd better get into it. And damn soon too."

A light clicked on at Camp Bob Howser. The guard came through the barracks, rousing the men for their fifteen-hour

day. In the kitchen, with the blackout curtains still pulled
tight and the air heavy from last night's mess, the men ate a
breakfast of cold toast and warm mush. Dulaney heard the
truck pull up outside, and he faced the coming day.

(((7)))

HE dropped off the truck as the sun hit the eastern sky and lit
up the earth around him. The guard riding in back with the
men turned his face to the west and Dulaney was gone.

He rolled into the ditch and splashed face first into a pud-
dle of standing water. He elbowed up the ditch, ready to jump
up and make the forty-yard run to the woods, but the outcry
he expected never came.

Slowly he raised his head. Some of the prisoners on the
flatbed were watching him but no one gave him away. The
guard looked over the top of the cab, the shotgun resting on
his shoulder, and the truck turned up a rocky trail and disappeared into the trees.

He ran due east. It was a risky move that would take him
right past the work site. Maybe he'd be bold enough to walk
up and ask 'em the time of day, like Rebel pickets did with the
Yankee enemy in the woods around Charleston eighty years
ago. They might not expect that. The dogs would know better, but often simpleminded men wouldn't listen to dogs if
the dogs didn't do what struck them as logical. Think that and
be caught, he thought.

The ground sloped down and he heard water rushing. A
stream would be good when they set the hounds after him,
but he never came across it. His need to run east was urgent,
and gradually the sound of the water faded away.

A vision of Holly chased him down the gulch. He had a
sharp premonition that he'd never see her again if he got caught,
so he wouldn't get caught. This is how simple life can be.

The sun was now well over the hills ahead. It shone through the trees and cast the forest in an eerie silver blue haze.

He was good with time and he knew when he'd been running ten minutes. He was good with distance and direction and he knew the work site would be coming up on his left any second now.

He thought of Kendall and the car. His confidence in the existence of a connecting road was not strong. There was a certain logic to it but it could be a mile away or twenty, he had no way of knowing. At best he'd have a forty-minute lead. Without a stream to wash away his scent, the dogs would run him to earth in two hours.

The woods thinned and he heard voices. He was close enough now to see the men. The truck was gone, the third guard with it. One of the remaining guards stood among the men; the other circled the clearing with his shotgun, coming within spitting distance before moving on past.

Dulaney eased away and ran hard to the east. Ten minutes later he saw a power line in the distance, then a narrow gravel road. No telling if Kendall had come, but he turned north with his hope running high.

It was a simple country road, just wide enough for two cars to pass. He kept to the woods, hidden if a car should come from either way, near enough to run out if Kendall should come in the Essex. Underbrush raked his arms and face, drawing blood, but he ran this way for many minutes. Then he heard a car coming and he dropped to the earth.

He ducked his head as the car came in sight. Not the Essex: couldn't miss that fire engine red. It was a black Ford; he saw no more before it was past and gone. Black Ford with a sticky valve, heading north into the deep woods.

He was up again and on the move, jogging through the brush. Made half a mile before he stopped in his tracks to listen. Heard the same car, same sticky engine, idling in the woods just ahead. The brush was very thick: he had to move slowly so as not to make a rustle. But as he eased ahead he saw what had to be the Essex, its bright red finish flashing

through the trees. Then the Ford, which had pulled along-
side and stopped with its motor running.

He saw two men but just shapes through the brush;
couldn't get closer without being seen himself. They seemed to
be looking through the car, had the trunk up, and when they
spoke he heard what they said.

"At least we know where he's goin'."

The Irishman.

"What do you want to do?" said the other after a moment.

"Poot everythin' back, just as it was, and let's get out of
here."

The trunk slammed shut. The Irishman came around to
the shotgun side of the Ford. "If I get me hands on that fooker
again it'll be more than a few bad ribs he'll be havin'."

The car backed into the road and drove away south.
Dulaney stood still, his nerves tight, until the sound of the
engine faded away.

He picked his way into the clearing and looked into the car.
Kendall had left the ignition key and some clothes for him on
the front seat. He changed quickly, rolling his prison grays
into a ball and stuffing them under the seat. He opened the
trunk and there were his papers from the hotel: just inside the
box, his notebook. He opened the notebook and found a hundred-dollar bill and a note from Kendall.

Jack,

 *If you've made it this far, I'm glad. I think we will have a
lot to talk about when we see each other again. I'm sorry I was
such a rotten friend but maybe I can make it up. I'm going to
tell you what I know.*

 *If you read this in time, check into the Franklin Hotel in
Sacramento. Use the name Jerry Sellers and I'll try to call you
tonight. If not, I know where you're going and I'll see you
there.*

 *The car's full of gas and I've left you some money for the
trip.*

         Marty

A vision of Kendall's face wafted up from the trunk. Dulaney had a sinking feeling as he listened to the breeze. Then he heard the baying of the dogs.

((8))

HE didn't stop in Sacramento. Kendall would call and then move on, and if they were lucky they'd meet at Holly's house in Pennsylvania. He had a need now to get there, and this was stronger than his other needs, to find Kendall and to hear what he'd say.

He drove through the day. Slowed by hairpin curves on both sides of Donner Pass, he felt his spirits rise as he crossed into Nevada.

On the other side of Reno the car broke down.

He got his papers out of the trunk. Somewhere ahead he would mail them to himself, at general delivery in Sadler, Pennsylvania.

He pushed ahead on foot.

((9))

SHE drew him on. Her face billowed out of the clouds at sunset and her voice beckoned him across the black wasteland. He walked on the edge of the highway, the great U.S. 6 that stretched across Nevada to Denver and points east. A million galaxies lit up the road. Ten billion worlds showed him the way.

A cowboy took him into Elko with its neon-lit whorehouses and its honky-tonk gambling parlors. There was a prewar gaiety to the town, a striking contrast to the tense, embattled climate of the coast. The next bus didn't come through till nine in the morning, so he bought another canteen in an all-night gas station, filled it with water, and pushed on into the night.

He had rid himself of his papers and now carried only the canteens, slung over one shoulder. Time was no factor. He had slipped into that meditative state that enabled him to stop the clock and shut his mind to anything that turned him from his purpose. If his muscles ached, he wouldn't feel them. He wouldn't be bothered by the pain in his feet, or think of food. He was young and powerful, with deep stores of energy that had never been tapped.

Ghosts rose out of the desert.

When they were ten years old Tom had cut their hands and tied them together for an hour. They were blood brothers now. He thought of Holly and heard Tom say, *Don't beat yourself up over something that couldn't be helped. She was never really mine.*

A car came past, slowing as if to pick him up. He hoped he'd get a ride as far as Wells, where he could jump a train, maybe a cattle car going to market in Chicago. But suddenly he cringed as he heard that engine with the sticky valve. Maybe just chance: might be thousands of cars on the road like that, but he braced himself for whatever might come. Then the car went on, and he saw little more of it than a black shape going by.

He caught a ride and walked the last two miles into town. A pale rosy glow had begun in the east.

At a gas station he filled his canteens and headed over to the train yard. As he reached the corner he heard that car again. The ping of its engine caught his ear almost too late, but he looked up to see a black '35 Ford swing into the next block. He got a glimpse of two men, dark shapes seen from behind.

And a license plate from the state of New Jersey.

He walked across the road and squatted in the bushes. He waited for a long time but the car didn't come around again.

An hour later he hopped a train, heading east.

((**10**))

THE train took him to the stockyards in Denver and another train took him on across Kansas.

In Missouri he saw the effects of war. Long lines of trucks, and troops marching beside the road. He turned north and caught a ride into Illinois. He thought of the Carnahans as he trudged through the darkness, and the thought of her lightened his step and helped him forget that he had not stopped: that he had slept only briefly in the cattle car across Utah.

He had little hope of catching a ride before daylight. But his luck had turned and a salesman with a car full of dresses took him into Pennsylvania.

He walked up Keeler Avenue with his heart pounding hard and his knees buckling with fatigue. He knew her house: Tom had taken a picture on a trip here in 1939. It was a cracker box, Holly had said: respectable enough as long as the paint held up, but shabby now in hard times. There was a giant elm in the yard with a swing hanging from its lowest branch; a fence separating the house from its neighbor to the west and a hedge to the east. But the hedge was dying and the swing gone, a rotted remnant of rope the only trace of it. The front yard was deep in weeds and around the side a window was broken.

The house was abandoned. She was gone.

He clumped up on the porch, walked to the edge, and looked down the far side. The grass was parched, littered with cans and broken glass. The windows were so murky he could see nothing of the inside from the porch.

She was gone, though. Now he would have to find her.

Common sense told him what to do next. He bought some clothes, took a room, shaved, got a shower, rested, and ate.

Five hours later he walked through Keeler Avenue looking and feeling like a new man. He talked to everyone he met and knocked on every door but no one knew where she'd gone. The neighbor across the fence was not home; the neighbor across the hedge had not seen her in many weeks.

He went to her church. The minister had known her most of her life but had not seen her since January. She had always been a loner: long periods of absence were not unusual, and he had never known her to have a confidante or a best pal. She sang like an angel but never stayed around for social activities or Bible studies. The minister hoped she was a believer but you never could be sure. She had always been something of a mystery.

Her life had been full of tragedy. "I heard she had a fellow but he died at Pearl Harbor," the minister said. Dulaney wondered if there'd ever been another fellow, before Tom, someone she might turn to in a bad moment. "She did have a boyfriend years ago. It was very serious. They had grown up together and everyone knew they'd marry. But he got killed in an automobile accident. Horrible thing, plowed his car into a trailer truck, went underneath, and took his head off. That's what I mean by tragedy. It's been a string of things, starting with her sister."

Dulaney had never heard about a sister. "What happened to her?"

"Swimming accident at the lake when she was ten. Holly nearly drowned trying to save her. Their mother never did get over it and Holly always took the blame on herself. Makes you wonder—doesn't it?—why God picks some people to suffer like that."

"Yes it does," Dulaney said. "It really makes you wonder."

He walked up Main Street. Everyone knew her and no one had seen her.

Early that evening he was back on Keeler Avenue. Lightning flicked above the trees and thunder rumbled over the earth. He thought of Kendall and wondered where he was, and what he'd do when he arrived and found the house deserted. Move on, most likely: maybe head for Chicago where there might be radio jobs he could do. He wouldn't wait around long. And neither can I, Dulaney thought. But I don't know where to go.

He went around the house and climbed the steps to the back door. It hung loosely on its hinges, the wood splintered and smashed. He stepped into a musty kitchen littered with trash. The remnants of a dining table were pushed into a corner and three half-broken chairs were scattered about. There was an icebox, its door open, with tongs hanging on a board beside it and an ice pick on the floor. The sink had no modern plumbing: just a rusting hand pump, with brown streaks where the tile had chipped away. He touched the pump and it squeaked and gave off a puff of dust.

Across the hall someone had ransacked her bedroom. Pictures stripped from the wall, the floor covered with papers, the bed destroyed, pillows and mattresses cut open and thrown about. Everything was pulled out of the closets—dresses, shoes, a coat. He picked up one of her dresses and held it while his eyes scanned the room. He saw a map pinned to the wall—a road map of New Jersey—and a picture in a broken frame. He recognized a young Carnahan with a woman who had undoubtedly been Holly's mother. He found a magazine, *Metronome,* with articles on the Goodman, Ellington, and Casa Loma bands, and he carried it for a while with the dress.

He crossed to the window and looked out. Lights were now on in the house across the fence but he had no reason to imagine that whoever lived there would know where she had gone. He felt a deep turn into despair as he began to pick up her things and put them in some kind of order.

Her books were pretty well ruined: cheap editions of Thomas Wolfe and Henry James, Djuna Barnes, Katherine Anne Porter, and Emily Dickinson.

In the parents' room he found a treasure: a picture of Holly, torn and weather stained, but it lifted his spirits for a moment. He tucked it into the least damaged of her books, the Dickinson, wrapped that in a piece of tablecloth to keep the rain out, and put it in his pocket.

For once in his life he didn't know what to do. He wanted to spend days here, fixing the house up and making it whole. But there wasn't anything left to save.

He moved into the front room and there in the fireplace, hidden under a pile of ashes, he found the remnants of an envelope. As if she had thrown a pile of papers in the fire and a few singed fragments remained. Magazines. Bills. Junk. One piece got his attention: just a newspaper headline and a small bit of type:

RADIO ACTOR MISSING FIVE YEARS
March Flack, British Air Thespian,
Disappeared in June 1936

There was part of a picture—an eye, a cheek, an officer's cap—but no text remained. He pulled it out to save and under it found a charred piece of notepaper with a chilling line in Holly's hand: *Don't you people have any conscience?*

That line kept playing in his head. He thought of it now as he finished his search of the house.

There wasn't much more to see. A basement at the bottom of a creaky stair. A coal room with an outdoor entry. A crawl space that ran deep under the house, dank-smelling, with an earthen floor.

He went next door, to talk to the neighbors across the fence. Bill and Maude Potter were in their early thirties, working people who had come to Sadler just last year. They had not known Holly well. A few pleasantries, an occasional word passed, then she was gone, they had no idea where. Potter had hardly seen her, yet his was a typical working-class, male-dominated household, and he did the talking. The woman stood in the kitchen doorway, a little girl of ten clutching her dress, saying nothing until Dulaney turned to leave. "Tell him about Hartford, Bill," she said suddenly.

Potter seemed annoyed and said there was no truth to it.

"Then tell him and let him decide."

It was the little girl who had told them about Hartford.

"Her name is Holly," Mrs. Potter said. "That's one reason they became such friends, because they had the same name."

"She's got a bad habit, though," Potter said. "She fibs too much."

But the woman persisted. The child had told them about Hartford after Holly disappeared, last December or January. Sometimes in the early evenings little Holly would crawl through the fence and they'd sit on the porch eating the apple pie that Holly baked in her kitchen. On this one night she had heard about Hartford.

"What do you think she meant? Was she talking about the city up in Connecticut? Is that where she went?"

Potter scoffed. "Who knows what she meant? Maybe she didn't say any of that stuff at all."

"Bill, you can't send him away like that," Mrs. Potter said. "Holly honey, let's go back and get you ready for bed."

With his wife and child gone, Potter was more reasonable. He offered a drink and Dulaney took a small one to break the ice. They sat and talked baseball. Ten minutes later Mrs. Potter returned.

"Bill doesn't like to encourage her if she's been lying to us." She looked at her husband. "But I think we've got to tell him about Hartford."

Hartford wasn't a city. It was a man's name.

The light was on in Holly's kitchen that night, and the child had climbed to the landing and looked in through the glass. Holly was sitting at the table and there was a man in the room with her. A scary man who talked in a low voice and never smiled.

There had been a threat hanging over that room. Potter sneered but the child could sense such things. "I know that for a fact," Mrs. Potter said. There was a threat in the room. "Argue with me if you want to, but that's what she said and I believe her."

The man wore a dark suit and his tie was knotted tight at his neck. He had taken off his hat, but that act of good manners made him no kinder to Holly, who sat huddled at the table across from him.

Mrs. Potter paused.

Potter leaned into the light. "Well, go ahead, tell him the rest now."

Mrs. Potter sighed. "The man was blind."

Potter looked at Dulaney. "Did you ever hear such a bunch of cock-and-bull? A blind bogeyman came and scared her away."

The man was blind, but when he left he walked straight out of the room, as if he knew it well. Outside, down the front porch, and into his car.

"A blind man driving a car," Potter said.

"What made her think he was blind?"

"He wore a blind man's glasses," Mrs. Potter said. "Dark . . . black glasses, even at night."

The child had gone into the room. Holly saw her but seemed incapable of speech. Her eyes were watery, her hands trembled, she was in pain. "Some children are sensitive," Mrs. Potter said. "They know these things."

I wanted her to feel better, little Holly said. She climbed into Holly's lap, hoping to make her feel better, and Holly crushed the child against her and held on as if for dear life.

I'm sorry you feel bad.

My father died, Holly said.

Dulaney felt the shock of it. He stared at Mrs. Potter.

Little Holly asked if her father had been old.

No, she said. *Hartford killed him.*

Then she seemed to get hold of herself. She smiled at the child as if she had only then realized where she was.

You'll have to go, sweetheart. I'm not myself tonight.

"The next day she was gone. No one's seen her since."

((11))

HE stood on her porch in total darkness with the sound of the rain heavy around him. The lights had gone out next door: the Potters were in bed by ten and both houses, shrouded by trees, had gone instantly black. In a while he sat against the front door but the wait was miserable. A cold wind blew the rain across the porch and soon he was slick with it. He kept thinking Kendall would turn up, but this seemed far less likely as the night went on and the rain got worse.

He had no clear idea where Holly had gone and no good way of finding out. The map on her wall matched the license plate of that '35 Ford, but little New Jersey is plenty big when you've got to walk it searching blind. Kendall was still his best bet. But if he didn't show up tomorrow . . . The thought trickled away. Dulaney didn't know what would happen tomorrow.

Sometime after midnight he gave it up and went back to his room. He hung his wet clothes over the radiator and fell into bed, intending to sleep only a few hours. But he was still tired from his long journey and he fell at once into the sleep of the dead. He awoke with a start. It was midmorning at least: nine o'clock by the clock in his head, and he jerked himself into his clothes and checked out. The rain had stopped but the sky remained overcast, and now, as he turned into Keeler Avenue, the house was as empty looking as ever. Kendall wasn't coming: the thought that he was adrift, with damn few clues and a whole country to search, sobered him sharply.

But he climbed to the porch and sat there, and as the hours crept by he tried to devise some plan. He would go to New York and try to get a line on Carnahan, beginning at the place where he'd worked two years ago. At the same time he would track Kendall through his radio connections. But this was an idiot's plan and he spent the rest of the day trying in vain to improve it. At five o'clock he decided to leave Kendall some kind of message, hope he found it, and move on.

Again he went in through the back way. He had seen a pencil in the kitchen, but now as he stood over the sink he was aware of all the shortcomings of what he'd been thinking. Where would he leave such a note, so that only Kendall would see it? There was no place, so there could be no note. He would wait another hour, then move on alone, now truly cast adrift, as solitary as those continental explorers four hundred years ago.

He turned away from the kitchen window and his eyes drifted back through the house, as if the spirit of Holly could rise up from those dim shadows and tell him something.

Suddenly he froze. Someone had been here. Something, he couldn't say what, had been moved. Then he saw what it was, a swirl of papers kicked aside, the ice pick that had lain almost in the center of the room gone, then seen a moment later where it had clattered against the door. Signs of a struggle, continuing into the back rooms. And there was Kendall, thrown into a corner, his hands clawlike, clutching nothing. The rope that had strangled him was still around his neck.

"Oh, Marty!" Dulaney fell to his knees and grabbed Kendall's hand. It was stiff and cold. He sucked in his breath and trembled.

Slowly his wits came back, pushing away the sickness.

He looked in Kendall's pocket and found a fat wallet. The mysteries began anew.

Cash. Two hundred dollars in twenty-dollar bills. Kendall had always claimed to be broke, yet he had left Dulaney a hundred-dollar bill, and here was three months' pay in his billfold.

Driver's license. Issued last fall in Kendall's name by the state of New Jersey, with a street address in a town called Regina Beach. New Jersey! Kendall had never said anything about New Jersey. He had been gone from the East for two years, he had said, and had lived in Connecticut when he'd worked in New York radio.

Hot walker's license and stable area pass from the California Horse Racing Board. Only the one track validation, Santa Anita, beginning last November. Kendall had said he'd come down from Bay Meadows.

Dulaney took the money, the cards, the wallet, everything. Suddenly he knew he couldn't leave anything here.

God knew what he'd touched, going through the house yesterday. He had left his prints on everything.

He manhandled the body down the stairs, across the basement to the crawl space. It was very stiff. *Probably dead about eight hours, killed while I was out on my ass sleeping.*

His movements were now instinctive. He heaved Kendall up into the narrow crawl space: had to bend his arms down and force him in, then crawl in himself to push him back as far as he would go.

Ten feet, fifteen. He wrestled the corpse through the earthy darkness. Then he found what he could—a pile of burlap sacks, an unused bag of fertilizer, and finally a fat roll of tar paper—and these he pushed into the crawl space to cover up the body.

And he got the hell out of there.

A stroke of good fortune—he passed the post office on the way out of town, otherwise he'd surely have forgotten. He slipped a note through the slot, asking that his papers be sent on.

He had a destination now. Regina Beach, New Jersey.

((12))

HE walked east, into the coming night.

In the morning he saw increasing signs of war fever. On a billboard in the middle of nowhere someone had plastered the words IF YOU SPREAD RUMORS, YOU'RE ONE OF HITLER'S BEST SOLDIERS. Still, people talked. They agreed that spreading rumors was un-American and then they spread them. He heard talk of spies everywhere.

He crossed the Susquehanna at Harrisburg and pushed on toward Philadelphia. Bought a newspaper in Elizabethtown, startled to see a front-page story with a Regina Beach dateline. Yesterday, ten miles off the pier, a German torpedo boat had sunk an American tanker going south from New York. Bodies were washing up and a heavy black oil slick had covered the beach.

He caught a good ride, which took him almost to the coast. Soon the taste of the sea was unmistakable and for the first time since California he saw antiaircraft guns on rooftops. He had hoped to reach the town before dark, but the rain had slowed him. Dusk found him trudging south on a narrow blacktop,

somewhere near the coastal highway. The sunset was spectacular, with streaks of fire shooting through clouds over terrain
that was quickly breaking into marshland.

He had bought a flashlight and picked up a free map in a
gas station, so he had a good sense of the town. It was on a
long skinny island between New York and Atlantic City, five
miles off the main highway on a two-lane paved road that cut
through a thick woods. He saw no houses going in, no lights
on either side. The land was deep and dark, the clouds were
dense, and his vision was limited to the small arc of light that
his flash threw before him.

A fog closed in and the woods broke up in pockets of
marsh. The air was salty and cold. Far ahead he heard a ship's
horn, and then he reached the bridge. It was an old narrow
job of wooden planks with rusty steel supports. He could
hear the surf as his feet clumped on the planks, and soon the
road dead-ended into a north-south street. The sea was probably fifty yards away but the fog had locked in everything
beyond the reach of his arm.

Dunes appeared to his right, and he sensed a vast presence
in the night beyond them. He felt suddenly dwarfed without
knowing why.

Then he heard music, wafting out of the surf on the opposite side. He heard the sound of hoofbeats coming, and he
stepped off the road and dropped into the sand as two horsemen came riding past on the edge of the road. In the glare of
their lights he recognized the uniforms of the coast guard, but
to him, now, they were just cops. He pushed on south. He
could still hear that music, a clarinet wailing and a swing band
driving the melody. The song galloped through the air—"The
World Is Waiting for the Sunrise." In the dunes a red light
flashed, flashed again, again. From the beach the music came to
a frantic climax with screaming applause. Then he saw what he
was hearing, a small party of jitterbugs on the deck of a beach
house, with a radio playing in an open window.

"You are listening to WHAR, your Blue Network voice of
the eastern seaboard. August Stoner speaking . . . correct eastern wartime is twelve o'clock."

The light across the road flashed again and the giant took shape in the fog. It was the radio station, with a tower so high it disappeared in the clouds.

(((13)))

HE opened his eyes and in the half darkness saw the shape of books on a shelf across from the bed. Slowly he remembered where he was.

A plain room in a hotel on the north side of town. He had signed in after midnight, scrawling his name illegibly in the register.

He was on the second floor looking south from the east corner of the hotel. The road rolled out of his left elbow: beyond it, the beach was an impossible mix of reds and blues. The surf was rough. In the distance he could see the town, lit up like a sapphire in the last long moment before the sunrise.

The hotel wasn't bad for two bills. The bed was hard and the building was quiet and cool. The owner was considerate: the books on the shelf were cheap editions, throwaways, library discards, put here to help a sleepless traveler get through the night. START A BOOK, TAKE IT WITH YOU, said the sign thumbtacked to the wall. The authors were America's writers: Hemingway and Caldwell, James Fenimore Cooper, Gene Stratton Porter, and Faith Baldwin. Nancy Drew, Tom Swift, Marjorie Rawlings—something for everyone.

Toss out the Baldwin and the Nancy Drew and he had read them all at some time in his life. Books had always given him a sense of destiny, of self. Maybe now they'd give him more than that.

He would need a new name. It would be beyond stupidity to get caught now because of carelessness. He looked at the names on the spines.

Hemingway spoke: first, of course, and loudest.

Not Hemingway. Too famous, too literary. A name should attract nobody's attention.

He thought of the people they wrote about. Robert Jordan and the Spanish war. Jody Baxter of the Florida wetlands, and his brawling friends the Forresters. Old Grandma Hutto.

What's your name, boy?

The voice in his head had a badge pinned to it.

Jordan, he thought.

He looked at the books and thought of their characters. Corny Littlepage from that dusty novel Cooper wrote that no one but himself had ever read. Corny and his Dutch pal Guert Ten Eyck.

I'll be Dutch, he thought. Not Old World Dutch—a family of transplants in teeming America. Now he could answer a cop's question.

My name is Jordan. Jordan Ten Eyck.

The rest of it came in a flood.

My parents were immigrants from Holland before the last war. They settled in the South. Not Charleston, not that close to the truth, but near enough to peddle this soft Southern accent.

My family settled in Savannah. We still have relatives in the old country. I've got cousins and an uncle in the Dutch resistance.

My father worked on the docks of the Savannah River. I had a brother but he died. My father insisted that we be raised in the customs and language of our new country. We never spoke or learned Dutch in our house. I was given my first name from the last name of the first good friend my father had in America.

Call me Jordan.

((ı • ı))

ONE DAY IN THE LIFE OF JORDAN TEN EYCK

(((**1**)))

HE walked across the road as the sun floated over the sea and turned the sky pale. He could smell the oil from the torpedoed tanker and he saw dead fish coated with black scum. The sand ran clear for a stretch, then oily, and puddles of oil were trapped in the gullies as the tide went out.

Teams of men were out in the water, rolling barbed wire and giving the town the look of a war zone. The coast guard again, keeping the Hun at bay. Or so they thought. What were they going to do, fence the whole East Coast, or would they finally have to face the obvious?—that if someone wanted to get into a country as big as the United States, he'd find a way.

The town was a typical Atlantic beachfront resort, with a boardwalk and amusement park. The pier jutted a quarter mile out to sea and had a pavilion the size of the *Titanic*. To the north, the radio tower seemed small now in the distant sunlight.

In a beachfront diner he ate breakfast and read yesterday's P.M. daily from Newark. A boxed sidebar told of operations at Regina Beach to contain the oil slick, but Jersey had been lucky. Most of the oil had been unloaded in New York and the tanks had been less than 10 percent full. But the town's Festival of the Sun might be shut down for the first time in its eighty-year history.

He talked to the waitress, a woman in her fifties with a tired face. He showed her Holly's picture but she shook her head. Her world was this diner, this counter, that kitchen, and a small flat off the beach. She had two sons in the service and on Sundays she rolled bandages for the Red Cross. "I'll bet ten thousand women like that come through this beach every summer." She wished him luck and he hit the boardwalk.

He hit the pier, the beach, the streets. He looked in every face and said her name to everyone he met, and he showed her picture everywhere.

He was stopped on the beach by the mounties, who were courteous but inquisitive. Where had he come from? What had he been doing there? What did Dick Tracy do yesterday? No offense, but it was wartime and they were asking these questions of many new people on the beach. They asked his name and he looked in the man's eyes. "My name's Jordan. Jordan Ten Eyck."

He moved on, climbing to the sidewalk that led into town. Nothing was open yet. He passed some people and showed them Holly's picture.

He was crossing the street when he saw a car pull into a parking lot. The car got his attention, then the man, then the building. It was a twelve-cylinder Packard, a seven-thousand-dollar automobile. The building was five stories high, unusual in a beach town of this size. His eyes scanned the building's facade and a shock went through him. The legend over the door said HARFORD 1937.

Harford, not Hartford.

Not a city. A building.

And the man wore dark glasses, and looked like a blind man.

((**2**))

SOMETHING moved on the southwest corner of the rooftop, and Jordan stood still and watched. There seemed to be a utility room, a tin shed at the far edge. Telephone wires crisscrossed above it, and suddenly a man appeared near the edge, there only for a moment at the eastern rim.

Jordan moved on past. Judgment warned him to tread softly until he found Holly.

The sound of a small jazz band pulled him into a one-block court, packed with bars and swing joints on both sides of the street. The sign said Chicago Avenue, and his heart quickened with the certainty that she would come here. He followed the music into a room where daylight never came and saw a small swing combo jamming away. They were playing a head arrangement, with clear touches of "Somebody Stole My Gal" rippling in the riffs. It was the kind of red-hot number that wrapped up a set, bringing a crowd to its feet as the clarinet locked horns with the tenor and dueled him to a raging finish.

But it ended in silence. There were a few scattered coughs from the bandstand and a laugh from the clarinet at the expense of the trombone. Jordan could see the stage and the empty tables around it and the bar across the room with its row of stools, also empty. The men were bathed in a ghostly velvet light, cool looking now that the spotlight was off. The trumpet called for "After You've Gone," with something new from everybody, and they exploded into it, infusing it with tradition and an occasional shot at the moon.

When it ended, the silence again was sudden and deep. It was so quiet that the voice in the dark place just inside the door seemed amplified.

"We're closed, pal."

Jordan didn't need an introduction: he had seen enough bouncers. A wiry fellow, young, with muscles.

"I'm looking for somebody."

"You won't find him in here. We're closed till three."

"This would be a young woman, possibly a regular. Twenty-six, pretty, with long honey-colored hair, sometimes tied back." He took out the picture and held it into the light. "She might've gotten to town in February, or anytime since then. Her name's Holly Carnahan."

The pause was long enough: she had been here but the bouncer wasn't telling. "Come back at three and we'll be glad to serve you a drink. But listen to what I'm saying, Kilroy. Don't come in here pestering customers with a bunch of questions, or else you'll be talking to me again."

"My friend's name is Holly," Jordan said.

"I heard you the first time. Look, the boys've had a long night. They just want to jam a little and let their hair down. Now, you look like a smart customer. I don't need to draw you a picture."

He reached out as if to grab Jordan's arm. "I wouldn't do that," Jordan said, and something in his voice made the bouncer hang back. He leaned into the light so the kid could see his eyes. "I'm an easygoing fellow, but I don't push easy. The good part is, we don't need to push at all. You could answer a civil question and I'd go on about my business."

The bouncer made a show of making up his mind. "This woman . . . you say you're a friend of hers?"

"I may be the only one she's got."

"Maybe I'd be her friend too if she'd let me. I see a lot of women in here, but she's really something. The caterpillar's kimono."

"I'll tell her you said that. She can be a little slow warming up to people but she's worth the trouble."

Jordan leaned back in the dark and waited. The rest of it was coming now. The bouncer said, "Yeah, there's a woman like that on the beach. The name she goes by is Holly O'Hara, but she's the one you want. Loneliest goddamn eyes I ever saw. I bought her a drink when she first came around but I never could get her to sit still for a repeat performance."

The kid coughed. "She's got something else you didn't mention—a voice that'll stop time dead. She's a singer in a joint up the street. Place called the Magic Carpet, halfway down on the other side."

((3))

THE Magic Carpet was locked and dark in the early morning. It didn't seem to matter now. She was here. She was safe. He would see her.

From a sign in the window he learned that she sang here weeknights with a group called the Windy City Seven. On Saturdays they could be heard from eleven thirty till midnight on WHAR, the local radio outlet.

He decided to approach her cautiously, choose his time with care, contact her quietly, and then let her come to him.

He didn't like this decision much. Something told him to find her now, with no more delays, and it was only calm judgment that held him back.

In the department store he bought some clothes: jeans and shirts, shoes, socks, underwear. He stopped for a respectable haircut and in a pharmacy bought a razor, lather brush, toothbrush, and shoe polish.

He checked into the same hotel and rented the room for a week. Told the old man he'd be needing a radio and got the one behind the counter, four bits for the week.

His room faced north, on the opposite end from where he'd been last night. The window gave him a clear view of the road and the radio tower looming over the dunes. He plugged the radio into a wall outlet and listened to what came out of it—some fellow in Washington talking about sugar rationing and the fuel cutbacks scheduled to begin in a few days. Now everyone would need a ration card to buy gasoline. Even Mrs. Roosevelt was learning to ride a bicycle and would get by on her three gallons a week.

He sat at the open window and tried to curb his uneasiness until tonight. He had deliberately not thought of Kendall but now he did, and he faced his conscience as he thought back over what he had done. It was too late for that now, but he would think about it in times to come. Until I put it to rest, he thought. Until I find out who did that thing and why.

He told himself he was doing right by waiting. It made no sense to stir up the town looking for her now. He opened Holly's Emily Dickinson and sat staring at her picture and, beside it, that scrap of newspaper headline. March Flack, British radio actor, missing since 1936. Suddenly it all seemed to jumble—Holly, Kendall, Harford, Carnahan, March Flack—and the day seemed endless.

In the bathroom at the end of the hall he shaved and took another shower. Now his room seemed different, as if someone had been in here. He had been foolish, given all that had happened, to leave his door unlocked. It was a habit that came from

living in tack rooms, which were never locked, and he stood for
a moment wondering if he had imagined some intruder out of
his own immediate past. Then he realized what was different.
It was the radio . . . someone with two good ears had turned the
volume down, not by much, but the sound had been part of the
room and it had changed. He cocked his head and listened, then
slowly turned up the volume until the room felt right again.

Suddenly he knew why: they turned down the radio so
they could hear me coming, so I wouldn't walk in and surprise 'em. Then, when they left, they turned it back up, but
not far enough.

So they know I'm here.

He sat on the bed. The rationing show was gone, and a
local announcer was talking about the oil slick and the
prospects for the Festival of the Sun to go on as scheduled. An
exciting Saturday lineup of local and national programming
was promised, with afternoon music by Jimmy Dorsey and
Lionel Hampton. At six thirty those funny fellows from Pine
Ridge, Lum and Abner, would kick off the Blue Network
evening schedule. *The Green Hornet* would air from Detroit at
eight, and Ripley's *Believe-It-Or-Not* from New York at ten.
He turned off the radio, closed the window, and locked the
door as he went out.

The sun was hot on his skin. The beach was crowded now,
the road into town clogged with cars. The stores were all open
and even from this distance he could see people congregating
on the pier. The pavilion beckoned, promising cold beer and
talk with interesting strangers. But he turned north, surprising
himself.

There were a dozen reasons why he should lie low till
dark, but it was too late for reasons. He felt the sand under his
shoes as he hiked across the dunes toward the radio tower,
shimmering in the noonday heat.

((4))

THE radio station was in a large building a quarter mile off the main highway on the west side of the island. The parking lot on the north end was almost empty; a smaller lot to the south was half full. Beyond the building was the tower, with a small tin shed at the base of it. A stand of trees ran along the creek and around the point to the north.

He started down the hill without a plan; then, as if on demand, he was struck by a dangerous notion that grew as he walked. He would present himself as an old friend looking for Kendall. He knew he was playing blindman's bluff with killers but he didn't see much added risk in it. Kendall's enemies would know him on sight anyway, so what good would a lie do?

He had a few small advantages. He had smelled them out back in California; he knew they were there but they didn't know that. And he figured they wanted him alive yet. They could've killed him in Nevada, on that lonely desert road, if that's what they'd wanted.

He crossed the oyster-shell road and was suddenly aware of the island's marshy back side: the almost seminal scent of mud and a faintly sweet decay where sea things had died and dried out on the bank. The building was impressive: it rose at least thirty feet above the cars, tall enough for three floors but apparently only the two. There were steel doors at opposite ends of the building with no handles on the outside. Each bore a sign that said FIRE DOOR/NO ENTRY. The windows on both floors were heavily curtained.

A redbrick walk skirted the building, leading through a rock garden around the corner. The lobby opened from the west side, facing away from the highway. He absorbed this instantly, but what he saw was two women sitting at a picnic table. One was reading a magazine and eating something from a brown paper bag; the other had her head down across folded arms as if taking a nap in the sun.

He started across the gap and now saw other tables off in the trees. It looked more like a campground than a radio station, with at least two brick barbecue pits and a volleyball net staked out in the sand. He heard music, then he saw a battery radio playing softly at the end of the table. The woman reading the magazine was just into her early twenties, with an exceptional face set off by short black hair. She grew prettier as the gap between them narrowed. Her friend at first seemed plain, but as he came closer he knew that this was a comparative effect. She wore a man's clothes, pants and a flannel shirt, sandals, and no jewelry.

The beauty spoke. "Here comes another actor, Liv."

Jordan laughed sociably and the young one decided to smile slightly. She had a Gibson girl loveliness, an almost aching perfection like the faces painted by Harrison Fisher long ago.

"So, stranger, what's your specialty?"

"Haven't got one. Just drifted in looking for an old friend."

"Friend got a name?"

"Fella named Marty Kendall."

"Oh, Kendall hasn't been here in ages. We were talking about him just last week. Somebody thought he might've gone to Chicago. There are still lots of soap shows coming out of Chicago, but I know Kendall's voice. I know all his voices and I don't hear him on any of those shows."

"Then where do you think he went?"

"I'd say he's on a bender somewhere. Would that be fair, Liv?"

The other woman said, "I guess that's the way to bet." She sat up straight and was very tall. A torrent of tawny hair tumbled down her back and her eyes were so pale they were almost gray. She looked his age, thirty-two, maybe a little older: she had crow's feet around her eyes and her mouth was a little too wide. There was nothing remarkable about her face except that it was unforgettable, its exotic prettiness pulling his attention away from the classic beauty beside her.

"Seems strange for Marty to drop off the earth," he said.

"Well, he did," said the tall one. "Not so much as a 'Doodah' or a *Vaya con Dios* to anybody."

"He'll probably come back the same way he left," said the beauty. "If he lives through it."

The tall one sighed and the beauty said, "If he's a friend of Kendall's he can't be too surprised. He's got to know that Kendall had a problem."

"He didn't drink around me," Jordan said.

The beauty changed the subject. "So if you're not an actor, how'd you come to know Kendall?"

Keep going, he thought: do what comes naturally. "I'm a writer."

She said, "Oh," as if that explained everything. The tall one was more impressed. "Are you looking for work?"

"I wasn't but I might be."

"Because they need writers here like Hitler needs a new attitude."

"If he's a good writer," said the beauty. "Why aren't you in the army?"

She was so young and sassy she made him laugh. But her esprit seemed genuine, so he told her.

"Lucky you," she said. "That means you'll probably live to celebrate your next birthday. I'd trade an ear for that."

He gestured at the table, a courtesy. Both said, "Sure," and he straddled the bench and sat. Beauty closed her magazine and turned off her radio. "So, what do you say? Do you want to work at Harford, or not?"

The word made him flinch. "What's Harford?"

"You're sitting in it. That's what we call this station. It's radio shorthand, insider talk."

"Most stations have nicknames," said the tall one.

"Usually it's the last three call letters. But 'Harford' is easier to say than 'H-A-R.' "

"Didn't I see that name Harford on a building downtown?"

"Now you've got it," said beauty. "Harford runs the world."

"And Harford is a man, right?"

"That's what they tell me." She cocked her head slightly. "Did anyone ever tell you you look like a workingman's Gary

Cooper? . . . A nice homely plainsman, long and lanky and quiet. My name's Rue Nicholas."

"Jordan Ten Eyck."

The tall one offered her hand and said her name—"Livia Teasdale"—and her grip was strong and firm.

"So, Kendall's not here," said Miss Nicholas. "What are you going to do, keep moving or work awhile? For a writer you seem damned independent."

"It's sure not that. But I've never worked in radio before."

He saw the question reappear in their eyes: *Then how'd you come to know Kendall?* He groped for a lie, something he'd never been much good at, but she let it go. She said, "If you're fast and you can write the way people talk, you're ahead of the game before you start. We've got a new station manager. Behave yourself and I'll introduce you. Then if you work out he'll owe me one."

"What do you do here?"

"They say I'm an actress. Sometimes I work, sometimes I don't. On nice days I sit out here and wait for the man to call me." She nudged her magazine. "Sometimes I find them a story they can use, something the networks haven't beaten half to death. If they can get the broadcast rights for next to nothing, they'll usually let me play some part in it. Welcome to my office."

He looked at the tall one. "Is this your office too?"

"No, what I have is a workroom. I do sound effects. With two kids I need a real job."

Miss Nicholas broke open her lunch bag and offered him a banana. Livia had some nuts in a cloth sack, and in the sudden intimacy of shared food they were friends. Rue asked what he'd written and without thinking twice, he told her. One novel long out of print. Two stories in *Esquire*, another in the *Atlantic*, two in *Harper's*, one each in *Collier's* and *Cosmopolitan*. In the silence that followed he blinked at his own stupidity. Nothing he had just said could be proved in the name Jordan Ten Eyck.

Again Kendall was there. They would be wondering what Kendall had been doing with a literary writer, but they didn't ask.

"For what it's worth, probably nothing, I am truly impressed," Rue said. "I never knew anybody who could write a novel."

"Now you see it's no big deal."

"Don't run yourself down, Jordan. When you get in there, smother that part of yourself that wants to apologize for living."

"When I get in where?"

"When you go in for your tryout. They try anyone who asks, and they will fall all over themselves giving you a chance to pan out for them. Shall I tell you what to expect?"

"If you don't think that's cheating."

Livia laughed. "Gosh, you really are something. Honesty, modesty, and manners in one package."

"He'll never make it in radio," Rue said.

"They'll give you a short test on world affairs," Livia said. "Do you know who Pétain is?"

"French traitor."

"You'll be fine. They don't get any tougher than that."

"They'll ask you to write some continuity," Rue said. "Do you know what that is?"

"No idea on this earth."

"It's just balderdash," Livia said. "The stuff they say between things. We come out of the network every half hour with thirty seconds to fill before the next show comes down the line."

"All of it's got to be written," said Rue.

"Maybe they'll ask you for a schedule teaser," Livia said.

"Or a plug for a new client," said Rue. "Just be conversational, don't get cute, and for God's sake don't be literary."

"If you run into a difficult name, give them a phonetic in parentheses."

"There's a book in the desk that tells you how all the tough names must be said—people, countries, everything. If they like you, they may call you back, maybe for several days. But you won't get paid unless they actually put you on staff."

"That's the bad news," Livia said.

"That and the pay you actually do get," Rue said. "If working like hell for next to nothing's your cup of tea, you'll be in hog heaven. So, what do you say? I'm meeting with the man this afternoon. I'll sic him on you if you want to take the test."

"What have I got to lose?"

"Nothing but your soul, Jordan. Most of us lost that long ago. Now we're all slaves to the great god radio."

In a while a surly-looking young man came out and stood at the edge of the yard watching them.

"I guess that's my cue," Livia said.

"The hell with him," Rue said. "If he wants you, let him come over and say so."

The kid lit a smoke and said nothing till he'd smoked it down. He flipped the butt into the sand and called across the gap. "Well, are you coming, or not?"

"Of course I'm coming," Livia said.

"If you'd rather stand around shooting the breeze all day, I can do this alone. Makes no damn difference to me."

Livia smiled sweetly. "Nice to meet you, Jordan. See ya later, Rue."

She walked away and the kid let a long challenging moment pass before he turned and trucked along behind her.

"There's a boy who needs to be taught some manners," Jordan said.

"He will be. Wait till the army gets him in boot camp next week. I'd just love to be a mouse in the corner of his barracks."

They sat quiet now, the serendipitous texture of the hour broken. A few minutes later the kid came out and pulled a wood-paneled truck to the fire door. Then Livia appeared carrying a shotgun and a rifle and two pistols tucked in her belt. Jordan said, "Looks like they're gonna start their own war," but a long moment passed before Rue replied. "They're going down to the beach to record some gunshots," she said. "He's supposed to be teaching her the finer points. I think I'll throw up. She's already forgotten more about sound than that little prick, pardon my French, will ever know."

"Smells like company politics brewing."

Rue smiled bitterly. "Livia's marvelously creative and that makes them nervous. And she's a woman, and *that* makes them nervous. And she's beautiful. Don't you think so?"

He took too long to answer and she gave him a look of disgust. "You men all think alike. You always go for the Dresden dolls like me. I'd give anything for a face like hers."

Jordan found this remark endearing. Rue cast her eyes at him and said, "The prick's father runs the sound department. Old Poindexter's been here since Jesus was a cowboy. He was one of the original soundmen, back when it looked like this station might set the world on fire. Somehow that never happened and now the old man's a worse drunk than Marty Kendall. So Poindexter's son Alger was being groomed to take over the department. What that means is a continuation of the same old stuff. The gunshots sound just like they did in nineteen thirty-two, and this little masquerade they're doing down on the beach won't change that a goddamn bit. It's just a finger exercise, something to keep her in her place. Don't do anything really innovative, that's the rule of the day. Don't do anything the old man can't do, or wouldn't think of doing in a billion years of firing shotguns into the sand. And the kid would've been thrilled to continue that glorious tradition, except for two things—his number came up, and now he's gone in the draft—and Livia's gonna keep his job warm for the duration. They just want to make sure she doesn't do it too well."

She sighed. "I don't know, Jordan. You'd probably be better off moving on. This place used to be first rate. The talent that's gone through here is a crying shame. You can't retrieve that, and the waste has been tragic. We should be setting the radio world on its ear every night. But it never happens. Harford lost interest in this place and everything else about five years ago."

"What happened?"

"His wife died. One day she just got sick and died. It was very fast." She shook her head. "You never know, do you?"

She waved at someone in the distance. "If you want to know more about this place, dig out the local newspaper from a couple of weeks ago. They had an excellent recap. There's probably a copy around somewhere."

She reached over and patted his hand. "Gotta go, they're giving me the high sign in the window. Time and the new boss wait for no one."

((5))

THE clock hummed faintly as the red hand made its sweep and slipped past the black hand with a little bump. It was two o'clock and the man, Mr. Jethro Kidd, had not yet returned to check his test. Nothing to do now but wait, think, endure the silence. There had been a janitor emptying wastebaskets across the hall but he was gone now. The hush had settled in gradually: it was his awareness of it that was sudden, reaching an instant peak as he finished the test and the typewriter ceased its furious clatter. Then he heard the floor creak and he pushed his chair back and looked around the edge of the cubicle.

He was in an upstairs room on the southwest corner of the building, sitting in a circle of light. Only the light above him had been turned on: the far reaches of the room, away from the wall with its shaded windows, remained in deep shadow. On any given weekday this room would be alive with people: billers and bookkeepers, copywriters, salesmen, and job hunters, all elbowing one another for a flat surface with a typewriter and a telephone where an hour's work could be done. Now there was only Jordan, and some spook back there in the dark.

He had been given a test, two dozen questions challenging his knowledge of world leaders. He had been given the station's schedule and told to write a few lines for the four o'clock break. He had been given the morning newspaper and told to steal from it liberally.

He had been given a time limit—thirty minutes for both the test and the finished copy—but almost an hour had passed and the man had not come back for him. Too bad, he thought:

he believed he had done well, and now they'd probably make him do it over again. But he would do okay: he had always read a daily newspaper and he had a good handle on the fools who ran the world. The test had taken ten minutes and he'd used his full remaining twenty minutes to write his copy.

At four o'clock the network would break away from a band remote and bring a show called *Club Matinee* down the line from Chicago. All he knew about *Club Matinee* was what was written on the continuity sheet. The host was a fellow named Ransom Sherman and he'd be followed at four thirty by the Jimmy Dorsey band. He turned his pages down, noted the time he had finished, and hoped the man would take him at his word. But he was a compulsive rewriter and now he rolled another sheet of pulpy newsprint into the machine and began to play with it. He looked outside and wrote a weather squib with a dig at Japan, then worked Dorsey into it and nailed it down in three lines. "It's getting hot in the Coral Sea, if you happen to be a Jap. On the Jersey shoreline the weather's naturally warm, with temperatures peaking into the high seventies and more warming expected tomorrow. Stay tuned for Ransom Sherman, and don't forget Jimmy Dorsey plays a red-hot clarinet just thirty minutes from now. It's all on WHAR, your Blue Network voice of the eastern seaboard, in Regina Beach."

He read it over, timing it by the clock's red hand, then added the tag line: "It's four o'clock, eastern wartime." In the margin he noted that he had finished this draft at one forty-three, well after the time limit.

Again the floor creaked behind him. He rose from his chair, so slowly that his eyes peered just over the tops of the cubicles. He saw no one, but someone was there. He kept his eyes on the far wall, where the door lay hidden in shadow, then suddenly he squirmed out of the cubicle and walked boldly up the narrow walk.

He reached the corner and at that moment someone stood up near the door and slipped out into the hall.

He hurried to the door and pulled it open. Another steel door halfway down was just clicking shut. He covered the distance in a few long strides, opened the door, and heard feet clattering down steel stairs. He looked over the rail and saw a man hurrying out of the stairwell. An outer door opened, light poured in, and he got a glimpse of blond hair as the man flashed past, into the south parking lot.

He scrambled back through the hall. Crossed the room, parted the curtains, and there below him the fellow stood staring back at the door. Jordan got a good, long look at his face. Early thirties, handsome features, and the stocky shoulders of a woodsman.

The man looked troubled, indecisive. But suddenly he turned and ran to his car, the same black '35 Ford that had followed Jack Dulaney from California.

Jordan thought he'd seen the face of Kendall's killer.

Woodsman, he thought. That'll be his name till I find out who he really is.

((6))

JETHRO KIDD was bony and tall, fifty years old, with spectacles perched on a head that seemed too big for his body. He looked like Ichabod Crane as he read Jordan's test. But when he spoke, his voice was a steely tenor packed with authority.

"This is the first time you've ever applied for a radio job, is that right, Mr. Ten Eyck?"

"That's right."

"What made you choose Harford?"

"Actually, I came here looking for a friend."

"Mr. Kendall, I believe you told Miss Nicholas. I know Kendall by reputation but he was before my time. I only accepted this job a week ago. Officially I'm not due in till Monday. Thought I'd drop in this morning, shake a few hands, get the lay of the land. Big mistake. I haven't even had lunch yet."

Kidd gave him a cool look over the rims of his glasses. "At least you seem to know who the president of the United States is," he said, turning the test down on the table.

"It's getting hard to remember when he wasn't president."

"Miss Nicholas tells me you've written for some national magazines."

It was too late to back out of that. He repeated his literary résumé and hoped Kidd wouldn't ask for proof.

"Why did you rewrite the continuity after the deadline?"

"Thought I could get it better. And I had time on my hands."

Kidd had not apologized for the delay and did not do so now. He had arrived at two thirty looking like a man in a hurry.

"That's the kind of writer I am," Jordan said. "I'll always use all the time I've got. If you give me five minutes, I'll get it done; if I've got an hour, that's how long it'll take. I don't bill for rewrite time."

He grinned, hoping to prove he wasn't taking himself too seriously, but Kidd wasn't looking. He read the continuity again, took a fountain pen out of a well-starched shirt, and struck through a line. "Don't play games with the weather. The navy doesn't like it. It might seem harmless enough on the face of it, that business with the Japs in the Coral Sea. But don't do it again. Radio's out of the weather business for the duration."

He started to say this made sense but Kidd cut him off. "If you want to work in radio you'll have to learn what the Office of Censorship expects from us. So far they're letting us censor ourselves and that's how we want to keep it. If we don't want Roosevelt to nationalize us, we've got to act responsibly. Don't make 'em mad over little things like weather. Save your energy for the big fights."

Jordan had no idea what that meant. Kidd looked up and said, "Miss Nicholas tells me you've been classified four-F. Something about a deaf ear."

"I can hear just fine, I just can't tell where sound is coming from."

"But they're not going to draft you."

"Not for this war."

"The war's playing hell with everybody. Most of the talent that was here a year ago is in the army. Women are plugging a lot of the holes. They've got a woman doing sound effects. Miss Nicholas says she's better than the man she's replacing. We'll see. One of our production men is now a woman. Another woman composes music for our two locally produced serials. But for some reason women haven't applied for the writing jobs."

"Maybe they think it's too easy, too much like secretarial work."

"Is that what you think?"

"No, but I'm a writer, I know better. I think women want to stretch their muscles, try out for jobs that've always been closed to them."

"Maybe they don't know that the entire sound department at the Columbia Network was set up by a woman, must be at least ten years ago."

"I wouldn't've known that. If I were a woman, that's why sound might seem more exciting than writing continuity."

"Continuity's just the beginning. There's an opportunity here that should excite anybody who ever wanted to string words together. Our contract with NBC runs through August and there's a good possibility that we won't be renewing it. That means we're going to need writers who can do drama as well as continuity. That's one reason you strike me as being worth a look. Miss Nicholas tells me you've written a novel."

Jordan nodded warily.

"They've never had much luck enticing dramatists to come down here. Our writing staff as of today consists of one very tired and overworked continuity man. That's what I mean when I say you have an opportunity here. But I have no idea if you're the right man."

Jordan clasped his hands and leaned forward on his chair. "Well, I can probably write a sentence that won't stink up your air too bad. But I'd be starting right from scratch."

"That might turn out to be an advantage. It means you haven't learned all of radio's bad habits yet. It can be damned difficult to unlearn something, once you've had success doing it the old, tired way."

This struck Jordan as a profound thing for a manager to say. Abruptly Kidd changed the subject. "How are you at taking orders?"

He had to think about that. The safe answer struck him as kowtowing, and he didn't think Kidd would be impressed by an ass kisser. "Most of the time I take orders fine. Generally speaking, I don't work well for fools."

"Generally speaking, I try not to hire them."

Kidd fingered Jordan's test paper as if the words could be absorbed through the skin and tell him what he needed to know about the man who'd written them. His eyes were like his voice, steely gray. "Radio's full of stories about people who had never given it a thought, or who came in on a dare because they thought they could do better. Some of them are national stars today." He picked up Jordan's two station breaks. "We'll use your original in the four o'clock slot. Give you a chance to hear how your words sound on the air."

But Jordan sensed before Kidd spoke again that he was still being tested. "Here's a hypothetical problem for you. Somebody gives you a script. It's great, it's true, it cries out to be done. But it's political dynamite, especially in wartime. It could be embarrassing to us or our closest ally. What do you do—bury it, or argue to put it on?"

"That's hard to say without knowing what it's about."

"Then let's narrow it down. I'm sure you've heard the horror stories of German concentration camps and their treatment of Jews in Poland. What if we had a script with the action set in a concentration camp? . . . Only the masters weren't Germans, they were Americans or British."

Jordan thought at once of the Japanese being processed into Tanforan: an almost impossible thing for radio, and yet . . . what was Kidd getting at? "I don't see how it could be done," he said. "Even as an allegory."

"I'm not talking about an allegory. Assume it's real."

"Then my natural inclination would be to try and do it."

"And how would you do that, without getting the station shut down by federal marshals and all of us thrown in jail?"

"I don't know."

But suddenly he did know. Once the question had been asked and the elements defined that made it impossible, he saw the faint shape of an answer. "I think I'd try to submerge it in theme. Give it context, so maybe it wouldn't stand alone as an attack against us or England." Kidd sat stony faced and Jordan went on to the next logical step. "Context means you'd need more stories."

"Could you write them?"

"Maybe." He nodded. "Sure."

"What would these stories be?"

He didn't immediately say: his mind had leaped ahead to the bigger picture. "A limited series," he said; "probably no more than half a dozen stories. Tales of wartime incarceration, each with a point about the horrors of being a prisoner."

Kidd was watching him intently now.

"I think I'd start with the German camps. It would almost have to start there. And end with the Japs on Bataan. That way you've got the Axis like bookends, like lightning rods at both ends of it."

"How would you write it? We don't know what's going on on Bataan."

"We can imagine. All of a sudden the Japs got tens of thousands of prisoners. What will they do with them? Build a camp somewhere and the men will be marched there; that's what always happens." He thought of his own country and its vicious Civil War. "I'd have to fictionalize it. Infer the panorama through one pair of eyes."

In the middle he would put in stories from various lands. Maybe something on Andersonville in 1865. Of turncoats and the makeshift justice of the camp. A lynch mob rose up from some dank place in his Southern heritage, but a split show suddenly occurred to him as having more thematic strength. People are the same all over and we never learn anything from history. A single hour with two stories, prison camps North and South; then plunk Kidd's piece, whatever it was, down in the third or fourth show.

"I'm guessing . . . is your script about our camps for American Japs?"

For a moment he thought that what he had said had taken Kidd's breath away. "Actually, I hadn't even thought of that," Kidd said. "Jesus, what a thing that would be. Talk about getting us all arrested."

Jordan sat forward on his chair and waited. Kidd said, "I wouldn't mind reading your book," and Jordan said, "Wish I had one to give you."

It didn't seem to matter now. Kidd said, "Are you going to be in town awhile?" and Jordan said, "It's beginning to look like it."

"What about this afternoon? Can you hang around?"

"Sure."

"There's no guarantee I'll even be able to get back to you today."

"All I'd be doing is looking at girls on the beach."

"I might ask you to come down tomorrow. I know it's Sunday but the show goes on. And you'll be working for nothing until I decide if I can use you."

"Writers are used to that. It's called writing on spec."

"There's one thing you can do right now if you want to make yourself useful. I'm talking about heavy lifting, not writing."

"I'm no stranger to that."

"Go ask Miss Nicholas if she can run you over to the office. When you get there, ask for Mr. Stoner. He'll tell you what he needs."

((7))

Out in the yard the picnic tables were now crowded with people, but Miss Nicholas was not among them. It looked like a party building, and the talk revealed a mix of specialists in the single-minded search for the compelling half hour of air. Salesmen talked with their own or with clients, and off at the table abandoned by Miss Nicholas a group of actors rehashed last Saturday's horror show. The show had gone well and surprised them all. The idea of boring out Easton's heart with an electric drill had sounded corny at the table reading, but on the air the bloody thing had come so vividly to life that two dozen listeners had called to complain. "You can't ask for a better reaction than that"—this from a middle-aged woman who had obviously been part of it. Jordan, standing nearby, learned that her name was Hazel.

No one questioned his presence. It was an open affair, come as you are, and a stranger among them was nothing unusual. The grill had been stoked and a cloud of rich gray smoke carried the aroma of cooking franks over the trees and down to the inlet. Jordan helped himself to a hot dog and beer. Drifted past one conversation and into another. Asked about Miss Nicholas, but she had not been seen in at least an hour. But she was doing a commercial at five, so she couldn't be far away.

He felt an almost constant unease now. A cold prickly undercurrent had planted itself under the hazy warmth of the bright spring day. The chain of events he had started was out of his control. At that moment the wind swirled the smoke across the yard and the Woodsman appeared. First there was only a ghostly presence beyond the pits; then he came through the knots of people and the smoke wafted past him. He had changed his shirt: now he wore a bright red short-sleeve of some thin, cool material, open to midriff to show off a barrel of a chest, shaved like Charles Atlas, smoother than the underarms of Rita Hayworth. He was a genial fellow, a born lady-killer, not at all the nervous creature Jordan had seen from the window.

The man started across the yard. Jordan hadn't been seen yet and there was a moment when he might have slipped away undetected. Instead, for some reason, he dropped his half-finished beer into the wire trash basket and circled the tables on an intercepting course.

The moment was less than that—part of a second when the man saw him coming at the edge of his vision. He turned his head and looked: their eyes met, but it was Jordan who broke stride and balked.

This was not the Woodsman. This was someone new.

A brother, he thought. They were too much alike not to be related.

They nodded to each other, the polite, impersonal greeting of strangers. Jordan recovered his pace and followed the man into the building, past the empty receptionist's desk, and on across the lobby to the men's room.

They stood side by side, alone at the urinals. The man stopped at the washbowl and ran water over his hands. He was suddenly tense: the air between them had changed as awareness set in. This man never saw me before, Jordan thought, but he knows me now.

He stepped up to the second bowl and their eyes locked in the mirror. They were just a word away from mortal combat.

Then the man looked away, intimidated for all his hard male strength. He fumbled at the towel dispenser but it jammed and he left dripping water.

Jordan opened the door and watched him cross the lobby.

Suddenly he was on the man's trail again—through the door and out, bird-dogging him across the yard. What was he going to do now? He didn't know.

A hand reached out and grabbed him. He spun around, ready to fight.

"Good grief," said Miss Nicholas. "Where's the fire?"

When he looked around again, the second Woodsman had disappeared in the smoke.

((8))

THE Harford building was a little less rosy in the fading afternoon, and there was still only that luxury Packard in the parking lot. Miss Nicholas pulled in beside it. "I'd better come in with you. I can run you back if this doesn't take too long."

The building was locked. She rapped on the glass and Jordan cupped his hands and peered inside. He was looking down a hallway with darkened offices on either side.

"Let's look around back," Miss Nicholas said.

On the west side they found a loading dock and ramp, with a pickup truck at the ramp and a row of wooden crates, some as large as small refrigerators, lined up on the dock. "We're making progress," she said. "That's Stoner's truck."

They climbed an iron stair to the dock and squeezed between the crates to a dark steel door half hidden in the shadows. She opened the door with a loud metallic snap and they looked into a dark back hallway.

"Gus!" Her voice had a slightly hollow sound in the cavernous building. "Hey, Gus!"

They stepped inside and moved deeper into the back room with only a gray shaft of light to guide them. "It's an elevator," Jordan said. "For freight, from the look of it. Should we go on up?"

"Didn't Kidd tell you what to do?"

"All he said was ask for Stoner."

"Hard to do when there's no one to ask."

"Then let's go up."

He pushed a button and there was a whirring sound. A large wire cage, lit on both sides by bare bulbs, floated down the shaft. It thumped on the ground and she stepped in. "You know how to run this thing?"

"Sure I do."

"God help us."

He pulled the cage shut and gripped the only visible means of control, a lever, and they started up with a jerk. He maneuvered the cage to a quivering stop at a large number 2 painted on the wall, and opened the door on another hallway, dark for the weekend.

The third floor was no different. But in its stillness he could hear music coming down the shaft. A swing band, playing a number so familiar he could almost call it by name.

"Listen."

The lift started up again, the music got louder and clearer, and then he knew it. "All the Things You Are." The door opened on the top floor and that voice came out of nowhere, nowhere and everywhere. It electrified him, chilled him, raised the hair on his neck. He forgot about Kidd and Miss Nicholas. He stepped out of the elevator, shook off the hands that grabbed him, and walked up the hallway.

He came to a crossing ablaze with coppery light. To his left was the sun, beaming through the windows from the west; down the other way, a closed mahogany door with a brass plaque, the lettering sharp in the sun.

LOREN HARFORD
PRIVATE

He turned away from the office, and at the end of the hall found a small radio studio, twenty by forty feet. The room was empty—no singer, no band, no audience—and the red-glass sign that said ON THE AIR was dark above the door. He opened the door and stepped inside. Clutching shadows were all around him: microphones, he saw, standing like scarecrows between himself and the windows. Now another surprise: the music didn't fade as the door swung shut behind him. The singer sang and the band played on, and the constant rumble was the noise of a live dancing crowd, as if a world of ghosts had filled the room, and it pulsed with the same color and life on both sides of the glass.

The spirit of Kendall seemed to be there, telling him things he could not have known. To the left is the director's booth, dark behind its own soundproof window; to the right, a production room. The piano's for fillers, and for cheapskate clients who won't foot the bill for an orchestra. The drapes hanging in the windows, now drawn back to give the room a sunbath, can be closed during a broadcast and will affect the sound accordingly. It's up to the director, what he wants to do and how good his ear is. He thought these things first in Kendall's voice, then he was vaguely aware that the voice had become his own. He sensed the two long microphones, suspended from booms over his head, and it seemed he had known they were there long before he looked up and found them.

There was a cheer from the crowd and another song was announced. "This was a hit on Broadway a few seasons ago, then Helen Forrest put it on wax with Artie Shaw. Holly and the boys give it the full treatment, right here on the beach. 'It's All Yours,' Holly."

Listen to them yell, listen how they love her. Who wouldn't love her? What's not to love?

"Jordan!"

Miss Nicholas.

He smiled and beckoned her but she grabbed his arm and bullied him out of the studio. As she pushed him down the hall, Holly began to sing, and Harford's door was now cracked open.

((9))

FROM the rooftop he could see the whole town and the miles of beach north and south. To the west, the ramshackle huts of the off-beach dwellers, the cheap rooming houses, the hash joints; then the creek and the marsh with its sloughs and mud banks, and a long crooked finger of hard dry land that made a road back to the deep distant woods of the mainland. To the east the empty sea, and far down on the southern tip, at least three miles away, the lighthouse, rising out of a shoal that hooked half a mile into the ocean. Night was hours away yet, but already lights were coming on downtown, on the street of clubs, on the boardwalk, and out along the pier.

The elevator had let them out in a small vestibule facing the sea. The wind was now billowing in from the southeast, rattling the cage as it squealed to a stop. The roof was cluttered with tools and equipment, boxes, canvas, aerials, and wires. A catwalk took them to a tin shed on the southwest corner. There they found Stoner, hunched inside, rocking back and forth on a squeaky chair near the far wall as he listened intently through a set of earphones.

"Hey, Gus, I brung you a fellow toiler."

Stoner held up a finger and cocked his head at something that had been said. He listened for another few seconds, squeaked back in the chair, and gave it up. "The man really is a lunatic," he said.

"What man?"

Stoner threw a switch, amplifying the program, and a flood of screaming German invective filled the room: the unmistakable voice of Adolf Hitler.

"You're a little slow on the uptake, Gus. The rest of the world realized he was crazy seven or eight years ago. So, what're you doing listening to that crap?"

"Putting it away for posterity—if we have any." He looked at Jordan.

"This is the man I brought to help you lug all that junk up here . . . Jordan Ten Eyck . . . August Stoner."

They shook hands. Stoner was shorter than Jordan but bulkier, in his fifties, with thick slate gray hair and the pan-flat face of a street pug. "Sorry," he said, "you caught me in the middle of something. But maybe we can work around it."

He gestured at the recording machine, which was etching the speech onto a large black disc. "This will make a great recording for the sound library. Just in case Harford ever does get this station on an even keel again. Maybe we could do a political play and use this for background noise."

Jordan came to the door and looked in. "How can you listen without a translator?"

"Gus is a genius," Rue said. "He speaks about a hundred languages."

"Includink der master tongue," Stoner said, with a good accent. "This is a rebroadcast of the big speech in Berlin a couple of weeks ago. I'm taking it off the shortwave from Cologne. They've been playing it somewhere every other day to remind the good people exactly what they've allowed to happen to them."

Jordan had read some of it in the papers but it took on a greater dimension when you could hear the monster's words in his own voice. The gist of the speech was simple: After ten years of encroachment, Hitler was taking absolute power. All existing law was suspended. For Germany this was life or death. People who failed would be eliminated.

Stoner flipped off the switch. "Now he's going to annihilate his own people. What else is new? What do you say, Jordan, let's get that junk up here, then the three of us can go somewhere and get looped."

"Can't do it, Gus," Rue said. "Duty calleth. The man's got me doing Little Miss Nicotine at five. And I'm screaming for them again on the horror show."

"He wants me to come back too," Jordan said. "I'm not sure why."

"These are exciting times we're living in," Stoner said. "It says something about the national character when people are too busy to drink."

"You're one to talk," Rue said. "We never see you around the jailhouse anymore."

"Too busy keeping you on the air. And doing my own little gig."

"Gus does the insomniac hour, starting at midnight. Reads poetry and prose in that great pugnacious voice, and plays the damnedest lineup of music you'll ever hear. Tchaikovsky by the Boston Symphony followed by Louis Armstrong. He's great company for nighthawks like me."

She looked at her watch. "Well, gentlemen, I've got to go."

"Don't worry about Jordan, I'll get him back to base camp."

She waved at them from the elevator.

"What a gal," Stoner said. "Sweet as a plum, pretty as a summer sunrise. That's her problem, she's too pretty for radio."

Jordan laughed.

"You'd be surprised," Stoner said. "Radio directors don't trust a really pretty woman to get a line straight. They figure if she was any good she'd be in Hollywood wiggling her heinie for a camera. What they want in radio is a blind man's dreamboat, a sweet voice and no face at all. I keep telling her she should think about the screen, but she's got radio in her blood. And she will be good if they let her. If she stays away from Clay Barnet. He's our program director. Pomposity in motion, dispenser of more bad advice than we got in the entire Hoover administration. It'll be interesting now that Kidd's here and apparently been put in charge of the whole shooting match. Clay won't think much of that."

He flipped the amplifier and found Hitler still raving in Cologne. "From one son of a bitch to another," he said. "This could go on for two hours. I've got a disc switch coming up, then we can get moving."

He sat at his table and Jordan watched from the doorway. The cutting head etched its way toward the center, carving the voice into the wax and leaving behind it an unbroken strand of residue that Stoner had twirled around the spindle in the center.

"What'll you be doing here if Kidd does hire you?"

"I'm a writer."

"Ah! This is your lucky day. Writing's a seller's market around here." He leaned over and looked at his work. "Come on in, watch what I do here. This might help you if they put you into anything sophisticated."

In fact he was fascinated by the scribbling movements of the machine, making its cold objective affidavit of the day's events from the day's air. Stoner eased over onto a straight-backed chair and Jordan sat beside him in the squeaky recliner.

"We get fifteen minutes on each of these transcription discs. If a program runs longer than that, I've got to find a place to break it. So I wait for crowd noise, laughter, or applause, and I open the pot on my second machine and let one disc blend into the other. If it's played back by an engineer with a good sense of timing, the audience won't even know there's been a break. Later I'll take you through the system, give you the grand tour."

"That'll be great. If I get that far."

Stoner waved this off, a mere formality. "It helps if you're a writer to know what the capability is. There's no sense writing something we can't do, but I'll bet between Livvy and me we can make up something to cover just about any situation. Do you know Miss Teasdale?"

"Met her a while ago."

"Amazing woman, incredible talent. She should be at NBC, but that's another story. Get her to show you how she makes the latch on a briefcase sound just like a car door closing. Christ, she drives old Poindexter crazy. A great example of what this station was and could be again. Did you see the article the *Beachcomber* did on us? . . . It's in that drawer over there. Take it with you, it'll give you an idea what you're getting into."

Jordan folded the sheets and tucked them into his shirt. Stoner leaned into his desk. "Here we go now . . . you can hear him building to a pitch."

Hitler pounded the podium. An ovation filled the shed and Stoner opened his second machine, giving the discs a five-second overlap. He took a paintbrush and guided the string of residue to the center, where it wrapped around the spindle and kept the cutting head clear. "Perfect," he said, shutting down the first machine. "Now, if you write us a play about patriots under the iron boot and you think a bit of bellowing Hun might be just the ticket for background, a competent engineer will know exactly how to cue it up. So, let's get out of here. I need to be back in fifteen for another disc hookup."

In the elevator Stoner continued his monologue about the station's capabilities. "We've got a fully functional microphone studio in this building. We can switch over at a moment's notice, and that can be a real plus if there's trouble at the main plant. If a listener got up to take a leak, he wouldn't even know we were off the air. And talk about class, it's got cork floors. You don't want any noise in a studio, and when Harford built this place six years ago, he had the whole floor corked. It's so quiet in there you can walk right up to someone before they know you're there."

They floated past the fourth floor. Holly's voice boomed into the shaft and the light flashed in Stoner's face.

"It's not quiet now," Jordan said.

"That's coming through the door, not the wall. Even then you wouldn't notice it if he didn't have it cranked up like that."

"What's that all about?"

Stoner shrugged. "God knows. He's been playing it all day. He can't get enough of it. Sometimes I can feel the beat coming right through the ceiling."

They bumped on the ground. Stoner walked through the dark chamber and pulled up the ramp door. "This is the job, champ—plain old grunt work. This stuff's heavier than *Our Gal Sunday* on a Friday afternoon. Whadaya say let's take the biggest of these bastards first?"

They manhandled the crate onto a dolly, then into the building, then onto the lift, and on up the shaft. The music came and went again.

"That's my most important job right now," Stoner said. "I take that baby off the line and make two virgin masters every week."

They reached the roof. Jordan said, "You've got me feeling pretty ignorant. I guess I don't know what the hell you're talking about."

"No reason you should. Harford wants a line check made of that show every Saturday night—no excuses, no failures, no acts of God permitted. He wants it done and it better be right. So I take it off the line and leave it for him first thing every Monday. The best sound money can buy."

"And then what? He sits there all day and just listens to it?"

"Some days he does. I guess he can't get enough of the singer. Strange, huh?"

"I didn't say that."

"No, but I don't think you'll argue much if I say it. Some people think he's a little crazy anyway. Did you hear what happened to his wife?"

"I heard she died."

"Sleeping sickness, they call it. She went to visit her family in Virginia and came home with a terrible headache. Lay down in her bed and never got up again." Stoner shook his head. "They say a mosquito causes it. Imagine losing your wife to a mosquito bite."

"I guess that's enough to make any man crazy," Jordan said.

They worked up and down through the darkened building, and with each trip Stoner captured another segment of Hitler until he had it all. Jordan felt a superficial bond forming between them, something that always happens when two men struggle on a four-man job. Stoner was naturally gregarious and didn't mind talking about himself. He had been here ten years and had learned what he knew from scratch. "I didn't know my keister from a kilocycle in nineteen thirty-two. But I'm a quick read and it wasn't long before we had this station booming up and down the coast. Now we're louder than the Feds like us to be, and every once in a while they send inspectors over to make sure we're not cheating on our wattage."

They traded stories, and he told Stoner his fiction of the Ten Eyck family, transplants from Holland.

"Do you really speak a hundred languages?"

"Rue exaggerates. Counting sign language and dialects, it's closer to fifteen."

"You speak to deaf people?"

Stoner made signs with his hands. "That means, 'Don't ask me, I just work here.'"

Jordan laughed and the fellowship ripened between them.

"Once I was offered a job as a translator in New York. But I'm like Rue, I like radio."

Jordan told of working on the racetrack, years ago at Belmont and that one summer at Saratoga. That seemed safe enough. But then Stoner said, "How'd you end up here?" and he knew he had to tell about Kendall since he'd already told Livia and Rue. "I came looking for a friend. Fella named Marty Kendall."

Stoner jerked upright as if he'd been slapped. "Jesus Christ, Kendall! How the hell did you know Kendall?"

He launched into a new mix of truth and lies: how he'd met Kendall on the racetrack, but he moved the locale to Hialeah in Florida. He told how they'd shared a tack room and a winter in their lives, how Kendall had spoken so fondly of his radio days, and how one day, without a word to anyone, he had simply vanished. Stoner looked incredulous, as if he couldn't accept what he was hearing. "What was he doing on a *racetrack*, for Christ's sake?"

"He never explained that."

Suddenly Kendall's spirit was there on the roof between them. "He must've cracked up," Stoner said. "How else can you figure it?"

They stood there for a long quiet stretch. Then Stoner gave a helpless little shrug and said, "Let's button this place up and get the hell out of here." But Jordan knew they were not yet finished with Kendall. Stoner fidgeted at the elevator landing, and the ride down was sober and quiet and dark. Even Harford had left the building, and they slipped past the fourth floor with the silence broken only by the whirring elevator.

"I've got one more grunt job, if you will," Stoner said. "Couple of barrels to go to the dump."

They got in the truck and drove north out of town. At the station, Jordan could see that the party he had left earlier was still growing. The place was swarming with people, the parking lots were half full, and cars were still coming in a steady stream. "This is one of the good traditions that they've kept going," Stoner said. "Harford always puts on a big feed just before the summer starts, something to kick off the season. Half the town'll be here tonight."

He pulled around to the east side and backed across the hard sand to the fire door at the end. In the glare of the headlights Jordan saw two fifty-gallon drums filled with trash.

"This is where you've got to have some balls," Stoner said. "Nothing to do but lift those babies up there."

They got out and Jordan looked at the junk—rolls of old wire, broken glass, and the remains of shattered transcription discs.

"Old sound effects records that've seen better days," Stoner said. "We'll be getting some new ones from New York in a couple of days."

They got down on either end and heaved the barrels onto the truck.

"I'll come with you to the dump," Jordan said. "Might as well see it through to the end."

The road north was relatively quiet. The early dusk was pushed by a gathering cloud cover and the sea was purple, the sky in the east like deep velvet. Far away a light flashed, some gallant skipper braving the U-boats. They passed the cutoff to the bridge, the pavement ended, and the truck rumbled over the washboard ridges of another oyster-shell road. Houses gave way to huts, and in a few miles the huts disappeared as well.

Stoner found the road he wanted, a pair of hard-packed sandy ruts cutting back through the trees to a landfill near the creek. He backed the truck around and stopped. "I knew Marty when he was still in New York," Stoner said. "I was at WEAF then. I had quit here, wanted to see what the big time felt like, and Marty showed me around. He was happy-go-lucky then. I knew he drank too much, but he always seemed to enjoy life, till it all started coming apart. By then I was back here again. I had had enough of the big city, and I was able to get Barnet to bring Marty down and give him a chance for a new start."

"A good friend'll do that."

"We became very good friends the last year or so. That's why I don't understand any of this. I still can't believe he walked out of here without telling me anything."

"And yet he did."

"And apparently did the same thing to you." Stoner took a deep breath. "I was thinking about him just this morning. I thought, He's got to be dead. Why else would he not call or even drop a postcard?"

"Shame, maybe. If he'd gone back to drinking. But you never know about people. Maybe he'll show up here yet."

"Somehow I don't think so. I've got the damnedest feeling none of us is ever going to see him again."

Suddenly Jordan thought of that half-charred newspaper clipping from Holly's house, and he said, "Maybe because it's like that other one."

Stoner turned and looked at him.

"Kendall told me about a man named March Flack. A radio actor who disappeared years ago. I assumed that was here."

"It was here. But that's been so long ago, how could that have anything to do with it? Jesus! March Flack?"

"What happened to him?"

"Nobody knows. He just dropped off the face of the earth."

"Did you know him?"

"Sure, everybody did. You couldn't be in this town and not know March. One of those bigger-than-life boys."

"And nobody ever—"

"Nobody ever found out anything. March did a broadcast one night and left the station late, to walk home. Nobody's seen him since. His wife's still here, living in the same house on the beach. Still waiting for March to come tell her where he's been the last six years."

Jordan didn't say anything and after a while Stoner made a little gesture and they got out of the truck. They climbed into the bed and wrestled the two barrels back to the tailgate. "I got 'em," Jordan said, and he pushed them off, scattering hundreds of little acetate pieces across the pit. He jerked the barrels free and tossed them, empty, back on the truck.

He asked to be dropped at his hotel. There, in his room, he stripped off his sweat-soaked shirt and sat on his bed. Across the darkening dunes the station glowed with lights and life. Here I am, he thought, not at all sure where he was.

He got out some fresh clothes and took a shower and made ready for the evening. But suddenly he remembered the newspaper story. He got the soggy clips from his pocket and flattened them against the table, and there before him was the story of Harford, from the *Regina Beachcomber*, dated April 23, 1942.

(((10)))

BEACH RADIO STATION
OBSERVES 20TH YEAR

WHAR turns 20 this year, a fact that puts it in the same historical ballpark as those pioneering beacons of the New York air, WOR, WEAF and WJZ.

But the station's history is like no other. Its technical excellence, nationally renowned, lets it play in New York "just like a local station," said a staffer requesting anonymity, in an interview.

"We've got an incredible directional tower, a location on the water that takes us straight up the Narrows into the city. On a strong night they can hear us in Maine, and as far south as Wilmington. And we're going broke."

Hardly a man among us can boast of hearing that first broadcast, Sept. 15, 1922. It was founded as experimental station XJ12 by inventor Frank Dressler, its average day then just two hours long. News, chats and phonograph records were aired over the lunchtime.

In the fall of 1925, Dressler sold his station and all its equipment to erstwhile industrialist Loren Harford, who installed it at its present site, on Beachfront Boulevard north of town. In 1927 he assumed the current call letters and established a hookup to the Blue Network of the fledgling National Broadcasting Company. In 1937 he moved most of the station's business functions to a new office complex closer to town.

Rumors abound that Harford, heir to an aluminum business based in Richmond, Va., has squandered much of his family fortune in a lifelong infatuation with radio. "To pursue it at the level of his ambition requires a deep purse," says George Rawlins, a *Radio Guide* reporter who wrote of Harford's adventures in the early thirties.

"We're talking network capability, and that means a staff of up to 85 employees. If you add a studio orchestra, the weekly payroll could go well over 100."

Adding to Harford's problem is his naturally reclusive nature. "He's got no sense of public relations," said Rawlins. "The pieces I wrote had to be compiled mostly from hearsay, and few of his employees want to be quoted by name."

Harford came here soon after the World War, having served as a lieutenant in the U.S. Army's First Division in France. Some say his love affair with radio began in 1910, when Caruso and others made their historic experimental broadcast from the stage of the Metropolitan Opera.

"Almost no one heard that broadcast," said Rawlins. "But for many of us, just the fact that such a thing was possible lit a fire in our hearts. People born since radio came of age simply can't imagine what it was like when it was all new and just beginning to happen."

"What Harford really wanted was to buy a New York station," said Lawrence Bills, Harford's station manager from 1927 until he joined the network in 1936. "Lacking that, he wanted a station that could be heard there."

Directional radio signals are nothing new, having their roots in the Marconi trans-Atlantic experiment of 1901. A more modern example is the 1939 Admiral Byrd series on NBC. Shortwaved from Little America to New York via Buenos Aires, it was then beamed southward from the powerful WGEO directional tower in Schenectady. In Antarctica, 10,000 miles away, the Byrd party could hear its own program, instantly and on ordinary radios, as clearly as if the transmitting tower had been broadcasting from the ice floes half a mile away.

"As far as Harford is concerned, his 5,000 watts easily had the clout of 10,000, especially when you beam it over water with a specific purpose in mind," said Bills. "We played louder downtown than anyone but WOR. And WOR had 50,000 watts to our five."

In 1933, the station began airing an electrifying series of dramatic broadcasts. These had many times the realism usually encountered on the air. They were also controversial, putting Harford in the crosshairs of the newly created Federal Communications Commission.

"He nearly lost his license to broadcast," remembers Warren Nelson, then radio critic for the New York *Times*. "My understanding was that he was one vote shy of becoming history. You can't fool around with the federal government and expect to stay on the air."

But what about the philosophy of a free radio? Wasn't that one of the cornerstones of radio law, adopted in the twenties in response to runaway technology?

"Believe what you want," says Nelson, "but radio in the United States has never been free. The idea of freedom has been set down because it looks good on paper, but in real life the F.C.C. has powers that scare radio people to death. The commission always holds the trump card, which may be played at its discretion every three years, whenever a station's license comes up for renewal."

Any station may be called into question and asked to prove that it has operated "in the public interest." Challenges to a station's license may be filed by anyone— listeners, rival broadcasters, or by members of the commission itself.

"The term 'in the public interest' means whatever the F.C.C. decides it means," said Nelson.

"You can't have anarchy on the air," says Rawlins in the F.C.C.'s defense. "But I can certainly understand how a man of Harford's ambitions would find arbitrary regulations intolerable. In the hands of a timid commission, the term 'in the public interest' can only lead to bland, unexciting radio."

Specifically, Harford was charged with undermining national morals by airing dramas with bold adult themes. "We're not talking about dirty radio," said Nelson. "But that's what some people thought, in a medium known most of all for its purity."

Harford came under fire for two weekly shows, an anthology aired under the title "Soundstage," and a half-hour continuing drama, "Home from the War."

" 'Soundstage' adapted short stories by gifted but unsung writers," said Nelson. "I remember one piece that had prostitution as its central theme. You can imagine how that played."

But it was "Home from the War" that drew the most wrath. The serial was denounced by church leaders, leagues for decency and by many members of Congress, who later admitted they had never heard the show. Bills, who directed, remembered it well.

"The hero was a veteran of the World War who had seen so much savagery that he had lost his faith in God. We had him come right out and say this in the first episode, and I felt the shock waves all the way up in the booth when the actor got to those lines. This just isn't done in American radio—not unless you're giving them a dyed-in-the-wool all-American villain.

"But this guy was our hero. And slowly over that first month we built his character till you couldn't help but love him. That's what they never forgave us for. We made them love an atheist.

"Then we took on real political issues, like the Bonus March in 1932. That whole bonus fiasco was a disgrace to this country and to the men who fought for it. It was an embarrassment to our government and it should've been. Here we had Herbert Hoover dining on pheasant with a Marine honor guard standing at attention, and outside thousands of vets and their children were starving."

"They had this actor who could do General MacArthur to a T," says Nelson. "They didn't even change the names! When Hoover sends MacArthur out to roust the vets and burn their shantytown, you just lived it. I wrote a column about that show. I couldn't believe what I was hearing."

Says Bills: "I think the only reason Harford survived that incident was that Roosevelt was in by then and the makeup of the commission had changed. Even then it was close, but Harford thrived on that kind of excitement. Let them dare try to take his license! That was a fight he was ready to take all the way through the courts."

This kind of legal fight is seldom seen in radio. As Waldo Abbott notes: "The industry has adopted the attitude of peace at any price," and no one wants to tackle the F.C.C.

Harford hated the "peace at any price" doctrine. "I worked for the man nine years," says Bills, "and I still can't say I knew him. I do know he was a radio animal. He believed that radio was the most powerful instrument for social change that we would ever have in his lifetime.

"He couldn't sit on a story because of someone else's politics. That wasn't in his makeup. If the story struck him as true, he was going to air it come hell or high water."

This era of daring and high creativity ended abruptly in 1936, when Harford's wife, actress Jocelyn James, died of encephalitis in the prime of her life.

"That's when the guts went out of this place," said one Harford staffer who shall remain nameless. "We've been going through the motions ever since."

"She was wonderful," said Bills. "We used her on everything and she could do anything. She could play little girls, old ladies, just any nationality or ethnic group.

"She was the atheist's wife in 'Home from the War,' and part of the reason why people came to love the hero was because they loved her so much."

Not much is known of her life with Harford. Apparently they were lifelong sweethearts, having shared the Richmond childhood and an early vision of what radio could do.

"They were just getting started when that awful thing happened to her," said Bills. "She wanted to start an actors' colony out at their estate on the mainland. Harford had an old-timey village built out there in the woods so her friends could come down from the city and be on the air and have a place to stay for as long as they wanted.

"It was a great idea. But it all ended when she died."

On the eve of its 20th birthday, the station is still on the air. But it's been a long time since its glory days.

((11))

JORDAN arrived at the station at ten o'clock and found the party in full swing. The clearing was mobbed with people, the tables and grills obliterated in a crush of bodies. He was handed a beer by a man in an apron and he stood at the corner of the building watching the people and the lights twinkling off in the woods. He recognized only a few faces from the afternoon: those who had come and gone and come again, in tweeds now rather than jeans.

He was surprised by the number of young men. Many were in uniform, perhaps on a final fling before shipping out Monday for the great adventure. How many would be dead in a year? He listened to the crowd and was saddened by the swagger. It was too easy to talk at parties, to add your voice to the weight of public opinion, to take your pride in the other man's risk and bandy words like "glory." He had eaten only lightly since dawn but there was still much food to be had. Another hot dog, an ear of corn basted with butter, sprinkled with salt, and handed to him, steaming from the fire, on heavy brown paper. He stood apart, drinking his beer, eating his corn, watching the passing parade.

Rue appeared out of the crowd. "Well, there you are. I was beginning to think you'd left us."

"Not a chance. I can't remember when I've had this much fun."

She smiled somewhat scornfully. "My dear, you haven't seen any fun yet. How'd you like to help a lady in distress?"

"Doing what?"

"A gentleman wouldn't ask. Do you want to help, or not?"

"Sure, I think. I'd probably be honored."

She grabbed his arm and pushed through the crowd toward the trees by the creek. They broke through a wall of smoke and came to the volleyball net, staked out in the sand, with just enough light from the south parking lot to reveal the shapes of people around it and make a game of some kind possible. "I have found us a player," she announced to the crowd. "The good guys are back in the hunt."

He didn't want to be a player but suddenly he was stuck with it. A warm voice nearby said, "Welcome to the ranks of the damned, Jordan," and Livia clapped him on the shoulder. "Don't worry, it won't last long. They're beating our brains out."

He was to replace Evie Overdier, a dangerously fat woman who was still breathing hard. His other teammate was Jimmy Brinker, a thin man in his late twenties who wore a baseball cap and had a soft, shy handshake.

Three shadowy men emerged from the crowd across the net. "So, who the hell is this?" said a voice, and Livia made the introductions. "This is Jordan Ten Eyck . . . Jordan, Clay Barnet." Barnet turned his back and walked away. Off to his left stood Alger Poindexter, and in the right court was another fellow he knew. Peter Schroeder, Livia was saying . . . one of the two Woodsmen, he couldn't tell which in the poor light.

So now he had a name. Barnet turned and came back to the net, closer now, for a better, second look. He wore a neatly trimmed beard, a man of middle age playing a young man's game. Schroeder stepped back, just out of the light, and Poindexter stood his ground. Livia drew her team together about ten feet behind the net. "Jordan, you start against Clay at the net. You're the only one with the reach and we can't afford to lose another point. Clay's been humiliating Evie, so if you can just make him eat a little sand I'll die a happy woman. Have you ever played this game?"

"A long time ago. Don't expect any miracles."

What difference did it make? He'd be badly out of practice now, and it was a sandlot game with a dime store net, and lines drawn in the sand. Did it matter who would win? But there was Barnet, a predator stalking the net, and Jordan knew nothing was ever just a game to a man like that.

"They're ahead twelve-four and they've got the ball," Livia said. "Let's see if we can make it respectable."

The game began and Barnet scored immediately, punching the ball past Jordan's outstretched hands. Poindexter and Barnet did a little war dance, hand-slapping and yelling taunts over the net.

"Thirteen-four," Barnet said. "Two points to game."

Barnet served to Livia. She tipped it up and Jordan punched it over Barnet's head, making Poindexter come up fast. The ball dropped between them.

"Goddammit, Alger, I had the son of a bitch!"

Rue laughed and moved over. "No point, our ball."

She served a sizzling shot that cleared the net by half an inch. Barnet got a fist on it and popped it over Livia's head into the backcourt. Brinker kept it alive, Rue tipped it, and Jordan slapped it across. Now he was ready. He knew exactly what Clay Barnet would do, what the Barnets of the world always do. How they always go for the throat.

He faked left and doubled back at once as Barnet took the bait and slammed right. He tipped the ball and Livia was there at his shoulder, banging it past Barnet's hands for the point.

"Hot damn, sucker slam!" Rue cried. "Thirteen-five!"

Her next serve was hard and fast. Barnet attacked the ball, skimming it just over the net. Jordan went headfirst after it, getting under it in the last second and looping it back into play. Brinker made the save and Livia batted it across. Jordan was on his feet, ready now as Barnet sent it whipping into his face. He punched it back, took it again, punched it back: three, four, five times, like warriors in the ring they slugged it out at point-blank range. Barnet wavered and missed, and Rue screamed, "Thirteen-six!" and clapped her hands.

Jordan heard Barnet say, "Son of a bitch," and when he looked again Barnet was staring into his eyes. He glared back, said, "Are you talking to me?" and now Barnet wilted under this challenge as well. "Your ass is mine, cowboy," Jordan said in the same tone of voice.

It was ugly now and the crowd was getting into it. People were two deep, shouting and cheering him on. The serve was broken, back and forth, the players rotated, and the Woodsman was flushed out into the light . . . the second Woodsman, Jordan could now see: the one of the bathroom mirror. He danced constantly, as if in the unceasing movement he could put off the moment of recognition that had already occurred. Jordan held him with his eyes. He had two of them on the run now, for reasons that had nothing to do with this silly game.

He served to Poindexter and again they won the point when Poindexter went back for an easy return and got tangled with Barnet, who was out of place in his eagerness to get at it.

Rue cupped her hands for a bullhorn effect, and when she bellowed, "Thirteen-seven!" the crowd laughed and cheered all at once.

Livia zipped the ball over the net. Barnet made the return and suddenly found himself in another standoff with Jordan. A frenzied volley of shots brought the crowd to a screaming pitch, but Barnet choked and missed again. Jordan knew then that the game was all but won.

He was everywhere now. He had taken away Barnet's game and was running him ragged. His legs were young and his heart was strong, and Barnet looked older with each point he lost. When Poindexter came up to help, Barnet pushed him away. Jordan took the point and glared through the net. He could see the pain in Barnet's face and he knew how desperate Barnet must be to call time. But when he said, "You'd better take five, old man," he knew Barnet would die first. When pride calls the shots, judgment goes out the window.

The score was thirteen-all when Barnet twisted his ankle and came up limping. Enough, Jordan thought: I've made him eat enough for one night.

"I think we have a draw here," he said to Livia.

"Absolutely." She was flushed with victory. "It's a draw, Clay."

"The hell with that. You stop, you fault. You fault, you lose."

"Then that's what we do."

She gave Rue a hug and walked off the court. Jordan went around the net but Peter Schroeder had already disappeared.

((« 12 »))

"STAY with me," Livia said. "I'll get you in ahead of the crowd."

They were checked through the door by a pert redhead wearing a badge that said HI, I'M BECKY HART. "Hullo, Liv. I hear you dropped anchor on the all-American boys tonight."

"This is our anchor. Mr. Jordan Ten Eyck."

The redhead's tiny hand disappeared in his. "My spies tell me your performance was virtuoso, Mr. Ten Eyck. Welcome to the club."

They walked across the lobby to the door marked STU-DIOS. The hallway beyond was still half dark, with some light coming through the glass in the studio doors. "This is Studio A," Livia said. "We do the band broadcast here. In ten minutes this place'll be a madhouse."

They stepped into a large room, two stories high with an observation balcony stretching around it at the second-floor level. The soundstage was flanked by a bandstand, with a banner on the wall behind it that said JUD WILLIAMS AND HIS WINDY CITY SEVEN. There was a small open dance floor and beyond that, an audience section of two hundred seats. Off to the right, the director's booth was alive with lights. Stoner sat behind the glass, talking with an older bearded man who kept demanding microphone levels through an intercom speaker. "The director's a fellow named Dedrick Maitland," Livia said.

"We just got him from Chicago. Supposedly he's good with audience shows like this one."

Behind them the door opened and Becky Hart came in. "Gangway, mates, we're about to unleash the mob." She moved along the far wall, turning on the overhead lights and picking up scraps of trash. "The band must be here," Livia said, and Jordan felt his heartbeat.

"Come on, we've got a little time left. I'll show you the other studio." She squeezed past on her tiptoes, her hair brushing his cheek, and talked her way out into the hall. "We've got a pretty good group here, Jordan. Gus and Rue and Jimmy are wonderful people. So is Becky. She wants to be a producer, a tough racket for a girl to crack. But she knows a good half hour when she hears one."

"Don't believe anything she says, Jordan," said Becky, coming along behind them to light up the hallway. "I'm only in it for the money."

They laughed as Becky moved past. "We've got two distinct camps here, as you may have begun figuring out. On our side it cuts across all the disciplines. The common ground is that we all love great radio. Rue, Gus, Becky, me, Jimmy—we meet once a month and eat dinner together. Read to each other—anything we've picked up that has unusual possibilities for the air. Of course, then the problem is actually getting it on the air—the age-old battle between money and art. Trying to convince Barnet that something can be intelligent and still be salable, and hope he'll let us steal an hour from the network and dare the wrath of the gods. That's what Becky meant when she said, 'Welcome to the club.' You're one of us now, whether you like it or not."

She pushed open a door and they went into a small room filled with the sounds of shoveling. First a shovel, then a spade in hard earth, the steel singing as it cut the ground under the boot. "We're burying a man alive tonight," Livia said. "This is Studio B. We do the horror show here every Saturday night, right after the band broadcast."

The room was in darkness except for a small circle of light around the soundstage. Two full-length microphones were set up about five feet apart, and two suspended overhead. The room had a standard single-floor ceiling and no section for an audience. Some of the cast had already arrived and were seated around a table across the room. Jimmy Brinker was there, still wearing the sweatshirt and the baseball cap. Poindexter was now decked out in his army working dress and looked more openly hostile than ever. Jordan recognized some of the actors from outside—the two men and the woman named Hazel—and another woman, in her sixties, with elegant silver hair. The director's booth was dark yet, but off to one side, in a cordoned area packed with turntables and gadgetry, sat an enormous fat man sipping from a coffee cup and playing with sound records. "Old Poindexter," Livia said softly. "My boss."

The shoveling went on, with various tools in various earths as the fat man lifted the needle and tried one band after another. At last he found a spade to his liking and he let it run, like an announcement of the grave diggers' ball, while he got up and refilled his coffee cup with something from a brown paper bag that probably wasn't coffee.

"The story's about a man who disappears," Livia said, "and how they finally learn what really happened to him."

"What did happen to him?"

"Got buried alive near a swamp in Louisiana. Voodoo country."

He didn't know if he should say what he was thinking. Then he said it: "He's got the wrong shovel."

She looked at him sharply. He shrugged and said, "I wouldn't tell you your job, but you don't find many stones in the ground down there. He's got some pretty hard spadework going on for that kind of earth." Shrugged again. "For what it's worth from a guy who doesn't know much about radio but has done a bit of shoveling."

She didn't say anything at first. Then: "You're right, of course. I tried to tell him this afternoon it didn't sound right. But what do I know? Besides, I've got other things to worry about."

A long pause, then she said, "Actually, this is a pretty unhappy show all around. I had a fierce argument with Clay when the script came down from mimeo. Right away he wanted Pauline to play the missing man's widow. Pauline's the older woman with the gray hair . . . Pauline Flack. Her husband did disappear, in real life. I think it's unconscionable to put her in that part and I said so. Even if she does need the money."

"What did Barnet say to that?"

"Just that I should shut up, mind my own business, and do what I'm told. And he's right, I've got plenty to do without worrying about Pauline. We've got a graveyard scene with all kinds of sound going on at once. We've got wind, a church bell, people walking, and clods of dirt hitting the box. The sounds of the box itself bumping against the sides of the hole. Dirt crumbling and falling down. The preacher rustling the pages of his Bible. Then there's thunder and it starts to rain, and I've got the sounds of all those damn umbrellas going up. It's not my job to worry about Pauline, but I like her. She's a lovely woman, and it annoys me that Clay won't use her for anything and then calls her for a part like this. She must be damned desperate for the money."

Rue came in. "Got any miracles for us tonight, Liv?"

Livia shook her head and Rue went on down to the soundstage. Someone up front laughed and the grave digger started anew. Livia said, "Come on, I'll introduce you around. You can form your own opinions from here on."

He met the acting aggregation: Hazel Kemble, Grover Eastman, and Tate Stallworth. Hazel was a woman of fifty-something with a puckish face and piercing blue eyes. Her chestnut hair was beginning to pale as the Japs closed off shipping routes from the Far East and put dye on the short shelf with stockings and spare tires. She had once played a monarch on NBC for Ponds cream: "Maude Adams was the star and I was the queen," she said. Livia said, "Hazel comes from a long line of theater people," and Hazel said, "Yes, my great-great-aunt was Fanny Kemble. My family is as distinguished as the Barrymores."

"You know the crowd," said Eastman; "the Staten Island Kembles and the Barrymores of Myrtle Avenue." He was tall and thin, slightly puffy under the eyes, and even before he spoke, his presence seemed that of a mean spirit. "Don't let her feed you that malarkey; she tries it on everyone. The closest she ever got to Maude Adams was when she went to see *Peter Pan* in nineteen-oh-two."

Hazel gave him a smile laced with acid. *You fool,* she said with her eyes.

Stallworth was in the same age bracket, faintly reminiscent of Kendall with his thick speckled mustache. "Don't get the wrong idea about these two," he said. "They've been having a mad love affair for years."

Eastman gave a barking laugh and blew a kiss.

"You've met Jimmy," Livia said, and he shook hands with Brinker.

"And Alger," Livia said, but he felt no encouragement from young Poindexter to do more than a slight nod.

"This is Pauline Flack."

Mrs. Flack said, "Hello," and shook his hand. Livia said, "Jordan is a writer," and Mrs. Flack asked what he'd be writing. Her voice was very British and genuine. Jordan told her that he hadn't actually been hired yet, and as they talked he noted that her elegant dress was fraying at the edges and the stitching was starting to go in the toe of her left shoe.

"This is our little company," Rue said.

"All enjoying our lean years together," said Hazel.

A sudden silence fell over the room. Then old Poindexter started the shoveling again and Hazel's temper boiled over. "Well, what are you all staring at? We're all in the same boat here and there's no use crying over it. None of us will ever see New York again."

"Some of us never have," Rue said. "But we will."

"Then you'd better get on the next bus north while you've still got your looks. If you're willing to sleep around, maybe you'll get somewhere."

"That's our gal," said Eastman. "Always in form."

"Some of us are going to do wonderful things," Rue said. "Jimmy is a shining talent. And Tate can do any dialect." She looked at Jordan. "He can play a Chinaman with a shirt laundry or a colored porter on the fast train to Chicago."

"Yassah, boss," said Stallworth, a mockingly bad Negro. "But tonight I play the hero, an all-American white boy. I get the girl too."

"But not before she's ravished by the monster," said Hazel in a soft voice so different from her own. "Please, Mr. Wyent," said the young virgin who had taken her over. "Oh, *please* don't hurt me again."

"Isn't she a goddamn marvel?" said Eastman.

Mrs. Flack looked from face to face, her own face impassive.

"I play the heroine," Hazel said. "I'm the daughter of the missing man. Rue screams for me at the climax. Nobody screams like Rue."

"My one great talent," Rue said with a sour little grin.

The door opened and in came the fat woman of the volleyball game.

"I believe you've met Evie," Livia said.

"Hi, Jordan, nice game," said Evie with a wicked laugh.

"Evie does the cooking show. And a few voices here and there."

"On the air I'm Laura Leaf," Evie said. "I am eternally slender, my loveliness the stuff of legend. I will cook for you all year, Jordan, if you can get Rue to send out her picture to my fans."

The shovel sounds had stopped and now old Poindexter pulled himself out of the chair and came over to join them.

"Jordan . . . my boss, Maurice Poindexter."

Hazel launched another attack. "Maurice makes us sound so good. Of course, Livia helps him enormously. She's a towering talent, wouldn't you say so, Maurice?"

Young Poindexter bristled. But the old man sipped from his cup and said, "Oh, she's an artiste, no doubt about it."

"Livia came up with the crowning touch last week," Hazel said. "The hot water bottle filled with motor oil sounded just like a real heart bursting. Didn't you think so, Maurice?"

"You're far more expert on that subject than I could ever be. I've never heard a heart burst. If you say that's how it sounds, who am I to argue?"

"Livia's been taking classes in the art of sound effects," Hazel said. "Did you know there's a class up at NYU? Who would've believed it, that our little business would come of age in such a big, big way? And Livia's so dedicated, as I'm sure Maurice will tell you. She goes up to the city twice a week to learn her technique."

Livia moved out of Poindexter's vision and made a cut-it motion across her neck. But Hazel just smiled and said, "She's learning things that might otherwise take her years to know."

Rue cleared her throat. "So here we are. Where's Clay?"

"Went to get his ankle taped," Evie said. She put a hand to the side of her face and said, "Personally, I think he's faking."

Old Poindexter looked at Jordan. "So, you're our new writer."

"I wouldn't say that yet. I talked to Mr. Kidd, that's about all."

"Do you write drama?"

"Prose till now."

"But you do deal with the stuff of human nature."

"I try."

"As a student of human nature, what's your opinion of Mr. Barnet's injury? Do you think he was faking?"

"I was kidding, Maurice," Evie said.

"All I'm doing is asking Mr. Jordan for his opinion."

"It looked real to me," Jordan said.

"Let's get a cross section of opinion," Poindexter said. "Let's hear from Mr. James Brinker on the subject of Mr. Barnet's injury."

"Leave him alone, Maurice."

"Miss Nicholas enters the fray. Why is it that every time Mr. Brinker is asked a difficult question, Miss Nicholas leaps to his rescue? What about that, Mr. Brinker? What's your opinion of Mr. Barnet's injury?"

"I don't know," Brinker said.

"He doesn't know," Poindexter said.

"He never does," said his son. "He never knows anything when it comes to putting up or shutting up."

Jordan couldn't stop what he said next. "Why don't you save some of that piss for the jerries, kid? You'll need it when you get to France."

There was a moment of shock. He could feel it going around the room. The kid said, "Listen, you," and balled up his fist and started around the table. But a motion from his father brought him up short.

"I heard some news today," said old Poindexter as if nothing had happened. "I think Mr. Brinker will find this interesting. They've changed the rules for the conscientious objector status. It's not going to be enough anymore to profess a profound moral aversion to war. Now you'll have to prove a belief in a transcendent creator deity as well. Do you believe in God, Mr. Brinker?"

"Sure. Doesn't everybody?"

"I sense a facetious undertone there, Mr. Brinker. Perhaps you'd rather not talk about God, now that we're in a real shooting war. But what about Mr. Jordan? Do you believe in a transcendent creator deity, Mr. Jordan?"

"Jordan is my first name."

"Mr. . . . what is it, Ten Eyck? Mr. Ten Eyck, then."

"Mr. Ten Eyck was my father."

The old man smiled venomously. "A clever man we have among us. He should do well writing Harford's radio plays. But does he believe in God?"

"That's between me and the draft board."

"He looks able-bodied enough," said young Poindexter.

"Be careful, boy," Jordan said, pointing a finger. "I'm damned able-bodied, if you really want to know."

"Yes, Alger, hush. If Mr. Jordan doesn't want to discuss his beliefs, let him hold his peace. It's Mr. Brinker's beliefs I'm interested in just now. He wasn't shy about expressing them last year, before the war became our war. Perhaps you remember that day. Some of you were discussing religious philosophy and Mr. Brinker certainly sounded doubtful about the transcendent deity then. What was it he said? . . . That perhaps some space traveler stopped here a billion years ago and emptied its garbage on the landscape. And our species was spawned in a garbage dump."

"We were kidding around that day," Brinker said.

"Well, I'm sorry I'm not laughing. You see, my son is about to go off to war, where people will try to kill him. I don't seem to be amused by much these days."

Brinker smiled sadly. "I wish I could help you with that. Would it make you feel any better if I went too and got myself killed?"

"Actually, you know, it would."

Rue stiffened. "You're a pig, Maurice. That's an awful thing to say."

At that moment Barnet arrived, hobbling in on crutches. He saw Jordan at once. "What the hell are you doing here?"

"We've just been talking," said old Poindexter. "You were the topic of the moment, Clay. You and volleyball."

"Goddammit, Maurice, are you drunk again?"

"That's rather a harsh term. Given my body weight, I might drink all night without reaching that happy state of oblivion. Besides, Miss Teasdale is working your show."

"It's a two-man job. As you damn well know."

"Oh, bosh. What she lacks in experience she will counter with brilliance, as Lady Hazel so charmingly put it. Now, if you all will excuse me, I'm going home."

Both Poindexters left the room and Barnet pushed his way to the front. "What the hell was that all about? Goddammit, I've got a radio show to do in just over thirty minutes." He looked at Livia. "How the hell are you going to do a scene that's got fifteen goddamn effects in it?"

"She will do it brilliantly," Hazel said.

"Well, she'd better figure out how to grow two more arms and another leg by eleven thirty." He glared at Jordan. "As for you, how'd you like to get the hell out of here?"

Suddenly Kidd was there on the soundstage, as if he'd materialized out of nowhere. Everything came to a stop for perhaps ten seconds while, one by one, they noticed that the door to the darkened director's booth was open.

"I guess I fell asleep in there," Kidd said.

No one believed him. He said, "Well, it's been a long day and I'm tired," but he didn't look tired. His eyes were clear and alert as he looked from face to face. "So," he said, "have a good show and I'll see you all on Monday."

There was a chorus of "Yessir's" and Kidd said, "Walk out with me, Mr. Ten Eyck."

In the hall, Becky Hart was ushering the last stragglers into Studio A. The building rumbled with crowd noise.

"Were you going to stay and watch the show, Mr. Ten Eyck?"

"I thought I would."

"That's fine. Hold that door, miss." Kidd stopped and studied Jordan's face. "There isn't much contentment here, is there?"

"I think there are frustrations."

"Very diplomatic. Say what you think, isn't that what we said?"

"I'm not entitled to an opinion yet, I just got here. But some of these people might surprise you."

"They'd better." Kidd's eyes were steady, his face unfathomable. "Tomorrow, then," he said, and he went on through the doors to the lobby.

Becky was tugging at his shirt: the downbeat had begun. "Hurry, Jordan, the warm-up's starting! We're going on the air!"

His heart turned over as he stepped into the studio. He burrowed into the crowd at the back of the room.

And there she was.

(((13)))

THIS must be a dream, he thought. That woman on the bandstand can't be the country girl I knew.

She sat in a strapless Alice blue evening dress, looking casual and thoroughly professional. This is unreal, he thought again. I am dreaming it all.

The man with the clarinet stood and looked at the clock. Seven minutes to airtime. The doors were locked and an announcer came to the microphone.

"Good evening, ladies and gentlemen! Thank you all for coming!"

The cheering rose to a roaring peak.

"My name is Bill Van Doren. It's going to be my pleasant task tonight to introduce these seven marvelous musical talents, and to announce the numbers they will perform during the half-hour portion of the program that we will broadcast. The show will continue after the broadcast, for those who want to dance or just sit and listen. This is our gift to you, in these trying days we're living in."

The crowd yelled. It was eager, enthused, hot.

"One of my functions," the announcer said, "is to host what we in radio call the audience warm-up. But if there ever was a crowd that needs no warming up, this is that crowd!"

The place exploded.

The announcer held up his hands and began his intros. The clarinet man bounded up and the audience shrieked its approval. The sax player stood to the right and did a little riff, and the clarinet chased him for a playful bar, and the crowd laughed. The trumpet man joined them, giving out with the thinnest wah-wah ever heard, and the crowd laughed again when they saw that his mute was the business end of a toilet plunger. The rhythm section trickled in: a bass and guitar and finally the drummer. With two minutes left, the announcer turned to Holly.

"What can I possibly say about the lady who sings for us? I could tell you that she's one of the most amazing people it's ever been my good luck to know, but that doesn't begin to tell her story. Many of you know it already. Two months ago she'd never sung a note professionally. Then one night during the amateur show at the pier, she came up and asked for a tryout. Those of you who were there that night will never forget the high voltage that ran through us all at the first sound of that incredible voice. But it's more than that. She's got style, class, and grace: an infallible ear for rhythm and a commanding instinct for whatever the boys throw at her. Without a lick of training, with no rehearsal whatever, she held us spellbound for almost an hour, till she ran out of songs. She's got a fabulous future—we knew it then and we know it now, and I'm as overjoyed as you are to have been here at the start of it. A real Cinderella story. Ladies and gentlemen, I want the biggest hand you've got for the best band singer I know . . . *Miss* Hol-*ly* Ohhhhh-*Har*-ra!"

The place went nuts. Bedlam, riot, hell breaking loose—nothing in his vocabulary fit the celebration he was watching.

The clock was down to fifteen seconds—no chance of bringing the crowd under control for the opening—but somehow Jordan knew that proper was not what they wanted. In the booth the director raised his arms for more noise and Jordan thought, Christ, no one will hear the show.

The announcer took the cue and stepped to the microphone with five seconds showing on the clock. "I've just been given a message!" he shouted to the crowd. "The Festival of the Sun *will* go on as always!"

The red light flashed, and on this note of mindless joy they took to the air.

The show opened at the peak of its chaos and he knew the timing had been masterful. The announcer boomed the opening signature across the studio—"The Windy City Seven is on the air!"—and it rode above the noise. Up came the theme, "Love Walked In," and in the booth he could see the two men working: Stoner with his head down; the director talking tensely, calling the announcer back to the microphone with a gentle motion of his fingertips. It was all in the fingers: the director controlled the announcer, and the announcer controlled the crowd. Down went the noise: again came the introductions, the mischief laced with a bit of on-the-air formality. The first number began: "Sweet Lorraine."

Holly had four numbers in the half hour. She sang "The Glory of Love" and Jordan was amazed at her polish. She had a sixth sense for when to move and how: when to rise from her chair and start across the stage so that her song began exactly as she arrived at the microphone; when to whirl and toss her head to the crowd; when to bestow that radiant smile. The vocal ended, the announcer came and went, the band played again. Holly sang "These Foolish Things Remind Me of You"—wonderfully, he thought, able, now that the novelty was fading, to enjoy her startling artistry. She was singing "I Can't Give You Anything but Love" when he happened to look up and see a man watching from the balcony. The man was alone in the shadows, the whiteness of his hands the most visible feature as he gripped the railing. Then his body leaned forward and for a moment his face passed in and out of the light. A slim man in a sport coat and dark glasses.

The little girl's blind man.

The man stood still as Holly did her final number. She sang "I Didn't Know What Time It Was," and in the closing chorus she turned her face upward toward the balcony, where even the knuckles had drawn back in the dark.

In the booth, Stoner and the director were laughing gaily, pleased with themselves. People milled about, thrilled with the broadcast and with the news that had launched it, and up on the soundstage the musicians were playing a soft interlude, setting the mood for the postshow.

A mob had gathered around her, many pressing close, asking for her autograph as if the fame that had been promised was already a fact. This is the time, he thought: go to her now, hidden in a forest of strangers.

His head loomed above the crowd. She would certainly see him if she looked this way. Now he could hear her voice: she had said something to the man who had asked for her signature, and it was that speaking voice that took him back finally to the girl he had once known.

There were a few dawdlers, tedious bores who tried to stake out the floor and regale her. She handled them masterfully, as if they were old friends or favorite uncles she hadn't seen in ages, shaking their hands with both of hers and letting them go with a cocked head and a sad little frown, so perfect with the smiling eyes as they were pushed aside by the current of the crowd. He heard her say, "Hello, what's your name?" There were two men ahead of him now and his heart was going like a jackhammer.

Then she was there. She looked in his eyes and he saw . . . nothing.

She took his hand. "Hello . . . what's your name?"

"Jack."

"You're a big fellow, Jack. I hope you liked our music."

"Your music is incredible."

"Why, thank you, sir, that makes me feel just fine."

He handed her a paper he had picked up and a pencil he had in his pocket. Saw her write, *To Jack, on a very special night, warmest regards, Holly O'Hara*. She looked up and smiled and he was moved on by the current. Not once did she look in his wake. She had passed him through as if she had never seen his face before that moment.

((14))

BY one o'clock it was over. The doors had been thrown open, the band was packing its instruments, and the crowd was breaking up and drifting reluctantly out of the building. Studio B was dark, the horror show now history and the cast long gone. Out in the yard a few people lingered, talking in twos and threes until the lights began blinking out.

He saw the band leave in a small bus parked at the side door. Holly made her escape, bounding into the bus, and Jordan stood in the trees near the volleyball net and watched them drive away.

There was no use trying to figure it out. There was nothing to be done until she came to him and told him what she wanted. But he couldn't shake the chilling effect of their meeting.

In his hotel he wished vaguely for a bottle of whiskey. It had been a long day and he craved something stronger than the brackish tap water from the room at the end of the hall. Tonight he would bed down with a troubled heart. There was no help for that, but he hoped sleep would find him, for he was usually disciplined enough not to brood over things he couldn't change.

The vision of Holly at the microphone was still vivid, but he found himself thinking about that man in the dark glasses. There was a feeling of compulsion there, a human bondage worthy of Maugham.

At some point he locked his door and went down the hall to the bathroom. Brushed his teeth, drank some water, and then, coming back along the hall, he was gripped by that feeling he'd had this morning, that someone had been here. He felt sand under his feet and it was wet to his touch. Sand from the beach, not the dry stuff he might've brought in on his own clothes from the dunes.

He listened at his door. Tried the knob and found it still locked. Let out his breath, took out his key, and opened it.

At once he saw the note, a cheap notebook sheet folded twice and slipped under his door. It said: MEET ME LIGHT-HOUSE 2 AM HOLLY.

Beyond the town the landscape was darkly extraterrestrial. The beach was densely overcast and the sky broken only by occasional lightning far away. He had no light and his journey was impossible except for the lighthouse, which cast its powerful beacon four times a minute.

He knew there were beachfront bungalows all along this stretch south of town, but they were dark now, hidden without lights back in the trees. There was no sense of earthly reality: the terrain was starkly polar in the momentary flashes of black-and-white relief, but the wind off the sea was warm. The tide was out and coming in, the sand hard and damp, with only an occasional gully to slow him as he picked his way along.

He was two miles south of town when he saw lights dancing ahead. It was the coast guard patrol, looking for little Hitlers crawling ashore from submarines. He scrambled up into the dunes and lay flat in the sand, and a moment later the horses passed less than twenty yards away. The man with the big light swept his beam across the water, out to the rolls of barbed wire and back. Pieces of conversation floated on the wind. "Man, that gal had a nice ass," said the big light, and the others laughed. There was always some kinda nookie going on down at the point, and catching a pair of lovebirds in the middle of something was apparently high sport. Thoughts of nookie kept them from seeing his prints in the sand.

He rolled out of the dunes and sprinted into the wind. A few minutes later he came to a deep gully. Water swirled around his hips.

On the other side the lighthouse was suddenly upon him. The beam passed over his head and the blinding contrast was gone, as if he'd stepped through a prism from that harsh snowy frontier into a mellow navigable twilight. He could see the lighthouse half a mile away, the cylindrical shape of it rising 150 feet over the edge of the hook. He saw the hook itself, a long crooked piece of land clutching at the sea. And the coastland, vastly changed, with fewer trees and then none at all. There were no houses south of the gully. It had a wild, barren look, tidal and near the end swampy. Marsh pinched the beach to its last faint trace, a trivial sand spit that finally gave up and melted into the water.

A soft rain had begun falling and the wind was dying in the east. The water in the cove was eerily calm, while waves rolled past on the other side to crash on the mainland a mile away. Now he saw the road, a plank-covered causeway that spanned the marsh, connected to the mainland by the bridge he had seen from the roof.

Still there was no sign of life: no lights in the dark recesses of the lighthouse, which he guessed were windows in rooms below the lamp. He climbed an artificial embankment lined with stones, bringing him to the catwalk that led out to the lighthouse. A gate hung across it, locked with a chain, and there was a sign he was just able to see:

U.S. COAST GUARD
NO TRESPASSING

His sense of unease was now acute. It had to be two o'clock—the clock in his head told him it was later than that. What if she'd been here and gone? If she had come and not found him here, would she have waited? He was willing to sit in the rain till dawn, but what troubled him now had little to do with wasting time in bad weather. This didn't smell right, and that was it in a nutshell.

He took her note out of his pocket but the cheap paper was breaking into soggy fragments impossible to read. It fell apart in his fingers—gone, he thought, which is what I ought to be. His gut told him to leave but his heart said stay. How could he leave till he knew why he'd come?

He settled into a wide crack between two posts and he huddled there, a third post, deciding for want of a better answer to wait it out.

The rain was steady now, pelting the water inside the hook like birdshot. Only his eyes moved, scanning the beach and the dunes. Occasionally he let his head turn slightly, to watch the marsh where it grew thick around the causeway. He didn't know how long he'd stood there when he saw a flash of light. Imagination, he thought: that could happen even to a levelheaded man on a night like this. Ah Holly, he thought, and in that moment he saw the light again.

The headlights of a car, unmistakable now, far back in the marsh. Two bold flicks with less than a second between them, then nothing. He eased down from the catwalk and followed the sandbar out to the edge of the causeway. This is it, he thought, looking into the pale, blurry road. That's all there is. Take it or leave it.

Of course he had to take it. But he couldn't shake the notion that it wasn't Holly waiting for him in the marsh.

The causeway swallowed him whole. A hell of frogs rose up around him. He could feel the rain but it made no sound. The surf dropped away, the wind dropped away. Nothing had the reality of its own noise in the land of the frogs. The place where you croak.

And wasn't it crazy how he couldn't see three feet ahead but he could clearly make out the woods on the mainland, half a mile away? The light would come round and burn off the dark: his shadow would leap down on the bleached-white planking and then, before his eyes could adjust, the light would be gone again, leaving false bottoms under his feet and a sense of hills rising around him. The planking was uneven and he had the illusion of a railing, though he knew there was none.

His sense of distance told him the car was parked a hundred yards deep in the marsh, at the edge of the island, just below the bridge. The road doglegged to the northwest, an immediate relief from the glare, though the causeway itself was now in continuous blackness. He felt himself rising through the marsh: his head came up out of the reeds on the long, gradual incline to the bridge. He had a tingling awareness of his naked vulnerability. Though he could still see nothing ahead, he himself must be starkly outlined against the light to anyone on the bridge, or even to a sharp pair of eyes in the woods across the creek.

He could see the bridge now, the ghostly steel supports rising above him. And there was the car, looking like a toy left near the workings of a child's Erector set. Nothing moved, on the bridge or beyond it, around the car or anywhere near it. It was less than thirty yards away. He stood in the half crouch, his muscles taut, waiting.

Don't move, he thought. Then he realized this had not been a thought. It was a voice.

"I said don't move. I've got a gun here."

The voice came from everywhere: the curse of the one-eared man. Bluff him, he thought: maybe it's just some kid. "You're buying a lot of trouble, pal."

"Shut up. Do what I tell you."

"What's the idea? I'm nobody special. I lost my girl down here and all I'm doing is looking for her."

"She's not coming. She sent me instead. I know who you are, Dulaney, she told me all about you. Move on up to the car."

He groped along the causeway. Now he recognized the car, that '35 Ford again, and he knew he was in deep, grave trouble.

"Put your hands on the hood."

A flashlight beam danced around him and he heard footsteps on the planks. He felt the man's free hand around his waist, slapping his pockets. Where was the gun? he wondered, but then the man stepped back and the chance was gone.

"That wasn't so smart, coming out here without a weapon. But I forgot, you were expecting Holly, weren't you? That's too bad—Holly doesn't want to see you. She sent me out to tell you that. In fact, she wants you to leave town right now, tonight. Are you hearing me? You're to leave now and never come back."

The voice sounded strongly German, the accent bumping over certain phrases. Again he said, "Are you hearing me, Dulaney?"

"Sure."

"Yes? What does 'Sure' mean?"

"Just that I'd like to hear it from her, that's all."

The blow took him off guard, sprawling him onto the causeway. He rolled over on his back and saw the Woodsman standing over him, holding an evil-looking gun by the barrel.

"Don't sit up, Dulaney. Don't do anything yet."

It was the first Woodsman, the jittery one he'd last seen running out of the fire door. The man leaned over him, switching the gun from the pistol whip to a more deadly grip. "I don't like doing this. I don't like hurting people, but I will. I'm at the end of my goddamn rope."

Dulaney shook his head and stared into the barrel.

"I want you to understand something. When I tell you to leave town, you had better do what I say. Don't say, 'Sure,' and think you can lie to me, because you know what? I've got to kill you if you do that."

The Woodsman prodded him. "Now you can get up."

Dulaney got up.

"Now, what do you say?"

"I guess I'll leave town."

A long moment passed. "You're lying," the man said. "I can see it in your face. You say you'll leave but you won't."

His voice was suddenly unstable, trembly and nervous. "You're lying," he said again. "You won't tell the truth about anything."

He's going to kill me right here unless I can get some leverage, Dulaney thought. He grabbed at straws. "I'd like to level with you."

"Yes? What does that mean?"

"You're not making it easy for me to leave, you're making it harder. I'd walk out of here tonight if she'd just talk to me."

"That's impossible."

"Five minutes alone with her, that's all I'm asking."

"Don't you hear good? I said it's not possible."

"Then at least tell me why."

"You forget who has the gun. I don't have to tell you anything."

Dulaney groped for some logic that might appeal to the man. On a whim he said, "I don't think you want to use that gun."

"It's you that's making me. You're leaving me no choice."

"I'll tell you something, friend. You sound like a man in trouble. I saw you this afternoon. Upstairs, at the radio station."

"Yes, I thought maybe you had."

"You looked like a man in trouble. Like maybe you'd come to tell me about it. Why don't you tell me now?"

"Oh yes, what a good idea. Then you can be a witness when they strap me in the electric chair."

Dulaney took a deep breath and a big risk. "Was it you who killed Kendall?"

The man flinched. "Don't you *dare* say that!"

He cocked the gun. Dulaney tightened up all over.

"Don't you ever say that. Don't you ever dare."

"Sure, pal," Dulaney said numbly. "Consider it unsaid."

"I've had nightmares about that. I can't get it out of my mind."

"Hey, I believe you."

"I never killed anybody."

"That's good. And you don't want to start now, do you?"

"You think I *like* this?"

"I can see you don't. That's what I've been saying."

The Woodsman said nothing. The gun bobbed in and out of the light.

"Was it the Irishman who killed Kendall?"

"Christ, no. He's just a mindless thug."

Another moment passed.

"What do you know about the Irishman?" the Woodsman said.

"Nothing. Kendall said a mulligan roughed him up, that's all."

"Forget him, he's nothing. I wish I'd never seen his stupid face. Let's shut up now. I'm tired of talking to you, you waste my time. Get moving."

They crossed the bridge, a slow surrealistic journey with mist swirling beneath them and the lighthouse now a soft, looping silver rope in the night sky. The Woodsman's light led the way and their feet made thick clumping sounds on the planks.

If there was any chance now, the slightest bobble with the gun, he had to go after it. His mind was focused on a single track, survival. He knew from the footsteps that the Woodsman was three paces behind him, eight feet back, still too far for a sudden rush. But time was running out: he had to try it, even if it looked like certain death. Wait till we get off this roadway, he thought. Give yourself the best chance, hope for a flesh wound and no broken bones. Be fast, he thought: fast and decisive. This seemed about the best he had going for him.

They had crossed the mudflat and were heading into the woods. The causeway ended on a narrow dirt road, the ruts filling with water and disappearing into long stretches of slop. They walked along a grassy ridge and the trees grew taller and closer to the road. "Turn here," the Woodsman said, and they hiked across a wet grassy meadow and down into a slough.

"Stop."

He turned around. No chance, he was too far back. One last try to talk him out of it, then have a go at him no matter what.

"Listen, pal . . . you can still talk to me."

The Woodsman laughed, a harsh, bitter sound. "What good will that do?"

"I'll try to help you. I can see you're in trouble."

"What if that's true? What do you think you can do for me?"

"I don't know yet, none of it makes any sense to me. I don't know what you did or where you came from. I don't even know how you found me."

"That doesn't matter now, does it? Let's just say your friend Carnahan told us. Let it go at that."

But almost at once he said, "No, that's not true. Carnahan wouldn't tell us anything, I'll give you that. He was your friend and you should think well of him. A brave man. Far braver than me."

Dulaney could see that something had changed. The Woodsman had begun to tremble and the gun wobbled in his hand.

"You can't blame Carnahan," he said again. "We took his key, after."

"After what?"

"We went to his room and found some papers. A half-written postcard to his daughter. Some undeveloped film, some notes. A spool of recording wire, still on the machine. Enough to tell us who you were and that he had sent you the rest of it. To some goddamn racetrack in Florida."

"Tropical Park. I wasn't there long."

A moment passed. "So don't blame Carnahan," the Woodsman said. "He was a good, brave man."

"Tell me something. Who are the others?"

"I can't say any more. I've got family in New York. They could be in terrible danger because of what I say."

Dulaney saw the gun move up. He braced for a charge. But then the Woodsman gave a long shivery sigh and said, "You're right, Dulaney, I don't want to kill you," and Dulaney let out a long breath.

"When you feel trapped, there seems only one way out," the Woodsman said. "Then you get down to it and you find out there isn't any way."

Then he said: "You're right, I don't want to kill you."

Then he said: "Can't."

He said: "Thought I could do it. Told myself I could."

He shrugged. "Can't."

Then: "I'm sorry I hit you, Dulaney. I didn't want to do that either."

Then he put the gun in his mouth and pulled the trigger. His head exploded and the light flew off in the trees.

An Open-
and-Shut
Case

THERE was never any doubt about the dead man's death. A clear case of suicide, said the coroner. Yes, there were mysteries, but all the facts leading to a suicide verdict were there.

A gun had been recovered, easily established as having belonged to the deceased and positively identified as the weapon that had fired the bullet. Evidence of intent had gone well beyond the gun. A packet of cyanide had been found in the glove compartment of the '35 Ford belonging to the dead man. This is not unusual in suicide deaths, said the coroner. A man despairs and decides to kill himself but he can't decide how. Most people seek a painless exit: most but not all. Suicides have been known to chop off arms and legs, then sit calmly and bleed to death. Death defies easy answers.

There was a catalogue of facts—where the gun was found, the absence of defense wounds, the powder burns on the hands and face—on and on, and all of it led to suicide.

The dead man's name was George Edward Schroeder, twenty-six, of second-generation German American stock. This made it news, for without the German angle it might have been reported as a mere incident, lost on an inside page. The newspaperman made some calls and quickly corroborated what the sheriff told him; the rest he filled in on a trip to New York, turning the death of a troubled young man into a first-rate piece of front-page propaganda. The headline was startling in the third week of May: THE LONG ARM OF ADOLF HITLER sold out the issue, and the piece was picked up by the Associated Press and carried verbatim, with the editor's byline, to newspapers across the nation.

Gunter and Hannah Schroeder had married in Bremen in 1912 and had immigrated to America two years later. They had settled in New York's German community, that section of the East Eighties known as Yorkville. Gunter opened a bratwurst-

and-sauerkraut eatery on Third Avenue, which he ran with his wife for twenty-five years. They had two children, but the daughter had married a German national and in 1935 had gone with him to live and raise their children in the old country. George, the son, had always been high-strung. He had few friends in his life and he worried about vast world problems, such as man's brutality to his fellow men, until he grew despondent and sick of his own race. It was said in the neighborhood that his despair had begun with the loss of his older sister, Gerda Luise, who had confided deep doubts about the path she had chosen, even on her wedding day and right up until the hour of her departure for Germany.

He took some solace in his work. He had been hired as an engineer at WQXR, New York's classical music station, and at night he would sit alone in the dark production room off the main studio and listen to the melodies of the great German masters. "Georgie was a born technician," said one man at the station who professed to know him well. "He could fix any transmitter problem, he had no peer at patch work, and so was one of those unsung heroes who quickly become indispensable. He could usually keep you on the air till a permanent repair could be made, and his greatest sense of accomplishment was that his work made it possible for people to hear this glorious music."

But his spirits sank again after the pilgrimage he made with his parents to Germany in 1939. "He came home brooding for his sister and her children," said his unnamed radio friend. "He didn't want to talk about it but one night we got drunk together and he told me what had happened. His sister, Gerda Luise, lived in Braunschweig, where her husband had been employed at Volkswagenwerk, the people's automobile factory, but had recently lost his job. Soon after his arrival, George was picked up by the Gestapo, was put in a small room with a picture of Hitler on one wall, and there for twelve hours two interrogators questioned him sternly about his allegiances. Was he a German, or an American? And what was he going to do about it when the chips were down, was he going to deny his blood, and didn't he realize what it meant to be alive and German in these exciting times? Even then, three years before the United States became their shooting enemy, they were looking for people to spy for them."

You've got to choose, they said: choose now, declare your loyalties, or have them declared for you and find yourself an enemy to both sides. Did you think you could hide forever in America, denying your heritage and cringing behind that paper they gave you? If you think that, my fine German friend, think again. We have people everywhere. We remember our friends *and* our enemies forever.

Ask your sister. Ask her husband. He had his chance to join the Nazi Party three years ago and he refused. Well, now *we* refuse *him*!

But perhaps you can help him redeem himself.

(A carnivorous smile in the hazy light beyond the cigarette smoke.)

Look at this as an opportunity, George. The chance of your life. How many people are ever given the chance to become national heroes?

Back in America, a group of German American militants had risen in Yorkville, demanding German support of the Fatherland in its war with the hated British.

There were visits in the night. Once he was seen being roughhoused by a gang leader who called him worthless. What have you ever done for Germany, Schroeder? Your whole family has betrayed its blood.

It's hard being a good American when windows are smashed and fires are started in the night, when the business you've built for half a lifetime dries up in a month. We tried, said old Schroeder, but no one came to eat with us anymore.

He closed his café and moved to the midtown West Side: found work in a Horn and Hardart Automat, clearing tables and washing dishes. His wife mopped floors and emptied wastebaskets in an office building. But the bund found them, and George quit his job at QXR and left the city.

"I was glad to hear he had found the job in Jersey," said his friend. "George was a born radio man."

"He was a good American," said his father to the newspaperman. "We don't have nothing to do with that bund business and I don't let nobody say nothing bad against my boy. He's dead now. For God's sake, can't you leave him alone? He was a good American."

"He was a good guy," said Rue Nicholas, an actress who became his friend. "Maybe it's not smart to admit being friends with a German boy, but I liked him. We were both insomniacs. Once we sat up all night on the pier, listening to the music and talking about what a sad, wonderful place the world is."

"He was high-strung, that's for sure," said August Stoner, his immediate supervisor at WHAR. "But he did his job and did it well. He was a real good kid. When I told him to do something, he did it right."

George Edward Schroeder was buried in a family plot bought by his father twenty years ago. Stoner, Miss Nicholas, and a few people from the station went up for the funeral.

The facts continued to beg the question: Did the long arm of Adolf Hitler reach across the sea and into this noisy little American beach town? Had the Nazis hounded this troubled American of German blood until he'd finally put a bullet through his head?

"You'll have to ask Hitler when you see him," said the sheriff. "As far as I'm concerned, it's an open-and-shut case."

But there are still those mysteries. Why would Schroeder drive his car over the beach, leave it, then walk back a mile and kill himself in the woods? Who was the caller who had found the body? Why would he not give his name, and what was he doing walking in the deep woods on a pitch-dark and rainy morning in May?

"It doesn't matter," said the sheriff. "It's an open-and-shut case. The kid killed himself."

((2))

THE kid killed himself. Jordan had seen it, there was no doubt of suicide, it was open-and-shut.

If the sheriff wanted to close the book on it, if the only real link to Hitler was the wishful thinking of a newspaperman, this whole incident would soon fade away from lack of interest. In the absence of fact, there was still no mystery, only the last tragic moments of a foolish and troubled young man.

But there were questions that the newspaperman could not ask. What Jordan knew would cast this halfhearted investigation into a darker light, suddenly more sinister and far more difficult to dismiss. Knowing that Marty Kendall had something to do with it, the sheriff might wonder why Kendall had disappeared, turned up in California, and then got killed in Pennsylvania. Hearing the true story of Holly O'Hara, the sheriff would certainly be interested in the fears of a child in that same Pennsylvania town. Then, because no lawman likes coincidence with his murder, he might reopen the file on another disappearance, now six years old. This would seem to undermine the newspaperman's German angle, for there was no war in 1936 when actor March Flack disappeared coming home from a broadcast. Eventually it would lead back to here and now, and the sheriff would have another German to find—Peter Schroeder, cousin of the deceased, who walked away in the smoke that night and has not been seen since.

Jordan had seen him vanish—one minute there at the volleyball net, the next gone without a trace. The German angle again, but it lost its sex appeal if he picked at it. One of the Schroeder boys might only be tied to the others by family, not by any activity in cloak-and-dagger. But what could he do?—one wrong word would send him back to California handcuffed to a deputy, to go quietly crazy in a jail cell. Holly was maddening. Three times they had come within speaking

distance on the boardwalk and she had given him nothing—
not a hint that she wanted him here or had any idea who he
was. Of all the possible things he could have imagined, this
did not even make the list. He was so certain she'd have
found some way to talk to him, but she never did—not a gesture, not a cough or a lingering look. She kept him a stranger
and this forced him to act like one. And as time went on his
fear deepened. He waited and watched.

((•   ))

THE
BLACKOUT
WALTZ

((1))

THREE weeks had passed since the Schroeder boy's death, and in that time his life had changed.

He had a paying job now, and the work was so challenging that his days often obscured what his real purpose had been in coming here. Every morning he opened his eyes with the same conviction—today he'd find a way to talk to her. He'd drop by the little club where she sang, find a way to send her a note, perhaps wait in the dark place near the edge of the bandstand, and then, when she came off between sets, say something that she'd have to answer. His faith was always strongest before the dawn, but once the day began his sense of purpose slowly drained away. She was so incredibly distant that speech seemed impossible, so much like a stranger that he never once caught her acting. After three weeks he could think of just two possible reasons for her behavior—that she was afraid or that something had happened to her mind. If she was afraid she was very much afraid, and anything he might say could only make matters worse. Her silence gave a powerful message: stay away, don't even begin to approach me. And so he did, and so he had to.

His days were full. Six days a week he wrote continuity at Harford's radio station, and on the seventh day he faced the horrors of the damned. Sundays stretched on in endless, lonely boredom, desolate and bleak. He was adrift in a sea of willing women and he cared nothing for any of them. It was his time off that drove him to despair: the Sundays, the nights, the mornings when he'd wake hours before the dawn and not be able to sleep again. In the stony darkness of his room he would make plans for the day, knowing that his best-laid schemes would come to nothing by nightfall.

((2))

THE day began. In radio lingo it was called the dawn patrol, a term that defined the skeleton staff that was in the building when the first announcer arrived to put the station on the air. Radio had its own language and he had absorbed it. Chimes were the sounds that closed all shows on both NBC networks, and his continuity could not begin until they were heard. He knew what a board fade was—the gradual potting down of a scene till it faded from the air, indicating a time transition—and a cross fade meant less time passing or none at all, perhaps a shift of locale as one scene was potted down while another came up to replace it. A clambake was a show full of mistakes, and a cornfield was a soundstage filled with standing microphones. He had learned the importance of dampening the studio, hanging drapes to absorb sound, and a live studio was resonant as it stood. A good director like Maitland could walk into a room and clap his hands and know what needed to be hung or taken down, and when the director said, "Coming up," he meant now, you're on the air in ten seconds. Microphones were either hot or dead, but there were many varieties. There were directional mikes with three dead sides, eightball and saltshaker mikes, ribbon mikes and bullet mikes, dynamic mikes and parabolic mikes, and each gave a different sound from the same input. Jordan now knew how to make the sound of an actor talking in a cave, how easily a makeshift echo chamber could be devised by having actors speak into a microphone dangled inside a piano. He had learned these things as part of his job but they were also his diversion. It filled up the days.

He had a routine. The daytime schedule was his responsibility, and from three o'clock on it was handled by the other writer. Phil Carmody was forty-five, a bleary-eyed veteran of the newspaper game who had matriculated in the Buffalo office of United Press. Barnet continued to function as program director while Kidd got his feet wet, and it didn't take long for Jordan to fall under his thumb. "Do it again," he would say, throwing Jordan's continuity in the wastebasket. Never a hint of what was missing or wrong, just "Do it again." Later, with Barnet well out of earshot, Carmody would tell anyone present that "this kid's a helluva lot better writer than I am." He needed Jordan to preserve his sanity. "Man, they've been working my ass off since the other guy quit last Christmas. My kids've forgotten what I look like."

In addition to everyday continuity, Carmody and Jordan wrote occasional commercials and scripted anything local that popped up in the schedule. Today, Monday, he knew without thinking that Evie Overdier did her Laura Leaf cooking show at ten fifteen. She did this three times a week, while on Tuesdays and Thursdays the same quarter hour was filled by a pair of retired vaudeville comics who sang Gay Nineties evergreens to their own piano accompaniment. Most of the other daytime slots were network originated, and his biggest challenge was making the continuity sound like something that hadn't been said a thousand times before. This meant he had to listen to everything. Jokes that were ancient when Joe Miller wrote them down two hundred years ago. Musical hucksters, farm news, and *The Breakfast Club*. Continuing melodramas so fantastic that they defied any possibility of truth. He listened to junk he couldn't have imagined, just so he could hoodwink the dependable nonthinkers from Maine to Virginia.

At night he'd have dinner, sometimes with Carmody and his family, once or twice a week with Stoner in a downtown café, most often alone in his room. The station went dark for four hours each twenty-four-hour day. It signed off after Stoner's show and came on again at sunrise. The two announcers Eastman and Stallworth alternated in the early morning: one or the other would arrive at five thirty, fire up the transmitter, log in on the F.C.C. sheet, and using the same small upstairs studio that Stoner had vacated a few hours before, put the station on the air as the sun broke over the sea.

The first hour was a potpourri of recorded music, personal chatter, and occasional snatches of verse. Yesterday's headlines, cribbed from the *New York Times,* filled the top of the hour, all read by the personality on duty. The whole package was billed as the *Rise and Shine with Uncle Wally* show. Both Eastman and Stallworth played Uncle Wally, and even people who knew them were amazed at how they could assume this singular fictitious entity with one perfect voice that was so unlike either of their own speaking voices. "I swear to God, I can't tell the difference," Rue said. "I get up and turn that show on and I don't know which one of 'em's doing it."

The network schedule began at eight o'clock, with Morgan Beatty and his world news roundup from New York. Most of the later morning was consumed by the soap serials: awful, mind-numbing things with titles like *John's Other Wife* and *Amanda of Honeymoon Hill.* He knew Kendall had worked some of these shows and he'd been trying to pick out Kendall's old roles where they still might exist. It was almost as if the man himself couldn't be gone if a role he'd originated was still alive. He listened and tried to remember the names Kendall had told him, surprised at his own primitive superstition. The story lines came and went. The characters cheated, lied, flimflammed, and some of them got killed. At the turn of the month Kendall was still dead, without a trace of his life left on earth or in the air.

It was clear by now that the station was undergoing some vast change that had been in the works for some time. The word was out that they were either giving up or losing the network, and a steady stream of job hunters had passed through the doors. By the end of May they had thirty employees, only a third of what Harford had employed in 1933 but up by 25 percent in just a month. A third announcer had been hired; there were bookkeepers and secretaries, new salesmen, and a traffic clerk. There were two telephone operators, a production man, and a new assistant engineer to replace Peter Schroeder, who had not returned. In early June, Kidd hired an organist named Leland Jewell, who could also play piano and didn't seem to mind what strange hours he was asked to work. Jewell told Carmody that Kidd intended to hire an orchestra as well, and new rumors got started from that.

To the actors the most exciting new arrival was Maitland, the director who had come in from Chicago just ahead of Kidd. "They seem to be old pals," Rue said over beer. "Whatever's happening, it's almost like they're coordinating it between them." Maitland looked like Walt Whitman and had a reputation as an actor's director. He was easygoing and friendly but he had clashed at once with Barnet over details of the band broadcast. "You want it done that way, you talk to Jethro," he had said. "On my soundstage we do it my way."

Of course, Barnet never took anything to Kidd, Rue said. "Everybody's a little afraid of Kidd."

But Kidd's arrival had brought them a semblance of cautious optimism. This morning he had reinstated staff meetings for the first time since Mrs. Harford's death in 1936, and the big studio was packed with staff from both buildings. Kidd came in exactly at seven thirty, taking his place on a stool at the edge of the soundstage. He opened with a brief statement, introducing himself as if no one had heard of him, nodding his head slightly at the uneasy laughter, then telling them about his program to bring them to network capability. He asked for questions.

Rue: "What about the rumor that we're losing the network? Is that what this is about?"

"That's not a rumor," Kidd said. "But like real rumors, it's a little wrong. We're not losing the network, we're giving it up."

Barnet cleared his throat. "There's a concern that we won't last two months without NBC, even the poorboy side of it."

Kidd nodded. "A blind man can see that we're losing money hand over fist. Just look at the log any morning—money is pouring out of here faster than the man can count it. What I can tell you for sure is that we are not going broke in two months. But our only long-range hope of making it is to give up the network. It may be our biggest asset but it's also our biggest liability. The network affiliation is just killing us."

"How do you figure that?"

"It's obvious. We can't sell local time because the network's got our best time slots locked in by contract, and the network doesn't like us anymore because our signal's so good that we're encroaching into New York with the same national programs the home station carries. We can't compete in New York with WJZ, and if we don't get at least a piece of New York, you're right, we can't survive."

Kidd looked around the room. "That's it in a nutshell. We've outgrown our local market and we never made those inroads in New York that were planned six years ago. Never mind why that didn't happen—reasons don't matter now. What's important is what we do in August when we head out on our own. I've already told the sales staff and now I'm telling you all—do not think locally. That's a fatal mistake; we're too seasonal down here. Every year our advertising gets thinner and our expenses go up. That's why we're going our own way, and that means I'm looking for ideas. We need commercial shows we can sell, but I also want controversial, hard-hitting things that make people talk. I don't care if you're a secretary or the man who plays the organ, if you've got an idea, I want to hear about it."

The meeting broke up. In the hall Rue gripped his arm. "Hot damn, Jordan, did you just hear what I heard? Hot *damn!*" Her voice quivered and her face was flushed with excitement.

(((3)))

HE was living in a rooming house now, a dreary place downtown. He was a block away from the club where she sang, yet he never went there. A dozen times he had gone to the door and turned away, pushed back as if some physical force had wedged itself between them. There was something so eerie in her behavior: it went beyond the strangeness of what she had done and even how she had done it. She seemed to be holding him back with the force of her will, and he walked on eggs, so wary of compromising her that he felt frozen, forever rooted in the woods at two o'clock in the morning.

He had a car, a Hudson rattletrap ten years old, bought cheap from a newspaper ad with Kendall's money. He didn't drive it much—with an A-card he was entitled to only three gallons a week—but it gave him mobility. He had followed her home one night and had been past her house a hundred times since then. She lived on the beach south of town, in an older house well off the road. Several times he had seen her on the boardwalk but he never approached her. He watched from the entrance of the penny arcade, and she passed so damned near that he could see the breeze stirring the fine hair on her arms. Just a word from a well-hidden place might change everything. She would turn and their eyes would meet and she'd be forced to say something in a place where no one would see them. But suddenly Mrs. Flack appeared, coming up the boardwalk with an old man at her side. Jordan hadn't seen her since that night of the horror show but he knew her at once. The old man had a limp and a chronic cough, which sounded from a distance like a series of small explosions . . . a casualty of the old World War, Jordan thought at once: a man damaged by shells and gas, he guessed; shells and gas and God knew what else. Holly walked past and there was nothing between them. Jordan stepped out of the penny arcade and they came toward him, but if Mrs. Flack recognized him she gave no sign. Holly was now far down the beach. Jordan turned into the square, and to the casual eye they were all strangers of the morning.

(((4)))

ON Tuesday he found a note on his typewriter summoning him to Barnet's office. It was paper-clipped to his Uncle Wally script, demanding a rewrite, so he did that first; then, because it had thrown him behind, he had to hurry through the morning and would be under the gun all day. By the time he got to Barnet it was almost noon.

"You certainly took your goddamn time getting here."

"Sorry. I got behind."

"Do it right the first time and you won't always be in a pinch."

Barnet leaned over his desk. "For some reason Kidd wants me to push you into dramatic script writing. I'm going to give you a show to write that you can't possibly screw up. Are you familiar with *Freedom Road*?"

"It's a Negro show, isn't it? . . . airs Sunday morning."

"It's a Negro show and we air it Sunday morning. You should have heard it by now."

He shrugged. "Sorry."

"Well, you'd better get familiar with it because you're going to be writing it, starting a week from Sunday. It's a quarter hour now but Kidd wants to expand it to thirty minutes. You'll need to come in this week, meet the cast, and get some idea what they're doing. We'll need to change your day off."

"I don't need a day off."

"Your day off will be Saturday. Don't try to impress people by doing more than your share, Ten Eyck, just do what you do and do it right."

"I'll do my best."

"That's what I'm afraid of. I read your rewrite for this afternoon. It stinks. Do it again."

((**5**))

HE worked until five and faced the bleak night alone. Maybe later, if he got groggy enough from too much beer and too little rest, maybe then he could flop in his bed and get a few hours' sleep before his phantoms came calling. He walked out on the pier and listened to the music, had himself a sandwich, and tried to turn off his mind. But nothing worked, and two hours later he faced the same desolate night with the same desperate problem.

Home. It could be worse. He came into the foyer and thought of jail.

The landlord's door was open as usual. The man was a sentinel, always alert when someone came into his hall.

"Mr. Ten Eyck, I believe. Yes, you had a call this evening."

He felt a mild shock. Who would call him, and why?

"A man. Wouldn't leave his name, but was fairly insistent that you get the message. Said he'd call you again tomorrow night at ten, on the phone box in the square."

"Did he say anything else?"

"No, but I can tell you this. It was a long-distance call."

Up in his room he lay in darkness, thinking about Holly and Kendall, a pair of Germans and an Irish thug, Mrs. Flack and her dead husband, and the little girl in Pennsylvania who had seen Holly talking with a blind man. At some point he fell asleep.

(((**6**)))

IN the morning he was always at the front door by five o'clock. Everything ran on schedule at Harford. The janitor, a young black man named Eli Kain, came in at four fifteen, had the five-gallon coffeepot on by four thirty, and was always at the door to let him in. His first stop was the kitchen, where he'd sit and have his two cups and read the main section of yesterday's *Times*. Sometimes, if Eli was on top of things, he'd follow Jordan into the kitchen and allow himself a cup. But he always drank it standing up, and always from a paper cup, never from one of the porcelain mugs used by the staff. Every morning the mugs were piled high in the sink for Eli to wash. This morning they gleamed on the shelf above the icebox.

"Siddown, Eli," Jordan said. "Rest your feet."

But Eli wouldn't do that, and Jordan couldn't insist without acknowledging the racial pecking order that had embarrassed him in his earliest days down south. You couldn't assume the authority to grant him a chair; that was worse than the unspoken tenets that made him stand. He refolded the *Times,* careful to put it back in order. It was Eli's newspaper, bought each morning for its theatrical section at the all-night newsstand on Chicago Avenue. By eight o'clock it would be appropriated by the staff—clipped and ripped, its items marked and passed around and often rewritten for radio use. But Eli always kept the Broadway page, and at eight o'clock, when the morning crew was just shifting into high gear and Eli's day was half finished, he could usually be found alone, at the most distant table in the yard, eating from a brown bag and reading about the new plays opening in the city.

Now he was drawing water for his mop bucket. Jordan had lingered a moment to ask a question. "What do you know about a show called *Freedom Road,* Eli?"

Eli looked up, obviously surprised. "It's a colored show. They play it Sunday mornings."

"I was wondering if you listen to it."

Eli nodded. "Sometimes I work on it."

"Really? What do you do?"

"I sing the theme song. And whatever else comes up. My uncle started that show. He's been doing it eight years now."

Jordan could see the questions in Eli's eyes. "Well," he said, "I've been told I'm going to write it, starting next week."

Another surprise. "That'll be news to Waldo. That's my uncle, Waldo Brown."

"You mean he doesn't know about it?"

"He didn't say anything to me when I talked to him last night. I can't imagine something like that and he wouldn't even tell me about it."

"Who writes it now?"

"Waldo does. What writing there is. A lot of it's just talking."

Jordan gave an apologetic shrug. "I'm sorry I'm so ignorant, it's just that they've got it tucked away on the schedule and there was never any call for me to listen."

Eli nodded. "We tell tales about the black race. What you might call oral folklore. I sing 'The Freedom Song' and Waldo sketches out some notes, and we just take it from there. It goes pretty fast."

"I think they're going to expand it," Jordan said, surprising him yet again.

Eastman came bursting through the door with a bleary grin, a look that said, *Don't say a word till I get my heart beating.* He poured himself some coffee, sipped, sighed, and stood staring at nothing. Eli wrung out his mop and disappeared into the utility room. A moment later Stallworth arrived with a bag of doughnuts. "Hello, Jordan. Good morning, Grover," he sang as he reached for a mug. Eastman looked up sourly. "They should pass a law against people like him. Nobody should be that goddamn cheerful before nine o'clock. Gimme one of those doughnuts."

"Absolutely. Here, Jordan, you look like you need some fortification."

"Don't mind if I do. What happened, you boys mix up your days?"

"We're double-teaming it today," Eastman said.

"Who's Uncle Wally?"

"We both are. Which will be interesting as hell if we both happen to talk at the same time."

"You can have the first hour," Stallworth said. "I'll do some other stuff. I'm gonna put on some blackface around seven fifteen. Don't worry, Jordan, it's an old script, you don't have to write a thing."

"What's the idea?"

"Don't ask me. The man says be here, here I be."

"It is strange, though," Eastman said. "They've never asked us to do it together. Something's in the wind."

Stallworth grinned. "Maybe they're gonna let one of us go. Better be on your best this morning, Grover, somebody's out there listening."

"Laugh if you want to, but something's up. Lotsa changes all of a sudden. I hear you're gonna write the colored thing, Jordan. That's kind of a comedown, isn't it?"

"From continuity? I wouldn't say so."

"By the way," Stallworth said, "where's Eli this morning?"

"Back here," Eli said from the utility room. "You need something?"

"Just wondering how you'd like to be on the rahddio today, kid."

Eli came out looking wary. "Doing what?"

"Whatever the script calls for, that's what. Pull up a chair. I'll give you a table reading right here and now—your first big radio audition. If you work out, I'll pay you myself—three dollars out of my own pocket."

"Do I get to see it first?"

"Look, either you want to be on the air or you don't. Don't do me any goddamn favors, Eli. If you want to work in radio you've got to be able to do everything. Even Ira Frederick Aldridge had to start somewhere."

"Yessir . . . I just can't do . . . you know . . . Hamhocks and Butterbeans. I can't do colored talk."

"Just forget it, then. Craziest damn thing I ever heard, a colored man who can't do colored talk."

"He doesn't *talk* colored talk, Tate," Jordan said. "He doesn't talk anything like what you do on that Hamhocks and Butterbeans."

"Now, don't *you* start looking down your damn nose at Hamhocks and Butterbeans. Everybody likes those skits. You should see the mail I get, and lots of it from colored people too. Hell, I don't need any help, I can play Hamhocks, Butterbeans, *and* their cousin Marcus. I've done it a hundred times before."

"Well, I'm glad you've got it settled. Now I can go to work."

Upstairs in his cubicle the new day began, and almost at once he was fully absorbed. The cubicle had a strong motivational effect on him. It had become his place of work.

He never wasted time, he never stalled. Rolling the paper into his machine was an immediate reflex, drawing him straight into whatever the job was. For once Barnet left him alone, and his words came easy, and the stuff he wrote was breezy and quick.

He worked until eleven; then, as he often did, he walked on the beach and let the sun clear his head. He'd be back by one, to help Carmody get a leg up on the afternoon and early evening.

Sometimes he walked past Holly's house, but for now he stood on the boardwalk and thought about this strange world he'd come to: he pondered what to do, but there were only the same two choices and she had given him nothing, not a glimmer of an opening for that other choice. But in this void one good thing had happened: he believed he was reclaiming his growth as a writer.

Last week his papers had arrived at general delivery, bounced across the country from Nevada to Pennsylvania and now here. The package had been broken apart and retied. It was still a good omen, he told himself. This morning as he arose from his bed he had jotted a few notes for his novel; then, opening his papers, he had found his racetracker story still fresh and alive, waiting to be finished.

He was on better terms with his new name. He had a driver's license now in the name Jordan Ten Eyck. He needed a solid identity; he had no idea how long this might last. On his good days he still believed Holly would come to him: that at least she would give him some sign. Perhaps this would be a good day. He climbed down from the boardwalk and walked south along the beach.

((7))

HE walked the beach barefoot, his pants rolled almost to the knees, sleeves rolled to the elbow, shirt open to the belt, and a wide-brim straw hat casting his face in shadow.

He knew Holly often slept till noon. He had made this walk many times, and usually her curtains would be drawn. If he went down to the lighthouse and back she might be up when he returned. Sometimes her doors were open and the rich smells of her cooking would waft along the beach.

Today he walked on the high soft sand, on a course that would bring him within a few feet of her door. A sudden premonition drew him on, and as he came around the trees her doors were open. He was close enough to hear the gush of her coffee perking and look straight into her kitchen. She flashed past and went out of sight; then, as if she'd been gripped by the same electric hunch, she returned to the doorway and stood watching him through the railing. Her face as always gave away nothing but in the suddenness of the moment, she paled.

Talk to her, he thought; for Christ's sake, say something.

But from somewhere in the room another voice spoke. "I hope you know what you're doing."

A man's voice.

Whoever he was, she didn't look back at him. Her eyes stayed fixed on Jordan's, and the moment stretched until she herself broke it. She glanced away toward the beach, a sign for him to keep moving. He touched his hat, nodded the polite morning greeting of a stranger, and moved on.

(((8)))

SHE had recognized him. She was not sick, there was no amnesia, she had known him. His first reaction was elation but this diminished throughout the day. Was it really as he had perceived it? . . . Had she dropped her guard just long enough for that energy between them to connect? A ten-second encounter. Was that enough?

Carmody had the kiddie hour done by the time he returned, and was working on the two late-afternoon quarter hours that were locally sponsored and performed. At five thirty they'd rejoin the network for a pair of thriller serials, and there was nothing but straight continuity from then on. Jordan settled in his cubicle and tried to work on tomorrow's Uncle Wally, but his concentration was shot. The afternoon went badly, and at three o'clock Barnet returned and had him do it all again.

His spirits were low as he walked home to his rooming house. What had happened at noon seemed years away, its significance lost in trivia. He heated some canned food on a hot plate and this was his supper. The food made him suddenly tired; there had been too many bad nights, and now he had to force himself to stay awake until he could see what would happen at ten o'clock. He tried to read but this only increased his weariness. He tried listening to the radio, but Harford offered a paltry menu on Wednesday nights, and in a while he dozed, roused himself with a start, and finally went out to walk the beach again.

At quarter to ten he came into the square and sat on the bench by the phone booth. The telephone rang a few minutes later; an operator said, "Please deposit forty cents," and he heard coins dropping in a pay phone on the other end. "Go ahead, sir."

A moment of dead air. "Dulaney?"

He said nothing.

"Goddammit, don't play games with me. Is this Jack Dulaney?"

"My name is Jordan."

The man laughed. "Go ahead, stick to that cock-and-bull story. Don't you know who I am?"

Yes. Peter's German inflection was stronger than his dead cousin's had been, but he would have figured it out anyway.

"You're early, Dulaney. You must be nervous. Have you been sitting there all evening, waiting for me to call?"

"I can't help being curious."

"I'll bet you are. Do you have any idea what you're doing here?"

"Not much of one. No."

"Maybe I'll tell you. Would you be interested in that?"

"I'm sure I would."

"Good." There was a pause, then he said, "Good," again. His breath was clear at a distance of forty cents. "I need some money."

Dulaney knew he wasn't being told this as a point of small talk. He tried to remember how much he had in the bank back home.

"I've got to get out of the country," Schroeder said. "Do you think you could help me do that?"

"I could put my hands on a few hundred but it would take some time."

"How much time?"

"I don't know. My money's in a bank in South Carolina. There's bound to be some red tape, getting it here and cashed. A week at least. Maybe ten days."

He didn't like it, Dulaney could tell by the silence. At last he said, "Okay, I've got things to do also. It's not easy getting passage anywhere in this goddamn war."

Suddenly, off in the dark, an air raid siren began wailing. At once lights flickered off and people began milling about.

"What's that noise?"

"Just an air raid warning."

Schroeder laughed. "You crazy bastards. You Americans are silly, you know that? Do you really think Germany is going to drop bombs on you?"

"I guess some of us do."

"Stupid. No wonder you're losing the war with all the stupid people you got. Germany will get you in other ways, not with planes across the Atlantic."

He breathed. In. Out. Dulaney pictured Nordic nostrils flaring.

"What do I get for my money?" he dared to ask.

"Only everything you came for. How much is that worth?"

"More than I've got."

"I thought so. Then you'll be hearing from me, sometime next week. What's your extension at work?"

"Thirteen."

"Unlucky number. Makes it easy to remember. When are you there?"

Dulaney told him but he didn't hang up quite yet. He said one more thing, which Dulaney would remember many times in the days to come. "I'm going to tell you everything, Dulaney. I've thought about it and now I'm going to do it. So you get that money and in the meantime you walk very carefully. That's a piece of advice I give you for free. Don't make waves. Then, when I've told you what I'm going to tell you, you grab that girl and get out of here. Kidnap her if you've got to, because I'll tell you something, we are all in danger—you, me, that girl—we're all in trouble. Are you hearing me now?"

"I hear you."

"Good. Good boy, Dulaney."

The phone went dead.

Beyond the square the whole town was dark. He saw people, dusky shapes pressing close around the phone box, shadows filling the square. The siren had faded but now it came again. He pushed through the crowd to the boardwalk, where people swarmed facing the black sea, waiting for something to happen.

Somewhere close a woman spoke, saying how deep the night was since they'd begun blacking out the lighthouse. "It must be a convoy going out," she said, and in the lull Dulaney realized she'd been talking to him. He felt her nudge close, seeking his body heat on a warm June night filled with phantoms. "I heard they're going to black us out if there's any shipping coming or going. The lighthouse is shut down for the duration. But I guess we're not even supposed to say that, are we?"

"It's okay," Dulaney said. "I won't tell Adolf."

"If I don't talk to someone, I think I'll go crazy."

He let her snuggle into his arm, the kind of detached intimacy that could happen only in wartime. "This is so damn spooky," she said, this woman he would never know.

"We're losing everything," she said. "The whole world's gone mad."

She was shivering violently now. "Please . . . do you mind?"

He put an arm over her shoulder and she huddled gratefully, this woman whose face he would never see.

((9))

ON Saturday night he ate with Stoner in a teeming fish house just off the boardwalk. The place was smoky and loud, always crowded, the fish cheap and abundant and unrationed. Every table was occupied, but they pulled themselves into a foursome with Becky Hart and their new director, Maitland. "It's good to meet you," Maitland said, shaking his hand. "I've seen you in the hall a few times, but either you've been on the run or I have."

The waitress brought water and almost at once he found himself dodging questions. "Jethro tells me you're a novelist," Maitland said, and Becky was immediately on his back. "That's fantastic, Jordan, what books have you written?" He shrugged. "It was a long time ago and it was just one book." But she refused to let it go. "You've got to let us read it. I'll bet we can get some radio out of it." He tried to dodge—"Like I told Kidd, it's so obscure even I haven't got one, and the subject's way too saucy for radio anyway"—but she was not put off. "Now we're really interested. What's the title? . . . I'll call some of the secondhand bookshops in New York and see if they can track it down."

He was saved for the moment by the waitress, a nice-looking woman in her forties with a nameplate that said TRUDY. She and Stoner seemed to have an acquaintance of some standing, as he joshed her freely while Maitland glanced over the menu. "Nothing for me but the clam soup tonight," Maitland said. "I never eat full meals at night anymore—my blood pressure's too high and the doctor says I must lose forty pounds."

"I don't know what my blood pressure is," Stoner said. "But I never wanted to live forever anyway, so I'll just take the usual."

"Two sharks and a potato field," Trudy said, and Stoner faked a slap at her backside.

Jordan tried to keep the talk away from himself. "She's got her eye on you, Gus. Her intentions would power the pier in a blackout."

Maitland laughed but Becky was still watching him. "We were talking about your book. You still haven't told me the title."

"Maybe because I don't want all my immature ramblings splashed on the radio."

"Think of it as opportunity knocking. Rewrite it into a masterpiece for us. How many writers get to rethink old work like that?"

"Maybe I don't want to rethink stuff. Right now I'd rather fix Gus up with the girl of his dreams."

"Save your energy, kid. Trudy and I have too much fun poking fun."

"But there's a lot more fun to be had."

"Jordan's right, Gus," Becky said. "Though for the life of me I can't imagine where he gets all that wisdom. You don't see him making any time to play with us girls."

"I'm too big and ugly," Jordan said, and Maitland's laugh boomed across the table. "Gus, on the other hand, could be a real ladies' man."

"You really could, Gus," Becky said.

"Get outta here, all of you," Stoner said. "I like Trudy, but listen, there was just one woman in my life and she's been gone twenty-four years this fall."

A silence fell over the table and Stoner's eyes, now sad, looked at them one after another. "You all heard about the flu epidemic. My Jeannie died November fourth, nineteen eighteen, at two thirty-two in the morning. She was twenty-four years old."

"My daughter died in that," Maitland said. "That goddamn flu. My wife's never been the same since that goddamn flu took our Sarah away."

"What a world," Becky said. "Sleeping sickness, flu, polio, war."

On that sober note she put away her pen, and their food came.

★ ★ ★

Jordan liked Maitland at once. He had a jolly demeanor that was infectious, a robust optimism that the best years of man were straight ahead. Radio was booming and television was still just a theory, a few watery pictures whose transmission range was far from certain. Even if television did someday prove feasible, it would always be a poor second cousin. "Once the novelty wears off it'll be finished. As far as drama goes, I can't see the picture boys ever doing what we do. They may think a picture will expand their horizons, but all they'll do is reduce it to the size of a seven-inch screen. I'm staking what's left of my career that there'll always be a market for a good half hour of radio. And listen, the best that radio can do hasn't even begun yet. Think of it in the Darwinian sense. Radio crawled out of the sea in nineteen twenty, and all this time we've been struggling to breathe air, not water. We haven't even gotten our legs yet, but maybe it's time we at least begin the struggle to stand."

"Maybe Harford's trying to take those first steps," Becky said. "It's pretty clear something's going on."

"We shall see."

"Come on, you old bastard," Stoner said. "You know way more than you're telling."

Maitland remained deadpan. "Let's just say I know enough to bring me here, at a time in my life when I'm getting damned selective. I could've had a job at CBS in New York but I'm here instead. That should tell you something, if you put any stock in what I do. There's not a network job any-where that could pull me away from here, and that's all I'm going to say about it. If you want to know more, ask Jethro."

"Oh yeah, I can see us doing that," Becky said. "Most of us are afraid to ask him the time of day."

"Oh, come now, Kidd isn't that fierce."

"He does seem interested in us, I'll give him that. About a week after I got here he called me in for an interview. I was sure I was going to be fired but we just sat and talked. He wanted to know what *I* think, what *I* want to do, how *I'd* define an exciting half hour."

"Good for Jethro. What did you tell him?"

"Told him what I think. A great half hour is a piece of shining truth, told in the most powerful way possible."

"That's a perfect answer! You couldn't have said it better if you'd taken two weeks to think it over. I'll bet that was the highlight of his day."

She blushed under his praise but her eyes were wary. "How can you tell? Who knows what he thinks?"

"That's why he's such a good manager, his expression never changes. But you can tell you've pleased him by what he does later. What did you tell him you wanted to do?"

"Said I'd like to produce." She blushed again.

"And what beyond that?"

"I don't know. There's no way a girl could ever direct."

"Why not? . . . just because it's never been done?"

"The guys won't take direction from a girl."

"Then you get some guys who will."

A long tremor went through her. "God, I couldn't tell him that!"

"Actually you could. Maybe you'll realize that, and sooner than you'd believe. Don't be surprised if he starts letting you try your wings."

"Maybe he already has. He's got me reading scripts now. We still get things from freelancers, and he's got me doing follow-ups on old scripts in the files that were never produced for one reason or another. You wouldn't believe what's in there—stuff from six and seven years ago, and some of it's very good. Kidd says he wants me to separate the wheat from the chaff."

"Then take him at his word."

"Mmm-hmm. But I don't want to send him something that can't be done."

"Why couldn't it be, if it's good enough?"

"I'm thinking of a particular piece. It's been there since nineteen thirty-six. I can't imagine why they didn't do it then. It's just . . . devastating . . . I can't get it out of my mind. Like it sets up a ringing in your brain and you think about it all the time."

"Then why do I sense a 'however' coming?"

"Yeah, there's a problem. A big one." She sighed. "It was probably doable in nineteen thirty-six. Today it's political dynamite. It scares me to think about it."

"What's it about?"

"It's a war story. A lot of it is set in a prison camp."

Jordan stirred. "I think he already knows about that play."

"How could he? He just got here and those files haven't been disturbed in years."

"All I can tell you is, that's one of the first questions he asked me—how would I get a prison camp story on the air?"

Maitland smiled. "You see, Rebecca? He's waiting for you to discover it. Show him how smart you are."

"I don't know. I'd like to find the author first so I can give it to Kidd as a whole package. Apparently the writer was a visitor from overseas somewhere. Have any of you ever heard of a writer named Paul Kruger?"

"There was a statesman named Paul Kruger," Maitland said. "A famous man, oh, forty years ago."

"No, this was a writer. I just thought maybe he had come to something, his play is so good."

"Did he accept Harford's check?"

"Oh yeah, apparently it was cashed."

"Then what are you worried about? For the purpose of onetime radio adaptation, we own the script."

She took a deep breath. "All right, I'll confide in you guys, but on your word of honor nothing gets said till I decide what I want to do. I'd like to find this guy, see what he's been doing all these years, mainly to see if he's got any more where that came from, like maybe he's sitting on a hundred of these things and I'm on the verge of a major discovery. Does that sound silly?"

"Not at all," Maitland said. "It sounds exciting."

"And it may be just a matter of going up to New York and knocking on a door. I've got a street address but it's six years old, and getting away has been damn near impossible. And if that's not enough, I think Paul Kruger may have been a— what do they call it?—a nom de plume? The check was signed over to a third party. Someone named Riordan."

Jordan felt shaken. At once it occurred to him that Kruger sounded German and Riordan was definitely Irish.

"Maybe I can help," he said.

"Yeah, like *you've* got so much time on your hands, what with Barnet on your back twelve hours a day."

"I'd like to read it, though. When you're ready."

"Okay, I'll make you a deal. You read my script, I get to read your book."

Stoner said, "Sounds like she's got you there, champ."

"Meanwhile," Maitland said, "how would you like to help produce something for me?"

Becky touched her heart. "You're kidding."

"Do I look like I'm kidding? Now, I'll tell you a secret. We're going to do a big war bond show a week from Saturday. Kidd wants to see if a little station like this can sell bonds. An hour of music and prose, lush inspirational stuff. He's going to bring in an orchestra and chorus—really pulling out all the stops. We'll have to use both studios, so we'll need two directors. Barnet and I have both been assigned to it."

"Barnet won't be happy unless he's running it."

Maitland smiled, the soul of patience. "We'll survive each other. He's got his ideas and I've got mine. I know he wants an opera singer for the national anthem, but I'd like a voice closer to common people. I like that girl who sings for us on Saturday nights, that incredible girl with the big voice. I talked to her yesterday but she turned me down. She says she's just a band singer. Thinks this is beyond her."

"She's crazy. She can sing anything."

"That's what I told her. I want her to sing other songs as well, stuff from the heartland. She could really carry this show, Rebecca, so there's your first job as producer. Produce Holly O'Hara and get her to sing 'The Star-Spangled Banner' on my show two weeks from tonight."

"I'll get her." She was visibly thrilled. "By God, that's a promise."

(((10)))

THAT night he stood in the back row and watched the band show, and in the crushing void of her departure he made a decision. He had hung back long enough; he would find a way to approach her. Now he faced another endless night, full of evil spirits, and he drifted upstairs to the bullpen. Perhaps he could write something, and in work find the release to go home for a few hours' sleep.

He began with raw notes, and soon he had a beachfront town with glitter and noise, the crush of crowds and the frantic pace of wartime, a lonely sailor on his last weekend home, and of course, the enigmatic woman. Soon a kind of white heat arose in his chest, and in a while the keys on the old Royal outran three teletypes in the room across the hall.

It was the age-old story of animal magnetism. The sailor, brash and full of immature posturing, turns out to be the frightened virgin; the girl, on the face of it elusive and shy, is a woman of the world. Shyness is just one of the masks she wears, and at the end her character remains dark and full of mystery. The sailor is forever touched: he loses the girl, she disappears into a ladies' room on the pier and never returns, and the boy squanders his leave searching faces on the boardwalk.

Who are these people? The girl leaves few clues and we never hear her voice again. The boy reminds me of myself, Jordan thought: me at eighteen with Tom's bravado. In the rewrite I will make him part of my racetracker clan, complete as he stands but part of a larger story for anyone who has heard the others. It has nothing to do with horses: only that the kid has come from the horseman's world and that's his back story. He's the horse trainer's son caught up in the war. This war and that girl might happen to anyone his age. That's what I want the listener to know.

He sat quiet, his fingers momentarily stilled. But as soon as he quit working his own loneliness invaded the cubicle and attacked his momentum. Suddenly his story was in grave danger. The spirit of the girl had occupied his workplace, and she was no longer fiction but someone he knew only too well. He held his pages over the wastebasket, poised to tear: a telling moment, perhaps the watershed of his writing life. But the change that had begun against his will had finally come true. His concept of the reader had been fading and had finally vanished.

He was writing for the listener.

Now he saw that what he had was the rough draft of a half-hour radio play. He felt a surge of inexplicable excitement as he took the next logical step, prose into script in the middle of a page, and again his fingers were flying and all his new awareness was there in his words. He understood demands and restrictions that had never given him a conscious thought, and he saw the story anew. The opening could not linger. Leisure was fine for depth in prose but a story for the ear must begin with the first spoken word of the encounter that will drive it.

He was not so much writing his play now as hearing it. The characters floated above his head and directed his fingers, and all he had to do was follow them along the boardwalk and tell what they did by what they said.

He knew it was too carnal for radio. He actually laughed when his characters closed the door in the shabby seaside hotel and the girl tugged hotly at the young man's bell-bottoms. He'd never get that on anybody's air. But he went on gamely to the end and finished sometime before two.

It felt good, a solid little lightning strike, done in a sitting. The impossibility of the subject matter meant nothing compared with what doing it had taught him, and a flood of new ideas came swirling through the enclosure. Every image was pure radio, each a compact slash of life that could be done nowhere better than on the air. For twenty minutes he took rough notes, as fast as he could type. The walls disappeared and he was ready to start again, take up a new idea and work it through the night. But the writer in him said it was time to stop, to leave something in the tank for the next sitting. He had a show to do tomorrow, a new cast to meet, but now as he gathered his pages and put them in a file folder, the act of quitting brought down his defenses and the ghosts of the night invaded his cell.

He tucked his folder under his arm and turned off the lamp, went down the fire stairs and over the dunes toward the glow in the south.

Slowly as he walked his faith returned.

He didn't know why. Something about the healing virtues of work was the likeliest answer.

Or maybe this: nothing could turn away the fact that she had seen him. Their eyes had met, she had been unable to look beyond him, and never again could she go back and hide alone in the shadows.

The dismal day was charged with new hope. He reached the road, bright under the moon. The ghosts had vanished, leaving him with one of life's smallest truths. Sometimes you've got to hurt before you can heal. That's why the trainer puts the hot iron to his colt's sore ankles. If you fire the horse, nature sends its healing properties rushing to the spot, to make him well again.

(((**11**)))

SUNDAY morning. Eli met him at the door but there was a difference to the day and both could feel it. "Coffee's ready," Eli said, but this morning Jordan drank his coffee alone.

A few minutes later he backtracked up the hall to Studio B and stood watching them through the glass. There were five of them on the soundstage. The old man with the gray hair would be the uncle; the others, including Eli, were all in their twenties. He opened the door and slipped quietly into the studio, and their concentration remained unbroken; they had not seen him come in, and he had a few moments to watch them when they didn't know they were being watched.

A young woman stood at the center-stage mike reading something. Then he saw that she had no pages, she was not reading at all but was acting out a piece she had committed to memory. The words struck his ear with an eloquent, easy familiarity, and then he had it—one of Richard Wright's stories from *Uncle Tom's Children*. But what really struck him was her style. She had a natural way about her that touched him across barriers of race and sex.

She saw him suddenly and broke off her monologue. The others followed her distraction, and the gray-haired man came out to meet him.

"You would be Mista Jordan."

"Just Jordan's fine. And you're Waldo."

"Waldo Brown. You know Eli. That child over there is his sister Emily. The fella behind her is Rudo Ohlson. And this is Ali Marek."

He shook hands all around and looked into the very dark face of Ali Marek. "I hated to bust up your soliloquy like that. Is that what you're doing this morning?"

"Oh God no," she said.

"That's way too strong for this show," Waldo said.

"We just messin' around," Eli said. "Doing play radio like it's real."

"I thought it was great," Jordan said. "Any of those Richard Wright stories would make good radio."

They seemed surprised that he knew the material and considered it suitable and even possible for the air. For his part, Waldo was relaxed and easy. "So, what's up?" he said. "What's goin' on?"

"They still haven't told you yet?"

"Nobody's told me a thing, except what I got from you, through Eli."

"That's all I know too."

"Eli said you're gonna do what? . . . write it?"

Jordan thought he had to watch what he said; he couldn't come in here like a boss man taking them over. But the news was good, at least he could tell them that.

"I think they're expanding it. They sent me over to see if you need a writer."

There was now a moment of such deep silence that he felt the need to put his thoughts into words. "Nobody intends to take you over."

"No, no . . . I never thought that. It's just been a long time coming." Waldo smiled warily. "Six years ago they were talking about expanding it. Putting in music and writing and sound."

"Do you know why that never happened?"

Waldo shrugged. "Miz Harford died. She's the one wanted to do it, but after she died this place went into . . . what do they call it in Buck Rogers? . . . suspended animation."

"Did you know Harford?"

"Sure. He's the one that put me on the air to start with."

"Tell me about it. If you don't mind."

"I wanted to do a radio program about the struggles of the Negro. I tried getting it on in New York but nothing ever came of it. One of the fellas I met made a call, and Mr. Harford invited me to come down."

"When was that?"

"Long time ago. Summer of nineteen thirty-four."

"I'm sorry I'm so ignorant. I've never heard it."

"We keep it real simple. We just tell stories, stuff I dig up."

"True stories, you mean."

"As true as I can make 'em. Some of it's . . . you know . . . folklore. But I try to stick with the truth as I know it."

Jordan looked at the cast, none of them old enough to have been here in 1934. Waldo caught his drift. "I've gone through twenty or thirty people over the years. It's a lot to ask 'em to drive down here from Harlem just for a fifteen-minute show, to speak a few lines. So they don't stick. Heck, I don't blame 'em, but I still think the show's important. Maybe I'm kidding myself, but I don't think you'll find anything like what we do at any other radio station in the country. Even if we are stuck away on Sunday morning."

"Well, then," Jordan said. "I'll just watch, if it's okay with you."

Today they were telling the story of Mary Ann Shadd, the Negro abolitionist who moved to Canada in the 1850s, established a newspaper there, and pushed for the rights of fugitive slaves. At quarter to eight Waldo gave a few last-minute suggestions. The cast made notes and that was their script. In the booth Waldo lowered a microphone. He does everything, Jordan thought: runs his own board, gives what direction he gives, and speaks his own lines from there. At thirty seconds Waldo fitted a pair of worn earphones over his head.

Upstairs in the second-floor studio, Eastman would be finishing an hour of gospel records. Waldo waited with his finger up, listening for the station break. Then he gave the simple announcement: "You are listening to *Freedom Road,* the oral history of the Negro people." Eli sang "The Freedom Song" and the story began.

There wasn't time for much, only the highlights of that long-dead woman's life. It was simple and crude, without music or sound, like watching a stage play without costumes or scenery. But it had warmth and a certain appeal, the five of them creating variety in shades of voice. Now they'd have to be more structured. Now they'd have to learn to read a script and follow real direction.

"Well, that's it," said Waldo as he came out of the booth. "It ain't exactly the Ziegfeld Follies, is it?"

"It's fine," Jordan said, warming to it. "All you need to decide now is whether you want to do it the other way."

"I want it to be heard, that's what's important. Anything that dresses it up is fine with me."

"Then the next question is, do you want to write it yourself?"

"I'm no writer, I don't fool myself about that. I'd be grateful for any help I can get in that pit of snakes."

"Then you get me. If that's okay."

They spent the morning roughing out ideas. Jordan was no stranger to the unwritten history of the black race, but in Waldo he had met a walking almanac. For their first show, one week from today, they would do Blind Tom Bethune, the musical prodigy born in slavery on a Georgia plantation. It was one of the stories Jordan knew well enough to write on short notice. For their second week he suggested Isom Dart, the black cowboy— expert roper, bronc rider, cattle thief, and according to legend, murdered by Tom Horn. Half a dozen true-life black stories raced through his mind, and Waldo added a dozen more.

Waldo would remain the driving force. He had collected enough material for years of radio. He knew his way around a library, knew where dusty tales and memoirs were buried, and had an acute sense of what a drama required. "We'll be hard pressed next Sunday," Jordan said. "I'd suggest coming early to iron the bugs out." They decided to meet at 5 A.M. "We'll do two or three table readings, till you're all easy with it. Then at seven the organist and the sound lady will come in and we'll have a dress rehearsal just before we go on."

After that it would get easier. Jordan would also have the Isom Dart script finished and back from mimeo this Sunday. "That'll give you a week to play with it in New York. I'll try to keep at least one-up after that."

They left around noon with everyone feeling high. At one o'clock he settled into his cubicle to write his first show. The magic began: the spirit that had touched him last night ignited again and he stepped across a century and out of his white skin, and became Blind Tom Bethune. By five o'clock he had a finished script, and in the late afternoon he walked alone on the beach, south toward Holly's.

((12))

IT was Tuesday before his chance came. He walked up the beach at noon and there she was. She was dressed not to be noticed: scarf, plain blouse, long skirt. No shoes, he guessed, as the surf was breaking over her feet and she made no effort to avoid it. Beyond her house the crowds thinned and she stood out clearly in the bright sunlight. No one was swimming: the rolls of barbed wire kept them back and there was still a faint hint of oil on the sand as the tide went out. A body had washed ashore last week, many miles from here, but half a dozen of the sunken dead had never been recovered and that was enough to keep even serious grandstanders out of the water on this hot day.

He felt no urgency. She was trapped on the beach and there was no hurry to catch her. The barbed wire petered away and the sea to the south was clear and bright as she moved on toward the gully that fronted the hook. She was less than a hundred yards from the cut with the distance between them half that, and a small party of people on a spread of blankets was all that kept them from being alone.

She splashed into the gully to her ankles. She hadn't yet seen him, except possibly as a dark shape at the edge of her vision. Then she did see him and knew: she looked straight into his eyes ten yards away and she knew him. Her face was scrubbed free of makeup: she seemed almost like a child until her eyes gave away her age. Her dress was wet to the knees, flattened against her by a stiff wind that set the curves of her legs and the deep furrow of her backside in bold relief, as if she'd worn nothing beneath it. He veered away slightly, intentionally passing between herself and the people on the blankets. There was a hail of "Howdy's," the common manners of strangers separated from the anonymity of the crowd. She looked expectant but he continued giving her whatever space she might need, speaking to them all as a group. He said, "Isn't this a wonderful day?" and the woman on the blanket said you couldn't ask for better, if only the war would go away. "It will," Jordan said. "One day you'll wake up and it'll be gone like a bad dream."

He splashed into the gully, out to the edge of the sea. So far the encounter felt right, to that happy part of his mind that had pushed him into it. It was his cautious half that begged to differ. Caution said she was halfway back to town by now.

But she hadn't moved. She stood watching him and he knew he had to speak but he had no idea what he'd say till he opened his mouth and said it.

"I believe you're the woman who sings on the radio."

She shook her head, the movement barely perceptible. The people on the blankets were watching her curiously, not yet sure if they should be impressed. Jordan came back up the cut, holding his hands over his eyes as if to get a better look. "Aren't you Miss O'Hara?"

"You're thinking of someone else," she said.

The woman on the blanket wiggled around to face them, draping her arm over the shoulders of the man beside her. "We tried to get in last Saturday," she said. "Didn't come close to making it. You'll have to tell us how you do it."

"I work there," he said, looking at Holly.

"Isn't that fascinating!" The woman laughed. "Too bad you're not that singer. Wouldn't you find that just fascinating?"

"To her it's probably just a job," Holly said.

"Anything can get that way," Jordan said. "I think I'd be ready to move on myself if something more important came along."

"Isn't that just like a man," said the woman on the blanket. "Wonderful job like that and he wants to move on. I think it would be so exciting to watch them put on the shows."

"There's really nothing to it. The listener does all the work."

"I listen to the radio all the time. I never thought of it as work."

"That depends on what you listen to." He moved away as something caught his eye, a shell tumbling in the foamy surf. He picked it up, a flawless little moon snail, he thought it was called. Holly still hadn't moved from the spot where she'd first seen him, and he came toward her with the shell held out like a calling card.

"Here you go, miss. A remembrance of the day."

She took it and their fingers touched. Her eyes probed his face and he gave her finger a little squeeze and smiled so only she could see it.

"Some people think it brings luck," he said. "But you've got to give it to the first person you see while it's still wet from the sea. Do you believe that, miss?"

"No. But I've never been one for superstitions. I'd rather just take it because it's beautiful."

"I'll make the formal gesture anyway. To Miss . . ." He tilted his head and blinked at the unfinished statement. "I almost did it again. Almost said Holly O'Hara, that's how much you remind me of that singer."

"Then the charm wouldn't work, since my name isn't O'Hara."

Caution held him in check. Then she said, "It's Carnahan," and his heart fairly rumbled with hope.

"To Miss Carnahan, then. Go in beauty and good fortune."

She said nothing. Her hand had closed around the shell and when she opened it, it was still wet. She slipped it into a pocket as the woman on the blanket spoke again. "I saw a radio show in New York last year. My sister took me to Radio City and we got in the audience for an *Ellery Queen*. Have you ever heard that show?"

"That's on the Red, isn't it? We're Blue, y'know, and I'm kept pretty busy with what's on my own air."

"What do you do there?"

"I write the continuity. The stuff they say between things."

"What's your name, if you don't mind me asking?"

"Jordan Ten Eyck." He looked at Holly. "My name is Jordan."

"I was never so surprised as I was when I saw them do that radio show. None of the actors look like the parts they play and it's amazing watching them make all those sounds. My sister can't listen to it anymore."

"The illusion is gone."

"Exactly. Now when she's supposed to be picturing a thunderstorm, all she sees is a man shaking BBs in a drum."

"That's probably the danger of having any kind of magic explained. It's better not to know."

"Not always," said Holly, coming out of the water.

She came past him very close: a nape of neck, a swirl of honey-colored hair. She stopped on the sand and wrung the water out of her hem, and her eyes came up and she smiled the way a stranger might. He asked, "Are you leaving us, miss?" and she said yes, and, "Thank you for the lovely charm." Now he took another chance, letting his bold side run mad. "Say, miss . . . do you think it would be proper to ask if I might walk you back up the beach?" She stood up tall and smiled. "It sounds very proper when you put it that way but it's not a good idea. I'm meeting a friend and he gets . . . well, you know how some men get. But thank you for the thought."

When she was fifty yards away he threw her another good luck wish and she waved over her shoulder. Behind him, the woman on the blanket said, "What a lovely girl. I was pulling for you there, but I guess you win some and lose some. It's too bad, though, a woman like her with a man like that. Such a pretty girl and all."

She was gone when he came back up the beach. The crowd was growing and she had lost herself in it; her cottage looked impregnable in the noonday sun and he tried to hang on to the thought that he had made some kind of progress. He slogged through the soft sand and climbed to the boardwalk south of the Ferris wheel, and there, when he turned, he was shocked to see her out on the beach again, coming along behind him.

She had changed her clothes and now had a dark scarf and a parasol to hide her face. She stopped fifty yards behind him, as if waiting for him to move on. He passed the amusement park and headed up toward the pier, and when he stopped again and looked casually around he saw that she was doing the same. Keep going, he thought; that's what she wants.

He clattered down from the boardwalk and crossed the graveled square, passed the phone box, and sat on the farthest bench in the park. For a long time she watched the sea, occasionally turning her back to it so she could look across the square where he sat. What was she telling him? . . . what was she trying to say? She wants to talk but not here in the open. So he got up and walked out of the park, across the street to the beer garden, through the cluster of outdoor tables, and into the building. The cool, damp beer smell closed around him. The place was dark and uncrowded, with only a sprinkle of faceless talk from shadows hunkered along the bar. He sat and ordered a draught.

The mirror behind the bar gave him a perfect wide-angle view and he nursed his beer as he watched her. Suddenly he made a new decision—he would speak to her, this time alone and of things far more important than seashells. If she left now he would get up and go after her. If she went home he would knock on her door. Perhaps he would do none of these things, but the beer was cold and it was a good way to pass the time. At least she would understand that. She had always admired his patience.

Half an hour passed before she came. He saw her cross the park and duck her head under the canopy. He didn't move except for his heart. He heard her footsteps and felt her looming presence, then she was there. She had come from his left but she went around and sat on the stool to his right. She had remembered his bum ear.

"Well, Jack Dulaney."

"As you live and breathe," Dulaney said.

"What's all this Jordan Ten Eyck business?"

"It's whatever you want it to be."

They were looking at each other in the mirror, their faces deep in shadow. Dulaney kept his there but she turned slightly as she spoke, becoming a pale crescent moon, a sliver of some old dream in the light reflected from the street.

"I guess it finally dawned on me, Jack. I should've known we had to have this talk. It was just a matter of time."

He turned to her now but she had looked away, leaving him a shadow to talk to. "I've had a hard time figuring you out," he said.

"It's simple, really. I kept thinking you might leave town."

He didn't like the way this was going. He liked it less when the bartender asked what she'd be having and she said,

"Nothing, thank you, I won't be here long enough." A powerful sense of doom came over him as he waited for her next words.

"Couldn't you see that's what I wanted you to do?"

"Is that what I was seeing?"

"Oh, please. Let's not fool around anymore, Jack, I don't have the time for it. I'm supposed to be rehearsing in twenty minutes."

"Then you tell me. Is that what I was supposed to think when you looked right through me? . . . that you wanted me to leave?"

"What else?"

"I thought lots of things."

"What things?"

"Everything but that. Everything from threats . . ." He shrugged and gave a friendly laugh. "I even considered that you'd lost your mind."

She didn't share the laugh but there was a hint of distant amusement, of the old Holly. "That's really disappointing, Jack. In the first place, who would threaten me, and why? And you should know better than anyone how mentally tough we Carnahans are. Haven't we weathered famine, war, death, and loss of faith? What else can happen to us?"

"I won't make that mistake again. I knew you could sing but I had no idea what an actress you are. That first night you had me believing I really was a stranger. I don't think I could've done that. It takes a cool head to pass an old friend by without blinking an eye."

"You're making more of it than it is. You didn't quite catch me flat-footed, I knew you were there. When we got off the bus I saw some excitement behind the building. Just a silly volleyball game. But imagine my surprise when I saw who was playing."

"Just killing time. The real question is, what happens now?"

"Nothing." She looked at him, then away. From the dark she said, "I don't mean to sound cold, but my life is very different now."

"So I noticed. Congratulations."

"Now who's being cold?"

"That's the last thing I ever imagined, being cold with you."

"Be happy for me. I'm having the time of my life."

"If that's true I'm damned happy. And listen, in case enough people haven't already told you, you really are something wonderful. The best part is, you just keep getting better."

She coughed softly. "I guess none of us knows what we've got inside us till the moment comes. You think you know yourself, and suddenly you learn you're deeper than that. And no matter how deep you go, there's always more. I'm learning something new about myself every day."

"And you think . . . what? . . . I'm gonna get in the way of that?"

"You could. Whether you mean to or not. I've got an opportunity here, the chance of a lifetime. But I could lose it all if I'm seen with you."

He laughed. "Hell, I knew my reputation was a little rough in some places. Didn't know it had followed me this far."

"Not just you, any man. The gentleman who's going to mold my career is a jealous master."

"Well, you haven't been seen with anybody yet. You've got to admit I've kept my distance."

"You've been very discreet. Thank you for that."

"Oh, my pleasure. I was never quite sure what I was being discreet about, I was just following your lead."

"You always did have such great instincts, Jack. Such wonderful judgment. Such a grand sense of what's the right thing to do."

"With one great and shining, thundering exception."

"Well, we won't get into that now. It's water over the dam, all finished and done with."

"I never really felt it was."

"It is, take my word for it."

He could feel her tensing up beside him. She reached over and took a drink of his beer. "You made that choice, Jack. You chose, remember? You were the one who packed up and left town. You, not me. You made your choice and that was the end of it. It wasn't my fault if it never had any real beginning. You cut it off and now we'll live with that, so please don't come vaulting back into my life at this late date and tell me you never considered it over and done with."

She took a deep, shivery breath. "What do you want from me? Do you want me to say I loved you? What good will that do now? If I said yes, I loved you so desperately that I wanted to throw myself in front of a subway that night, would that make you feel better? Do you have any idea what you did to me, how desolate I was when you left me there? All you ever thought about was you and Tom, what was right for you, and I was just the spoils. And when I finally did the only thing I could do, you were both gone. But I didn't die, Jack. The old Carnahan backbone bucked me up and I came out of it stronger than ever."

"There's a lot in what you're saying. Some of it I didn't know then."

"You didn't want to know."

"Holly, I couldn't know. So I made sure I wouldn't."

"Goddammit, even then you had to know."

She gave him an angry look in the glass. The look he returned was only sad. "I plead guilty," he said. "I was a damn fool. Deaf and blind, mostly dumb."

"Well, it doesn't matter anymore, you can put it to rest. I've learned how not to be in love, and life's a lot better this way. I've got a program now, I can see where my life's going. The man who's handling me won't tolerate any changes in the program and that's just fine with me. So that's what I came to tell you. I don't have time for a personal life and I don't care. I can't make it any clearer than that."

"No, that's pretty clear."

"Then all we need to do is say good-bye."

"And I leave town."

"Please." She leaned toward him and for a moment he thought she might take his hand. But she leaned back and said, "I just don't need you here complicating my life."

He finished his beer. "There is one other thing. I heard your father died."

Her mouth opened but nothing came out. The shock went on: ten full seconds. Then: "My God, where'd you hear something like that?"

"I went to Pennsylvania looking for you. The little girl next door said you told her that yourself."

He stared at the mirror. Her face was now cloaked in darkness.

"It's one of her stories," said the voice from the void. "She lies through her teeth. She's a sweet child and I love her but she just won't tell the truth. Her parents must've told you how she lies."

"That was mentioned."

"Then there you are. My father's never been better."

"I'm glad to hear that. I'd like to see him again."

Her response was slow in coming and struck him as cautious. "He always did like you, Jack. You two had a special friendship."

"Then I think that's what I'll do, go visit your dad, see if he can help me put some ghosts to rest. See where the road takes me from there."

"I'm sure he'd love that. Finding him might be a problem. The last I heard he was traveling in Texas."

"Really? He used to keep in touch all the time, as I remember it."

"Things change—isn't that what we've just been talking about? I'm not a child anymore who's got to be checked on every week. I've got my life, he's got his. That's how it ought to be when you grow up."

He said nothing and the silence turned prickly. She picked up the talk: anything to break the mood and give her a legitimate exit. "If I could tell you where he is, I would. I'm sure I'll hear from him eventually. That's how he is these days, still a rolling stone, but he only calls me when he moves. Three or four times a year I'll hear from him."

Her voice droned on till he was aware it had stopped. When he said nothing she rose from the stool as if to leave. But there was one more shock to come and he timed it like the telling moment in a radio play. "What I still don't understand," he said into the mirror, "is how the kid knew about Harford."

She took a step backward and almost fell. He gripped her wrist and leaned into the light. "How would the kid know that name, except from you? Why would she say Harford had killed your father?"

"I have no idea what you're talking about."

But she knew exactly what he was talking about. She knew why he was here and how impossible it was for him to leave. She had to know that he loved her and would walk into hell to save her, even from herself. If she needed a knight, here he was, his life at her service. But his arrival had only brought her fear.

No chance now for a graceful exit. "The hell with it," she said, pulling away from him. "The child lies. My father's fine. Believe what you want but that's how it is. Now stay away from me."

She was gone. He watched her in the mirror as she crossed the street. She popped open her parasol and quickly became part of the faceless, madding crowd.

(((13)))

HE now knew that she was driven by fear. He knew the child had not lied. He believed everything was connected: Carnahan to Kendall to the Germans to March Flack, and all of them to Harford. He thought his best hope was to dig out the truth quickly. Caution was not working and time was becoming the great enemy.

He found Mrs. Flack in her yard on the beach. He approached on the path through the dunes, and as he came around her house he saw her standing a few feet away, painting a picture. Her canvas was propped on an easel in the bright sunlight and she was wearing a large straw hat and the same faded dress. She saw him and for a moment her brush hung suspended.

"Do I know you?"

"We met one night. I work at the station."

She put down her brush and looked at him hard, and suddenly a look of excitement spread across her face. "Did they send you to fetch me? Have they got something for me to do?"

"No ma'am, I'm sorry. I was just passing by, thought I'd say hello."

The light went out of her face and she shrugged. "They don't use me much, unless they need a good Yorkshire accent. I used to do all those, but Hazel and Rue have got the general British accents fairly well. Once in a while someone wants the genuine article, and that's me. But not today, I guess."

She took off her hat and looked at him in the full glare. "I remember you now. It's Mr. Jordan, isn't it?"

"Jordan Ten Eyck."

She smiled in faint apology. "I'm sorry, I just remembered Maurice calling you Mr. Jordan. Would you like something? A Coke perhaps?"

"If you're having one."

"Come up to the porch where it's cool."

He sat in a rickety chair at a plain table while she disappeared into the house. She returned with a bottle in each hand. "I'm afraid there's no ice."

"It's fine like it is."

She opened the bottle and the yellow foam ran out on her hand. "I've become addicted to these damned things," she said. "They're called Dopes, you know. There's a rumor that they're laced with drugs to keep you coming back for more."

Jordan nodded—he had heard this for years—and he sipped the warm syrup and licked his lips. "Here's to dope," he said, and she laughed merrily and touched her foaming bottle to his. Her face contained touches of mischief, nothing like the queenly presence he had met in the studio. "God, look at us, swilling it down like pagans. I can't believe I didn't even offer you a bloody glass."

He took a chance and said, "It's okay, Mrs. Flack, a bloody glass wouldn't be very appetizing anyway."

She roared with laughter. "Oh, you!" she cried, and she barked like a hyena. "Oh, you silly Americans! My God, that was a good one! Haven't laughed like that in ages. You shouldn't spring something like that on an old lady, Mr. Jordan."

"You're not an old lady, Mrs. Flack."

"Well, thank you. Did I just call you Mr. Jordan? My gracious, where have my manners gone?" She sniffed and smiled and said, "Would you like a proper glass, Mr. Ten Eyck?"

"It doesn't taste the same in a glass."

"That's the bloody truth. You've got to have that sucking sensation or you lose the kick they put into it. But I do wish I had some ice to offer you. Don't have much in the way of frills these days. I get by, though. In a way it's good not to have all those modern trappings. You feel closer to the earth when you've got no gas or electric."

"You don't have electricity here?"

"Haven't had for three years now. At first I missed it terribly, but I'm used to it now. Got my oil lamps and an old wood burner to cook on. And Thomas brings me all the wood I need from across the way."

"Thomas?"

"He's my friend. Thomas Griffin, formerly of the New York stage."

"I've seen you walking with a fellow. Man with a limp and a cough."

"That's Tom. Got the limp and the cough both in the war. His lungs were frightfully damaged at a place called Cantigny."

"Mustard gas," Jordan said.

She nodded. "He can't work anymore. Couldn't get two lines out without those coughing fits coming over him. But oh, you should've seen him in his good years. He was a glorious Hamlet. And he's such a dear friend. Don't know what I'd've done these six years if not for Tom."

He was struck by a flashing memory of his own Tom, and he wondered how he'd get into things. But she opened the door herself. "I suppose you've heard the stories."

"You mean about your husband?"

"Well, of course *every*body's heard *that* story. I mean about me, Mr. Ten Eyck. The crazy woman who lives alone, waiting for a ghost to come back and tell her where he's been the past six years."

He shrugged. "That's just gossip. Not worth worrying about."

"It is if it affects your livelihood. You can see for yourself how little work they give me. I think I make them uncomfortable. And that's a shame, you know, for them and for me, because I was a pretty fair radio actress in my day."

"I'll bet you still are."

"I'll bet I am too. I was good enough for the BBC ten years ago. I've got good air presence, I can sight-read with any of them, and I know what the limitations of the microphone are. This must sound terribly vain."

"There's an old saying, Mrs. Flack. It ain't bragging if it's true."

"All I want is a chance to compete, to be judged in an honest audition rather than by Mr. Barnet's notions of what I can and can't do. I get nothing but stuffy old English dowagers or widows of Regent Street shopkeepers. And not much of that anymore."

He thought a moment about what to say next. "I'll tell you something if it won't offend you. I don't mean it to."

"Oh my, that sounds dire."

"It's not, really. Just a little observation. I think they see you as a recluse. That's what I've been led to believe, that you'd rather not be bothered with the day-to-day stuff of radio."

"That's not true."

"But I think that's the perception."

"A perception that begins and ends with Mr. Barnet. He's been running things for so long, now it's spread to the rest of them. The fact is, I'd love to be one of their insiders. But it's not going to happen."

"Why couldn't it?"

"Ask them that. Barnet would tell you he doesn't have that many roles that call for British accents, which is ridiculous.

As if the ability to do dialect is solely an American accomplishment."

Jordan was struck at once by the truth of this. "You're right, it makes no sense."

"It's ridiculous. Why should my ability to talk American be any more in question than Hazel's skills with British? We're both actresses! I can do American! I can do Brooklyn! I could do a gun moll right out of Damon Runyon if they'd let me, or a Negro from the South if they needed one. But when they did *Uncle Tom's Cabin* last year, I wasn't even invited to a reading. Barnet was afraid I'd play Topsy like Alice in Wonderland, I suppose."

"This might be a stupid question, but have you ever told them this?"

She gave a sad little half laugh. "You've put your finger on my problem, all right. I'm too proud for me own good. Too proud to go groveling to the likes of Clay Barnet."

"He's not the whole ball of wax over there."

"Well, he almost is. Or was, before Mr. Kidd arrived. I keep hearing rumors that changes are in the works. Do you think that's true?"

"I hear the same rumors."

"Let me know, would you, if Mr. Kidd plans to audition people. You'd be in a position to know, and I'd be thrilled to try out for something, especially one of those meaty continuing roles. Something like that would turn my lights back on."

"We've got a new director now," Jordan said. "I don't know if you'd heard. His name is Maitland. He's been here a month."

"Maitland! You're kidding!"

"Do you know him?"

"Of course! I worked for him in New York in nineteen thirty-four! He was at WOR and we were fresh off the boat from Liverpool. He was wonderful!"

"A big teddy bear, gray and easygoing."

"Yes, yes, what splendid news this is! My God, how could I not have known this?"

"You've got to get out more, Mrs. Flack." He smiled shyly. "You don't want to become a self-fulfilled prophecy. A recluse because they think you are."

She gripped his hand. "Jesus, that's *exactly* what I'm doing! This business of Maitland proves it. Jordan, you've saved my life!"

"Really, Mrs. Flack . . ."

"No more 'Mrs. Flack.' Please, you must call me Pauline. Oh, Jordan, do you know what this means? All the rumors are true! Harford *is* coming back! It's all happening again! The promise of those old days is finally going to be fulfilled."

His silence cast her hope in doubt and she was immediately desperate to retrieve it. "But what else could it mean? With Maitland here again, what else could it mean?"

He sat up in his chair. "Was Maitland here before?"

"For a little while, yes."

"What was he doing here?"

"Just filling in. Our program director was leaving for New York and Dedrick came down as a favor to Harford."

"So he didn't intend to stay."

She furrowed her brow. "I only talked to him a few times then. I remember he was tempted to stay, but he had another offer in Chicago. And Harford seemed to be retreating. I guess Maitland didn't see the commitment he needed."

"So Barnet was made director instead."

"Yes, and nothing's been the same since."

Jordan sat still and let this play in his mind.

"Those were such exciting times," she said. "There wasn't anything Harford wouldn't try, no taboos he wouldn't challenge. Our morale couldn't possibly have been any higher. We had a lot of people come through here then."

"What kind of people?"

"All kinds of talent. Not just Maitland—Harford brought in actors and musicians and directors and programmers. And there were lawyers too. That's when we knew he was serious about seeing what could and couldn't be done on the air. The place was alive with activity and ideas. But then Jocelyn died and it all just fell apart. She was a glorious person, Jordan, and she took to radio like no one I've seen before or since. There are people like that, you know, dyed-in-the-wool radio people. They come to it whole, with such infallible instincts, they don't need any apprenticeship because it's so natural to them. It makes me sad just to think of her. A very kind and lovely lady, and Harford just worshiped her. This place was supposed to be a tribute to her talent. They were going to take on the world together. They brought in a programmer to help them plot the station's direction. I remember seeing the four of them walking together on the beach—Harford and Jocelyn, Maitland and this new man who was going to run the station."

"Did you ever find out who the new man was?"

"He wasn't here long enough. You'll have to forgive me . . . I haven't thought of him from that day to this."

But she thought of him now and a sudden flash of surprise crossed her face. "He was a thin man, I remember that. A tall man, thin and serious, with a rather large head . . ."

They looked at each other. He waited and let her say it.

"Kidd."

She said it again. "Kidd. Who else could it have been?"

This discovery thrilled her anew. "Now do you see it? Do you understand it now? The station is truly coming to life. It's taken Harford all these years to get past that tragedy and now he's ready again."

Jordan sipped his Dope, took his time. Then he said, "Do you remember when that was, when you saw them walking together on the beach?"

"Of course. I remember exactly. The first week in June, nineteen thirty-six. I'll never forget that time. It was just a few weeks before my husband disappeared."

(((14)))

FOR a few minutes at the turning of the tide the sea was glassy and still. The wind had died to nothing and the waves lapped listlessly at the shoreline. Jordan sat still, thinking vastly different thoughts from what Mrs. Flack must be thinking as she stared past his shoulder at the gulls dipping over the beach. Leave her be for a few moments, he thought; let her savor her brighter prospects and she'll be happier when the hard questions come. But when it started again, the talk between them was as natural and easy as it had been from the start.

"It's not like what you've been hearing. I know what they say about me—that crazy woman, pining away for a man who's gone and left her—but it wasn't like that. March and I had a fairly stormy life together. I knew he had lots of affairs. I don't think there was a time in the twenty years we were together when he didn't have something going on the side. He got in a terrible scandal in England. That's why we came over here, but it never stopped. I threatened so many times to leave him, but he was in my blood and I was in his, and after a while it didn't seem to matter so much. I know he loved me, it just wasn't in his nature to be faithful. And though I raised hell when he dallied, we always made it up, and I knew I'd never leave him and he'd never leave me."

"Then what do you think happened to him?"

"He ran afoul of someone. I can't think of any other answer."

"Any idea who might've harmed him, or why?"

"No, and believe me, I've thought of everyone."

"Was there an investigation?"

"Such as it was. The sheriff here isn't exactly Scotland Yard."

"Same sheriff then and now?"

"Yes, he's a hail-fellow-well-met, pals around with everyone, and seems to be in the job for life. The less work he does, the better he likes it. From the start he leaned toward the easy theory, that March had left town with a young woman."

"Any particular young woman?"

Her cheeks turned red. "March had, uh, known one young woman for two months. She had just left town and the theory was that March had gone with her."

"Did the sheriff ever talk to her?"

"Says he tried. Tracked her to Detroit, all on the telephone, talked to her sister there, learned she'd been through town a few days earlier. Supposedly she'd gone to Canada to start a new life. And she had a man with her. The sister had never met him, and he might have been anyone from Winston Churchill to the man in the moon. But based on that, with nothing more to go on, he concluded that it was March."

"What happened the night he disappeared?"

She looked at him hard now. "You're beginning to sound like a detective yourself, Mr. Ten Eyck."

He shrugged. "I'll tell you the truth, then. The real reason I came here was to find a friend of mine who disappeared. Fella named Kendall."

"I knew Kendall. Not well, but I was in a few radio shows with him. I didn't know he'd disappeared. I thought he'd just . . . left."

"Then I learned that another man disappeared around the same time. A handyman named Carnahan. Did you know him?"

"Just to say hello to. He was Livia's friend."

"You mean . . ." He let this trail away into a question.

"That's what I hear."

"He was quite a bit older than she is. From what I've heard."

"Well, what of it? Girls are always throwing themselves at older, world-wise men. You should've seen the girls who chased after March."

"Is that what Livia did?"

"I'm just saying that age isn't the barrier it's cracked up to be. She and Carnahan were very good friends. They'd walk on the beach just before dawn, when there was nobody but me to see them. I saw her kiss him once. Not the way you'd kiss your father. But what are we getting at here? Do you think March was connected to these others?"

"I don't know. What would you think if you were me?"

"But that's preposterous. Whatever happened to March, that was so long ago."

He shrugged. "What about the night he disappeared?"

"Well, let me think. We had an early dinner. March was doing a play that night at nine and there was to be a microphone dress at seven thirty. So we ate and March left for the station at seven. I never saw him again."

"But he did arrive."

"Yes, I heard the play. They were doing the life of Lord Kitchener, with March in the lead. He had to carry it, he was in almost every scene for the full hour. He was magnificent, if I do say so, but March was always good in those roles of British pomp. He could really project that bellicose authority, if you know what I mean."

"So you heard the play. Then what?"

"Nothing. I waited up for him but he never came home."

"No calls? . . . to say he might be stopping somewhere?"

"Not a word. We had a telephone then and he certainly would've called if he were going to be very late. The show went off at ten. He should've been back here by ten thirty, eleven at the outside."

"What did you do when you didn't hear from him?"

"At about two o'clock in the morning I decided to go over. By then I had gone through all the natural reactions—I'd promised myself I'd kill him if it turned out he'd gone off with some tart and fallen asleep—but by two o'clock I knew something was wrong. I remember that thought flashing through my head, that something had happened and I'd never see him again."

"You walked over?"

"Yes, I'd had this horrible thought—what if he'd had a heart attack in the dunes and was lying out there helpless? So I walked the way I thought he'd go—we'd gone that way dozens of times—up from the beach to the road, then over the dunes to the tower. I took a flashlight and called his name. But there was nothing . . . except . . ."

"What?"

"I did see his footprints. But only going."

"Then he didn't come back that way."

"Not exactly that way. But it was very dark. You know how it gets here on those murky nights. And my light was dim."

"Was there fog?"

"No, just dense clouds. I could see where he'd gone well enough, those big feet slogging along. But if he came back across the dunes, he crossed in a different place."

"What happened when you reached the station?"

"Nothing. It was all locked and empty. I banged on the door but I knew there was no one to hear me."

"Then you didn't see anyone or anything unusual?"

"Just some lights across the way. But only for a moment."

"Across what way?"

"Over on Harford's property, far across the marsh near the woods. Might've been headlights of a car on one of the dirt roads, or maybe just torches—flashlights or whatever."

"Did you tell the sheriff about that?"

"Of course. He didn't think much of it. We got a better investigation out of the newspaperman than we did from the sheriff."

"What did he do?"

"For one thing, followed up every lead I gave him. Went out and tried to talk to Tom, actually did get a statement from Harford, and tracked down that woman March was supposed to have been with. She was still up in Canada with her boyfriend. Who wasn't March, by the way."

"What was the sheriff's answer to that?"

"Some nonsense about a philanderer never changing his spots. Just because March hadn't run off with one woman didn't mean he hadn't run off with another. And when push came to shove he could always fall back on the no-body argument. If there'd been a murder, where was the body?"

"But you said yourself, he didn't set any world records trying to find one."

"I suppose in his own mind he did try. Give the devil his due, he deputized some people and they combed through the marsh. Went all through the woods and searched the island with a dog. But by then a week had gone by and any trail there might've been was cold."

"I hear those dogs are great, though, even with old scents."

"The sheriff certainly put a lot of stock in it. I was asked for something March had worn, some piece of clothing that hadn't been washed, so the dog could pick up the scent. But the silly dog led them into town, then turned around and came straight back to the station."

"What did they do then?"

"Tried again, this time from here. Same thing happened, the dog made a beeline straight across the dunes to the station."

"Then what? What did the dog do then?"

"Went down to the foot of the tower, where the little utility shed is. Nothing in there but some tools, a wheelbarrow, and some old machinery. The sheriff thought it was obvious that the floor had never been taken up but they pried it up anyhow. Nothing under it, just that hard sand, but the damned dog kept going back there. As if March had been sucked up into the tower and on into the radio cosmos. God, what a chilling thought."

Jordan thought about what to ask next. "Getting back to the Kitchener broadcast. Do you remember who else worked that show?"

"I think Hazel was there . . . no, wait, for some reason she couldn't do the show and they had some other woman doing the female voices. And I think Barnet directed. Maitland was here then, but it had to be Barnet. I remember now. There was some kind of row between Barnet and Hazel over the script. That's why she didn't do the show. It would also explain why I didn't get a call. I wasn't getting along with Barnet even then."

"Do you know what the fight was about?"

"Can't imagine. I do remember that Stallworth announced it."

"What about Kendall?"

"Oh no, this was years before Kendall got here."

"Was Harford around then?"

"We never saw him. Jocelyn had just died, you know."

"How about Eastman?"

"He was here then. Whether he worked that show I can't say."

"Rue was probably in high school then. How about Brinker?"

"I can't remember. He's been here quite a while, you know. He's older than he looks. I think he was here at least by thirty-seven."

"Poindexter would've done the sound, and Stoner worked the board."

"Almost surely. Poindexter's son wasn't old enough and Livia hadn't arrived yet. Or had she? God, my memory's turning to mush. But I do seem to recall that someone else was on the board. March told me they'd had a frightful row the day before and Gus had walked out too. You see, Jordan, our program director isn't the easiest man to work with, and he and Stoner have never gotten along."

"Could the man on the board have been either of the Germans?"

"Oh no. You'd have to ask Gus, but I don't remember seeing either of them until a year or so ago."

He finished his Dope and put the bottle down beside hers.

"So, what's it all mean?" she said. "And what can be done about it at this late date?"

"I don't know, maybe nothing. But I'd like to nose around, if that won't bother you."

"Be my guest. Nobody else seems to care."

"You wouldn't have a picture of your husband handy—just something I could look at?"

"Of course. I'll get it for you."

She left him to mull over what he'd learned. He heard her footsteps cross to the front of the house, then a deep quiet came over the porch. But the tide had turned and the wind picked up; a small set of chimes began to jangle at the edge of the porch, and turning to look at it, he saw the limping figure of the old man coming up the beach. A chilling apprehension blew over him, a harbinger in the wind.

The old man walked with a determined shuffle, fighting his way through the soft sand on his way up to the house. Now Jordan could hear him breathing, a wheezing *aaahhh-aaahhh-aaahhh* as he came. He stopped at the fence and looked up. Jordan waved a friendly greeting, but the old man turned quickly away: down through the soft sand to the hard beach.

Mrs. Flack came out with a photograph in her hand.

"Your friend was just here. I think he was upset when he saw me."

"He probably was." She sat at the table. "Now he'll sulk for days."

"Sorry. Didn't mean to cause you a problem."

"It's not your fault. Tom sees things, or imagines he does. He's fine with me but he can't function with strangers anymore. He had a god-awful time in the first war, aside from being gassed. He has hallucinations. Imagines himself back in France."

"That's not uncommon. They call it shell shock."

"I'm afraid he's getting worse. Some days he's almost his old self, then he'll get lost in some fantasy. He's been in and out of sanatoriums since the armistice."

Jordan felt a new wave of questions. She sensed this and said, "You're fishing around. Looking for a tactful way of asking me if Tom Griffin might've killed my husband."

"You're a smart woman, Mrs. Flack."

"I'm not all that smart; common sense would lead anyone to that question soon enough. We had all the makings of a classic triangle: the husband who treats his wife shabbily, the other man who loves her, the hot tempers of creative people."

"And you did see lights that night in the marsh."

"Yes, and Tom and March did sometimes quarrel. But I could say the same of March and me. There were times when I felt like killing him myself. All I can tell you is, I didn't, and I know Tom didn't either."

"Do you mind, though, if I ask you a few more things?"

"You may ask me anything."

"Where does your friend Tom live?"

"Across the marsh, at Harford's. There's a road, and he keeps himself a little boat hidden in the brush by the inlet. Harford lets him live in one of those thatched-roof Shakespearean cottages that were built for Jocelyn's friends. I don't know what Tom would have done except for Harford. I imagine that surprises you. You've probably heard all kinds of things about Harford that may or may not be true."

"Actually I haven't heard much of anything."

"Then let me put this in your hopper. Tom came home from the war in a basket and Harford sent him to a place where they put him back together again. By nineteen twenty-one he was so much better that he was able to act again. He had a good season in New York, then made it to London for two years, and that's where we met him. He's had some good years since then, but sooner or later the nightmares come back—the shakes, the midnight sweats, the visions of death. Then he's got to go away again. But he always goes first cabin and Harford picks up the bill."

She waited for his reaction. "Harford's a strange man, Jordan. He's distant and full of mystery. But his loyalty to people who have been in his life is absolute."

"Was Tom in his life? . . . before the war?"

"Tom was in Harford's unit in the war. I don't know what happened, I never talk to Tom about those places and times. But here we are. Harford takes care of Tom, and because of Tom—and March, to a lesser degree—he takes care of me as well."

"You've lost me now."

"That's because you're making a false assumption. You're thinking, If Harford's taking care of this poor woman, he's making a rotten job of it. But he can only do what I allow him to do."

"Which is what?"

"Nothing too obvious." She blushed and laughed self-consciously. "He buys my paintings. My awful so-called art."

"Maybe it isn't so awful."

"I don't fool myself much about that. Mainly I dabble to pass the time." She laughed and looked away toward the sea. "Harford buys my supplies, my canvas, all under the guise that it's Tom who's doing it. Once a month Tom will come by and select some piece, and leave me an envelope with some grocery money in it. And that's how it works. Harford does only what necessity dictates. If he leaves too much money in the envelope I won't take any of it. If he intervenes on my behalf at the station I won't stand for it. I will not be rammed down Barnet's throat like some charity case. But I will admit there were times when Harford's money kept the wolf at bay." She looked at him across the table. "You probably think I'm a silly old woman awash with false pride."

"I think you're the last woman I'd ever accuse of having anything false, Mrs. Flack."

She handed him the photograph and he stared down at the quintessential British authority figure in full-dress splendor, with war medals splashed across his chest and a perfect set of seven-inch mustaches. "In his war uniform March even looked like Kitchener. He dressed for the show that night—there was an audience and Barnet wanted it to be colorful. The last thing I said to him was how unfortunate that it wasn't a stage play so a real audience could see the old bastard in all his color and pomp. I was joshing him, you see. We'd had a terrible fight that afternoon and I wanted to get past it. He laughed and swatted my bottom and I knew it was going to be all right. Then he walked out of my life."

((15))

HE had no illusions about approaching Livia on the subject of Carnahan. His luck with Mrs. Flack had been extraordinary. This would be tougher.

He knocked on the sound room door, then opened it. Poindexter was standing alone in the center of the room, wearing earphones and holding a pistol of at least .38 caliber in his right hand. Suddenly he fired—four shots in rapid succession; then, as if he'd sensed an intruder, he took off the phones and turned slowly, stopping with the gun pointing at Jordan's chest. He smiled venomously through layers of fat and said, "Stick 'em up."

His voice was hard, full of malignance. Jordan waved at the ceiling. "You got the drop on me. Now let's put the gun down."

"Does it make you nervous? They're only blanks."

"Put it down anyway."

The gun clattered on the table. "What do you want here, Mr. Jordan?"

"I'm looking for Miss Teasdale."

"Of course you are. But you can't have her, she's gone into the city for her class. She's such an ambitious woman . . . wouldn't you say so?"

"She tries to do a good job, if that's what you mean."

Poindexter picked up the gun. "Actually I'm rather busy. If there's nothing else, how about getting the hell out of here?"

He now faced a bleak afternoon. By three thirty he had tomorrow's Uncle Wally roughed out, lacking only the headlines from the morning *Times*. He hung around, helping Carmody with the night work, dreading the time when he must go home to his empty room.

At six o'clock he went looking for Stoner but no one had seen him. He looked for Becky but her office was closed and dark.

He went to the pier and sat at the end of the bar, drinking beer and watching the women dance. Hours passed; he lost count of the beers he'd had but he knew he'd had plenty when the midnight festivities began with a musical game called the Blackout Waltz. Without warning the lights would go out, partners would change, people would grope toward each other with waves of uneasy laughter, the music would begin again with a soft murmur beneath it as the people drew together and enjoyed the delicious and titillating fun of dancing in the dark with a stranger. He heard a voice at his side: "Come on, big man, dance with me, I've been watching you all night." The next thing he knew he was out on the floor with some full-bodied woman in his arms, shuffling and bumping against other laughing couples as the band played on. He felt the smoothness of her cheek against his neck and smelled the fragrance in her hair. Suddenly he felt sick and the room began to spin, and he pulled away and blundered through the swirling strangers.

He walked out on the beach. His legs felt weak and his stomach queasy.

He sat in the deserted square near the telephone box.

At last he stood in his room and looked at himself in the mirror. Fool, he thought.

* * *

He sat up suddenly after four hours' sleep. The clock in his head told him he was late. He got up, dressed, and struck out across the dunes.

He looked in through the front door. Eli wasn't there. The clock over the receptionist's desk told him he was thirty minutes late.

He rapped on the glass but Eli didn't come.

A moment passed and he heard the sound of tires on gravel and saw headlights swinging into the front yard. Stallworth, he thought, coming in for the dawn patrol.

The car door slammed. Footsteps came along the stone walk. But the man who turned the corner wasn't Stallworth.

It was Harford.

(((16)))

EVEN in the dark he knew at once who it was. Harford didn't offer his hand or introduce himself. "I see you've been waiting," he said by way of a greeting. "Where is the janitor?"

"I'm sure he was here. I ran late today."

"I'd think he would wait. Wouldn't you expect him to wait for you?"

"Not if he wants to get his own work done."

Harford opened the door and held it, allowing Jordan to pass through ahead of him. "Well," he said as they walked hollowly across the lobby, "we'll have no more of that. I'll have a key delivered to you before the day is out. It's absurd for you to stand outside waiting for a janitor to let you in."

Still no greeting: just the uneasy silence as they went into the kitchen. Harford went to the coffeepot and looked around for the mugs, but none had been washed yet; the sink was still piled with last night's clutter. "We seem to be in some disarray this morning," he said.

"He's always got them washed and stacked by now," Jordan said. "He's running late because of me. Here—I'll wash out a couple."

But Harford waved him back and washed two cups himself. He handed Jordan a steaming cup, threw one leg over the table, and they looked at each other for the first time in the full light.

He was older than he looked from a distance. His face was lined and his wavy black hair had tufts of gray on the sides. He was certainly no less than fifty. Jordan wished he could see the eyes. Harford must sleep in those damned glasses.

He looked at the clock: it was five forty-two.

"Uncle Wally isn't coming in today," Harford said. "He's sick."

"What about Eastman?"

"I don't think you're following what I'm telling you. It's not Mr. Stallworth who's sick. Uncle Wally is sick. *Capisce?*"

The Italian word washed over him and yes, he understood at once. He said, "O-kay," and couldn't keep the singsong question mark out of his voice. "So what about the show? Everything I've written is geared for that character."

"There won't be any script today. You can use it tomorrow. Just change the headlines and that ought to give you a pretty soft day."

He nodded slowly, like a man trying to be agreeable with a boss who has suddenly begun talking irrationally. "Then what are we going to do?"

"Talk."

"Who?"

"Us. You. Me. Miss Teasdale will be joining us, as soon as she can provide for her children. I'm afraid I woke her rather rudely. Maybe Mr. Kain will join us. And there may be a few surprises."

Jordan groped with all the potential disasters of such a grouping. "What about Miss Nicholas? We could get her and Brinker in."

"I don't want air people. We know what they can do. I've got a new idea I want to try—just a bunch of ordinary schlemiels sitting around on the beach, talking about the affairs of the day. Better yet, talking about what they *know*, and how that relates to what's going on in the world."

They looked at each other. "We're just going to chat?"

Harford nodded.

"For two hours."

"Maybe we'll throw in some music now and then. But no prearranged skits, no Hamhocks, no Butterbeans. If I hear that insipid nonsense one more time I may strangle Mr. Stallworth with my own hands."

The door opened: it was Eli, dragging his mop bucket. When he saw Harford, he stopped and blinked.

"Good morning, Mr. Kain."

"Morning, sir."

"Have a cup of coffee. Here, I'll get you a cup."

Eli looked at Jordan with wary eyes as Harford turned to the sink and washed out another cup. Jordan shrugged and tried to look easy.

"Thank you, sir." Eli took the cup as Harford passed it.

"Sit down, Mr. Kain. Over here, please. At the table."

Eli sat across from Jordan and tried not to look at anyone.

"We're going to have some fun this morning," Harford said. "I understand you're studying acting, Mr. Kain."

"Yessir."

"How far along are you?"

"Oh, I got a ways to go yet. But I work at it."

Harford looked up at the clock. "I'm going upstairs now and put us on the air. You gentlemen sit here and finish your coffee. Think about whatever makes your juices flow. Then mosey on up around five after six."

They looked at each other as Harford's footsteps faded down the hall.

"Might as well relax, Eli. No more mopping for a while."

"What's going on? If you don't mind my asking."

Jordan told him what Harford had said and they sat and sipped the coffee.

Ten minutes later they entered the small staircase concealed off the wings of Studio B and climbed to the second-floor hallway. They emerged into a world of glass, facing east over the dunes to the distant sea. The sun was just breaking and a bank of fluffy pink clouds made the morning spectacular. Music flowed down the hall, and as they approached the studio they could see Harford sitting in the slot of a triangular table behind the glass. To Harford's left was a spinning turntable with a transcription disc, the source of the music coming over the air. The music was soft and lilting: the march from *The Nutcracker.* Another record was cued and ready on Harford's right.

He motioned them in: Eli to the chair on his right, Jordan to the left. "Put your earphones on when we start. They'll give you a sense of presence on the air."

"I hope you know what you're doing," Jordan said. "I'm sure Eli will be great, but I can't imagine what I'll say on this thing."

Harford smiled and held up his hand for quiet. "We're almost on." Then, to Jordan, he said, "The current wisdom in radio is that people won't listen to classical music in the morning. Do you believe that?"

"I have a hard time believing any kind of so-called current wisdom."

"Good, so do I. We could talk for a few minutes about that. Pop culture, the national character, and why at least two generations must die before their own times can be honestly assessed. Is Dashiell Hammett more important than Dick Tracy, and will either be remembered with Dickens and Poe? What about you, Mr. Kain? What do you think of classics in the morning?"

"People might not sit still for *Night on Bald Mountain.* What you've got on sounds pretty good . . . sir."

"Let's dispense with the 'sir' business for now. Can we do that?"

"Yessir."

"Good. Don't forget. We're just three fellows sitting on the beach trying to figure out how the world turns. For the purposes of this little clambake—and let's hope it's not that—I will be called Gavin. A good Celtic name. Mr. Kain, you will be Roger. Originally from the Old High German, I believe. But it sounds Anglo-Saxon enough, in modern times."

He took off the glasses and they saw why he wore them. His face was startling: one eye dark brown, the other almost yellow. He looked slightly mortified, as if he'd just passed some test he'd been dreading.

He looked at Dulaney and said, "You we will call . . . Jack."

They met each other now, as if for the first time, across a broadcasting table, and for a moment Dulaney could only think, *He knows me.*

The music ended, the moment passed, and Harford—without breaking the eye contact—potted up the second turntable. The room was filled with the sounds of the sea: waves breaking on the beach and the cawing of seagulls. Harford opened his microphone, the red light flashed ON THE AIR, and he began to talk. "Good morning. You are listening to WHAR in Regina Beach, New Jersey. Correct eastern wartime is six ten. My name is Gavin, and this is Thursday, the eleventh of June. I'll be here on the beach until eight o'clock. We'll have news and views and straight talk from people just like you. No experts, no warmed-over vaudeville acts this morning. Just you, me, and whoever happens to come by. Perhaps that man in the distance, just starting up the boardwalk . . ."

He potted himself out and brought up the sound effect. Suddenly the gulls were louder than the surf, giving a good impression of ebb and flow. "You're the man on the boardwalk, Jack. You'll probably stop and enjoy the breeze, giving us time for a little news. Think about what you'd like to say. Maybe I'll ask a question or two. And you, Mr. Kain . . ."

"Yessir."

"Not 'sir,' not today. Just be yourself and there's no possible way you can be bad. Forget color, forget where you are. There is no color in radio, only when someone like Mr. Stallworth brings false colors into it. We'll have none of that this morning, Roger. Today you are not a colored man and we are not white. I do not own this radio station and you do not mop floors at my pleasure. Do you know how to read, Roger?"

"Sure," Eli said. "I read just fine."

"I don't mean that literally, so don't take offense. Do you know how to sight-read? Have they covered radio in any of those classes you've been taking?"

"It's been pretty basic so far. I do understand the concept, but I don't think they take radio seriously."

"Well, perhaps we'll make them sit up and take notice. Roger will read the news. Coming up."

Eli took his notes, pulled his earphones tight, and waited for the red light. His heart must be going a mile a minute, Dulaney thought. Then he was on, with no more time to think.

What a surprise. He is good. His voice ripples with character and intelligence, and he packs it with an authority that he certainly can't be feeling at this particular moment. He must know what a handicap he faces, how impossible this is. Harford can talk all day about radio being color-blind, but see if he can name even one working news broadcaster anywhere who is black. So where is it leading, what's he trying to prove?

Pieces of news force their way through a crowded mind. Again the RAF takes the war deep into Germany. More than one thousand bombers scorched Essen last night, just three days after the same bunch turned Cologne into a hellish graveyard of ashes. How do you like it now, Schicklgruber? Jews are said to be dancing in the streets at reports from Germany but there is also a chilling, dark side to the war. An underground socialist newspaper tells of mass murder by gas at Chelmno. Rommel steps up his campaign in the African desert. In Russia, the Germans are obliterating the last standing buildings at Sevastopol, and the people fight in the rubble where their city once was.

At the end of the news the studio was quiet and the war was suddenly remote. Dulaney watched Harford and wondered again what his game was. It seems impossible but I think he knows me. That Jack business didn't just pop up by chance. Can't shake it, that awful feeling that he knows everything about me.

(((17)))

Now the broadcast began to unfold. As Gavin, Harford pretended to follow the progress of this lonely-looking man up the boardwalk, speculating as to his nature and his outlook on life. His musings had an almost poetic flow, a rhythm of thought rather than words, and the fact that he spun this out without a script seemed remarkable. Suddenly Roger was on again. "I hear you're an avid follower of the doings on and off Broadway," Gavin said. "What have you seen lately that's worth talking about?" Roger immediately recalled *Harlem Cavalcade*, which unfortunately had closed almost as soon as it had opened at the Ritz. They talked about this, and Gavin had some thoughts about Harlem in general, how some of the most exciting music of the day was coming out of the clubs north of 110th Street.

There hadn't been much else to crow about in musical theater. On the legit side they had Steinbeck's play, taken from his book *The Moon Is Down*. Roger found this truly daring for wartime consumption but Gavin considered it tripe. Not that the idea of giving the Nazis a human side wasn't defensible, but Steinbeck had taken it too far. The decency of his one German officer reflected too favorably on the Reich as a whole, making it seem less evil than it was, and this was especially true in view of atrocities that were only now coming to light.

Without warning Jack arrived. "Here's the man we've been hoping to talk to," Gavin said, and he was on. He was surprised at the ease with which he took to the air, and for two or three minutes he and Gavin engaged in pure improvisation, just building his character. Jack was a longshoreman down for the holiday. "A shirtsleeve philosopher," Gavin said with a bit of happy mischief in his voice. "Perhaps you can settle the matter of John Steinbeck's most recent work." Jack hadn't seen the play but he had liked the book a lot. "It takes courage to do what Steinbeck did in wartime. I know there are men of conscience in the German army—don't ask me to prove that, but the odds against it would be too great for me to believe. And I know those men are just as distraught over Hitler as we are."

Gavin gave up with a sigh. "So Steinbeck wins, two to one. Let's get personal now. Do you mind if I ask you some personal questions?" Dulaney felt the first tweaking hint of an on-the-air trap and his answer was cautious. "That all depends on what the questions are and how personal they get." Gavin laughed and asked him to try this: "Are you currently in love?" Of course, Jack said, following Gavin's lighthearted lead. He was young and free, the days were long and warm, how could he not be in love? Gavin said, "Tell us the name of the woman you love," and suddenly the name Gloria was in his head. He had never known anyone with that name and he hoped this fiction would be his ticket out of here. "I ought to plead the Fifth," he said, "but her name is Gloria and I'm supposed to be meeting her up the beach just about now." This worked well: Gavin said, "Godspeed, Jack, and thanks for talking to us."

The hour ended with a visit from the man who ran the bowling alley, an enormous fellow named Albert Hocking who had a natural gift for gab and charm that could be cut with a knife. Roger's second stint with the news did not go as well as the first: he had had time now to think about it and let himself get nervous. But Harford seemed untroubled by a few blown words. At the end of it he reached over and shook Eli's hand. "Good work, Roger, thanks for coming in. Your future is bright." And Eli nodded and left the room, looking back over his shoulder just before he disappeared into the stairwell.

Music began the second hour. Harford looked at Dulaney and said, "What did you think of his reading?"

"Exceptional, especially considering the pressure he was under."

Harford seemed to be listening to his music. Then he said, "Pressure is part of this business. But you're right, he could be good."

Dulaney cleared his throat. He had never been able to let sleeping dogs lie and now he said, "Of course, that business about him having a future in radio is pretty doubtful."

"Is it? Who can say? Perhaps we're heading into a more enlightened day, once we get this war behind us. At least we can control what happens here, no? Actually, this may open up new careers for both of you. Miss Hart is down at the switchboard taking calls. If you'd like to know how you're coming across, I'm sure she'll tell you."

Dulaney shrugged and Harford leaned close, the chair straining at its hinge. The studio was absolutely silent—Harford had turned off the studio speakers and the only sign that music was still playing was the needle bouncing on the meter. "My advice is, don't ask," Harford said, and he leaned back in that same tomblike silence, rocking slightly. "Don't ever ask, not in your writing nor in anything else that you do from the heart. People will pull you down to their lowest tribal levels if you let them. Public opinion may keep you on the air, but it's hardly a reliable measure of what's good or bad about your show. And critics are just an extension of public opinion. Most of them are just glorified newspapermen, with no idea what goes into a novel or a play. Even when they praise you it's always for the wrong things. Here, our piece is ending. Maybe we'll find Jack strolling back up the beach with his girlfriend, if Miss Teasdale will get here and help us."

At the last second he changed his mind and brought up more music: Beethoven's Minuet in G, a piano without orchestra riding on the continuing surf effect. They listened for almost a minute, then Harford said the thing that shocked him all the way to the floor.

"Did you ever know a man named Carnahan?"

He groped for an answer, staring at his feet while Ludwig trilled above his head. At last he forced his eyes up and met Harford squarely—the small headshake, the quizzical look, and then, too late, his answer. "Don't think I've heard the name. Should I have?"

"I don't know," Harford said. "I just thought you might have."

Beethoven went out, Schubert came in, with a full orchestra and no sound effects. At that moment Livia arrived. She appeared beyond the window and Harford snapped to attention, grabbed up his glasses, and spun around in his chair, smacking his coffee cup to the floor. On went the glasses, his mask to the world. So he was sensitive about his eye, perhaps even vulnerable. He was nervous around women and maybe fearful. But none of that mattered in the enormity of what had just happened.

Livia came in, looking uneasy. Harford's chivalry leaped out at her—he was on his feet, holding a chair, apologizing elaborately for calling her so early. He sat and tried to explain. "I had this idea, it came to me just last night. A brand-new kind of morning show built around talk. Then I had a hunch that I had discovered something, that this is going to be the daytime radio of the future. It's cheap and fast, and a good host—certainly not me, but someone who knows how to do it—will be able to move it along without any kind of script. Have you been listening, Miss Teasdale? Do you know what we've been doing?"

"Yessir. But, Mr. Harford—"

He held up his hand. "I want you to be Jack's girlfriend, Gloria."

She was horrified, and tried to protest. She was no actress, she was deathly afraid of the microphone, of making a fool of herself. She was suddenly breathless—"Oh, sir, I *can't!*"—but he motioned her to get on her earphones. Schubert was tooting his finale, the air was ready to be filled, and when he said, "Come now, do me this service," his gentle tone offered no escape. She looked at Jordan with doleful eyes.

Harford brought up the surf effect and smiled at her over the table. "Just talk about who you are. What you love. There's no way you can mess this up. All right . . . coming up now."

Later she would tell them she couldn't remember half of it. Harford began asking questions, and the answers she gave were the real ones, out of her life. She was a farm girl from California. Her dad owned a bee ranch. She had six brothers and all of them had come of age in the late twenties on their father's bee farm near Bakersfield.

They talked radio but Harford steered her clear of her own involvement and let her speak as a listener. She thought radio was mostly junk, with flashes of quality and moments of unquestionable brilliance. Like any other art ruled by popular culture, Harford said, and she agreed. She thought the best show on the air was *Vic and Sade,* a quiet little quarter hour hidden away among the daytime soap shows. She listened to *One Man's Family* because it reminded her so much of her own people. Her father fussed like old Barbour and her big brother had frequent battles of authority with the old man on questions of discipline and faith. The concept of a large family would soon pass out of favor, Harford said—"After all, there are a hundred and thirty million of us now"—and she agreed that the postwar world would come upon them with a rapidly expanding and increasingly unruly populace. A terrifying thought, Harford said, and she nodded soberly. "Gloria nods," he said for her, grinning broadly. "She forgets where she is. The specter of the future leaves her speechless."

But the specifics of the bee culture were still at her fingertips, fourteen years after she'd left home. She remembered it all—the chores, the hours that never seemed to end when she'd been living them but now seemed so essential to the woman she had become. The image of that farm infused her dreams with color and gave her an almost mythic sense of loss. But you couldn't go back. No, Harford offered: Wolfe had it right. "I've never read him," Livia said, "but he does sound like a wise man. If you try to go home, you see that what you went back for isn't there anymore. It left when you did."

"Were you afraid of the bees? Did they scare you?"

She laughed and blushed. "Not half as much as you do with your microphone and your questions. I've had bees all over me and never got stung."

Her first job in the East had been in an amusement park. "I was the one in the fun house who went into the revolving drum to help all the clumsy people who couldn't get out by themselves. Then they put me on the air jets that blew the women's dresses up. I was good at that, much better than the boys. They were always too eager to turn on the air."

Lots of laughs. She was easier now about being on.

"How many children are you and Gloria going to have, Jack?"

"Oh, maybe a dozen."

"Dream on, cowboy," she said, and they all laughed.

He asked her opinion of Steinbeck but she had never read him. "Mostly what I read are the Victorians."

Victor Hugo was her favorite writer; *The Man Who Laughs* her best-loved book. Harford was touched. "That's a book I've loved as well. But I'll bet you won't find one person in ten thousand who's read it."

She shrugged. "I don't know. The hero's predicament has always appealed to me. Something about the hideous face and the tender heart never fails to move me to tears."

(((18)))

HARFORD disappeared at once as the hour ended. He shook Livia's hand, then Jordan's, and hurried to the stairwell.

"What on earth do you make of that?" she said.

"I don't know. I guess we're radio stars now."

They walked along the hall together. He asked if she'd be free for lunch. "There's something I'd like to talk to you about."

"Can't today. I'm juggling my kids all day, and Maurice has me hopping this afternoon and tomorrow. Look, you're coming to my house tomorrow—come early and we can talk then."

Back in his cubicle he tried to work, but Harford's voice lingered in his mind and the question was always the same.

At noon Becky Hart called, summoning him downstairs. When he arrived he found Holly sitting in her office.

"Jordan, do you know Miss O'Hara? I'm this close to having her convinced about our war bond show next week. We're all going to lunch and I need you to come up with the final irrefutable argument."

Jordan could get no sense of what Holly wanted. He wavered.

"I think I'd better pass. Got way too much work to do."

"The station's buying. You won't hear that every day of the week."

"I guess I'm doubly cursed."

"At least keep Miss O'Hara company while I go find Dedrick."

They were suddenly alone. Holly looked back at the door and her eyes moved around the room.

"So . . . Jordan . . . what kind of writing do you do here?"

He told her again what he'd told her yesterday.

"Will you be writing Mr. Maitland's show?"

"I'll probably work on it. Nobody's said anything yet. But it doesn't take long to put something like this together."

"You sound like an old hand at it. I suppose it takes years to learn."

"It's not very complicated. All I write is, 'Miss O'Hara sings the national anthem,' and you do the rest."

He sat with his back to the wall and opened his notebook as if writing the sketch now. What he wrote was the note CALL ME EXT. 13. He put the open notebook on the desk facing her and waited while she read what he'd written. Then he snapped it shut.

Becky appeared in the doorway with Maitland at her side. There was a warm exchange of courtesies. Maitland said, "It's so good of you to reconsider," and Holly said, "Becky is relentless . . . but let's see how I sound in the audition." This afternoon she would sing to a recorded backdrop in Studio B. Stoner would cut a disc, then they'd all sit around and talk it over. But her success was a foregone conclusion. "You are going to be sensational in this," Maitland said.

Jordan walked them to the outer door and Maitland told him to be thinking of other pieces Holly could sing within the hour. "Real Americana, stuff from the heartland. She's going to be the voice of this show, she's going to carry it, so see what you can come up with. In your spare time."

Becky laughed. "No rest for the weary, Jordan."

And on that note they left.

(((19)))

HE was early the next afternoon for the party at Livia's. Her house was far up at the north end of the island, beyond the end of the road. He parked in a little circle of trees and followed a path down to the beach. The only house in sight was a rambling cabin of uncertain age with add-on rooms that looked to have been built by different hands at different times. The house was ringed by a sun-bleached slat-board fence and was brought to life by the smoke coming from the chimney pipe in the roof. Livia's dilapidated car was parked to one side and he could still see the tracks in the sand where she'd driven up the beach on the outgoing tide. In the distance he saw two boys running along the edge of the surf in a futile effort to get a tiny kite airborne.

He walked up to the porch and she swept him into a room smelling of glorious food cooking. It was indeed a rustic place, with a few small rooms gathered around the original one-room cabin and a partition separating the living and eating areas. In the kitchen, Evie Overdier was minding an ancient wood-burning stove. "Laura Leaf is cooking for us," Livia said.

"Just don't think of touching anything," Evie said. "In fact, why don't you two take a hike up the beach?"

So they walked, following her boys up the wild beach toward the windswept point. At last they were alone and the thing had to be said. He couldn't let her get the wrong idea, but almost at once she began making small talk, as if they'd found themselves in a lull on a first date. She probed cautiously—where have you been, where are you going, who were your people?—then asked the first big question. "Ever been married?"

This was not going well. Now he felt obliged to inquire politely about her own ill-fated marriage.

"Blame it on the ignorance of youth," she said. "But two great things came out of it. I've got the world's most wonderful children."

"Then you're lucky it happened, no matter how it turned out."

"Don't worry, I know that. He was the bum of the year, but look what we made together. Someday you'll experience that—only the good part, I hope—and then you'll know."

"I won't count on it. I never had much luck with women."

"Luck's got nothing to do with it. All it is is chemistry."

"But chemistry's got to work both ways, so we're back to luck again."

She sighed. "Yeah, you're right. I can't tell you how many times I thought the chemistry was wonderful. But in the end the luck wasn't there."

He cleared his throat. "Listen, I've got to tell you something. I've been hoping we could talk."

She didn't know if she should be playful or wary. He pushed ahead, hoping for the best. "I heard you knew a man named Carnahan."

She stopped and looked at him coolly.

"It turns out I knew the same fellow," he said quickly. "At first I wasn't sure, but the more I heard about him . . . I knew him a long time ago in New York. We were good friends. Talked, shot a lot of pool, read the same books. Then lost track. But he was one of those special people in my life and I always wondered where he went."

"I thought you came here looking for Kendall."

"I did. That's what surprised me, that another old friend had been here too. Worked at the same radio station and one day left without telling anybody anything. Just like Kendall."

"Not quite like Kendall. Carnahan didn't drink."

She was clearly unhappy with this line of talk. He had expected that. People wouldn't all open up like Mrs. Flack.

She began to walk again. Far ahead, her boys had given up the kite and were coming back toward them.

"So. What brought you to me?"

"Just that I heard you were friends."

"Who'd you hear that from?"

"Just here and there. You know how people talk."

"What do you want to know? . . . was I sleeping with him, that kind of thing?"

He gave her a long look that said she should know better.

"But what else can I tell you? I don't know where he is."

"Let's forget it. I can see you don't want to talk about it."

"I just get so goddamned mad when people gossip. We went to great lengths to keep it quiet. But they find out and talk about us anyway."

"I shouldn't've brought it up."

"It's not you, it's everyone in this screwed-up world. I don't find it easy to talk about. It was the very same experience we were just discussing—great chemistry, rotten luck. So much for me as a romantic philosopher."

He waited but what came next was a turnabout. She wanted to hear about the Carnahan he had known, so he told her about the long talks, the book hunting on Fourth Avenue, and Carnahan's gradual transformation to a father figure. Occasionally she'd smile and he knew he'd touched something true; or she'd laugh softly and say, "Yup, that's him all over." She stared at the surf swirling at their feet, as if she could see the faint outline of a picture in the soup: the battered hat and the easy way, the hard hands, the gentle spirit, and in the sea those bottomless eyes that had seen a thousand years of hardship.

Her kids arrived, ending the talk. There was a year between them, though Jason, the younger, was as tall as Jeremy and apparently had been born with an inexhaustible supply of energy. Jordan suggested a lighter tail for their kite, some paper-thin cotton rag with just enough body to steady the stern, and suddenly they were off again, racing toward the house to see what they could find. "Stay out of that store-room!" Livia yelled, but they ran on. "They're fascinated with that room," she told Jordan. "They'll use almost any excuse to go in there because it's the one place I don't let them play. I throw everything in there, but there are some things they shouldn't see. Messy stuff from my divorce. It's bad enough they had to lose their father, they don't need to know what a bad man he was. I guess I should throw that stuff out. Someday I will. What's the use of having it—except that it's part of your life."

By then Brinker and Rue had arrived, driving up the beach to the front gate. Rue was taking some things out of the car, and in the distance he saw Stoner's truck just turning onto the beach. The subject of Carnahan was for the moment dropped. "There are only three commandments at these things," Livia said. "Eat, drink, and be merry."

They called themselves the Goodfellows because, as Livia explained it, they were all on the right side in the battle between money and art. Tonight, he knew, there would be intense discussions on possible ideas for the air, but it began with gossip and socializing. Stoner had brought the week's *Beachcomber*, just off the press. The editor had taken notice of Peter Schroeder with a short piece, boxed in the lower right corner of page one. The headline was provocative—SECOND GERMAN YOUTH GONE WITHOUT TRACE FROM WHAR—and there was a fleeting reference to the German angle in the text. The links between Peter and George Schroeder were told in a line. They were first cousins: Peter had come here in the mid-thirties with the Schroeders as his sponsors.

"He was like George, only more outgoing," Stoner said. "Not as good an engineer but okay. He got his work done."

"It doesn't say here if he'd gotten his papers," Jordan said.

"He told me he'd taken the oath in thirty-eight. I never had any reason to doubt him."

"What about his family in New York? Did anyone ever ask if they knew where he went?"

"I did, at the funeral," Rue said. "They have no idea where he is."

"Yeah, right," said Evie, who had come to the door. "Like they'd tell any of us anything. I think something scared the hell out of him and made him run. Maybe he got a tip Hoover was after him."

Livia shook her head. "You really think Peter was a spy?"

"Yeah, I do. I never trusted those boys, either one of 'em."

"Well, I don't believe it," Rue said.

The subject changed. Everyone wanted to know about the broadcast Jordan had done with Harford. What was he like? Had he actually put the janitor on cold and had him read the news? How had he gotten Livia to talk, and did he seem addled or deranged? But what they really wanted to know, he couldn't tell them—what Harford might do next.

"Maybe Becky can tell us," Rue said. "If she ever gets here."

"She had to pick up Maitland," Livia said. "And Maitland asked if he could bring Pauline, so Becky had to stop for her too."

Rue made a face. "Damn it, Liv, she knows the rules."

"What was I supposed to do, tell her they aren't welcome?"

Rue looked at Jordan. "We're supposed to keep these monthly soirees confined to our own little band of Goodfellows. They are strictly secret—no bosses, no directors to inhibit what we say, no strangers except by acclamation. There was never any question about you, sweetie. You qualified at once, for heroism on the field of volleyball."

Livia scoffed. "Honestly, Rue, you make us sound like a bunch of snobs. As if someone's got to qualify for our precious company. She doesn't mean any of this, Jordan."

"Liv is right, don't pay any attention to me, I'm just being difficult. I like Pauline. Maitland too. But let's face it, this changes things. Maitland isn't going to be honest with us; we still don't know why he's here, and that's a damper. That's one thing we all agreed we'd never let in among us. Secrets. Nobody holds back, nobody's afraid to throw out any half-baked notion that might, with a bit of help from the others, make a decent piece of radio. No Barnets, no holier-than-thou types like Eastman, no Stallworths . . . nobody who won't answer an honest question when it smacks him right in the mouth."

"No Poindexters," Livia said. "I'd rather eat with Hitler."

"And let's not forget what happened when Hazel crashed us two months ago. The whole damn evening was ruined."

"Somehow Hazel found out where we were," Livia said to Jordan.

"And wandered in, drunk as a skunk," said Rue. "If you haven't figured it out by now, Hazel is a very mean drunk. Gus had to take her home and sit with her while she cried in her beer."

"She really is a tragic character," Stoner said. "She's had a hard life and nobody ever asks her anywhere."

"Hard to imagine, isn't it?" Rue said. "She's such a goddamn delight to have around."

The others arrived twenty minutes later. Becky parked in the trees and they walked up the beach. Maitland ambled and the women walked on either side of him. Pauline looked almost young from a distance and Becky was elfin at Maitland's right. There was a chorus of hellos as they came into the yard. Pauline embraced Jordan, and Maitland shook his hand warmly. Wine flowed and the early talk was uninhibited enough even for Rue.

At eight o'clock supper was served. Evie had made a rich seafood casserole, which they ate on the beach. Brinker had built a bonfire and they sat around it on folding chairs, talking about the news and what they'd read that month and what could be made of it for the air. Ideas ranged from current affairs to the classic short stories of Guy de Maupassant and Frank Stockton. Stoner thought a modern variation of the old "Lady or the Tiger?" story might work well today, if the theme could be political rather than romantic. "Which door do you choose at the end, and who's behind it: Christ, or Hitler?" A brilliant idea, Maitland said—"We should really get something down on paper"—and at once Becky put down her plate and began scribbling furiously in a notebook. "It needs to be subtle, don't you think? . . . until the very end, maybe the final minute, when suddenly you know what the choice is. This is wonderful, Gus!"

Jordan agreed—the idea was perfect for radio. The difficult part would be the story, finding something that hit home and made the wartime point. But this came instantly. Rue said, "What about Georgie Schroeder? . . . He had a choice to make," and in the long silence Jordan saw the entire play unfold in his mind. "I think she's got it," he said. "A young German American who gets pressured by the bund. Visitors come in the night. Windows are broken, the old folks terrorized. The wife's threatened on the street by a pack of wolves."

"That's my part," Rue said. "I've got squatter's rights on it."

"Keep him much more American than German," Maitland said. "Not a hint of an accent; we want the listener to be on his side right from the start. Make the old folks Germanic, give *them* the accents, but even then make it crystal clear that they are true Americans. They came here forty years ago for all the things that are right with this country."

"Good," Jordan said. "At the end he has to make that choice. So he opens the door."

"Good!" Maitland thundered. "Can you write it?"

"We just did." He sat back, exhilarated. "I'll have it in script by Tuesday."

The talk turned to the war bond hour. Jordan had made a list of songs for Miss O'Hara to sing. He had her opening the show with "America the Beautiful," coming back at fifteen with an extended medley—"My Country 'Tis of Thee," "You're a Grand Old Flag," and "The Battle Hymn of the Republic." Then at midshow a collection of regional Americana—"Beautiful Ohio," "Carolina Moon," "California, Here I Come"—and for a smashing finale, "Dixie." Maitland wanted only to reverse the medleys. "The 'Battle Hymn' has more smash today than 'Dixie,' and that's what I want, a powerhouse effect as we get close to the end. I want every listener to sit up straight in his seat and think, Goddammit, that girl makes me proud to be an American—then get out of that chair and buy a bond."

There was more talk of drama. Brinker enacted a scene from a story he had read, did it in perfect Irish brogue and from memory, and again Jordan realized what a special talent he was: shy in life, easy on the air. Jordan had been asked to bring a script for his upcoming colored show and they gave it a reading, gathering around an imaginary microphone while Stoner stood on a chair with a flashlight and lit up the script. Brinker read Blind Tom's lines in a black voice as real as Eli's, and Rue played the missus of the white family that had stolen Tom from his real blood kin. Pauline played Tom's mother as if she'd been born in a Georgia slave shack and had never heard of England, and Rue stood mesmerized as these lines were read, and Jordan knew she had learned something tonight.

Maitland wondered if anyone had been assigned to direct. "I think it runs a little long," he said. "I didn't bring my stopwatch, but my gut tells me you'll need to make some cuts to get it down to twenty-nine and change. Give yourself plenty of time at the table reading."

That seemed to bring the evening to an end. Livia's boys were asleep on the blankets and the bonfire had crumbled into deep red coals. Stoner looked at Becky but she shook her head and said, "This has been lovely, people, but I've got an early day tomorrow."

"What's going on?" Rue said.

"Nothing. Who said something was going on?"

"Well, listen to yourself. You get a look from Gus and suddenly you get all jittery." She looked at Stoner. "Gus?"

"It's nothing," Becky said. "Kidd asked me to go through the files and weed out some old scripts. I found one I thought was special, and I asked Gus and Jordan and Dedrick not to say anything yet."

"So show it to us, we'll give it a reading. That's why we're here."

"I haven't got it anymore. Kidd saw it on my desk and took it away from me. Look, I don't want to talk about it. I'm a little disappointed that I lost it like that, so I'd just as soon we dropped it."

"At least tell us what it's about."

"I'm not supposed to."

"What do you mean you're not supposed to? You can't even talk about it?"

"Apparently not."

"And you're the only one who's read it."

"I guess Kidd read it. He seemed to know it well enough when he saw it on my desk."

"You mean like, Oh my God, what're you doing with that?"

"Something like that."

"And he didn't even know it had been there in the files, is that what you're saying? That means he's got another copy. What was yours, an original?"

"Mimeo."

"Which means they okayed it for production, way back whenever, and made at least one copy. Then never put it on. Is that what you're saying?"

"That was my impression, from the notes and correspondence that were there in the file with it."

"And you're not going to tell us about it."

"He told me not to. He was very clear about that. Do you want me to get fired, Rue, just so you can satisfy your curiosity?"

Rue looked at Livia. "Damn it, I hate stuff like this. Secrets. You see how it gets, Liv? You see how it gets? Something's going on and we're the last to know. Come on, Jimmy, let's get out of here."

(((20)))

FRIDAY was always his busiest day. Saturday, his new day off, that went on without end. He welcomed Sunday like a long-lost friend. He arrived in darkness, at four forty-five, and found his cast already at work on the soundstage. Emily Kain, Eli's sister, was reading from the script at the center mike. Occasionally she broke away from her reading to ask a question, and Waldo would do his best with it. Across from Emily, at a second mike three feet away, Ali Marek began the long, painful monologue that would close the show. Her role was pivotal. She was only twenty-three but she would play Blind Tom's mother, Charity Wiggins. She's going to be great, Jordan thought: she would be a superb actress if they let her.

Eli stood off-mike, his part done. Blind Tom was one of the Bethunes now as the play ended: his European tour alone had made them at least $100,000, but Tom and his blood kin had seen none of it. Eli was going to be the weak link, adequate maybe, but far too nervous to rise to the performance that Ali Marek would give as his mother. He's in love with her and that's a hindrance, Jordan thought; they are kindred spirits even to the sound of their first names, but he's thinking too much about acting and not enough about the man he needs to become.

The fourth player was Rudo Ohlson, a light-skinned Negro who spoke with a trace of Jamaican. This he lost in the role of Tabbs Gross, a black man who had filed a lawsuit on Tom's behalf, trying to get him away from the Bethunes. That had worked about as well in 1865 as a man of 1942 might expect.

He waited until Ali Marek had said her final lines, then he walked down to the soundstage in the sudden quiet. "Mornin'," he said, nodding to each of them. "Y'all must've slept here tonight."

He could see the fear in Waldo. It had probably been building all week. Waldo nodded distantly and said, "We been here awhile." There was an awkward moment as they all struggled with their barriers. "You're sounding good," Jordan said, and Waldo tried to smile. "I don't think we're ready to take it to Broadway yet. But that was a helluva play you wrote for us."

"I don't think the play's ready for Broadway either," Jordan said. "But you all sound great, and I think this may be the most exciting thing ever heard at eight o'clock on Sunday morning."

They all laughed and that got the ice broken. Jordan and Waldo came up on the soundstage and they sat at the table with the cast hunkered around. The first order of business was choosing a director. He had a hunch Maitland might show up and hoped he would, but they had to assume they were on their own. "I never done any directing, not for real," Waldo said. Jordan hadn't either but he had seen plenty done in the month, so the division of chores settled itself. Waldo would run the board and Jordan would point the cues.

The first table reading went quickly. Eli blew some lines but Jordan motioned for him to keep going. While they read he ticked off places where the script might be shortened. At six o'clock Becky Hart came in, wearing a stopwatch on a long string around her neck. Jordan felt a flush of gratitude. Livia arrived. She had already read her script and had marked it profusely for sound effects. She had never met the cast and Jordan made the introductions, and they all shook hands and tried to share a few easy moments over coffee. Then Livia moved over to the soundman's section and began rigging her microphones.

"Let's give it a dry run before the organ man gets here," Jordan said. "Then we'll do a dress and by then we should be ready."

They began. "Just keep it going," he said, warming to it. "Don't bother about fluffs, just talk over 'em. Keep it natural, Eli, just stay loose. You sound fine."

He began timing his cues and Livia started throwing them some sound. In the corner of his eye he could see her cuing up records and trying out some manual effects. They reached the midpoint break. There'd be no sponsor, just a pause with music between the acts. Jordan said, "Let's take five here," and when he turned he saw Barnet standing behind him.

"So the blind leads the blind. Who told you to rehearse the cast, Ten Eyck?"

"Wasn't I supposed to? You never said we'd have a real director."

"You never asked." Barnet came to the edge of the sound-stage and beckoned Waldo out of the booth. "I've got a good mind to let you people actually try this by yourselves. Then we'd see a spectacle. You—what's your name?"

"Waldo Brown."

"Well, Waldo Brown, do you have any idea what you're doing back there? Never mind. I've got one of Stoner's new men coming in to run the board. No offense, but it's a little more complicated now."

"I guess we had a communications problem," Jordan said. "It's my fault."

"Yes we did and yes it is," Barnet said. "Have you been taking the time, Rebecca?"

She raised her watch.

"Then let's go ahead from this point. See if it makes any sense."

They were all shaken now. Becky clicked on her watch and Eli began to read. He stumbled over a word and stopped. Becky clicked off the watch. Eli stood frozen. Barnet had hand-motioned everyone into silence. He stared at Eli without mercy, waiting for a voice to return.

"I need some water," Eli said.

"You listen to me now," Barnet said. "If you do this on the air I will strangle you with my bare hands. Do you hear what I'm saying?"

"You're not helping him much, Clay," Becky said.

"Let's move on."

Becky came up to stand beside Barnet now, encouraging Eli with her eyes and clicking off the watch whenever they broke away to discuss a point. When Ali Marek read her last line, Barnet spread his arms wide. "Hallelujah! Music up and out, over to the network, and thank God for small favors. How'd we do on time?"

"Thirty-three twelve."

Barnet gave Jordan a withering look. "Do you always over-write this much, Ten Eyck?"

"We were just about to make some cuts."

"Then let's cut the goddamn thing and get it done while there's still something left of the day. I think the mother's part's going to have to come way down."

"She's the best thing on the show," Becky said.

"Maybe so, but that closing speech goes on way too long."

"But it's the whole point of the play."

"We can cut it in half, save a minute right there, and still make the point. Some of her lines in the middle can be trimmed as well."

"I can cut it," Jordan said. "Give me a few minutes with it, I know what to do with it now."

"Cut the mother's part. No offense to you—what's your name?"

"Marek."

"Well, Marek, you read a line well enough, but this . . . story . . . isn't about your character, is it?" He nodded at Eli. "It's about his. It seems the author made an error in construction. In the throes of creating timeless dialogue, he forgot who his main character is."

"You're right," Jordan said. "I see that now. I can cut it."

"All right, the rest of you take five. I'm going to get some coffee."

Jordan sat at the table and in two minutes he had cut his script from eighteen pages to sixteen. He lost some of Ali Marek's good lines in the center, but by spreading the cuts he was able to keep the closing intact.

It was now quarter to seven. Leland Jewell came in, picked up his music, and sat on a stool between the organ and the piano. The piano was vital to this show: it was the spirit of Blind Tom Bethune, a fifth member of the cast. But when Leland spun into his piano and ripped off some of Blind Tom's old pieces, Jordan felt his spirits rise. Leland was a pro: the music would be fine.

The engineer arrived: some kid with a military deferment hired by Stoner just last week. They shook hands, the kid said his name, Joe Carella, and Jordan walked him across the soundstage making introductions.

Barnet came in and called them together. "How's the script looking?"

"It should be right on the money now."

"Then let's go through it. Cast, get your pencils and make the cuts as we come to them."

Jordan shuffled his pages. "Page seven, lines 156 through 161. All of page eight down to line 171. Two lines on page nine, 183 and 184. And there's a place on page ten that can be cut or left in, depending on the time. Lines 192 through 197."

"What about the ending?"

"This seems to do it. I don't think we need to mess with the ending."

Barnet simmered. "From the depths of his wisdom the master speaks. Did I not make myself clear when I said cut the ending?"

"You asked for a three-minute cut."

"Listen, you. When I tell you where to cut a script, I god-damn well want it cut there. Now let's go through it again."

"It's getting late," Becky said. "We've still got a dress to do."

"We can't rehearse until we've got a script."

"Excuse me," said Joe from the booth. "I need some mike levels."

"Just hold your horses." Barnet picked up his script. "Now. Let's put the cuts *back in* on page eight and *take out* everything on page eighteen after line 313."

"All right, Clay, you're the director," Becky said. "But I think it's a much weaker show that way."

"I agree with Becky." It was Livia, across the stage.

Barnet ignored them. "Now we have our script. Let's give the engineer his levels and get this done."

The cast took their positions around the three standing mikes. Each of the microphones was tested, as well as the two in sound and the two at the organ and piano. Barnet walked around, drawing a few curtains, and finally he joined Joe Carella in the booth. Rudo, who would also announce, came to the center microphone and nodded that he was ready.

"All right, cast," Barnet said through the intercom. "We're running late, so let's do this thing right the first time. Thirty seconds."

A spate of coughing. "Coming up," Barnet said.

It began with an old slave song and segued into a thunder-ing organ crescendo as Rudo boomed the opening title. Nice, thought Jordan: Leland had written the music especially for the show, and it gave them an important heft right at the top. But Barnet waved angrily and shut it down.

He stalked out of the booth and went over to confer with Leland. This went on for many minutes, with Leland improvising and Barnet waving for new silence. Becky looked at the clock as Barnet continued his harangue. "This is not the goddamn *Cavalcade of America,* Mr. Jewell, no matter what Ten Eyck may have told you. Don't make it boom, don't puff it up, don't give it any exaggerated importance."

"Come on, Clay, give us a break here," Becky said. "Just ease up a little. We're running out of time and everybody's tense. This is going to be a difficult, important show . . ."

"You've got that half right. It is going to be damned difficult, it's going to be just about impossible to make this thing into a half hour that anybody outside of Harlemville U.S.A. will want to listen to. Just don't try to attach any importance to it, Rebecca, because you risk your own credibility when you do."

Back in the booth then for a new intro. Leland played a watery variation of what he had done, and the story began.

It was good. Stoner had been right, it was going to be a decent show in spite of the tinkering. The cast was rising into it, even Eli sounded better. But again Barnet shut them down.

"You sound like you're reading, Mr. Kain. The trick is to read without sounding like it. Let's try it again, top of page two."

Becky clicked her watch, but Eli had been shaken and missed his cue. Ali Marek leaned in and whispered something behind her hand.

"No coaching, Marek."

They waited. Eli dabbed his eyes.

"Are you going to be all right, Mr. Kain? If you're not, now's the time to say so. It's a simple reading job, couldn't be easier."

"I got some sweat in my eyes."

"Don't sweat," Barnet said. A funny line but nobody laughed.

"Maybe Ten Eyck can read the part," Barnet said. "I hear he's a budding radio star. Apparently he wowed the morning crowd the other day."

Barnet made a what's-it-gonna-be gesture. "It's probably not too late to call Mr. Stallworth. He always does well in roles like this."

What an insult, Jordan thought. What an asshole this guy is.

"You . . . Waldo Brown. Can you play this role?"

"I wouldn't think of it."

"Then we're stuck with you, Mr. Kain."

Suddenly Ali Marek threw her script down. "For God's sake leave him alone."

Barnet blinked and leaned toward the glass. "What was that?"

"She said leave him alone," Jordan said.

He had had enough. He came across the soundstage and got up close to the glass. "I'd like a word with you, please."

"Oh, by all means, you can see we've got nothing but time. But Becky's fretting over the clock, so maybe you'd better catch me after the show."

"I'd really rather catch you now. Out in the hall."

They locked eyes through the glass and Barnet wavered. Jordan thought, *Your ass is mine, cowboy,* and Barnet's face withered slightly. Long seconds passed before Barnet leaned into the microphone and spoke. "Cast, we seem to have another problem. Let's take five."

He was aware of Barnet's footsteps behind him as he walked out. He heard Becky say, "It's twenty to eight, guys!" and something dropped, clattering to the floor. In the hall he turned, Barnet came past him, and Jordan pushed the door shut.

He didn't know what he was going to say until suddenly he was saying it. "If you keep this up we're going to lose this show. I can't stand still and let that happen."

"What's that supposed to mean? Who the hell are you to make decisions like that?"

"These kids have been working like hell for no money. The old man's been waiting for this chance for eight years."

"Oh, you're breaking my heart."

"So we're gonna give 'em their chance. Unencumbered by you."

"You must be crazy."

Barnet made a move toward the door. Jordan stepped in his way and cut him off. This is how Captain Bligh must have looked—shock, denial, outrage, and fear, all in one face. He can't believe his ship's been taken away from him.

"It's not you, it's the cast," Jordan said. "Look at it that way. This cast isn't ready yet for a director of your . . . abilities. You're used to working with professionals who can handle it. It's good that you came to realize that, just before airtime. A wise decision on your part. That's what I'll tell people, if they ask me."

"You'll tell them nothing. You won't be here to tell anyone anything. Just you dare try to go on without me. I'll cut you off the air."

"Then you'd better get ready to sing for half an hour."

Barnet was trembling now. "You're finished here. You can kiss your ass good-bye at this radio station."

"I'm really sorry about that. It was fun while it lasted."

Barnet stepped away and moved backward to the double doors. He stood for a moment, a silhouette, motionless against the pale gray lobby.

"Go ahead, do your show. You'll die out there."

He turned and walked out.

Back in the studio no one had moved. The clock on the wall was down to seven forty-five and Becky stood to one side, her stopwatch suspended, thumb poised on the button. He gave them the news from the edge of the soundstage. "Mr. Barnet decided we'd be better off without a director. We're on our own."

He motioned to Becky and drew her aside. "Listen, you've been great and I won't forget it. But you need to leave now."

"Jesus, Jordan, what've you done?"

"I don't know. I guess I finally reached my limit with him."

"Oh my God."

"Anyway, it's done now. But for the record, I think you need to be out of here."

"I'm not afraid of him. I want to stay."

"I'd feel better if you didn't."

There was no time to argue about it. He hugged her tight and said, "Talk to you later," and shoved her gently into the hall.

The clock said twelve minutes to air. He walked up on the soundstage. "All right, folks, here we are. Obviously we don't have time for the dress. But you know these parts, you've been up reading them half the night."

He looked at the piano man. "Leland, put the original music back in."

Back to the cast. "Let's go with the ending and make the cuts on page eight. And take those lines out of page ten, just to be safe."

Back to the piano man. "If that puts us short, improvise us up to the break."

He looked at the booth. Behind the glass, Joe Carella nodded.

"Livia?"

"I'm fine."

"I guess we're ready, then." He walked around the stage, looking at the microphones, coming back to the center to face his cast. "One last thing. You guys are all great. Eli, you are very good in this . . . very rich and strong, you make my words sing. Emily, Ali, Rudo, you're all fine. Watch me with your side brain and keep your focus on your characters. Don't look at the booth, I'll be right here on the floor with you."

We'll all die together, he thought.

He looked around and tried to remember all the things he had seen Maitland do. "Two minutes. Cast, take your places."

Rudo took the center-stage mike and held his script out, ready to go. Ali Marek stood on her toes and whispered something in Eli's ear. Suddenly everything got quiet. Only the clock moved.

"Ten seconds," Jordan said. "Coming up now."

The red hand moved past the hour, the light flashed ON THE AIR, and the song began. The organ swelled and the theme was magnificent, a powerful bed for the announcer's opening words.

Fade to night. Carella opened Livia's mike and the room became a country road in another century, alive with crickets and frogs and the bumping, turning wheels of a hay wagon. Jordan looked across at Ali Marek and threw his first cue, and Charity Wiggins came to life.

She was tight for only a moment: then the muscles in her arms and hips went slack and she began to relax. Her eyes searched for Eli but there was no time: she'd be on again in a minute.

Jordan felt the play unfolding in his mind, the cotton fields stretching across most of the known world. He moved his hand: the sun went down. He raised a finger: the new day dawned in an explosion of sound, of horses and rowdies and the unmistakable din of a railroad yard. He stood like God and the universe rolled out at his feet. If he pointed left, Livia gave him London, a different kind of clatter with steel rims on cobblestones and a British flavor to the babble. He swept that away with a thrust of his arm, and in the cross fade sat Charity, three thousand miles away.

They reached the midway point in half a heartbeat and none of them knew how they'd gotten there or how well they were doing. The short piano interlude brought them into the second half, and Jordan felt his heart going like mad.

Emily read her four lines to open the new scene. Rudo was good as old Bethune—maybe the first time anywhere that a black man has played a white man, Jordan had thought when he'd written it. Son of a bitch, he thought now: it's going too well, it's going too well. Haven't heard a bobble yet.

It all seemed so fast. Surely we'll run very short, he thought. Leland will have his hands full.

But then Ali Marek was there, full of fire and rage for her uncut finale. Leland brought the music up and out, and the clock on the wall showed them right on the button. Rudo read a flawless closing signature and the music rose again to trail away in a board fade. The clock said 29:30. Rudo caught Carella's thumb-and-finger signal for a station break and he talked them down to the half hour.

The red light flashed off. The room was eerily still. Only their eyes moved, searching their own faces for the answer to a question none of them wanted to ask. The answer came from a single pair of hands applauding and a soft voice somewhere in the darkness offstage. "Y'all can relax now. That wasn't nuthin' but nice."

Waldo Brown, the forgotten man.

Then the door slammed open and Becky shrieked, "It was great!" and suddenly they all knew they had survived. Ali Marek collapsed in a chair. Eli let out the breath he'd been holding forever. Joe Carella stood wearily in the open booth and even Livia looked shaken in her place among the gadgets. Only Leland Jewell, the old pro, had taken it in stride.

Jordan shook hands with everyone and thanked them all, and he felt a surge of pure joy.

Hours later the feeling hadn't diminished. He couldn't remember a greater moment as it grew into the evening. This was it. Live radio. What he'd been born for. It was everything he had ever wanted to do. He had spent a lifetime reading and writing and getting himself ready for something, and now here it was. This was it. If it had come too late, at least he hadn't gone through life without knowing of its existence.

(((**21**)))

THAT night he wrote what he now thought of as the Georgie Schroeder script. By midnight he had a polished piece, which he read aloud and timed to the second at 28:45. Allowing for music and signatures, it should be just right. It had a gripping, often touching story line, with the evils of Nazism shot throughout. He had given his hero an American-sounding name, Rudy Adams. His real name had been Rudolph Adler, but that was disclosed only at the end of the play, and by then he should have the sympathy of even the hardest-hearted haters of all things German.

On Monday morning he went to work as if nothing had happened. He put his new script under Kidd's door and sat with his coffee and Eli's newspaper. Up in the bullpen, he heard Barnet talking to a salesman a row away, but the confrontation he expected never came. Livia called at ten and invited him to lunch. Becky called from downstairs and told him he was the talk of the building. At some point he noticed that his telephone was beginning to malfunction, as a strange humming noise clicked in about ten seconds into each conversation. He screwed off the steel cap that covered the switching box but found nothing visibly wrong. The wire went down from his desk and disappeared into the floor.

Just before noon the phone rang again. It was Kidd's secretary, asking him to stop by the office. The shoe falleth, he thought.

But when he arrived Kidd was in good spirits. "I heard your show yesterday. I liked it. Heard you directed it as well."

"Barnet was there. You know, to make sure we didn't get off base."

"Really? That's not what I heard."

"He left just before we went on the air. I think he could see that the cast was too tense with him, so he left it to us. Waldo and me. And we had Livia and Joe and Leland. They're all solid."

Kidd said nothing for a moment. Then he leaned back in his chair. "You and Barnet don't like each other much, do you?"

"I can't speak for his part of it. Me, I've met guys I'd rather be around. But I can get along with him."

"All right. What about this Sunday?"

"We planned to do the black cowboy."

"That's fine. What about a director?"

"That's up to you."

"Dedrick would be available. If you want him."

"He's a good man. I like him. I'm sure he'd be great with the cast."

"Or," Kidd said, "you could do it again yourself. See how it goes."

"I'm willing to try that."

Kidd shuffled through some papers. "I got a call a while ago from the radio critic at the *New York Times*. He's already heard about your little adventure yesterday."

"News travels fast in radio."

"Well, it's a public medium. When people hear something that's so different from anything they've heard before, they tend to react. The *Times* had a dozen calls this morning. That's a lot, considering the source. We're not exactly NBC, and that makes the press curious. Sunday morning isn't what he usually writes about, but he wants to see the script of what we did yesterday. I'm going to send it to him."

"Okay."

"I think he'll be listening next Sunday. You still want to go it alone?"

"Whatever you want. I'm sure willing to try it."

Kidd found what he was looking for—the new Rudy Adams script. The pages were already marked for mimeo. "When did you write this?"

"Last night."

"You wrote this from scratch? In one sitting?"

"It just came together. Sometimes a piece of writing does that."

Kidd looked down at the pages. When he looked up again his face was flushed, and for the first time Jordan saw excitement in his eyes.

"I seem to be at a loss for words. It's an extraordinary piece."

"It was Stoner's idea. Maitland had some good input. And Miss Nicholas wants to play the wife. If it ever gets to air."

"Well, she'll get her chance. I want to do it next Saturday, as part of the war bond show. Expand that to ninety minutes and put this in just as it stands. Have Miss O'Hara sing just before and after. I understand you've been working on that war bond hour as well."

"I'm doing some of the continuity."

"I want Maitland to direct this. He's already handling the musical segments, and that'll fill up the big studio. But we'll need the dramatic cast nearby so they can be moved quickly in and out when the time comes. We'll take Barnet out of Studio B and have him broadcast the bond appeals from upstairs. With all this going on, Maitland will need an assistant director. I'd like that to be you."

Jordan nodded, and felt a quickening in his heart.

"There's a lot to be done. The orchestra won't get here till Friday. The conductor thinks he's doing a musical show, he doesn't know yet that we'll be asking him for an entire dramatic score as well. I'm going to send him a script today and we'll see what he comes up with."

"What can I do?"

"Get Miss Nicholas over here and see what she sounds like. Try any of the others that you think might work out. Then give Maitland your recommendations and we'll hear them all tomorrow. I want it nailed down by Thursday, who plays what, so we can start rehearsing them that afternoon. I want this to come off without a hitch on the air."

"It's going to be one hell of an expensive show."

"Tell me about it. It'll cost us as much to do it as we'll make for the cause. But what a way to start."

Oh yes. Jordan nodded. What a way to start.

((22))

He sat with Livia at a rooftop table under a flapping umbrella and they talked about Carnahan. Barnet had hired him last summer as the station's handyman, and she had been drawn to him at once. "I was amazed at how much he knew about the world and everything in it. To me that's what defines a man. Not how old he is or how he looks. What he knows."

She smiled faintly. "Talk about chemistry! I thought it was wonderful. If you're asking me what happened, don't expect any easy answers, because I just don't know. He was much older than me but you know that. I'm sure he was old enough to be my father, but I never thought of him that way. I didn't think the age thing was any kind of factor."

She shrugged. "Maybe I was wrong. Maybe it did bother him, how it looked going around with me. Maybe it bothered him about my kids. When a man gets in his fifties it's probably hard keeping company with a woman years younger who has two children. Most men his age are happy to be done with that. But he loved my kids, no one could fool me about that. And they loved him. They still ask about him, about when he's coming back."

The waitress came. They gave their orders and she sat for a moment, lost in thought, staring at the sea.

"You said the other day it reminded you of Kendall. But there wasn't any mystery with Carnahan. He left some notes that pretty well settled things. One to his landlord, saying he was vacating. A strange note to Barnet, quitting his job. Nothing for me. Not a damned thing."

She leaned into the table. "He was a good man. I'll always think that, even if I can't quite forgive him for the way he left. That's always the first thing I think about when I think about him. He was very decent.

"And he was great to talk to. We liked the same books, the same films, all kinds of music. He was full of surprises. When you first met him you saw a handyman. But then you talked to him, and my God, his general knowledge just went on and on. His opinions were always so well reasoned, so full of common sense.

"Rue discovered him; she got to know him before I did. He was like you, he came here totally cold, with no idea what radio was about. Then he began to see it. The whole world of it began opening up to him, and it was a very serious discovery. He was going to sign up for some radio classes at NYU, that's how serious he was about it. He was part of our little group almost at once; he brought in stories that none of us had ever heard of, things he'd read in *Scribner's Magazine* when he was a young man, long before there was such a thing as radio, but they worked so well on the air today. Gus thought he'd make a natural director. His voice was quiet but when he talked, everyone listened. He just soaked up life.

"We had a lot of fun for a few months. It probably wasn't his fault that I thought it was more than it was. That's an old story—girl gets too serious, guy moves on. Happens all the time. It's not the first time it's happened to me, if you want to know the truth."

Jordan said, "Still, the man you're describing and the man I knew doesn't just pull up and leave like that."

"Well, he did. Facts are facts."

"Maybe he meant to leave you something and you never got it."

She frowned. "Nice try, Jordan."

The food came and they ate quietly, enjoying the breeze. At last she said, "Nope, I think it's got to be the age thing. I've gone over it a hundred times and I think I miscalculated from the start how affected he was by that. If I'd been more sensitive it might have turned out different."

"Did you ever come right out and ask him?"

"Not in so many words. Why plant something that's not already there, right? But I guess it was there. Inevitably people mistook him for my father and he knew how annoyed that made me. And what must've made it worse, he does have a daughter almost my age. But I don't even know for sure where she lives, so I couldn't get in touch through her if I wanted to."

She sighed. "Somewhere in Pennsylvania. That's a big state."

The waitress returned and Jordan reached for his wallet but Livia wouldn't hear of it.

"Tell me about the last time you saw him," he said.

"We had a picnic. A great Indian summer day in the middle of November. He was off that day and I was working a show that night but I had the day free. We had been promising my kids we'd take them on an outing, so we did, way down the beach near the lighthouse. It was a perfect day—after the season, the beach was wild and deserted and we had a grand time.

There wasn't a hint of anything wrong. We were out all day and got back to town around four o'clock."

"And that's the last time you saw him, when you dropped him home?"

"I didn't take him home. He asked me to drop him at the post office north of town—he had something to mail but we had come out too early in the morning to do it then. I told him I'd wait and run him home but he said no, the Christmas rush was starting, the line in the post office was longer than his walk home. I got my last look at him in my mirror as I was pulling out. He was waving to me. I remember thinking how I'd love to have that image in a photograph, him standing there with his hat in one hand, waving with the other. I felt a rush of sadness, couldn't explain it and still can't, almost like a black cat crossing my path. Then I saw some people from the station and the feeling went away. I knew it was silly. I'd see him tomorrow, just like always."

"What people did you see?"

"George and Peter Schroeder, actually. They must've pulled in right behind us."

Now another cat crossed her path. The implication had been slow in coming but she was far too smart to miss it once she'd put it into words. George was dead. Peter was missing. Carnahan was gone, and now perhaps the links to Kendall didn't seem quite so tenuous. In her eyes he saw new trouble growing, and with it a hint of fear.

(((**23**)))

BACK at the station, Rue was waiting for him, sitting in his chair with her legs crossed primly.

"Becky called me in. She said you wanted to see me."

"I wrote the script," he said. "The one we cooked up on the beach. I told Kidd you were interested in the wife, and for some reason he thinks I should be the one who reads you for it."

She accepted this like an employee reporting for work. Reasons didn't matter. A decision had been left to him and it was a part she wanted badly without ever having seen a line of it. "So let's do it," she said.

They went to the small conference room just off the hall and he gave her her first look at it. She sat at the table and began her reading cold—not a hint of the old camaraderie, not a frivolous word—but she got better as she went along. Occasionally she looked at him as if asking for direction, but he only nodded to encourage her on. What did he know about acting? . . . how could he tell her how she must do it? But suddenly he did know. Who would know better than the man who'd written it?

"Let's try it again," he said. This time when her eyes probed his face, he too had abandoned their friendship. The role was hers to win but she would have to win it. Hazel was a call away. Hazel got all the choice, difficult parts. She closed her eyes and took a deep breath. He said, "Give it a stronger heartbeat," and she opened her eyes and looked at him.

"Give it more fear, right from the start," he said. "Remember, she sees the face of evil long before he does. She knows where it's going."

She nodded and did it. She nailed it. There in a room no bigger than the one where the Gestapo had interrogated Georgie Schroeder, she gave him what he wanted. Her voice was the essence of fear.

"Let me try it again."

"No, I think you've got it."

She was still unsure. "I want this part."

"I'll talk to Maitland."

"I want this. I can do it better."

"That's good," he said. "Save it for the air."

By five o'clock he had finished another script. He read it in complete amazement, the unfamiliar dialogue and strange images flowing through him as if for the first time. It brought his arms to gooseflesh, without question the best thing he had ever written. A dozen times during the day he had forced himself out of the Carnahan dream to look down on a new page that he remembered writing only vaguely. The power flowed and he drew from it, and he thought he could work forever. The power flowed, the cycle was endless, the energy never stopped. He thought he had come here with nothing but he'd had what he'd always had. He had everything.

(((24)))

THE Tuesday morning staff meeting was crowded. Kidd came in precisely on time and introduced some new faces. Monte Braxton was a writer-director just in from Chicago. Bruno Zylla had been a composer-conductor at NBC-West in Los Angeles. His orchestra would be here on Friday. Vick Waters and Bernie Roberg were writers who would work on continuity and special projects. "Mr. Ten Eyck is being relieved of continuity for a time, to work with Mr. Maitland."

There was a stir in the room.

"I think you all know by now that Mr. Ten Eyck has written us a play for Saturday night. It's a fine piece of work. It should make us some waves in the city, *if* we can get people to listen. I've been on the phone about it, and I think I can persuade Susan Daniels and Rick Gary to come down and do the leads for us."

Rue looked up as if she'd just been cut.

"I know this is going to disappoint some of you. This will be our first big splash and we badly need the experience and name recognition that they can bring us." He looked at Rue. "If you've got anything to say, I'll be happy to hear it."

"I've got nothing to say. What would I have to say about it?"

Jordan held up his hand. "I've got something to say."

"I see fire in your eyes, Mr. Ten Eyck. I appreciate that, but if we can get Susan Daniels and Rick Gary, I think we should do it. They are two of the best names in New York radio and they'll assure us an audience just by their presence."

"I know who they are. But you asked me to read Miss Nicholas for the wife and we did that in good faith. I think she's going to be great."

"I'm sure she would be, and I apologize. I asked you to do that before I knew that Miss Daniels and Mr. Gary might be available."

"You're missing my point." Jordan rose from his slouch at the back of the room. "Sure, you can buy an audience this Saturday, but what happens to that audience when those people go back to New York? Are you going to persuade this Daniels and Gary to give up their networks and move down here? I don't think they'll do that. Sooner or later you'll have to make it or break it with your own people."

Kidd looked around the room. "Any other comments? . . . Miss Hart, you look like an opinion just waiting to be asked."

"I agree with Jordan, sir."

"Count me in that camp," Stoner said.

"Mr. Barnet?"

"I'll be the devil's advocate and go with the network people. They'll give it instant credibility. Frankly, I'm surprised they'll even consider this."

"People will consider all kinds of things if you pay them for it." Kidd pointed at Hazel. "Miss Kemble."

"I just want it known that I can do anything Susan Daniels can do."

"Anyone else? . . . Speak up, nobody gets shot at sunrise here."

From the center of the room Maitland spoke. "We're all professionals, Jethro. The question of name recognition is a valid one, but you know Jordan is right. These people will be here for one night only and then we're starting from scratch again. We're going to have to earn our audiences week in and week out."

"If we do keep it in-house, who will you choose for the boy?"

"Brinker seems most likely."

Jordan raised his hand. "I think you'll need Jimmy in some of those Nazi roles. He's too good with dialect to put him anywhere else. Stallworth and Eastman can do some of those, but I think Brinker's got to be considered for the speaker of the Hitler Youth Movement and maybe one of those Gestapo interrogators in the flashback."

"Then who does that leave us for the lead? We really are thin on air talent here, Jethro."

"I'm aware of that. Rome wasn't built in a day."

Suddenly Rue said, "Maybe Rick Gary will come down and leave Susan Daniels at home," and the room exploded with laughter.

Becky said, "I think she deserves the role for that comment alone, sir," and the laughter went on.

Kidd waited it out. "Unfortunately, it doesn't work that way. But I want to be fair. Dedrick, can you audition the staff today?"

"Of course," Maitland said.

"And give me an answer by five o'clock."

"Absolutely."

"All right, then. It's your call to make."

Over in Studio B they began. An air of excitement came over the soundstage: Jordan could feel it as he sat alone watching them read his words. Even Eastman and Stallworth knew they had something they had not seen here in years. Hazel complained that she had not been allowed to compete for the lead, but Maitland shut this down at once. They had no time for grumbling: the part he had for her was small but choice. She would play Gretchen, the Nazi scarf peddler in Yorkville. She had been Rudy's childhood friend, but now as the story opened she was selling him out to the wolf pack.

Pauline would play Rudy's mother: "a German voice laced with Americanisms," Maitland instructed. Eastman and Stallworth would vary the one-liners of the mob. Brinker, for the purposes of this audition, would read three important roles, including the hero.

The first reading went well. Becky sat on a stool and timed them, and at the end said, "Steady as she goes, mates, it's going to be right on."

They went through it again. Rue rose to Maitland's direction and got better with each reading. They broke for lunch early, at eleven thirty. "Everybody back here at one," Maitland said. "We'll have a few director's nitpicks, then we'll run it through from the top and I'll go give Jethro the good news." Rue caught Jordan's eye, mouthed the words "Thank you," and blew him a soft kiss.

A small group of Goodfellows went to eat at the fish house. They sat at a table on the roof and there was such goodwill and open affection among them that Jordan forgot for an hour all the times when he'd been alone. There was a feeling suddenly that anything was possible, nothing was out of their reach.

Rue said, "So, Jordan, when are you going to write us something new and exciting?" Everyone laughed, but the table got quiet when he told them he had already finished another script. "It's for the Negro show. But there are a couple of white parts that might be pretty good for a rising young actress like yourself." He shrugged. "I know that's never been done, white players backing up a Negro cast."

"That doesn't bother me," Rue said. "But Harford doesn't pay for that show, we all know that, and it's against my religion to work free. It's just not a good idea to give it away; that leads to all kinds of bad stuff. So having said that, what's it about?"

He told them about Sarah Mapps Douglass, the Negro abolitionist whose friendship with the white Grimké sisters in the early 1800s had fired his imagination last night. He had written it for Ali Marek, but the two white women could be a challenge for Rue. He saw her in both parts, tempering her voice just enough to pull it off. "There's one tricky scene where the sisters get into a good-natured argument. Lots of instant voice changes, lots of nineteenth-century mannerisms. Lots of vinegar, I hope."

"It does sound perfect for Rue," Livia said. "She can argue with herself for once and we'll all sit back and see who wins."

"For what it's worth," Brinker said, "I think you should do it. I'd do it myself but women are a little out of my range."

Jordan said, "It would really expand what I could do with it if I had some white voices to play with. There's no way Emily Kain can handle this, she hasn't got the experience or the whiteness. You've got to have a sense of white propriety to pull that off. But I've got to be careful. The last thing I want is for them to think the whites are taking them over."

"If you could only get Kidd to pay me even a dollar for it," Rue said. "Anything to keep it professional."

"I think Kidd will pay you," Becky said.

"How do you know? Damn it, Becky, now what's going on? Have you been talking to Kidd about this behind our backs?"

"I had no idea there was even a script until just this minute."

"Then how do you know so much? Here we go with the secrets again."

"All right, I'll tell you what I know. But if you blab this around I'm going to be furious." She looked at Jordan. "This morning I heard Kidd talking to payroll. Your cast gets paid as of last Sunday. The checks will be in your envelope this Friday."

"You're kidding!"

"Nope. Ten dollars apiece. Less than scale but ten more than they ever made before."

"Are you serious? They'll be rich! This is great news!"

"Just remember, you didn't hear it from me."

"What about Waldo? He's got to remember to pay Waldo. I can't give out those checks unless there's one for Waldo too."

"What about you, Rue? Will you work for ten dollars?"

"Hell, yes. Jordan's got himself a genuine white woman, two for the price of one."

Maitland was still on the soundstage when they returned at one o'clock. He sat with Zylla, working on the maestro's script for the musical score. Leland would work the rehearsals on organ in the absence of the orchestra, to give Maitland a sense of timing and pace. "Dedrick's a heavy rehearser," Rue said softly. "He'll be changing stuff right up to airtime."

They began again. Maitland stopped often for suggestions on music or sound patterns, for new interpretations of individual lines. He coaxed Pauline into what he wanted, a good German mamma who loved her boy. Hazel as usual was perfect: she gave them a version of the scarf woman so true to the original that Jordan found it chilling.

At four thirty Maitland sent Becky to fetch Kidd. "Okay, people, let's give him a show," he said, and everyone got in place as Kidd came in and sat facing the soundstage.

The run-through was perfect. Becky clicked her watch and said, "Twenty-nine sixteen," and Kidd nodded curtly and got up from his chair.

"I don't need to ask what the verdict is. Miss Nicholas sounds superb."

Rue smiled, a little out of breath. "Thank you, sir."

"This is it, then," Kidd said. "What did you decide about the lead?"

"We still need someone," Maitland said. "Brinker's good but Jordan's right, we need him too much in those Nazi roles and I don't want to spread him any thinner than that. I know Rue was kidding but I'd like to try to get Rick Gary and give Susan Daniels our regrets."

"I talked to them both this afternoon," Kidd said. "Gary will come with or without Miss Daniels, so it looks like we can have the best of both worlds. But he can't get here till Saturday afternoon. You won't have time for much more than a quick table reading with him before the dress."

"That's okay, he's a pro, he knows what to do."

They began to break up. Kidd pulled Jordan aside as the cast drifted out. "Mr. Harford would like to see you tonight, if you're free. Just a friendly chat over dinner. Casual dress, no frills."

"Casual's about the best I've got."

"Seven o'clock, then. Come over to the office and ring the bell, someone will come let you in. I may join you, or maybe not. I've still got a mountain of work on my desk."

He sat at his desk in the empty bullpen, still tingly from the day, still caught in its spell. He closed his eyes to rest a few minutes, and the pictures began again.

He was in that meditative state, half awake, half asleep. He was aware of the clock though he didn't see it. He knew he'd need to get moving soon: go home, get a shower, change clothes. But when he opened his eyes, he grabbed a sheet of newsprint and rolled it into the typewriter.

He had a title for a story. "Dark Silver."

Suddenly he had the story as well. It had no ending but that didn't matter. It was a river of life.

It went like it always went: quickly, explosively.

Dark Silver was the name of a racehorse. The story would be a continuation, a weekly half hour with plenty of time to work in the characters. Open ended, sprawling, rich with detail.

He roughed out an outline, the action of the first five chapters, and his racetrack family came to life at once. He would need five weeks to set the central hook. To tell how this family of struggling racetrackers had had a succession of crippling setbacks, and now pinned the hope of their stable on an old stakes horse named Dark Silver. Five weeks would give him the luxury of getting the five main characters established, with a half-hour chapter devoted to the problems of each, while the larger conflict would slowly develop and build throughout.

Lee Brewer was the father, the central character. But he decided to begin with Nina, their fiery eighteen-year-old daughter. A great part for Rue. He would back into the main story in the second week, but for now Nina had the most immediate problem. She was desperate to become a jockey, which would break that all-boys clan and flout tradition. The entire action of the first episode would be set on the day of her license hearing before the Nebraska Jockey Club. Her brother Sam would support her, Will would be less enthused, and the sarcastically affectionate exchanges between these three would make them all sympathetic in different ways.

He sketched out a few more characters.

Melanie, their mother, who had been a schoolteacher twenty-five years ago. Pregnant with Will on their wedding night, he decided. He didn't know how such a thing could be used but it struck him as true and he wrote it down. Pauline would play this role.

Gill Dockett, the unscrupulous trainer who was Lee Brewer's archenemy. His son Al Dockett, cowed by the old man and thus a bully, in love with Nina, desperate to impress her, doomed of course to failure. Kyle Nelson, Lee's best friend and most serious rival in the claiming wars. And Job Hendricks, the veterinarian: a wise old hand who'd always been a listening post for the three young Brewers in times of trouble.

This was enough for the opening show. The climax was pure dynamite, with Nina brought to a raging fury by the arbitrary decision of those old bastards on the board, opening a rift with the powerful chairman that will bring new trouble to her whole family. He banged out some dialogue:

"The reason is simple, Miss Brewer. Girls do not ride. No girl has ever been granted a license, and properly not."

"And properly not? What does that mean? That's a hell of a reason! Damn it, this is my life you're fooling with! Who do you people think you are, gods?"

The cusswords were vital. She must swear at them, offend them deeply, and thus begin the chain of events that would start this vendetta against her. Even the words "damn" and "hell" would be shocking on the radio, and the shock would double if they came from a woman.

The telephone rang.

"Heeey, Dulaney! . . . It's about time you got back to that desk."

Schroeder.

"Where the hell you been all day? I been trying your phone every hour."

"We're rehearsing a play. It's . . . it doesn't matter."

"Did you get my money?"

He lied without thinking. "It's burning a hole in my pocket."

Schroeder laughed. "You'd better put out that fire, old buddy. How much you get me?"

He lied again. "Four hundred."

"Good. I'll need it all before I get where I'm going. I'm leaving the country tomorrow."

Dulaney gave a little grunt.

"What's wrong with you?" Schroeder said.

The line had clicked and there was that soft hum again, like a bad party line on a rural telephone hookup. "I'm fine, but there are people around. Maybe you should call me back on the phone in the square."

"I don't hear any people."

"Take my word for it."

"I take nobody's word. You're not trying to pull something now, are you, Dulaney?"

"What good would that do me?"

"Who knows how you crazy Americans think. You just come tonight. You give me my money and I give you your money's worth."

"I can't get away tonight."

"Well, you goddamn better, you hear that? You better come or I'm gone and you're a dead man. You got that, Dulaney? You got that? You and that honey of yours can take what comes."

Dulaney said nothing for a long time. Ten seconds.

"So, are you coming or not? Say it now, Dulaney, you got this one chance."

"Okay . . . I'm coming."

"Tonight."

"Yes. I'll be there."

"If you're late even by one minute I'll be gone."

"Schroeder, listen to me—"

"No, you listen. You come to a rooming house on East Eighty-fifth. Halfway down the block in the three hundreds. There's a window box on the first floor—the only one on the block. Ask for Richard in three sixteen; he will tell you where to go. If there's any monkey business you don't get past Richard, you got that? Come at eleven fifteen, no sooner, no later."

The connection broke. Dulaney sat listening to dead air. Then the line clicked and the hum went away.

((25))

HIS car ran hot in the wilderness, but sometime before eight he limped into Pinewood Junction, a jerkwater whistle-stop on the railroad. The town, carved out of a dense forest thirty miles west of the beach, was closed tight. Not a sign of life anywhere: not a gas station or even a bar, not a soul on the road or walking along the paths that seemed to be the town's only sidewalks. A few dim-looking houses back in the trees. A long brick building, closed and padlocked, with the single chipped and peeling word GARAGE clinging stubbornly to the bricks over the bay doors. Something that looked like a general store, a relic from the last century, locked tight and dark like the rest of it.

There was a railroad depot. He had been assured of that, and there it was, just beyond the town limit on the other side of the tracks. The platform was empty, the windows dark, but he clattered across the tracks, pulled into the dirt lot, lifted his hood, and diagnosed his own problem, a splitting radiator hose that might last another fifty miles or give up the ghost in the next ten seconds. Water dripped slowly on the engine, and the drips sizzled and danced into steamy oblivion.

He climbed to the platform and stood at the end of it. A large slate schedule revealed that the northbound from Cape May to New York was due in thirty-seven minutes, at eight thirty-two by the clock over the door. He pulled up the flag to signify PASSENGER WAITING, then sat on a bench outside the locked ticket room and hoped the conductor cared enough to stop for a single fare.

He thought about Harford and Kidd. How long had they waited for him and what had they thought when he failed to arrive? Standing them up was a minor worry, now that he was on the road with some kind of resolution in sight, but it was what he thought about, along with his telephone and the worry about that strange hum. The weather had changed. An early dusk was coming, the sun already down beyond the misty woods. The day had turned cold: not in actual degrees, but there was a chilling augury about his mission that extended to the environment. He couldn't remember when he'd been so jumpy, so impatient to get somewhere and get it over with.

The timetable unfolded in his head. The train would put him in New York at nine twenty-eight. Almost two hours to kill. At eleven fifteen he'd meet Richard in room 316. He knew this by heart.

Midnight. By now he'd have seen Schroeder, probably somewhere in the immediate neighborhood. Richard would certainly pat him down, so he'd have nothing more than his guts and his strength when the showdown turned ugly. And ugly it would be when Schroeder found out he had no money. He hoped he and Schroeder would be alone, but more likely there'd be a gang from the bund, there to intimidate him if nothing else.

First reason, then bluff. If that fails, fight. It wasn't much of a plan but it was all he had. "One way or another" was his byword. One way or another Schroeder was going to tell him what he knew.

What a plan. A great prescription for getting yourself killed.

It started going wrong before the train came in. Perhaps it was the deathlike stillness that made the movement catch his eye. Some little flutter in the woods across the tracks and beyond the glade: gone now as he turned his head for the full frontal look. Just the jitters, he thought: he'd feel better when he got on the train, better yet when the neon city pulled him into its vast anonymous hustle. A man could hide in that crowd forever if he didn't have to go up to Yorkville and put himself in a spotlight, betting on a blind hand and hoping he wasn't being lured there just to be killed like Kendall.

A covey of birds was his only warning. They flushed out of the thicket at the edge of the trees, banked north over the tracks, and glided into the grass two hundred yards away. A hunter, he thought. That inherited ability to read the woods drew his eyes back to the spot where the birds had jumped, and he saw a shimmery presence just into the forest. A hunter who flushed birds but did not shoot, visible for less than a second before vanishing back in the brush. A hunter hunting but not hunting birds, he thought, and in that second he knew he was in trouble.

The hunter's hunting me.

He was already moving when the crack of the rifle ripped across the clearing. He dropped to the cement floor as the second shot knocked over the bench in a shower of splinters. He rolled to his feet and scrambled behind the depot. A third shot hit the building, blowing half a brick out of the northwest corner.

He flattened against the wall and there, in the longest minute he had ever lived, he thought he could hear the mist falling in the trees. He peered around the edge. The woods were dense and darkening, primevally empty.

He looked through the depot window, through the dark waiting room, and on through the glass doors to the woods east of the track. Not a movement anywhere back there. That in itself meant nothing. But the thicket had gone back to its natural quiet. The birds circled and came home.

It looked like a nesting place. A nest would draw birds back, but they wouldn't come if the hunter was still there.

At least eight or ten minutes had passed: plenty of time for a shooter to change his position and have another try.

Where would he come from?

From the north it would be a difficult shot. The road into town was long and straight with a deep open stretch. From the south it would be easier, with ground cover that grew thick around the tracks almost to the edge of the depot. The shooter would have one short moment of exposure as he dashed across the tracks, but once across he'd have a clear shot down the west end of the depot.

He took a deep breath and stepped around the edge of the building. Stood in shadow, looking across the tracks where the shooter had been just a few minutes before.

Here he passed the time, standing in the depot doorway, waiting for the train. At eight thirty-four he heard the horn and it came in, hissing to a stop.

Doors opened. People stared through lighted windows.

He'd be open to one shot from the south as he darted away from the cover of the building. He leaped across eternity, into the waiting coach.

He took a seat and sat low. A few passengers looked at him curiously, then the newspapers went up. The shields of urban indifference.

The doors closed. The train rocked through the black Jersey woods.

A conductor came through and collected his fare. At nine twenty-five they rolled into Penn Station and Jack Dulaney walked into the warm Manhattan night.

((26))

A SENSE of urgency drove him on to Yorkville. If he was in danger, so was Schroeder. This bit of logic kept running through his head. I will lose him if I go early: we will all lose him if I don't.

A man on a train would almost certainly get to the city before a man in a car. But this advantage dissolved in his mind as he stood in the Lexington Avenue subway and waited for the uptown train. The lights of the Brooklyn express flashed over his feet, a caravan of people hurled through catacombs to troubles of their own.

Somehow he had to get to Schroeder: had to talk or bully his way past the sentry in 316 and make them listen. He got on his train and the next thing he knew he was getting off on Eighty-sixth. With luck he'd have an hour to work with: sixty minutes to persuade two jumpy Germans that they needed to hear what he needed to tell them.

He came up the steps to a far different Yorkville than the one he remembered. The glitter had faded from Hitler's Broadway: the gaiety had gone and many of the cabarets had closed. There was less to celebrate in 1942: Hitler didn't look quite as invincible as he once had, and the city's tolerance of un-American activities had expired with the German declaration of war last December 9. There were still traces of political sentiment—a swastika painted on a redbrick wall, a picture of their führer taped to a light pole, an anonymous handbill raving against the Jews—but the revelers of 1938 had apparently been arrested, dispersed, or driven underground. The street was so quiet he could clearly hear the footsteps of a man crossing half a block away.

The flag store where Holly had run afoul of the Nazi woman was vacant now. The grand meeting halls—Turnverein, Mozart Hall, the Yorkville Casino—were closed and dark. He passed the pastry shop where Tom had been challenged by the Hitler youth gang . . . still open, and nothing about it changed except now there were no customers. Even the waiter, he thought, was the same weary-looking fellow who had asked them to leave. The scene tugged at his heart, making him wish for another crack at better days and a chance to get it right with the benefit of hindsight.

He walked down Second Avenue to Eighty-fifth Street and a moment later stood outside the apartment house. There was no use planning it to death: all you could do was play it by ear and see what happened when you knocked on the door. The hallway was dingy, with uncarpeted stairs curling up from an aperture halfway down. As he came to the second floor he heard voices talking German, then music on a phonograph. The floor creaked when he went on up. He followed the numbers to 316 at the end of the hall. There was a window—one of those six-foot casements that open onto fire escapes—and he looked over the coaly gap between the buildings. He put his head to the door and decided not to knock. Not now, not yet—some unknown hunch stopped him.

He flipped the window latch and pushed it up. It moved easily in its sash and he guessed that prolific use was made of the fire escapes in the summer: that soon people would be hauling mattresses out of their rooms to catch any breath of air. But that wasn't the case tonight. There wasn't a light anywhere: not a sound or a hint of life until he stepped out on the landing. Then he heard a group of men singing harmony in some distant place: German songs in the German tongue. They were such gay people, such jolly good fellows. You had to wonder why they couldn't stop fighting the rest of the world.

Now he heard another noise, the rhythmic moaning of a woman. It grew in intensity until it seemed to fill the black gulf. He saw a bit of light from the street, just enough to make out the iron landings extending like steel skeletons full-length down each floor. The woman's voice had risen to a whimper: as if she's being killed, he thought, or beaten and left for dead. He touched the wall and the window to 316 was open a crack, raised about three inches over the sill. Was that where the crying woman was? But the room was blacker than the night, and when he leaned down and put his face to the opening he felt a stuffiness that said there was no one in the apartment.

Then the rickety platform began to rock and he knew what it was . . . a pair of lovers on the landing just above his head. The whole works clattered, creaking in a rhythm that was unmistakable, rising to a melting rapture and the deaf-and-blind fury of animals. Once in broken English the man tried to protest—*Hush now, hush! Someone will hear!*—but the woman cried out to Jesus and was already past caring. In the telling moment Dulaney had his fingers under the window. Only the real Jesus heard the squeak as he jerked it up and stepped into the room.

He took a long breath and pulled the window down where it had been. He touched an unmade bed . . . pillows strewn as if the lovers had begun their play here. The room was stifling. He felt his way around the bed, to the wall, then to the door. The front room led out to the hall, the thin line of light around the door his only guide.

The hall door opened into a windowless living room, with the bedroom on the fire escape and, he guessed, a kitchen and

bathroom on the other side. He groped his way along the wall
and wondered, did he dare use a light? Maybe, if he could be
sure of containing it. He found the switch and moved beyond
it: then, casting away from the safety of the wall, he struck out
across the room.

There were no obstacles to the opposite wall and he
moved along it to a doorway. Bumped past an icebox to a
small dining table with chairs. Felt an oven: his fingers
touched the gas jets, then the grates, and he felt his way
around that to another door. Pushed it open and the faint
smell of rust told him he had reached the bathroom. At that
moment the telephone rang, breaking the silence like a
bombshell.

He jumped away and spun into the room. Slammed
against the wall, said a soft "Jesus Christ," and stood breathing deeply while the phone went on ringing. He lost track of
how many times it rang, and when it was finally quiet, that
was somehow worse than the noise. He heard a clock ticking,
and this heightened his urgency and gave him a new awareness of time. It must be at least ten o'clock now and he was
burning up the minutes with no other plan if his meeting
with Schroeder should fail.

Unless he could find a lead, somewhere here in the apartment.

He turned on the bathroom light, an agreeably dim bulb
over a rust-colored sink. Again the phone rang, exploding in
the same split second as if the light had set it off. It jolted him
a second time and he cursed himself. Loudest goddamn telephone on the planet. But he had light now, and he was in a
large bathroom with a tiled floor that testified to better days.
He opened the medicine cabinet but it was almost bare: a
cardboard box of aspirin, a well-squeezed tube of toothpaste,
a bottle of disinfectant. One other item caught his eye: a
diaphragm, shoved into a corner of the middle shelf. Lusty
people, these Germans.

He followed his reflected light into the eating room. The
telephone kept ringing. Now he could see it, perched on a
counter a few feet away, and he had a sudden urge to answer

it—crazy, he knew, but it seemed less so as he stood there facing it. What could he lose? If it happened to be Schroeder
calling, maybe he could get it all said in one long piece—how
his phone had been tapped and even now someone might be
out in the street, gunning for them both. But he was spared
the decision when the ringing stopped.

He saw the clock on a shelf just a few inches from his face.
It was still only nine fifty-four, if that could be believed. He
peered into the living room, and the few pieces of furniture
looked spectral in the indirect light. There was a poor excuse
for a sofa with stuffing coming out of one arm. A console
radio across the room. A desk against the wall with a hard
chair pulled up close. That was it for furniture.

He sat at the desk and made a quick search of the pigeon-
holes on both sides of the writing surface. Nothing but a few
bills, all in the name Aleta von Papen. Nothing about a
Richard or any of the Schroeders. Could he have come to the
wrong place? He stared for a moment at the radio, a well-
used Zenith with shortwave and police bands, and something
caught his eye. The dial was set on Harford, the spot marked
with a small red slash.

All his doubts vanished in that moment. Suddenly his mind
was back at Harford. He knew the station's schedules well
enough to test that clock on the shelf. Right now Eastman
would be reading the closing of one of their few local nighttime
slots. Rue would be standing at the other mike, ready to do Miss
Nicotine for their one national account, Wings cigarettes. He
clicked on the radio and turned the volume low, little more than
a whisper, as he went through the left drawer. The radio whistled as he sifted through a wad of newspaper clippings, most of
them about G-man activity in Jersey and New York. Two Germans arrested at a farm near Elizabeth. Fourteen rounded up on
a sweep through Yorkville. German-Americans in sensitive
positions—in radio stations, post offices, shipping companies,
anyplace where they could see or hear things—placed under
increased security. Nazi sympathizers find little to cheer about
in U.S. courts as prison or deportation looms for most. Hoover
given prominent credit in every piece. He and Congressman

Dies, who reconvened the Committee on Un-American Activities yesterday, lauded for their eternal vigilance. A familiar voice burst out of the radio—Rue, just finishing her commercial. Good news . . . the clock was off by less than a minute.

There was a short break just before ten, which Eastman would fill with news, local spots, and schedule ticklers. Here he was now, telling listeners what was left of the Harford day. A band remote at eleven thirty, courtesy of the boys in Blue, followed by Stoner's *Scrapbook of Sound*. It all seemed so distant now. The station cut away to the network and he turned it off and went on searching the desk.

In the bottom drawer he found a stack of letters, some in German, some in English, all handwritten and addressed to the same woman, Aleta von Papen. Most were from family in Chicago and Milwaukee. *I still worry about Gerda Luise,* he read. *It's hard not knowing if she lives or dies, and now we won't know until this awful war is over.* The name teased him and then he remembered that story in the *Beachcomber.* The dead boy, Georgie Schroeder, had had a sister named Gerda Luise. She had married a German national and had moved with him to Germany. The letters deeper in the pile were all in German, mailed overseas before the declaration of war had shut down the mails last December. They came from a G. L. Nadel or a Gerda L. Nadel and had been mailed from Germany at regular intervals throughout the late thirties. He wished he could read them, because the ones in English were little more than family gossip.

These came from first cousins in Chicago and Milwaukee. Even Hoover couldn't make a case against them with this as his evidence. They seemed to be good naturalized citizens trying to love their new country enough without loving the old one less. A man like Hitler might make something out of that. You've got to choose, he would say: choose now or be branded a traitor. Good thing we're above that here, Dulaney thought, but then he had a vision of that Japanese family at Tanforan and he wondered what Hoover would say to him about that.

The family in Chicago had had a visit from George. He had come for a rest and needed it. Something very bad was going on with him; he looked terrible, his nerves were shot, he smoked all day, and his sleep was poor and filled with nightmares. Someone called Maynard had terrified him. One night he had cried out in his sleep and one of the words they heard him say was the name Maynard. He denied this, said he'd never known anyone named Maynard, but you could see he was lying.

Then, at the bottom, he found a long letter from George himself. *Dear Leta,* it began, and what followed was three pages of very cribbed and dense handwriting. Dulaney read the first paragraph and felt a thrill of discovery. Then he heard a clatter from the bedroom. Someone was coming down the fire escape.

((27))

HE shoved the letters back in the drawer—all but the letter from George. That one he folded and slipped in his pocket. He hurried to the bathroom and doused the light. He stepped behind the door and heard the window squeak as the woman climbed into the bedroom. She was alone, talking to herself. The light went on in the kitchen and a beam of it leaped into the bathroom and fell across the tub. Her shadow passed and he heard her open a cabinet. There was a clink of glass, a gush of water from the tap, the greedy gulping sounds she made drinking it. Another glass. The tumble on the fire escape had left her dry.

Her chatter stopped only while she drank: a stream of Germanic carried on in two remarkably distinct tones of voice. Her husky side was nasty and laced with sarcasm, at one point laughing outrageously at something the other voice had said. Her voice was young and she was high-strung and quick.

She banged her way into the bathroom, shoving the door back against his arm. Through the crack he could see her—a thick mane of auburn hair, a sleeveless dress, a hand on a hip, a leg propped up on the edge of the tub, and the other hand exploring herself under the dress. Another diaphragm: it came out with a rubbery sucking sound and she threw it into the sink. She leaned over and pulled something out to the middle of the room—one of those saddle-seated French bidet things for washing a woman's private parts—and she wavered between that and a full bath. She hiked up the front of her dress and sniffed, sniffed again under her arms, said, *"Du stinkbombe, Leta,"* turned on the bathwater, and kicked the bidet out of sight. Now she stood in full view, a beautiful girl whose sweaty face stared at itself in the mirror. She lifted her arms, felt for stubble, wrinkled her face, and began taking her clothes off.

He knew he had to move now. But the telephone rang and she whirled away with an angry outburst. In the sudden distance he heard her yell something that sounded like, *"Oh scheiten ficken Telefon!"* and she was already a room away as he nudged the door inward and stepped around it.

She was standing at the counter with him at her back, talking angrily on the phone. A hot mix of German and English with Peter on the other end, he would bet. He heard her say, "Didn't I tell you I'd be here? . . . So I'm here, so what more do you want from me?" A line in German, then, "There's plenty of time," then, "Stop acting like that, it's none of your business where I was, gottdammit, don't I have my own life to lead? You think my whole world must come stopping anytime you snap your Nazi fingers?"

She slammed her hand down on the counter. "Hey! You want to do this by yourself? You fool around witt me and I walk out of here right now, you can come over here and do your own gottdamn dirty work."

She slammed the phone onto its cradle and screamed a string of ferocious German obscenities. Then she turned and there he was.

She tried to blink away the shock. Her eyes leaped on to the open bathroom, as if what she'd seen just couldn't be. Then came a second shock. Her mouth dropped open for a few ticking seconds while the anger filled her up again. He was aware of his own voice, telling her he had come about Peter, but she screamed over the words. "Who der hell are you! What you're doing in my house!"

It slipped into madness. He heard a soft little growl and in her eyes the moment passed from anger to insanity. She was coming at him: less than half his size but stalking him like a predator.

He backed away, keeping the table between them. He kept trying to reason with her—he had come to meet Peter—and this time she heard him but it didn't matter. Her lip curled back as she circled to his left. He followed her step for step. A shift in her eyes was his only warning, and suddenly he saw the butcher's block with a ten-inch knife sticking up in the wood. She lunged at it as he moved to stop her. He caught her shoulders, she spun, the knife popped out of the block and clattered under their feet. He caught her under her arms as she went after it: she fought him back across the room, slippery, still slick with sweat. He tried to pin her hands and she hit him . . . a slap across the face, then a searing pain as she went for his crotch and got it. He tied her up with a bear hug and they fell to the floor. He had her then, wrapped in a fetal shape with his arms and legs around her. All she could do was buck and writhe and curse him hotly in German.

They lay still. Her breath tickled his arm and the aroma of sex and sweat was heavy between them. "You bastard," she said at one point.

Then she laughed.

At once she was convulsed, heaving in desperate mirth that went on for an impossible time. "Oh, you bastard. You big ficken booby, you should see your stupit face when I grab you by der nots. I bet we look like two dogs humping down here. Gottdamn Doberman and der poodle."

She went off again into fits of hysteria.

"Pity der poor poodle."

She shrugged against his arms. "So what you do now, kill me? Or we just gonna sleep togedder on der floor all night?"

"Nobody's going to kill you. I'm trying to tell you something."

"I heard you der first time. You come to see Peter and this makes it okay for you to break into my house."

She lay quiet for a moment. Then: "You bring der money?"

"Sure."

"How much?"

"Four hundred was the deal, wasn't it?"

"Deal was for you to come at eleven o'clock and fifteen minutes. Ask for Richit."

"Things changed. I had a good reason."

"Reasons can get your dick cut off."

He cleared his throat, made a little laugh out of it. "Well, it worked out all right. I'm here, still in one piece. Where's Richard?"

"Is no Richit. Just me you talk to. You gonna let me up?"

"Maybe. If you can behave yourself."

"I guess you gotta find out." She sighed and leaned her head back under his chin. "Come on, Delancy, my gottdamn tub's running over."

Now he was sitting on the closed toilet, telling her what he'd come to say while she mopped the floor and mostly said nothing. Her rage was gone, drained with the bathwater, but still in the air like the half-remembered tantrum of a child. At times she seemed absorbed in what he was telling her, then her mind would drift. She would become suddenly playful, splashing him with water from the draining tub and laughing explosively as he sat dripping before her. A crazy girl: fickle, gorgeous, scatterbrained, and horny, nutty as a chipmunk's den. Her madness filled a room, warping it. He had seen that flushed, heated sheen on a woman years ago, a lust that never cooled, preorgasmic even when she'd just been with a man. An older generation had defined it: nymphomania, the word for the sexual psychopath.

It left her no attention span for such matters as life and death. She seemed unfazed at the thought that killers might have her address: either she didn't believe it or she missed the fear in his voice for her safety. Her eyes would dart away—to the outer room, to the sink where her diaphragm still lay soaking, to the mirror for a glimpse of her own lovely face, which always made her smile—then her face would twitch and her gaze come back to the tight place below his belt. There was sex in everything she did. "How old are you, Delancy?" she asked at one point. When he told her thirty-two, she said, "I'm twenty-eight. That's good, huh?" There was sex in that too.

The room was suddenly quiet.

"Did you hear what I said? Did you hear any of it?"

"Yah, yah. Peter said you'd try something."

"What's Peter so afraid of? Did you ever ask him that?"

"Who said he's afraid?"

"He'd be here himself if he wasn't."

"Maybe he's got his reasons. You don't know everything."

He prompted her with his hands. For the moment now he had her attention and his best chance to keep it was to stay with the short questions, the confrontational responses: anything that forced her to answer and think about what he had said.

"What don't I know?"

"What it's like to be German."

"Is that what Peter's afraid of? Is he running from the law?"

Suddenly irritated, she shook her head. "I'm saying nothing about that. I don't know nothing and I don't want to." But her hands had begun to tremble.

"Maybe I should ask what you're afraid of."

She sighed. "Jesus Christ, Delancy, you're pretty stupit for an American. You need a picture drawn on you?"

He smiled. "Just a little picture maybe."

She said nothing and he pressed on. "I heard you talking to him. On the telephone you called him a Nazi."

The word shocked her, as if in the heat of the moment she hadn't known she'd said it. Her mouth opened but no sound came out. He sensed his advantage. "Are the police looking for him? Is that why he went into hiding? Is he afraid he'll be arrested because of his politics?"

"He tells me nothing. I don't let him tell me nothing. I don't know who's looking for him and I don't care. Peter's a bastard and I hate him."

"Then why do you help him?"

She looked at him: a quiet, fearful moment full of indecision. "Is what you do witt family. I don't like it but mine papa makes it a thing of honor."

"Does your father know Peter's a Nazi?"

She recoiled a second time, then pushed the air as if she could force the word back upon him. "You listen, you! I got nothing to do witt no gottdamn Nazis!" But her voice had dropped to a whisper and he had to lip-read the last word.

He repeated the question. "Does your father know about Peter?"

"Peter's his brother's son, that's what he knows. He doesn't think about me or der trouble I could get in."

Her attention was all his now, her madness and lust absorbed into something far deeper. The great fear of her life. Her eyes were clear, fixed on his face. Still trembling, she said, "Mamma Christ, what am I doing talking to you? I don't know nothing about what Peter does, I don't know no damn Nazis, don't you even *think* such a lie! Jesus, I could get in such trouble! Do you have any idea what Hoover would do to me?"

He had a very good idea. Hoover was her Fraunkenschtein, the little man with the cold eyes who made the trumped-up killers thrown at her by a stranger fade to nothing. She coughed and looked at him in disbelief, her face the oddest mix of pleading and menace. She seemed to be saying something—*How der hell did I get into this? How could that door blow open so fast? How could I be so stupit, tell my worst nightmare to a foreigner who is probably an enemy?* She knew he had found her weakness and now she must beg him not to exploit it. But the more she talked, the worse it got, the more she had to talk and the greater her fear was.

"You better not spread these lies, Delancy. You got to promise me, swear you won't say nothing if you know what's good for you." She touched her mouth with a shaky hand and said, "Please," a word he knew she didn't say often. "You be a good boy, huh? Be sweet and I'll take care of you. You'll be amazed at what I can do. But you got to promise. You don't understand about Hoover. He will think, Well, she's just German trash, he can do what he wants witt me, so I got to give him no cause to ever hear my name. He don't need proof, he makes it up. Who's gonna believe me?"

She droned on and it made him sad to hear her. What he was doing made him sadder; it felt dishonorable because what she was telling him was at least possible. But the clock was running so he said nothing and he knew this was more terrible than if he'd screamed at her in disbelief.

She was telling him what a good American she was. "I am going to night school, I'm learning about Thomas Jefferson, I learning to talk so I don't sound like such a kraut. I don't say 'dis' or 'dat' no more, only sometimes. I'm trying to get hold of my temper and be a good citizen. You think Hoover cares about that? I can swear der truth on a pile of Bibles and it don't matter what I say, Hoover won't care. I *hate* Hitler, I despise that son of a bitch, I got nothing to do witt them baby killers. I start off every day gottdamming Hitler and his war. I got my papers, I'm a good American, and Hoover doesn't give a shit. If it makes him look good to put me in jail, that's what he does. You people who were born here just don't know what he can do, all that power they give him. You can be a perfect American and still he gets you. He finds der evidence you never saw, der papers you never wrote, they find stuff under your bed or behind der wall, under der floor. They bring in people you never heard of to tell on you, and you're gone."

She sat on the tub, weak from fear and peaks of rage. Talked about her struggle, coming to a new land without a word of its language. "You don't know what it's like being a German girl trying to make her ends meet in this awful time. Everybody blames you for Hitler and every bump in der night means Hoover is comink to get you. I swear to gott I am going to kill Peter. If they deport me I will kill that penis-pulling swine witt my own teeth. Right into Hitler's front room I will track him . . ." She smiled. "But this is not going to happen, is it, Delancy? Tomorrow Peter's gone and you're not going to tell on me, are you? I know you're going to be a good sweet boy."

She gripped his shirt. "Dammit, say something!"

"It's not Hoover who's coming for you, Leta. Tonight Hoover's the least of your worries."

"You should walk in my shoes. . . . Live in my life. Then you can tell me about Hoover and his G-mens." Her smile flashed and the charm flowed again. He noticed how much more German she was as her nerves unraveled.

"So what do you want, Chack? See, I call you Chack—is your name, yes? What do you want, a nice little piece of German shortcake maybe? A hot bath and a douche. I could make it sweet again. Still lotsa time till Peter calls."

He leaned toward her. "You're a pretty girl, Leta, but you don't hear so good. I can't wait around for Peter to call. I want you to call him. Tell him I'm here. Tell him what I said. Tell him if he wants any of this money he's got to meet me right now."

"I can't."

"Then you're both on your own."

"I'm telling you I can't! He's got no phone, he's got to call me from a phone in der hall."

"Then you're out of choices. You've got to take me there."

(((28)))

THEY went out the back way, to a night so deep they vanished from each other. Down the hall to the back door, and through it to oblivion.

She clutched his hand and pulled him along the walk.

We made it, he thought. Nothing back there for a killer to find—just an empty flat and a fading whiff of a horny woman's sweat.

Suddenly she seemed to want this showdown, as if the rage had returned and broken the fear apart, refilling her with madness. One of us will kill the other, he thought: that's what she's hoping. But how she hoped it would turn out was the sixty-four-dollar question.

She led him off the walk, across a sandlot. This gave way to hard ground, and a narrow crack appeared between the buildings, with the dim lights of the street beyond it. "It's not far now," she said. "Just across der street and down der block."

She stopped. "You remember what you said, Chack? What you promise?"

He had made two promises: that he'd never give her name to Hoover, no matter what, and that he'd give her a minute, when they got where they were going, to go in alone and talk with Peter. He didn't like that but she said Peter had a gun, and if they should walk in together and surprise him, what might happen wouldn't be her fault.

Jesus, what a chance I'm taking, he thought. She confirmed this as if he'd said it aloud. "You know what you do, it's not safe. You know how Peter is. So just do what you say. Just go in and give him der money, then take what he gives you and get der hell out. Don't fuss witt him, don't give him no guff. You don't want to fool witt Peter."

"I hear you."

"Udderwise I think he is going to kill you. And this would make me sad, Chack, because I am comink to like you so much."

"This would make me sad too, Leta."

"Don't make jokes now, this is not funny. Is no time for bullshit."

The word was startling: it was a military vulgarity; an old one, he thought, but still largely unknown outside the army. He had never heard it from a woman. So she knew some soldiers. Did that mean she was a spy?

"Peter don't want to kill you, Chack, but he will if you try something. So just give him der money."

"That's what I came for."

"Just give him der gottdamn money, Chack, then get out of there. That's all he wants, just der money, but if you cross him I don't want to be there. I could tell you bad stuff on him."

"What stuff?"

"Stuff I'm not supposed to know. It's too dangerous to talk about and it's got nothing to do witt me. But I got good ears. I know what they do."

"What who does?"

"I shouldn't tell you. It's very dangerous, what I know."

"It won't matter. Tomorrow Peter'll be gone. He'll have my money and be far away from here."

She said nothing.

"It might give me an idea what I'm facing here."

"I tell you this much. I know a man was kilt in Pennsylvania."

His heart went up a notch. His mouth was dry. "Who was killed?"

"Somebody. I heard Peter and George talking one time. Poor Georgie is *so* upset but Peter just laughs. This is what I'm saying, you can't fool witt Peter. Sometimes I scream at him but I'm like everybody else. I get out of his way when he really gets pissed off."

There it is again, he thought. Army slang, latrine lingo as the dogface calls it. Words so rare in civilian conversation that the possibility she'd learned them by chance was like the snowball in hell. Maybe she worked the military at its weakest point, screwing her way up and down the chain of command and passing what she learned on to Berlin through the Schroeders.

"I shouldn't be telling you any of this. I do it for your own good and I could tell you plenty more. It wasn't just der one in Pennsylvania. Anudder man was kilt down in New Chursey."

"What man? . . . When?"

"A long time ago. Maybe last Christmas, around der new year."

"Who were these guys?"

"People who knew stuff. I don't know, I shouldn't be talking about it. I heard some names but it's hard to remember.

Der one in Pennsylvania was Prindle, I think. I can't remember der udder one."

"Carnahan," he prompted.

"I can't remember. Anyways, it's got nothing to do witt me. I'm just telling you so you know not to fool witt Peter. Just give him his money, Chack. Don't piss him off. And get der hell out of there."

She pulled him on, into the street and across. The hotel was a grim relic of an older century, five stories high with a portal in the center and a dimly lit drugstore on the ground floor at the corner. Where a room could be had for an hour if that's what you wanted, two bits up front, pay at the drugstore, no questions asked. A flophouse.

She turned him into the dark entry and hustled him through a foyer that stank of urine; on through a second door, which creaked inward to a dismal hall and a set of stairs. Two men sprawled under the staircase, passed out with an empty bottle between them, and as the door swung shut something crawled across one man's face and scurried away. "Rats," she said with a shiver. "Christ, what a place."

There was only one light, a bare bulb dangling from a cord that cast the deeper hall in dusty shadow, like an old sepulchre lit by a torch. He saw the telephone on the wall to his left, its brassy coin box as out of place here as he was. "This is where you wait," she said. "Don't move till I come back for you."

He got over by the phone and stood there. If this implied a promise, he would let her think that. In his own mind all bets were off once she had gone alone into that room. "You be good now, Chack." She kissed her fingers and touched his cheek. Such a good boy he was. A good big boy.

Then she walked away. At the crossing corridor she stopped and looked back once and he had the strangest feeling, one of those premonitions that had happened only a few times in his life. She waved to him and turned the corner and he knew he'd never see her again.

He hurried down the hall behind her. At the corner he heard her say, "Open der door, it's me." He made the turn and saw her leg disappear into a room halfway down the hall.

He heard the click of the door closing. Heard her shout.

She screamed and a gun went off. There was another shot, and another, as if a cannon had gone wild and begun blowing the building apart.

He reached the door in a mindless flash of motion. He knew it was locked: even as he rattled the knob he was hauling back on his right leg to batter it down. The door blew out of its frame, exploding in pieces into the room. He rolled away from it, ready for more fire, flattening himself against the outer wall, tensing to attack anything that moved.

He threw himself into the room and fell to the floor, rolling out of the light to the far wall. There he crouched, till a cooling breeze drew his eyes to the open window. Gone—out through the alley to the street. He groped at the wall and found the light, and there was the girl, pretty no more, sprawled in her blood, her one remaining eye fixed vacantly on the ceiling. What he hadn't expected was Peter, hog-tied to a chair a few feet away.

Peter. His fingers still twitched in death, and blood soaked through the gag in his mouth. It ran down his chin and dripped into his lap and was just beginning to pool on the floor under the chair.

((29))

HE heard footsteps, voices in the hall, and he stepped through the open window into the small yard behind the building. The night was dark but he could see enough to know that it was a typical New York tenement yard: a small oblong square fenced on three sides to keep the people of the opposite houses out. Nowhere to go, except over that fence—a formidable climb on short notice. Dulaney flattened himself against the building, watching for movement. But he was gone, as if he'd taken wings and flown over the rooftops.

That's what he did, he thought: went up the back stairs and over the roof.

He started up, and reached the rooftop a moment later. Nothing there. He pulled himself up and crossed from building to building until he came to the end of the row, and the fire escape that went down the front to the street.

He came this way, he thought, and that's when he decided to go back to the dead girl's apartment.

Down the fire escape to the second floor, then down the ladder to the street.

He turned north, up Second to Eighty-fifth. His mind still bristled with crimson violence and he walked with care, far from the curb, in the shadows of the buildings to his left. He stopped at the corner and took a breath, and he knew the memory of that crazy girl would be with him forever.

In another minute he had reached the apartment. He went in through the fire escape and the place was still, beyond quiet, just as they'd left it. Now he felt his first real wave of jitters. Now that it was over.

But of course nothing was over.

He looked at himself in her bathroom mirror. Looked down at her diaphragm, then up again, meeting his own eyes in her glass.

If it ended like this it wouldn't ever be over.

He came into the front room. Far away a siren wailed. In a while the cops would arrive. But it would take them some time to sort out who had been killed. Then they'd come over here and look at her stuff.

But would they ever solve this case? Would the cops care about a couple of dead Germans who were probably spies for the Nazis? Would it matter about the letters she had saved telling of a cousin's grief in Germany, or the newspaper accounts of Hoover's raids in Yorkville? They were Nazis and the cops would say good riddance to both of them.

There wasn't much to decide: he was going to take the letters. But when he sat at her desk and opened the drawers, they were empty.

He took a deep angry breath. "Son of a bitch."

Couldn't have missed him by more than a few minutes.

He slammed the drawers and jerked them open again, as if the papers could reappear like a magician's trick.

Then he noticed the pull-out writing board, flush against the right side of the desk. He pulled it out and found a single sheet of blank loose-leaf paper lying flat on the surface.

As if she'd started to write a note, then got interrupted.

And it wasn't quite blank. She had written one word, which made no sense. The word was *Whitemarsh*.

(((30)))

HE was able to get a train into Newark and south from there to Elizabeth. The train rocked through the Jersey suburbs and in a while he closed his eyes, as if he could push away the red horrors he had seen. But in the rosy darkness the girl's face came back to him, and he found himself staring at the country whipping past with no idea how long his eyes had been open or what he'd just seen. The train rolled through a cheery-looking township, and his thoughts turned back to the papers in the desk. He could almost feel the despair of George Schroeder, the nightmares leading up to his suicide. George had been menaced by someone named Maynard, a name burned into Dulaney's mind like Roosevelt's day of infamy.

He was somewhere on the outskirts of Elizabeth when he remembered the letter he had taken. He plucked the pages out of his back pocket. Again the opening paragraph gripped him as it had in the apartment. George had decided he wanted a record kept: some kind of document telling what had been done; something that would protect them because they both knew too much, they could never feel safe again, they must not make the mistake of thinking it was okay and they were all working for the same cause. They were *not* working for the same cause, never had been. *The only cause we must worry about now is ourselves, body and soul.*

A chilling sentiment, Dulaney thought. In the second short paragraph Schroeder had warned her to put his letters in a safe place. There would be more later, he promised, but she must be careful with what he wrote; its purpose was to save them, but if handled carelessly it might only lead them both to more danger.

And what had that crazy girl done with it? . . . Thrown it in a drawer and given it no more thought than she'd given Jack Dulaney's warning about a killer coming to get her.

But when he read the letter he was disappointed. The promise of that first paragraph dwindled and Schroeder seemed increasingly uncertain as he wrote his way into it. Schroeder knew this but he wasn't sure what to do about it. He was suddenly hesitant to name names, and he fell into the use of initials to identify people. This of course defeated his purpose, but a start was a start. Perhaps finishing and sending it to her would fortify his purpose and give him new resolve for what must come later. He slipped into narrative, as if he were writing not to the girl but to some unknown readership. And by the end of it at least one thing was clear. Dulaney knew what Kendall had done and why.

Much of it was easy to decipher if you knew the names. Kendall was K; Carnahan was C. But there were others who remained shrouded in murk. And some of the pieces weren't here. Dulaney remembered the last moment of George Schroeder's life and what had been said. They had gotten into Carnahan's apartment: they had taken his key and gone to his place and found some stuff. Enough, whatever it was, to set them on Dulaney's trail and trace him to Tropical Park. But by then he had moved on—where, they didn't know.

Hell, I didn't know my own self, Dulaney thought.

He had been at loose ends. Tom was gone in the navy, Holly was gone. Even in his mind Dulaney was drifting, as he drifted across the country.

It wasn't that difficult for them to find him. If he stayed with the horses they could follow his trail from Florida almost as if they'd had a map. Mix with the horsemen, ask their questions. Lacking anything definite, they could easily plot out where he must have gone. There were only so many racetracks in the United States with winter meets. The Fair Grounds in New Orleans (yes, he had been there, working for ten days before moving on). Hot Springs would be starting up but not until February. There would be short winter meets at Bowie, up in Maryland, and at Churchill Downs, in Kentucky. There was a bush league track in Phoenix, if he was truly on the move, and at some point it was suggested that he might even have gone to Tijuana for the racing at Agua Caliente. From there it wasn't far up the coast into California, where the fall season was just ending at Tanforan and the winter was beginning at Santa Anita.

George's absence from the station was explained away as a personal problem. His traveling partner was a man identified only as R, but this became clear almost at once. "That stinking Irishman," George had called him at one point; "Christ, how I hate that stinking Irishman." But he was relieved for a time when they were told to split up: George was to follow the southern route while the Irishman checked the racetracks in Maryland and Kentucky. All the work of a few days. *I picked up his trail in New Orleans,* George wrote. *I found him in Los Angeles.*

Now that they had him, what would they do with him? Whatever Carnahan had sent him, it had not caught up with him yet. *Otherwise we'd have heard by then.*

He's a rolling stone. He's probably careless about forwarding addresses. God knows where it is now.

They needed someone to get next to him. Someone American, of no particular nationality, someone he would never suspect. An actor who wouldn't ask questions if he was paid enough to do it.

At least, for a while, I was rid of R. Once we had Dulaney in our sights that hard Irish bastard drifted away and was gone for weeks. Fund-raising, he called it, raising money along the coast and in other western cities. Places he might not get to again if war was to break out and travel get difficult. I didn't see him again for more than four months.

There was only a single reference to the one who had sent them. He was called W.

((31))

HE got off the train at Elizabeth. The last train south had long gone and the schedule showed nothing more until 5 A.M. But he got lucky: found a cabbie in a stand near the station who for $20 was willing to turn off the meter and take him the thirty-five miles to Pinewood. He paid with the last of Kendall's money and most of what remained of this week's pay. They stopped at a gas station at the edge of town and he bought a five-gallon can and filled it with water from a pump behind the outhouse. Then he slumped in the backseat, discouraging the cabbie's attempts to talk, and the suburbs fell away and the big piney wilderness closed around them.

The town, when they arrived, was as black as the forest: still no sign of life as the cab pulled into the lot beyond the depot. He filled his radiator in the glare of the cab's headlights, then they went their separate ways and he was alone again.

The ride over to the coast wasn't bad: he could make it easy in thirty minutes at this time of night if his car held up. But he was tense as he headed east on the narrow state blacktop. He turned on the radio and a startling thing happened . . . Holly was on the air, as if he had leaped ahead four days to Saturday in one violent night. Her voice filled the car and the crowd cheered as the clarinet pushed the rhythm to a hot finish. Suddenly he knew he was listening to a recording. He heard Stoner sigh into the pot-down, then speak as the crowd noise faded.

"Man oh man, what a sound. Recorded four weeks ago this coming Saturday night. A great piece of popular music, a wonderful way to end the day."

Stoner took a long breath and let it tickle the microphone. It was a deliberate effect, done with the nostrils and a slight movement of his head, a thing Dulaney had heard him do with other artists he liked. Admire with a slender sound. Stoner was a master of dead air. He uses it all, Dulaney thought; he's the only guy we've got who dares to *think* on the air because he knows there's always something going on when the mike is open. You can almost see the wheels turning in his head: then, when he does speak, it's like he's gone into your own head, to think your thoughts. A sniff becomes a comment. If he moves his face you know it: if he scratches his cheek you can tell whether he needs a shave. Suddenly Dulaney loved radio, surrendered to it as Jordan Ten Eyck had already done. This is the most intimate medium that will ever be devised. It pulls people together, draws them into each other, makes them one.

Stoner spoke. "I sit in shame. What a fine natural talent she is, and I never knew it until tonight." He made a small sound in his throat, the quietest grunt to underscore his surprise. A man sitting across from him in the studio wouldn't have heard that, but the microphone caught it and took it to air, to be heard for hundreds of miles.

"I'm the one who makes these airchecks every Saturday night. Not that you care about that, but in this case it makes a point. How dense we can be sometimes. I've recorded that show for fifteen weeks, but this is the first time I've ever heard the lady sing. It's always been just a job to me, just volume levels on a meter. A close eye on the wax to make sure the cutting head's clear. In my mind she was just local talent. No big deal, so I never listened. Until tonight."

He took another breath and squeaked back in his chair. "Well, what can I say? Tonight you're listening to a very special *Scrapbook of Sound,* nothing at all like the stuff I usually do. For the past hour I've been playing some of the music that I've been putting on discs every Saturday night. It started out as a command performance—the boss made a gentle suggestion that it might be a good way to help us promote the big war bond show we're doing on Saturday. So consider yourself notified—Miss O'Hara will sing for us live, in a ninety-minute special that'll include music and poetry and an original drama that I promise you, people, will be worth your attention.

Meanwhile, let's listen to more of the pleasantest surprise these old ears have heard in a long, long time. Let's go back to the beginning. Let's reach all the way back to that very first broadcast, to the first song she ever sang on the air. Listen . . ."

The sound of the crowd came in, like the start of an earthquake.

"Listen," said Stoner over the rumble. "We've just stepped back to March seventh, and she's about to sing that good Helen Forrest number 'You're a Sweet Little Headache' . . ."

The quake deepened, a cheer went up, and there she was again, pulling Jack Dulaney through the midnight woods. To the east, to the sea, into the air. And such as it was, home.

He felt better now. The specter of death was somehow less cutting in her presence and the world was a better place. He wouldn't forget, but the raw edge would continue to retreat, and tomorrow he could face what had to be done with a cold eye.

The road dead-ended on the north-south highway and he pulled to the side and poured in the rest of his water. As he headed north the country became bright: the woods fell away, and the marshes broke the land apart, and the moon, floating over the tidal waterway, cast the sloughs in an almost surrealistic silver. Maybe that's what Whitemarsh meant. A place, a town, some district near here. He stopped the car for a moment and got out, and he stood looking over the white marsh to the glow in the east, where the town by the sea was.

But the dread of his room returned in a rush and he went instead to the station. The ghosts of Kendall and the girl had filled his car, and what he needed was the simple presence of another human being.

He let himself into the dark lobby and stopped at the desk. Someone was there, a pale figure in a shrouded corner just out of the night-light's reach. Hazel. He waved and said hello but she stepped away, back into the dark, and he heard the soft swish of the ladies' room door close behind her. He moved on through the double doors to the stairwell.

Upstairs, the music was loud in the air, and he followed it into the studio. Stoner's chair was empty, pushed back from the transcription that spun on the turntable. Holly's voice boomed from the speaker, but he moved on beyond it, into a dark hall that skirted the outer wall. Something fluttered a few feet away—some kind of opening or doorway that led outside—and as he came closer he saw a small balcony, recessed into the building in an L shape on the southwest corner. Stoner stood at the railing, staring over the dunes at the sea and listening to the music on a small speaker near the door.

"Hey, Gus."

"Hey, champ . . . what the hell are you doing here?"

"I don't know. Just restless."

"Me too."

"Must be a night for it. I just saw Hazel downstairs. She seemed pretty spooked about something."

"You probably spooked her. She's not supposed to be in here at night, Barnet warned her once or twice before."

"Does she make a habit of hanging out here?"

"She will if they let her. I've had her on my show a few times, to read some poetry or something from a woman's book. But she never wants to leave. She'll take over the show if I let her."

"I guess she's one of those people like me. Spooked by the night."

"She's a troubled lady. A remarkable talent, but she's not supposed to be here at night unless she checks with me first."

"That probably goes for me too."

"Yeah, technically, if you come in this late you've got to check with the man on the air. If you've got a key, you're probably okay."

"Maybe Hazel's got a key."

"Not a chance. The only people with keys are the ones who need 'em—the dawn patrol, management, and me."

"Then how does she get in here?"

"It's not hard. Just come in during the day, hide, and come out when everyone's gone. I'd better go down and see what the hell she's doing."

"Too late. I think she's gone."

He pointed out to the road, where a car sped away to the highway.

"I'll talk to her tomorrow. Don't say anything, just let me handle it. No sense getting her in trouble, she's got enough of her own."

He stepped out into the breeze and joined Stoner at the railing. From the balcony he got a good sense of the island at night. The view was panoramic, from the north bridge road to the lighthouse south, and west across the black marshes to the woods where Georgie Schroeder had killed himself. The lights of the coast guard flickered along the surf. "Lots of bungalow sailors out tonight," Jordan said.

"They're trying to make an impression on somebody. Some pompous beer belly from the big tepee in Washington is probably in town."

"Anyway," Jordan said. The thought trailed away. "I couldn't sleep. Thought maybe you'd like to have a beer."

"Sounds great but I gotta take a rain check. I'm coming down with some damn thing, and if I don't get some rest I won't be worth a damn to anyone. I'm learning I'm not twenty-one anymore."

Behind them the music had settled into a lively instrumental rideout. Stoner let it run, past the announcements toward the end of the program.

"This has been an interesting evening," Stoner said.

"I caught some of it. Heard your confession of . . . what would you call it?"

"Stupidity brought on by resentment."

Jordan laughed politely.

"I've been annoyed at having to aircheck this thing every Saturday night. It's a tense piece of work, a real pain in the ass. You feel like your job's on the line if you screw one up, that's how seriously Harford takes it. But I've got to agree with him now, it's worth it."

"She does have a voice," Jordan said.

"She'll go big time, there's no question about it. I've got it on good authority that some very important people were listening to us up in New York tonight. I'm talking about big names, champ, major attractions in the band business. Kidd told somebody and I picked it up from there."

"Did they say who?"

"The name I heard was Tommy Dorsey. It doesn't get much bigger than that. I think he'd be crazy not to hire her. That's where she belongs, with a real band, not this pack of beach bums. My money says she'll be gone from here in a week."

They went inside and down the hall. The sign-off was simple, quick and easy if you've done it a thousand times. Stoner sat in the slot between the two turntables, leaned forward, potted up his microphone, and faded the show to nothing.

"Miss Holly O'Hara," he said, and that was his closing.

"And now WHAR comes to the end of its broadcast day. Our studios are located at two-mile point, on Beachfront Boulevard, in Regina Beach, New Jersey. Our schedule resumes at sunrise with the Uncle Wally show. This is WHAR in Regina Beach. It's two o'clock, eastern wartime."

He watched as the second hand swept past the hour. "Our national anthem will be played by the Boston Symphony Orchestra."

The turntable started and a rousing anthem hit the air. Stoner hummed the melody, leaning back in the chair with his eyes half closed.

"You walking, or riding?"

"Walking, I think. My car's running hot. I'd better not push it."

"I'll drop you off."

Downstairs, he left a note for Maitland. *I know the timing's lousy but I've got personal business that can't be put off. Hope you can cover for me with Kidd. I'll try to get in late tomorrow and square things.*

Outside, he locked the door and they rode quietly into town.

"Sorry for the rain check, champ. Let's grab dinner later in the week."

And Jordan walked alone, feeling the horrors of the night closing in behind him.

There was a letter in his mailbox. What an irony. His money had arrived from South Carolina. A day late and a dollar short. But no . . . when he ripped open the envelope he saw that his balance was $400, almost to the penny. Another irony. Ober had deposited two checks to his account for magazine work he'd done in California. So he had enough to live on if Kidd should get nasty and force him to quit. He could live for months, if he lived that long.

Up in his room he rested, but sleep was elusive. His mind was on fire.

What do you do now?

What do you do, having seen what you've seen and gone where you've gone? He hadn't slept in almost twenty-four hours. Didn't know if he still had a job. He was a fugitive and now he had left that paper trail from South Carolina, so California could find him if California cared enough.

At the end of the hour none of that mattered. He had a killer to find and the two questions that had come out of Yorkville were his only starting points.

Who was Maynard? What was Whitemarsh?

In the bathroom at the end of the hall he took a hot shower and washed away the last faint trace of the dead girl's sweat. Then he slept.

(((**32**)))

HE slept till eleven, and twenty minutes later he was out on the street. He deposited his check, kept some cash, and stopped at a gas station just north of town. There he paid a fellow $5 to drive out to Harford and fix his radiator hose, a job the man promised would be done by two o'clock.

The *Regina Beachcomber* was located in a stone building that forty or fifty years ago had housed the jail. The office was in the front, with the print shop visible through an oblong window. No one was in the office, but through the glass he could see a man at work, moving back and forth between a press and composing table. A sign over the door said TAKE A LOAD OFF YOUR FEET, I'LL BE OUT WHEN I CAN, so he sat on a chair and waited.

Soon an old woman came in from the street. "I hope you're a paying customer," she said as she went behind the counter. "We're light on advertising right now, been that way all year long and I can't figure out why. With our stories on the Schroeder boy's death, you'd think we'd be jumping."

He came to the counter. "Sorry. I'm just a man with a mission."

"What does that mean? Is somebody suing us?"

"Not me. I'd just like to see your back issues. If they're open to the public."

She looked at him hard through thick spectacles. She was at least seventy, with curly white hair and a rosary hanging from her neck. "The back numbers aren't here anymore. Don't have room to store 'em, so we give 'em to the library. They were gonna have 'em all bound by years but they haven't done that yet. As far as I know they're still sittin' in the storeroom in boxes."

"Can they be seen there?"

"I doubt that, honey, they'd have to close the library down to take you over there. If you'd give me some help, maybe I could find something for you in the clips. Just what is it you're looking for?"

"About six years ago an actor disappeared from the radio station."

"March Flack. It's become one of our local legends." She went to a large black filing cabinet and pulled out an envelope bulging with clips. "This looks like a fat file but you won't find much new after the first year. We just rehash it every summer. People are fascinated by stuff like that, so it's always good for three columns under the fold."

The first story was dated mid-July 1936. Almost three weeks had passed since March Flack had disappeared and still he rated only two paragraphs on an inside page. The writing between the lines was clearer than the story: even the press had not taken it seriously at that point. Not until the end of the summer had the story reached page one, when the sheriff's theory was subjected to serious scrutiny. One by one the newspaperman had found and interviewed all the women March Flack had known in recent years. None seemed to be hiding anything. Readers would have to take the newspaperman's word for that, for the paper's policies in stories of sexual shenanigans was to protect the idents of women until a crime was shown to have been committed. The woman in Canada hadn't seen March in more than a month when he disappeared. At that point foul play had to be given serious consideration, but the sheriff's heels were entrenched in his usual pits of resistance. "Show me a body and I'll investigate it. Until then I've got to assume that Mr. Flack left here under his own steam. Especially under the circumstances."

The sheriff wouldn't elaborate on the circumstances but they were common knowledge by then. Mrs. Flack had been quite candid about it when the newspaperman had walked out to her beach house and asked the right questions. "We had an awful row that day. There was no use denying it, three dozen people at the pier saw me throw a glass of beer in his face." A third party at the table, the former actor Thomas Griffin, had then gotten into a shouting match with March, which had almost come to blows. "They had to be separated by one of our bouncers," said the bartender.

All essentially what Pauline had told him.

When the inevitable question came up, about Mr. Griffin as a possible suspect, the sheriff's long-suffering sigh seemed to hiss out of the newsprint. "A suspect in what? I keep saying this but you don't seem to get it. There is no evidence of a crime. And you can't say I didn't look."

He had searched the island from sternum to apex. He'd taken a large posse of men and combed Harford's woods across the way. He had searched with a dog and nothing had been found. And yes, Mr. Griffin had been interviewed by the sheriff, and no, he did not have a satisfactory account of his whereabouts that night, but people sometimes do retire early, and alone, and most of them are innocent. "And we still need a body, don't we?"

Mr. Griffin had refused to talk to the newspaper.

"Find what you want?"

"I don't know what I want. I'm new in town, I heard this yarn and I got curious. Disappearances have always fascinated me."

"Well, this is a good one. My guess is it'll never be solved. Not after all these years."

"You been around here long?"

"Only all my life, is all."

"You must know pretty much everybody."

"I didn't know you till you walked in that door. But I do tend to know the people who've been here awhile."

"You ever hear of anyone named Maynard?"

She turned the name over on her tongue. "Maynard . . . Maynard . . ." Shook her head. "Never been anybody named Maynard in this town, I'd stake my reputation on it."

"What about Whitemarsh?"

"You mean like a family name?"

"Could be that. Or a district. Maybe a township."

"I don't think so. Not around here."

Suddenly she said, "Maybe you got 'em backwards. There was a *town* called Maynard. Not a family. A town."

Jordan felt a prickly feeling at the edge of his scalp. "Do you know where it is?"

"Got your tenses wrong, honey. It ain't, not anymore. Hasn't been for years."

"What happened to it?"

"Burned to the ground. Everything in it lost to fire."

"When was that?"

"Oh golly, I was a young woman then. At least forty years ago. We did a story on it a year or two back. Wanna see it?"

She brought another envelope from the steel cabinet. This one was thin, with only the one clipping inside it.

THE STORY OF MAYNARD, he read. EXTINCT TOWNSHIP ON THE RAILROAD LINE FROM GOTHAM TO CAPE MAY.

There was a picture with a cutline. *Downtown Maynard in the 1880s.* It looked like a frontier outpost, with wooden buildings and muddy streets. A hotbed of gambling, a center of wild and woolly hell-raising in its day. The whorehouses were known from here to Philly—they had written this so cleverly, letting it be known without saying it in so many words—and there were fights every Saturday night. The town was entirely recreational, so to speak: hardly anyone lived there, and when it burned, on January 12, 1900, most people said good riddance. In a few years the forest had come back thicker than ever, and a new highway built in the twenties had skirted the area, and the old dirt road had begun growing over as well.

"Nobody goes there now," the old woman said. "But it's easy enough to find. There's still a sign on the railroad line, though the train doesn't stop there anymore."

This made his blood tingle. Something had happened in Maynard, and not forty years ago. Something recent, bad enough to give a man nightmares.

That's where I'll find Carnahan. And maybe March Flack as well.

He didn't want to go into the station, but the man was still working on his car when he arrived at two o'clock. He didn't want to be seen by anyone who might ask questions or slow him down. He had a couple of stops yet to make and by then it would be three o'clock, less than six hours of daylight left under the best of conditions. He sat in the car with both doors open, drumming his fingers on the steering wheel. He was impatient to get away, and he almost made it.

The repairman slammed his hood just as Becky walked around the corner of the building. On the path beside her was Holly.

"Jordan! My God, where've you been? Kidd's been asking about you all morning."

"Something came up. I left Maitland a note."

"But you need to be here. Surely you know that; we go on the air in just three days."

There was an awkward moment as she crouched in the door.

"I don't mean to sound like a mother hen, but we've got a lot riding on this show. We want it to be good. You remember Miss O'Hara . . ."

"Of course. How've you been?"

Holly nodded but said nothing. She knows something's happening, he thought. How could she not know?

Becky leaned into his line of vision. "Are you coming in now?"

"Not quite yet."

"What's wrong with you? Is there something I can do?"

"No. It's something I've got to do."

The repairman came to the driver's window. "I think that does you."

"Good. What do I owe you?"

"Your five covers it."

Becky hadn't moved. Holly's eyes hadn't left his face.

He shrugged. "I'm sorry. I've got to go."

He stopped at the hardware store and bought a shovel. Bought an axe and a gasoline lamp and some other things.

One more stop. He pulled in under a sign that said CAMERAS WATCHES FIREARMS JEWELRY. The south beach pawnshop.

Inside, he turned and looked back through the glass. A car had stopped out on the road and sat idling there.

He bought himself a gun, an old army .45 revolver, which came with its original holster and belt. Bought a box of shells, and as he paid the man he saw that she had turned in and parked beside his car.

He didn't try to hide anything: there wasn't much use in that. He came out, opened his door, and threw the gun on the seat.

They sat in their separate cars, a few feet apart with their windows down. Then her voice floated over the gap.

"What's going on, Jack? What's with the shovel? . . . What's with the gun?"

"I'm taking a little time off. Going camping. Clear my head."

She leaned toward him. The sun hit her face.

"You've found him, haven't you?"

He shook his head. "Not yet."

"But you know where he is."

"I know what I think. That's all I know."

"I know what I think too."

"Which is what?"

"Now they'll kill you too."

He shrugged and smiled. Said maybe they would, maybe they wouldn't.

"I'm coming with you, Jack. There's no way you can stop me."

"Hell," he said. "I wouldn't even try."

((**33**))

THEY had no plan. The sun had begun to settle in the west but this had no meaning. Time had stopped: there was no longer any day or night, there were no jobs urgent enough to draw them away, they had no duties except to this. A spiritual understanding had risen between them and there was no need to explain. She didn't ask how he'd learned what he'd learned and to him the mystery of her behavior had ceased to matter. Answers would come later.

He had stopped at the Pinewood depot, which was open at midafternoon, and asked directions from the ticket man. Eight miles straight back down the tracks, or if you wanted to go by car, five miles back to the old road trace and follow it in from there. "Good thing I've been saving my gas," he said.

He stopped at the general store but she had no interest in the bag of merchandise he had stashed in the backseat. She trembled briefly as they headed out on the road south but he made no effort to comfort her. They sat like strangers, separated by the full width of the front seat.

The cutoff was just about where he expected it, and they were swallowed whole by the forest, a vast timberland clogged with underbrush. The road was bad, with water-filled holes almost axle deep, in places little more than a trail. It would winnow down but then, as he nudged the car on into the trees, the branches would part and the trace appear again, and this kept happening until the branches would not move and the road choked off.

"I guess we walk now."

He had talked the shopkeeper out of a gunnysack to put his groceries in. It made a heavy bundle but he could carry it, hurled over his shoulder with the drawstring wrapped around his fist. She watched him strap on his gun but said nothing about it; only when he heaved the sack over his shoulder did she come to life. "What can I carry?" she said, and he gave her the axe. She asked what it was for and was satisfied with his simple answer: "In case we need it."

They struck out through the woods. The way remained dense but never impassable. There were paths left by hunters who had come and gone for years, and occasionally they came across traces of the road—short, clear stretches no worse than the road behind them. Here they made good time, until it vanished again in a snarl of saplings and underbrush. But there was always a path and he knew there would be.

It was getting on toward four o'clock by the clock in his head. The woods were pale but they still had five hours before the full night would catch them. He didn't have much hope of finding anything tonight, and meanwhile Kidd would be looking for him at the station and across town the same thing would be happening with her. The band would fret when show time came and there was no Holly to sing their songs. And what about tomorrow? Her absence would be noticed at the station as well, and people would put two and two together. Now we are linked, he thought. Like it or not, this will make our continued separation a needless gesture.

He guessed it was half a mile to the tracks and that was about right. Soon he got his first glimpse of the rails through leaves fluttering in the breeze. Still there was no talk: she followed him on the narrow path, keeping pace at a distance of twenty yards, and at this distance she followed him out of the woods and up the short incline to the roadbed of the New Jersey Railroad.

He turned south, walking just inside the rail, taking the crossties two at a time. She walked on the other side and the margin made a statement. *Don't talk to me, please, I couldn't bear it. Just give me these moments and this space to myself.* The funny thing was, he could say the same thing to her: that now, after weeks of longing to talk, the dark mission that had finally drawn them together had left him, for the moment, with nothing to say. He looked back over his shoulder. She was losing ground on the crossties, taking two steps to his one and watching carefully where she put her feet. Those shoes she wore were not for walking, and already her dress was torn at the hem and streaked with mud.

The tracks gave off a shimmery heat. The roadbed was long and straight and unpromising, stretching on for at least two miles without a turn. Surely they'd come to the old town site before then. Certainly the Schroeders had not come all this way with a prisoner or a dead man. Suddenly he had doubts, his first real bout of second-guessing. Then in the shimmer he saw the sign and his hunch came back with a rage of certainty.

He dabbed his eyes on his shirtsleeves, dreading what the next few hours or tomorrow might bring. In the distance the sign took on substance and shape. The letters began to form, M . . . A . . . Y . . . , and he looked back to find Holly far away but still coming.

He stepped over the rail and slid down the roadbed. Walked off into the woods and at once found the trace of the old road. It began to dawn on him now, the size of the job he'd taken on: how even a man who knew where a grave site was could miss it by being a few feet off in any direction. He put his bag on the ground and as a first step undertook a circumferential definition of the town on the west side of the tracks. He wasn't sure why he did this—even if Maynard meant what he now knew it meant, it was no sure thing that the grave was within its limits—but it gave him something to do until she arrived. He paced off the road and came back again, and she stood looking at the wilderness that surrounded them.

"Are we there?"

"I think so."

She hadn't questioned anything and didn't now. "Just give me a few minutes to rest in the shade. Then you can tell me what I can do and how we can get started."

He took a small roll of light canvas from his bag and spread it on the ground for her to lie on. She had a headache, which had begun on the long walk up the tracks, but he had aspirin and a soft drink in his bag. "You think of everything, Jack," she said, but he passed this off as the simple woodsmanship of a camper who had forgotten everything at least once in his life. She took the aspirin and he left her there, to continue his walk north along the trace.

He tried to imagine what the town had looked like sixty years ago, to see beyond that conglomeration of dots on a fading page of newsprint. He stopped and looked back, a sense of place came over him, and he could almost see that corridor through the trees by the traces that were left.

His first job was to walk it: north and south, then east and west, looking for oblong places, sinkholes that might have settled in six months, ridges of earth or uneven ground about the size of a man's body. Perhaps a break in the ground cover, a small patch that had grown back evenly or not at all, would tell him where to begin. He couldn't get careless and let impatience ruin it: had to walk over ground he had already covered, see with new eyes, not miss what he sought because he was too eager to find rather than see. His first pacings were in rows only a foot apart, up and down like a farmer behind a plow. An hour passed and the woods grew shadier. In another hour he had crossed the trace into continuous shadow and the going was slower. Now he needed to stop more often, get down on his knees and examine the darkening earth before moving on.

He carried a spiral notebook, marking possible sites on a crude little map. Nothing had grabbed him yet, but he'd come upon half a dozen places that had earned marks on his paper. These he'd revisit, probably tomorrow, if he found nothing better: do some digging and see what each of them held. He was well off the road in deep woods when he saw a little recess. He got down and dug his fingers into the earth and decided that this would be his main effort in the final two hours of the day.

He stripped off his shirt and went to work. Soon he had a hip-deep hole that quickly became impossible to see in its black bottom. But the work was discouraging: his shovel began hitting roots and other entanglements that had been in the ground for a long time. He thought he'd go on for a while longer and look at the evidence fresh in the morning. Then he heard something behind him and Holly was standing over him at the edge of the hole.

"God, I must've died. How long was I sleeping?"

"Oh, an hour or so." He stopped and rested on his shovel. "How's the headache?"

"I'm fine now." She leaned closer, her face a shadow now, her voice disembodied, coming at him from the trees. "Is this where he is?"

"I don't think so. It was worth looking at, but probably not."

"Let me shovel."

He shook his head. "Those shoes of yours wouldn't last five minutes. And if I can say so without tootin' my own horn, I was born to this labor."

"Then what can I do?"

"Go across the tracks and search the ground over there while there's still a little light. Look for anything that might be . . . you know."

"A grave," she said evenly.

She stood there for another moment as if she had something more to say but didn't know how to get at it. Then she looked at the sky, yellow over the trees. "We're gonna get rain." She smelled the air. "All my life I've been able to tell when rain's coming. It's a feeling in the air."

"I hope you're wrong this time."

"Yeah." She looked at the sky. "But I'm not."

Still she stood there. She said, "Jack, I . . . ," but when nothing else came he said, "Go on now. See what you can do while there's still a little light left." He watched her walk out toward the tracks, then went back to work. But soon he gave it up. He had hit a bed of clay, and there was no way anything would be buried under that.

The train passed, going north. They're late tonight, he thought. The clock in his head told him that this time last night he was already well on his way into town.

He carved out a campsite with his axe, deep enough in the woods that it couldn't be seen from the tracks. Then he built and lit a fire, broke out a fry pan and the half-dozen small pork chops that he'd had the storekeep pack in ice and wrap in butcher's paper. Soon he had supper going, with a can of beans simmering in the coals. The woods were dark, but if he looked across the way there was still a rosy light on the face of the forest. He took his flashlight and went to the edge and called her in.

She was nervous now and excessively polite. She praised his supper lavishly, touched by the trouble he had taken with the tin plates and the real forks and the real food. It was simple food, he said: it was the woods that gave it such out-of-this-world taste. In the quiet that followed he said, "We won't eat this well tomorrow night. If we're out here that long." Still nothing was said about their obligations. They sat cross-legged on opposite sides of the fire and occasionally their eyes met in the smoke.

"I wonder what they'll think," she said at last. "If we don't show up tomorrow. Or if we do."

"They'll have to seriously consider canceling that radio show."

"Or getting another singer." Abruptly she changed the subject. "I saw a snake, in the tall grass across the railroad."

"You'll have to be careful with those bare ankles."

"Are they poisonous?"

"I believe there are a couple that get up this far. Cottonmouths . . . timber rattlers. They're more common down south, but you'll see 'em occasionally right up into New England."

They seemed to want to talk about everything but the thing that had brought them here. Far away thunder rumbled. "That's the rain moving in," she said. "I told you we'd get it, the air's heavy with it."

He himself felt no such heaviness but he figured he'd better take her word. He fetched his canvas roll and walked out into the forest until he found a place for a lean-to, with a tie-up to two saplings and tall fat pines on either side. In fifteen minutes he had the canvas staked down and tied at the top, with a trench dug around it so the water would run off and not leak in from the bottom. He made her a soft bed of grass and leaves and gave her the gunnysack filled with pine needles for a pillow. He would sleep sitting up, propped against one of the pines about two feet away. "Just like the Waldorf," he said as the rain began.

She crawled inside. The darkness in the lean-to was infinite. He flicked his light to get his bearings and saw her stretched out on her side with her head propped up on her hand, watching him. "We should be fine here," he said, settling back against the tree. He turned off the light and was engulfed by the earth.

Her voice came out of nowhere. "How can you sleep like that?"

"I've been studying mind control. That's all it really is."

The rain hit the canvas in great fat drops, and soon he could hear the water running off into his little ditch. "Are you getting wet?" Her voice was everywhere in the black universe. He said, "No, I'm fine," and this was mostly true. A little water wouldn't bother him; he had slept in circumstances far worse than this, and he was tired, and tomorrow was going to be hard, and he hoped he had the strength of mind to put it all away for now and rest easy. He stretched out his legs with the flashlight at his side and the gun belt rolled up in his lap.

"Jack?"

He opened his eyes. Realized the silliness of that and closed them.

"I'm sorry," she said.

"Nothing to be sorry about."

"Do you want to talk about any of it?"

"We've got some things to talk about. But they've kept for a while, they'll keep a little longer."

The rain was steady. It was good sleeping weather but suddenly he knew that sleep would not come as easily as he'd hoped. He heard her stir on the bed and turn over.

"Do you really think he's here?"

"I don't know. I'm playing a hunch." But he couldn't leave it like that. "Yeah, I do," he said. "I think he's here."

"It's not going to be easy, finding him."

"It's hard to tell. We got such a late start today."

"The woods are thicker across the tracks. They grow right down to the road."

His eyes flicked open and he was wide awake. "What road?"

"There's a dirt road that comes in from the east."

"It's probably another one of the old streets."

"No, this is more than a trace. It goes way out, away from the tracks. I walked along it but I never found the end. I think it goes all the way to the sea."

He didn't say anything.

"Well, it goes somewhere. What else is out there?"

The town, he thought. The radio station, Harford's place. Old Tom Griffin's cottage not far from the white marsh district. All due east of here: a long ride on a bad country road, but some dirt roads will astonish you.

They were quiet now and in a while the rain passed. Her breathing was regular and deep. He rested but could not sleep. Always that road would appear and pull his mind back to full awareness. At last he knew he wouldn't sleep until he had seen it for himself, and he rolled out of the lean-to and followed his light down to the railroad and across to the other side. He found the road and followed it through the trees for a mile or more. It grew stronger as he went, leading him out of the woods at a little creek bed that opened into a long marshy slough. The clouds were breaking up and the world was silver, and the road went on.

((34))

HE opened his eyes after four hours' hard sleep. The world was dark but dawn was coming. The clock in his head never worked better than in deep sleep, a truth he had never understood. Day after day he would open his eyes and instantly know what the time was and how long he had slept.

He was lying on the mat in the lean-to and Holly lay sprawled across him with her arms around his shoulders. He had come in around one thirty and she'd been awake, insisting that they change places. "You sleep, I'll sit up awhile," she had said, but sometime in the night she had fallen asleep and here they were, locked together like old lovers, with his arms wrapped around her.

He shifted slightly and she turned over, releasing him. He pulled himself up and straddled her, swung his leg over, and got out in the predawn wood. The forest was like a medieval painting, drippy and gloomy with pockets of deep fog and, far out beyond the railroad, a rosy nimbus where the sun was struggling to break through. In the tent he heard her stir. "There's no rush," he said. "Just come when you're ready."

He walked out past the dampened remains of last night's fire, picked up his shovel, and headed across the way. He had a new hunch; the discovery of the road had given it to him, and now as he walked through the tall grass the hunch got suddenly stronger. It was too early yet for effective work: the fog was hanging on, getting thicker if anything, and choking off the sunrise. The woods were still locked in black shadow and he couldn't see much of the ground, but he walked until he reached what he thought was the edge of the old township.

When he turned he was looking straight up the tracks and the sign, MAYNARD, seemed to be floating in the soupy morning. But he could read the letters and that made it spookier as the hunch gripped him tighter.

This is where it happened, he thought. Not on the other side; over here, with George looking back up those tracks at that sign. He was a sensitive kid, that's why the word kept giving him nightmares.

Imagine the turmoil in a kid like that if he had to watch the killing of a man. Georgie surely would have turned away at the moment of death: turned from the horror of it and had the word MAYNARD burned into his mind by a gunshot. Then had to face the horror anyway and help with the burying, the body still warm, the blood still flowing. It was as good an idea as any and this was as good a place to start.

Holly arrived with their small bag of food. Nothing elaborate today, just canned goods from the store. She sat on a stump and gave him his choice and he said, "I'll take the peaches if you don't care." She cut the top out of the can and handed it to him, took the pears for herself, ate slowly, and waited for his thoughts on the new day. "This puts a little different slant on it," he said. "I think the sign plays into it; I'll tell you why later if that's how it turns out. For now let's just say that I'll start work down here, where I can look up that stretch of track and keep that sign in view."

The fog had thickened and the sign had an otherworld visage that he couldn't shake off. "You'd never know there was a town here," she said. "I wonder why they never built it back."

"They say it ran afoul of the good people. Too much gambling, drinking, fighting. This was the whorehouse district over here."

She laughed dryly. "God help us all when the good people get going."

He drank the juice from his can.

"It's funny," she said. "I haven't given a thought to my job or the guys in the band. Jud's going crazy by now."

"I don't think you need to worry about getting fired."

"What about you?"

He shrugged. "If they want to fire me, that's what they'll do."

"Does it matter? Do you really care?"

He didn't know how to answer that without getting into the need to explain. But he didn't want to lie, so he said,

"Yeah, it matters. For different reasons than you might think. Sometime I'll tell you maybe."

She kept looking at him in that curious way. He met her eyes and said, "I seem to've found something there that I didn't know I was looking for. Kinda like what you've found, if that makes any sense to you."

"Yeah, it does. It's probably too bad for both of us."

Dulaney picked up his shovel. "Well, this is nice but it ain't gettin' the work done." He moved off into the trees. Holly went the other way, north along the railroad tracks.

The rosy tinge had gone, leaving a gray pall over the woods. The fog was a nuisance: thick pockets of it drifted in from the east. Occasionally he could see across the glade at the east end of where the town had been, a hundred yards at its widest point. Once he saw Holly, like a fleeting specter in a ghost story, gone in a moment. He turned and came back across the town site toward the railroad, found the remains of a chimney and a trace beyond it. The trace might've been a street, maybe an alley behind one of the cribs, where the whores could stand and display their wares or gather for a smoke between customers. Dulaney stood still and in that moment he could almost see the guys milling around, hear the chatter of the dice, and smell the hard liquor. All of them dead now—the women and their pimps, the brawlers, the drinkers, the good people too—all dead and gone.

He went down a recess and up the other side, and the sign floated before him. There was nothing to the place and never had been, just a few wooden buildings on a piece of land no bigger than a postage stamp, but plenty big enough if you had to dig it up from one side to the other.

He found his first dig site, a small depression just into the trees, with the MAYNARD sign wafting in clear view up the tracks. Draped his shirt on a tree, and soon he was in his rhythm, arms and hips as relentless as a well-oiled machine. In half an hour he had an oblong pit, three by six, with piles of earth growing on both sides. It wasn't far to the grave digger's finish line: six feet under and still no break in the earth, no bed of clay or other change in texture, no discovery that might tell him something one way or another. Prudence told him to stop when his thighs caught a shower of breakaway earth. It would be easy to get in trouble here, have the walls come down and bury him. That's all she needs right now, he thought: to come back and find me dead under a cave-in.

A train passed, going south to Atlantic City. He stood behind a tree and watched it float along, the windows like a streak of light in the mist. The caboose flitted away and the fog sucked it up, and a moment later he started in again.

He was no longer fussy now that he had broken ground. If something caught his eye, he would dig it up and look. At eight o'clock he was again up to his knees in dirt. He could finally see the sun, a pale white ball floating out beyond the trees to the east. At midmorning, with three holes and half a dozen short digs behind him, he still had the hunch as strong as ever. He hadn't found the right piece of ground yet, but it was here, he could feel it. He hadn't seen Holly in more than an hour, but in a way he was relieved by her absence. With her standing watch he would feel a need to apologize, to be timid with strokes he now took at a rugged, fierce, white-hot pace. As if he'd hit the old man. As if the old man would feel it.

The clearing of the fog came suddenly, and within fifteen minutes, at about ten o'clock, the day went from soupy gray to a brilliant hot yellow. On and on he went, gaining strength as he always did in the face of a daunting physical battle. Soon, if Holly didn't return and break his rhythm, he would slip into that state of automatic reflex where the mind seemed to separate and steel the body against almost any punishment in pursuit of a goal. Ten minutes later he was lost in it, and he felt nothing after that, he shoveled tirelessly. The next time he looked at the sky, the sun was at noonday and he realized that Holly had been gone too long. He gave her one sharp shout but only the birds called back.

He threw his shovel down into the dirt, picked up his gun belt, and walked north along the railroad. He felt uneasy, the same prickly sensation he'd felt two nights ago standing alone on the platform at Pinewood. He didn't call out again, just headed off into the woods where he'd last seen her. He reached a wall of old growth, so thick she couldn't possibly have gone there, and pushed on north. Even after forty years he could see where the fire had gone. Brakes appeared in the old growth, and these had come back first as meadows and later as new growth, which had all but filled the open spaces with smaller, younger trees. He walked up the length of these pine brakes until the old forest closed him off again; then he'd skirt the edge of it and work his way back to the west, all the way to the railroad, where the zigzag process would begin again. The way was slow and tedious and the sun was over the top of the sky when he found her.

She was sitting on the ground in deep forest, very still, as if waiting for someone to come wake her. As he approached, her head turned slightly in his direction but she didn't look. She trembled and her face was ashen, and her eyes filled with tears when he came around and squatted before her.

He knew what the matter was. She had found her father.

She looked off into the glade and he reached out and squeezed her shoulder. He walked away and there in the glade was the grave site. He had no doubt as he kneeled and ran his fingers around it, just as she had known when she'd turned over the camouflaging bed of pine needles and exposed the slightly sunken trace. Dulaney got up and looked back through the forest and up the tracks. The word MAYNARD filled his vision.

He had had the right idea, he'd just picked the wrong side of town to start on.

After a while he went back to her and squatted in the dirt at her feet. Her face broke his heart: he had never seen such raw hurt in someone he loved, as if everything rotten that had ever happened to her had come to roost at once. Until now she'd been fooling herself: still half believing he'd be wrong and she could cling to that faint hope that the old man was alive. Now she'd have to watch while he was dug up and examined, and Dulaney didn't know what he could do for her. That was the worst part, he had no idea how to start trying to help her. He wanted to crush her against him and hug the pain out of her but

she invited no touch, encouraged no words, asked for no show
of strength to help her hang on to her own. He asked, "Would
you like me to leave you alone for a while?" and she gestured yes
and he rose from the dirt and moved away. "I'll be up where we
started."

There was no talk yet of digging up the grave and there'd
be none until she was ready. To keep himself busy he started
covering up his holes. An hour passed before she came to find
him. He asked if he could help her but she only shook her
head. She sat on the ground at the head of the hole, as close as
she could get without falling in, and watched him work. He
tapped in the earth and covered it with dead flora, and then,
when he was satisfied that he'd left no trace of a dig, he
moved on to the next hole.

At once she moved with him, sitting close on the ground
in that same meditative way, watching without looking. She
moved whenever he did, as if suddenly she didn't trust letting
him out of her sight. Right now I'm all she's got, he thought.
Maybe she's got a big-time career ahead of her, maybe she'll
meet a thousand people and marry one of them and have his
children, but right now, at this moment, I'm all she's got.
Everyone else from the old days is dead.

((**35**))

HE dug up the old man an hour later. An ordeal with her sitting close, watching every plunge of the shovel and every
heave of the earth.

There was no getting her to leave. He had tried that and
finally left her alone. She sat so still, moving only her eyes,
and he worked with care, intimidated as he knew he'd be by
her presence. It was a deep hole, a discouragement to preda-
tors, but his leisurely pace continued. It gave him time to
think, but what now arose in his mind was a whole new set of

problems with no easy answers. There was only one clear fact: he himself could not be tied to any official discovery of the body. That would lead only to jail.

He hit something solid, and as he scraped around it, it became a sheet of plywood. It took a while to dig that out, and the earth beneath it was rich and black, cool to the touch. That might mean anything from total decomposition to little at all. It was possible, he thought with a shiver, that the body would still be whole, the flesh intact, the gore still in evidence. He leaned on his shovel and spoke to her. "Why don't you go back to camp and let me finish here? I'll come tell you what I find." But she wouldn't go, and a few minutes later he found Carnahan's hat.

It appeared whole under a shovelful of earth. He picked it out and knocked off the dirt against his leg. He could see what had happened, how the hat had been overlooked until the covering up was under way, then tossed in on top. Holly said, "Give me that, please," and her hand quivered as she took it and her eyes filled with tears. God damn this, Dulaney thought: I'd give a thousand dollars and work all year to get it if she weren't here now. She looked in his face and tried to smile, a last small attempt to be brave, but it was doomed and she crushed the hat between her breasts and cried silently into the felt.

In what seemed like no time he had reached the body. It was wrapped tightly in canvas with the folds tucked under at each end. He handled it with care, working his shovel around the edges to free it from the earth without damage. When this was done he took it in his arms and hoisted it out of the hole, laying it gently on the ground. He motioned her to sit still: then he climbed out of the grave and carried it out to a flat place in the grass. There he unrolled the canvas and took his look.

The first thing he saw was the violence. Shot in the back of the head, like Peter: the whole forehead blown away by the exit wound. But the flesh had held. It was pale and leather-like, and Dulaney could still recognize Carnahan's face.

He looked at her and nodded. She got to her feet and came around the hole but he stood before her and blocked her way.

"You don't need to look."

"Yeah, I do."

"It's pretty bad. Take my word for it. You can trust me."

"I know I can, Jack. But I still need to look."

He moved away. Afterward she came to him and said, "You can put him back now." She dropped the hat near the grave and walked out of the trees, across the tracks, and up to the campsite.

She had broken down the little lean-to when he got back to camp; she had rolled up the tarp and put everything back in the gunnysack. Something about her had changed: something that had always been there, even in times of her greatest mystery, seemed gone away now. As if part of her had died with the old man, he thought.

He guessed the time at four o'clock. They had been here twenty-four hours, and it had aspects of both an eternity and an instant. He got out his canteen and put an arm over her shoulder.

"Oh, Jack, don't hug me. If you do I'll just break down again."

But he held her tight with the smells of the earth and sweat all around them, and after a while they sat in the shade and he gave her a drink from his flask. It took her breath away.

"Now sip a little. It's strong but you'll get used to it."

She sipped and sipped again. She passed him the flask and he drank a mouthful and passed it back.

"Oh God," she said, drinking. "Oh Christ, what am I gonna do?"

"I don't think you need to decide that now."

But of course she did. "We'll have to leave him here," she said. "I can't have them get their hands on him, I don't trust any of them. It's better to leave him, so they don't know that we know."

He didn't say what he was thinking: that leaving him here had risks of its own. Someone could come back and dig him up, move him where he'd never be found, and then where would they be?

But she had decided. "We'll leave him. And tell no one we know."

So he went back and buried the body. Put in the hat, then the plywood, covered it tight, and scattered the brown pine needles across it.

At seven o'clock they made the trek back up the tracks. The car looked undisturbed where they had left it yesterday, and he found a place to turn around for the bumpy ride out of the woods. Once she said, "I wonder if I've done the right thing." Dulaney nodded in understanding rather than encouragement. "Everything changes if you bring the law into it now," he said. She sniffed. "But would anything get resolved? I can't trust any of them. Harford runs everything."

At the road he turned on his headlights and started back to Pinewood.

"We've got other things to decide," he said as they reached the cutoff. "Everything's different now."

"Yes it is. We'll have to talk, but not now."

"I'm not going to leave you alone tonight."

"I won't be alone. I'm going to work."

"You've got to be kidding."

"I need to go in. For any number of reasons, not the least of which is my own sanity. The show must go on, Jack—how would it look if I missed two nights in a row?" She touched his cheek, then leaned over and kissed him on the corner of his mouth.

"Can I come watch?"

"Why not? What difference does it make now, right?"

"And afterward I'll meet you on the beach."

"All right. I can't promise when."

"It doesn't matter when. I'll be down below the pier, whenever you get there."

They headed up through the white marsh district, then east on the final run to the beach.

"He was a great man, Jack. But of course, you know that. Did you know about his women?"

He shook his head.

"Don't lie to me."

"I saw him with a woman once, back in Brooklyn. That's all."

"I never saw him with anyone. But I always knew they were there. When I'd come visit, there were signs that he had a woman in his life. I never said anything, didn't want to embarrass him. But I knew he didn't have an easy time with my mother, and now I wish I'd said something just to make him easier with it. Don't worry about it, Dad. Be happy. Life is short. Little did I know then how short it was."

He pulled into the lot where they had left her car. She got out and looked back through the window. "Don't trust anyone, Jack," she said. Then she was gone.

((36))

A SUDDEN splash of beach neon brought him back to reality: the festival had come, with barricades and noise, music and dancing and cookouts in the streets, and people swarming by the hundreds. The crowd had doubled in just two days and even now it seemed to swell before his eyes. Cars were banned from downtown until Monday and he had to park far away and walk in to his rooming house. It was sometime after nine when he got home.

In the bathroom at the end of the hall he got his shower and shave, and was there only long enough to dress.

The streets were full of hot raw energy as he headed back across town. He had a sense of more people accumulating unseen, growing like potted plants somewhere beyond his ability to make them out but ready to be turned loose upon this other mob, which had already outgrown its space. This is how the world really ends, he thought: not in a takeover by tyrants but with mobs of overpopulated animals shoving and clawing for the last inch of breathing room. He came past two sailors fighting in a circle of cheering women; then, at the newsstand, a headline from yesterday's *Daily News* caught his eye. DEATH IN YORKVILLE, it said. NAZI SYMPATHIZERS MURDERED IN HOTEL ROOM. Pictures of Peter and the girl in happier times. Quotes from Hoover, alleging their ties to the bund. "We've been keeping an eye on them for some time," Hoover was said to have said. But he refused to speculate on why they had been killed.

Dulaney reached Chicago Avenue in a swarming whirlpool of people. The clubs had all emptied into the street and the bands were out, blaring at one another from opposite sidewalks. A makeshift stage had been set up across the end of the block and the bands moved toward it, fighting their way to the high ground. He didn't see Holly yet but her boys were there, wailing away under the neon Persian carpet rider. People were packed too tight to move. They couldn't dance with anyone so they danced with everyone, a comical up-and-down jump that had strangers holding hands and beer sloshing over till there wasn't a dry shirt on the block.

Slowly he was able to wedge his way down the sidewalk to the dark place at the edge of the stage. He squirmed around it and found himself at the end of a short backstage platform, lit up by moonlight where the street dead-ended in the dunes. Holly stood a few feet away, staring off into space. He didn't move and she seemed frozen in time until her name was called from out front, almost a full minute later. She swished past the edge of the stage and her eyes met Dulaney's for half a heartbeat as her momentum carried her through the gap to the cheering throng.

He stood listening to her sing. In a while he climbed up on the back platform and looked out through the makeshift panels to where she stood at the microphone. She was outlined in a thin blaze of smoky light while gray faces looked down from rooftops and upper-floor windows. She sang half a dozen songs, one after another; then she moved out of the light and the crowd cheered wildly as another singer and another band struck up at the far end.

Dulaney backed up and eased to the side so he could stay in the dark and still see partway down the stage. She was standing about twenty feet away, talking to people in the audience, touching every hand that reached up to her. She looked for all the world like a poised young woman who had never had a heartache, who had never known a loss, or suffered a real brush with tragedy.

At the end of the stage she turned and started back across. Only then, with the crowd breaking up and moving away, did her eyes blink shut and a deep strain of weariness come suddenly upon her. She left the stage and was escorted into the club, and the people followed her in until the doorman began turning them away.

He came around the stage, and in the sea of faces crossing and moving away, he saw one he knew. Kidd.

"Hello, Mr. Ten Eyck. I thought I might find you here."

"Why is that?" he asked. But he already knew the answer.

"Word spreads fast. We heard the singer was back. Since you dropped out of sight at the same time, it was a logical guess."

Kidd came toward him. "Let's us take a little walk."

They went into the dunes, down a path toward the beach.

"So," Kidd said. "May I ask where you've been?"

"I had some business to do. An emergency came up."

"An emergency involving Miss O'Hara?"

"I didn't say that."

"Then what? Do you have any answers for me about why you've been gone for two days?"

"It's nothing I can talk about. It's a personal problem."

Suddenly Kidd was angry. "Goddammit, you listen to me. Do you know how important this is? We've got a very complicated broadcast staring us in the face and you pull a Judge Crater on us. What am I supposed to do about that?"

Jordan said nothing.

"I can't have you wandering off like that," Kidd said. "It doesn't look good, for one thing . . . let alone the fact that we needed you. It's just not right; it gives the staff the wrong idea about how the place is run. People shouldn't assume they can just come and go when they want to."

"I don't assume that. This was something I couldn't help."

"Then tell me it won't happen again."

"I hope it won't. I'm sorry I can't do any better than that."

Kidd rolled his eyes. "Do you know what I would do if any of the others pulled something like that? I'd fire them on the spot if they gave me such a half-assed answer. But you've got a gift, a talent for radio that'll take you anywhere you want to go. I know it when I see it because I've seen it so damned seldom that I can count on my fingers the number of people who have affected me that way. I read your stuff and I think, Where the hell has this guy been? Your third colored show is great, it's inspired. You're able to give these things the breath of life. And this is what drives us, Mr. Harford and me, this is what we want our radio station to be. Are you listening to me?"

"Yessir."

"Let me tell you where it can lead, then you decide. Because I *will* fire you, Ten Eyck, I don't care how good you are, if you disrupt my station. A year from now you could be making more money than you ever saw. Directing your own shows. Writing your own ticket. Or you can throw it all away."

"I don't want to do that."

"Good. I've got some news that ought to get your head back on straight. One of our salesmen sold your show yesterday. You're getting a sponsor, starting in August; a colored newspaper in New York is going to carry it for thirteen weeks. We're moving it to a prime spot, Fridays at eight. It'll cause a stink there and get people talking, which is just what we want. So, what've you got to say?"

"I don't know what to say. That's wonderful, fantastic. Does the cast know?"

"How could I tell the cast? This time last night I had no idea if you were ever coming back."

"I'm sorry. And I am excited. I'm damned thrilled at this."

"You should be all those things. For starters it means full-scale rates for everybody. It means you're going places, Jordan. The road ahead is bright. Don't screw it up."

(((37)))

It was three o'clock in the morning and he had been standing under the pier for two hours. For the fourth time the big band was playing that musical game, the Blackout Waltz. He could hear it all as it came down through the floorboards and washed in on the tide from a quarter mile away. The announcers called for the lights to go out and the partners to change, and there was a rumble and a shuffle as a hundred couples made the switch. The music flowed back at him over the water and the crowd was humming. It was exactly then, in the middle of the fourth Blackout Waltz, when he looked wearily to the south and saw her coming.

She was still a hundred yards away but there wasn't a doubt who she was: a lonely-looking figure in an evening dress, emerging from a beach still crowded with people. The moon was bright and as she came toward him he could see that her hair had come undone and one of her straps had fallen down around her arm. She was walking barefoot, carrying her shoes and swinging them gently in time with her hips. She dropped the shoes and peered into the gloom under the pier.

"Jack?"

"Hi."

She didn't seem to see him, but she covered the last few yards in a rush and collided into him. Now he saw what the matter was: she'd been blinded by tears. She gripped his shirt with a soft cry of despair and he wrapped her in his arms and drew her back into the dark. An explosion of lust broke over him, a longing so powerful it reduced to nothing the hundreds of times he thought he'd felt it. All the women in his life came together in his mind and were gone in a flash. Never again would there be such a feeling, never could there be another like this one.

His sense of time was all shot. The next thing he knew the pier was closing, the band was playing "Goodnight, Sweetheart," and the crowd was tramping out. The footsteps sounded like thunder on the planks over their heads. Laughter rippled up and down the beach and flashlights danced around them, but no one came into the dark where they stood. In a while she stopped shivering and put her hands inside his shirt. She said his name and he squeezed her shoulders, a loving, wordless reply.

"You're such a dear friend," she said. "You don't deserve the grief I'm going to bring you."

"Don't ask me to leave. That's the one thing I can't do."

"That's not what I meant. No, I'm all done trying to get you out of here. I'd have better luck getting Hitler out of France."

"Then what are we talking about?"

"It's me, I've changed, I'm not the same girl you knew. Even then I was having trouble believing in things like love and justice. Now I truly know better. Love does nothing but make you vulnerable, and I don't ever want to be vulnerable like that, ever again. Once I'm gone from here, I don't intend to be."

"Then what will you do?"

"Live for myself and don't be *un*happy. That's what I want now."

She shushed him. "Listen to me, you need to hear this. I know you came here to help me but what you've really done is make me vulnerable again. That means another loss coming, somewhere ahead."

"It doesn't have to be that way."

"It always is. Why should this be any different?"

Before he could answer, she said, "I've been thinking about this for weeks. About what to do with you. Today, coming back on the railroad tracks, I finally figured it out."

She touched his face. "The loss is already there," she said. "It just hasn't happened yet. Once I figured that out, and accepted it, the rest was easy."

Her fingers touched his neck. "I've got one more fire to walk through," she said. "I even know what I'm going to do if they kill you."

She moved away. "I want you to promise me something."

"If I can."

"I mean this, Jack. Otherwise keep your distance."

"Do I get to hear the promise before I make it?"

"I think you know it. When this is over I'm going some-where. Maybe to have a career in New York, I don't know, I haven't decided yet. But wherever it is I'm going alone, I'm going to start my life from scratch, and I'm not going to let anyone touch me, ever again. So that's the deal. Don't follow me, don't try to change my mind, just let me go."

"You might feel different then."

"Goddammit, Jack, I'm telling you *now* that's what I want. And I don't want to go through this again."

"All right. If that's the promise you need, you've got it."

"Good." She came to him again. He felt her hands inside his shirt, drawing him close. Then she pushed him away, then pulled him as if she had split into warring halves. On it went, like a mating dance between two animals. Suddenly she stopped and kissed him, went up on her toes, threw her arms around his neck, and crushed her mouth against his. A long mindless moment passed. His hand had come up to her breast and for that moment she let it rest there: then she backed away, breathless, and the dance went on until she could speak again. But all she could say was his name, just "Jack, oh Jack, oh Jack," in a rhythmic little singsong. Her head lolled over and her breath was hot in his ear, her cheek brushed softly against his face, her mouth touched his, she bit his lip. "Jack," she said, going up on her toes to kiss him again.

She stepped back and was suddenly gone. A moment later he saw her shadow, thirty yards away at the edge of the pil-ings. She was standing still, looking north up the beach, and he could only imagine the turmoil inside her. She moved and he lost her for a minute, then he sensed her there in front of him.

"I do love you," she said. "But I'm no good for anyone anymore."

"I don't believe that."

She went on as if she hadn't heard him. "Too many people I loved are dead. After a while you can't help thinking maybe it's your fault. Some of us are just . . . you know . . . unlucky. We bring bad luck to everyone who loves us. That's why I'm going to hold you to your promise."

She took a deep breath. "I don't know what happened to us. Somewhere back there we just went past each other. The stars weren't right, the world went crazy, God knows what happened. But we missed our chance and the world moved on. Everyone I loved died, everyone but you. And after a while I started thinking it was good you were gone. Away from my evil eye."

She pushed him and pulled him and started the dance again, their own little Blackout Waltz. "It's a damned sorry mess I've brought you, Jack. A past full of trouble, a miserable present, no future at all."

She pushed him away and pulled him back. When she kissed him again her hunger was fierce. She buried her face in his shoulder, said his name, tried to pull away. But her hands wouldn't let him go.

"I don't know what to do." Suddenly she was agitated. "I don't know what to do. I thought I knew and now look at me. I'm going to treat you so badly, and I don't know what to do."

"Don't think about it. Think about how you're going to get through this time and how I can help you."

"I don't know . . . I don't know . . ."

"Whatever you need, that's what I'll be."

She kissed his hands. Her own were trembling. She clutched his shirt and said, "What I seem to need most right now is for you to love me."

He heard a rustling, her dress coming up, and he thought his heart would knock him down. His mind groped with a last rational truth. He didn't bring anything, he'd never been one of those rubber-in-the-wallet boys, he'd always had to scrounge one at the last moment, and now, God damn his stupidity, where the hell could he go at four thirty in the morning?

"I don't care," she said. "I don't care what happens."

She went down on the sand and groped at his belt, fumbled at his buttons, got him free, pulled him down, and in the same quick movement he was inside her. Her face jerked tight against his ear and her voice was a crooning whisper—"Oh Jack, oh Jack, oh Jack"—in perfect time with his heartbeat. In the heat it began to fade until it was gone with his heart, somewhere far beyond his senses. Her legs locked around him and he thought, Jesus Christ, there is a God, and every drop of his life gushed into her. Ages later he heard her voice, still crooning, for it had never stopped, calling him back in the same loving rhythm.

She caressed his face and called his name and held him tight between her hips, rocking slightly where they were joined.

"Here we are," she said. "Here we are."

Here we are, he thought. Together at last.

HOLLY

HOLLY said:

This is how I met Harford. This is why I did what I did, and why I was so cold to you when I wanted to be just the opposite.

It began with that postcard sealed in an envelope. So strange that her dad would do that. A penny postcard would go on its own, but put it in an envelope and they'd charge you three cents to deliver it. She recognized the handwriting, and the shape of the card could be felt under the envelope. It promised secrets, something written for her eyes only. Alarming, like getting a telegram at midnight.

In the summer of 1941 he had been working at Bethlehem Steel. But a friend at the plant had given him a tip: a fellow from Easy Street needed a good workingman in the old hometown, a little beach burg down the coast in Jersey. I'd take it myself, said Carnahan's friend. But you know how it is. You can't go home again.

The job would be mostly maintenance to begin, but his friend had heard rumors. Stuff that only a local knows. There was going to be a lot of growth. The man, Loren Harford, had an estate of several hundred acres, and there was a radio station on the beach and an office building at the edge of town, and the grounds surrounding both radio properties. There wasn't much danger he'd run out of work.

Harford wanted a jack-of-all-trades and Carnahan was certainly that. He was at home with every tool, he could paint, landscape, and build from scratch. He was a good self-taught plumber and a good enough electrician to put in a fixture or wire a room. He could fix broken windows, take a power mower apart, repair a car. He was a fixer who had learned much in his years on the road, and it wouldn't be long before he'd acquire a nickname. Soon they'd be calling him the Magician.

He interviewed with Harford and got the job. *It's important to remember that,* Holly said. In one of his first cards from Jersey,

Carnahan had talked of his meeting with Harford. He got the job and seemed happy in it: contented with his life for the first time since he'd left home in 1932. Then came the postcard in the envelope, and nothing was the same after that.

> *Holly honey—*
>   *I wonder if it would be possible for you to put me in touch with Jack? I don't want to open old wounds but I'd give a lot right now for a short powwow. You know how I always admired his judgment.*
>   *If he can't come here I'd be willing to spend a good piece of my week's pay on a phone call. I've got his old address but I'm not sure if he's still there.*

Now she saw that he had written on both sides of the card. His writing covered the space for the address, meaning what? . . . that he never intended to mail it uncovered. She read the message on the face.

> *This is nothing to worry about. It's just that something about Harford bothers me suddenly and I need to figure it out. Jack would say I'm being foolish and that's probably all I need, the old voice of reason. Anyway, I was thinking about him tonight, wondering if he's still at the S.C. address. Don't fret over this—if you don't know, I'll figure it out.*

He had signed it, as always, *Old Me.*

There was a postscript in the margin, the words packed tight in an effort to convince. Unconvincing, of course. This was what haunted her.

> *I'll write you a better card next time. Why don't you burn this one in the fireplace? Promise me you will. And don't worry, this is really nothing. But if you know where Jack is, reply by letter, not open postcard. I'd rather people didn't know my business.*
>   *Love you, honey. Damned glad I'm your daddy.*

He had probably been in a hurry when he'd written it. If he had reread it he'd know how worried it sounded, and he'd never have sent it.

It was so unlike him that she immediately called the bus lines and asked about fares to New Jersey. *All that afternoon I tried to reach you,* she said. *All I could be sure of was that you weren't in Carolina.*

She would go to Jersey herself. But in the morning this plan seemed foolish. She would wait till Monday and the next postcard. If he didn't seem better by then, she would go to him at once.

No card came on Monday.

You've got to understand how he was about that. He was like clockwork with that penny postcard. Even after Mama died, he stuck to the ritual of the penny postcard. If anything it was more important, now that there were just the two of us.

She couldn't remember a single week since October 1932 when he had failed to write something. His postcards had formed a long continuous letter of his life on the road. He packed the tiny panels with news and he tried to be upbeat. But if life was hard he said so, told them why he had no money to send, and that he was moving on looking for something better.

If a card didn't come on Monday, it meant only that the mails were slow. Often Tuesday was a dead mail day, but by Wednesday at the latest her card would arrive.

On Tuesday morning the sunshine warmed her spirits. But no card came on Wednesday. She left that night, November 19, in bad weather.

Regina Beach, November 20. Arrived after an all-night, all-day train-and-bus ride across Pennsylvania and Jersey. The weather stayed miserable, wet and cold to match her mood. The night came early, without a hint of sunset. It was the off season: the town had folded its tents and rolled up its awnings by six o'clock, and an hour later the streets were deserted.

There were obvious places to go, people to ask. She knew the address by heart, a rooming house downtown. What a relief it would be to go there and find him, put fear to rest, and learn that all was well. They would eat supper together tonight and laugh over her sudden attack of cold feet.

But she felt a harbinger in the air as she came into the foyer. There was no name in the slot for room 214 and this rattled her. Still no reason for real alarm—there were other blank mail slots, and this was the off season after all. But why would 214 be blank when she knew for a fact that he'd been living here and getting mail since the end of August?

Upstairs, no one answered her knock. Downstairs, she could hear noise in the manager's room. When he didn't come at once she kicked at the door and battered it with her fist.

The door jerked open: a rat-faced man in his forties, not sure whether he should be angry or alarmed. "Jesus Christ, lady, where the hell's the fire? You trying to break that door down?"

She was combative and tense, but reason came over her and she forced a smile. "I'm sorry . . . I'm sorry, I was looking for my dad in two fourteen."

The man melted, a pushover for a pretty face. Looked over his shoulder at his own room, which she could see was a pigsty.

"My dad's name is Carnahan."

"Sure, I know him. He's gone. Left about a week ago."

"What do you mean, left?"

"Just put a note under my door. Said he won't be back, I should go ahead and rent the place."

The nagging fear turned suddenly cold and she shivered under his eyes. "Did you do that? . . . Did you rent it?"

"Not yet. I got other places to rent."

"Did he owe you money when he left?"

He took too long to think that over and lost what chance he might have had to lie. "Actually, he left with two weeks yet on his month's rent. That's why I haven't tried to rent it."

"Have you done anything to his room yet? Changed the bed . . . ?"

He laughed. "Lady, this ain't the Ritz. I ain't even been in there yet."

"Do you think I could look at it?"

He hesitated. "You're sure you're his daughter?"

She showed him a driver's license in her name. A picture of the two of them together. He went to get the key.

Alone upstairs, she found a dark room with a window looking down on a rain-slicked street. She turned on the light. It looked like any room of a workingman's means, empty and stark, offering nothing of the countless people who had lived there.

Empty closet. Nothing in the bathroom. The view was north, and far away she could see the flashing red light of Harford's radio station.

She sat near the radiator and turned the squeaky valve. Soon a heavenly ripple of hot air came up, but it took a long time to warm her.

Her eyes moved around the room. Speak to me, Daddy.

That's when she first thought the unthinkable.

He's dead.

Now when she knocked the rat-faced man came at once. He had combed his hair and changed his shirt, picked up some stuff in the room behind him. Now she could come in.

He offered coffee. She said, "Oh God, yes, thank you," and was surprised when it was good, rich and black the way she liked it.

"So what do you think?" he said. "Gonna be in town awhile?"

"Yeah. I think awhile." Her voice sounded numb in her ears.

"You could stay here. In his room, I mean. The rent's already paid."

"Thank you. You're very kind."

She finished her coffee, then remembered what she wanted to ask. "Do you still have that note he left?"

He didn't have to search for it. "You can keep it."

Upstairs, she locked the door and sat on the bed. Opened the note and looked at the handwriting.

It wasn't her father's. Jesus, it wasn't even close.

I had a dream once, she said. All the people I knew and loved were dead. It was a child's worst nightmare. Then I lived to see it come true.

My sister died, but you know about that. She was ten, I was fif-teen. I was a good strong swimmer and I was supposed to be watching her. But I got distracted and just that quick she was gone.

You asked about my other friend who died. His name was Emmett Huff. We grew up together. He lived next door, our bedroom windows faced each other across the hedge, and in the summers we could talk back and forth, till our parents made us turn off the lights and go to sleep.

If Emmett had lived we'd have gotten married and I'd have chil-dren by now. There's not a doubt of that in my mind. I'd be a happy working housewife, average as hell, in Sadler, Pennsylvania, and all my singing would be done in church. You and I would never have met.

But Emmett was killed. Of course he was.

I'm sorry if that sounded like self-pity, I hate that. But maybe it'll help you see what damaged goods I am, and why I'm going to hold you to your promise. How you stay with me at your own risk.

Emmett was just a great lovable boy and I loved him all my life. God knows he loved me. But he was like all of us then, he worked too hard and he was always tired. One night he fell asleep at the wheel and his car went right under the back end of a truck. I was supposed to meet him, and when I heard the sirens I got a cold feeling like I'd had that day at the lake. The same clammy shivers I felt years later when I stood in my father's room and read a note he'd never written. I walked out on the highway and got there just as they were pulling the car apart. Someone tried to hold me but I broke free as the door came off.

Emmett's head fell out and rolled between my feet.

She tried to make sense out of what she'd just said. Maybe God did it. For some reason that must never be questioned, God drowned my sister and killed my friend in that awful way. It makes no sense to have gods like that, unless there isn't any God, then it makes perfect sense. It's all the luck of the draw. Some people are lucky and some aren't, but there's nothing guiding us, caring, or watching out for us. Our lives are no more significant than ants on a hill. It doesn't matter how important you think you are, your luck can turn in a minute. Even the rich and powerful can be stepped on.

One of our presidents lost a son like that.

Franklin Pierce and his wife saw their son killed in a train accident. They watched his head roll down the aisle of a passenger car.

Mrs. Pierce went crazy. In the White House she wrote letters to her dead son, and wore black every day of her life.

I made myself a promise: I will not go mad. But you are probably the last to know it when you're going crazy. Tom knew there was something wrong with me. I could never give him what he wanted. I did try, I hope you believe that. But it just wasn't there.

Now he's dead too, so none of it matters, does it?

The hunt for my father was all that mattered. I was in a strange little town that might've been on the back side of the moon, I was that alone. I had to talk to Harford but I didn't know how to start.

Pardon me, sir, I'm looking for my father.

What've you done with him?

She anticipated trouble, then went out and found it.

"I'm sorry. Mr. Harford doesn't see people or give interviews."

She expected that. She looked at the woman, a sunny creature her own age, and said, "I'm not here for an interview. I'm looking for someone and I have reason to believe Mr. Harford can help me."

"I doubt that. Mr. Harford has led a secluded life in recent years. He sees no one."

"He saw my father."

The woman shook her head. But she said, "What's your father's name?"

"Carnahan."

"Of course. A nice man. We all liked him. We were surprised when he left us so suddenly."

She closed her eyes and saw a streak of red fury. Opened them wide again and said, "He didn't leave you suddenly. Something happened to him."

The woman tried for a look of sympathy. "I can see you're worried. But I'm sure he's fine."

"Oh good, I feel much better now. But I'd still like to see Harford."

"Well, you can't. I've tried to explain how it is, but you won't listen." The woman sighed deeply. "Look, I'll ask Mr. Harford if he knows anything. Best I can do."

"When can I come back?"

"Try me later today."

But it was the same later that afternoon. "It's just as I told you, Miss Carnahan. Mr. Harford never met your father."

There must have been something in her eyes, for the woman looked at her and wavered again. "I think you should see Mr. Barnet. He does a lot of the hiring."

Her father had never mentioned anyone named Barnet. But she said, "At this point I'll talk to anyone."

Barnet was a cold man, clearly annoyed at having to deal with her. "I hired your father. Not Harford—me. He worked for us five or six months and didn't give any notice when he left. I doubt if Harford ever spoke to the man."

They're all lying, she thought.

That afternoon she watched as Harford left the building. The next morning when he came in, she was there, watching from the woods fifty yards away. She learned his comings and goings. Discovered where he ate, by combing the beach looking for his car. You couldn't miss that big flashy automobile. The man was a walking self-contradiction. Equal needs for privacy and celebrity. Wanted to be known without all the trappings of fame, so he put his name in stone on the new office building and hid behind that battery of secretaries. Seldom appeared in public but had the station reflect his name in its call letters.

He wants to show the world what's possible with radio, Dulaney said. *Maybe that's how he wants to be remembered.*

She nodded. *Or maybe it's got something to do with his dead wife. But I didn't care about any of that. He had his problems, I had mine.*

The next day she waited for him outside the office building. When he came out at dusk, she stepped up beside him.

"Mr. Harford . . ."

He shrank away. Reached for the door of his car.

"I've been trying to talk to you, sir. Your people won't help me. You hired my father. His name is Carnahan. You hired him and now he's disappeared."

"You've made a mistake. I don't hire people."

"He wrote and told me about it. The meeting he had with you. And it *was* you, sir, he called you by name. Now he's missing."

He seemed to be looking at her: it was hard to tell with those glasses he wore but he seemed to be watching her intensely. She said his name, just a soft "Mr. Harford," but it was enough to break the spell. He opened his car door and said, "I can't help you. I never met your father." And he drove away.

The next morning she was waiting at the restaurant where he ate. He came in and went into a back room, passing not two feet from the counter where she sat reading a newspaper. She got up and followed him.

He was sitting alone at a table reading his own paper. No one else was in the room. He had taken off his glasses and had unfolded a *Times*. He didn't hear her coming, didn't see her, till suddenly she pulled out a chair and sat at his table.

What happened next would shock her and freeze her mind-set for months to come. She said his name: it was barely a whisper but he recoiled and cried out as if she'd shot him. He dropped his newspaper and spilled his coffee everywhere. For just an instant she stared into that yellow eye: then he jerked his face away and in the leap for his glasses his chair tipped over. The great Mr. Harford lay sprawled at her feet.

Just as quickly he was up and gone. Oh God, she thought with a sinking heart. Oh God, oh God, oh God. Is that the look of a guilty man, or what?

It was clear by then that she wasn't going to get anywhere with Harford. So she thought in early December 1941.

She went to the sheriff, who took her complaint, took down her address in Pennsylvania, assembled a sheet of vitals on her father. It took less than ten minutes and the sheriff's attitude wasn't encouraging. There was no evidence of a crime, and he certainly wasn't inclined to challenge Mr. Harford until he had more than she'd given him to go on.

By then she was thoroughly spooked. She had a nagging feeling that the sheriff would share everything with Harford, that she had done nothing but put herself in danger. She would approach no one else: not yet, not now. She would watch them from a distance and speak to no one. She learned who they all were: she became one of those people you never see. She did everything she could to make herself less than ordinary. Dyed her hair, made it mousy and straight, wore glasses from the five-and-dime and dresses from rummage sales. She followed the staff, watched them when they came and went. *Wherever they were, I was there too.*

It's amazing how obscure you can be, sitting in a restaurant so close you're almost part of them. All your attention focused on your newspaper when in fact you're watching them and nothing goes past you. My dad was a hot topic back then, mainly because of Livia. I guess they thought the world ended where my newspaper began. Before long I knew all about them.

I read all the history, everything that had been written about Harford and his radio station. I knew about March Flack. I bought the back issue of the newspaper with the latest recap, and I saw Mrs. Flack when she walked on the beach with that sick old man.

I saw Harford many times. I watched him constantly, and sometimes I'd let him see me. I'd stand still until it dawned on him who I was. Don't ask me to explain it, it doesn't make any sense. Nothing I did in those weeks makes any sense at all.

The next thing I knew it was Christmas.

December 24. A horrible day, with nothing open and no life anywhere. The wind cold, the sky gray, the beach stormy and deserted. Occasionally she heard Christmas carols as she walked through the streets. She longed for work, even the drudgery of washing dishes, but the hash house where she'd taken the job was closed today and tomorrow, leaving her alone till noon Friday. She wanted desperately not to think, but not to think was the province of those joyful creatures celebrating the holiday behind the frosty windows. She walked north on the beach and suddenly Livia's house appeared in the gloom. A rosy bungalow with smoke curling from a cinder-pipe chimney, yellow windows, and shadows dancing. A child peered out and she stood still, too far back, she thought, to be seen. She didn't know what kept bringing her back here—surely nothing could relieve the crushing loneliness she felt—yet so many nights she had come to watch these windows from the dunes. If she ever did break her silence, it would likely be with Livia. A hundred times she had thought of it, just walking up to that door and making the first human contact. Hello, I'm Holly Carnahan, I believe you knew my dad. So simple, so easy, the right thing to do. But if you ask her, seven busy months later, she will not know why she came, hesitated, and finally turned away.

That night fate almost changed it. The child at the window gave a little wave and suddenly the door opened and Livia stepped out. They looked at each other and Livia raised a hand and said, "Hello there."

Holly said, "Hi," but the step she took was backward, into the gloom.

"Are you lost?"

"No . . ." She drew her coat tighter. "I'm just out walking."

"Miserable night for it." Livia took a few steps and tried to see her better. She must be cold in that thin shirt, Holly thought. "Not many people come up this far," Livia said. "I guess you're a stormy weather gal."

She could see Livia didn't know what to do next. They were strangers after all, but you didn't close your door on anyone on a cold and stormy Christmas Eve. "I hope you're not alone," Livia said.

"No . . . I'm meeting someone later."

"That's good. No one should be alone at Christmas. I could offer you a warm place by the fire. Some hot apple cider with cinnamon."

"Thank you. But I can't."

"Santa's coming. He really is, he'll be here any minute."

Holly looked at her.

"It's a game we play every year for my kids. They get their presents on Christmas Eve. Some friends get all decked out and play the role." She beckoned with her fingers. "Come in for a while, warm yourself."

"Really I can't. I've come too far as it is."

"Okay, then. Happy Christmas, stranger."

"Yeah." Holly watched her go. "You too," she said after the door had closed.

Stupid, she thought, turning away. Dumb, dumb, stupid idiot. What harm would it have done to let her see your face? To have a cup of steaming cheer? To visit with her children? . . . or tell her who you are?

She saw headlights in the dunes: Santa coming, not in a sleigh but in a Dodge of mid-thirties vintage. Brinker's car. She knew them all, knew who they were and where they lived, what they drove, where they ate. She knew them even in their disguises. Rue and Becky dressed as elves. Rue's friend Brinker as a clown. The fat cooking woman, Laura Leaf, bundled up as Mrs. Claus in a Santa suit. And Stoner a splendid Santa, stuffed into his own red outfit with pillows and pads, his bearlike frame topped with white curls and a long flowing beard to match.

First Brinker went in, to dance and delight. Ten minutes later, the elves, carrying stockings with nuts and oranges and small wrapped parcels. Mrs. Claus arrived with cakes, rich devil's food for the kids, spiked fruitcake for the grown-ups. Stoner stood alone on the porch, timing his own grand entrance, loving the wait as he chuckled at what he was seeing inside. Suddenly he was discovered: a tiny face peered through the glass and screamed for joy. "Hello, sweethearts, hello!" he cried, clumping to the door with bells ringing and his bag brimming with boxes and teddies slung over his shoulder. Livia threw open her house and took his bag and the children leaped into his arms. "Merry Christmas, sweethearts! Merry Christmas!"

The door closed and they were lost in their holiday world.

The shadow woman watched them play. She was drawn to the glow and pushed to the dark. She wanted the light and wanted it badly; it drew her like the pull of the sun. But it was the darkness that claimed her.

She awoke in the darkness of her father's room with his voice in her head. She sat up in bed.

Nothing out in the vast blackness but the hissing of the radiator. You are going mad, she thought.

I had to get out of there. Go home, if only for a while. Once I had the thought, I couldn't get out of that town fast enough.

She threw her clothes together in a moment. In the closet her coat caught on the hanger and she ripped it free, tearing the lining and scattering dust everywhere.

Something fell. Some small thing, round and hard.

A roll of film.

She dragged the chair into the closet and got up to look. A bare light hung from a frayed cord and she held it over her head. There, where the molding made a little ridge over the door, in a layer of dust—a dark spot, about the size of a fifty-cent piece.

The roll fit the spot perfectly. It had hung over the lip by almost half, balancing there until she had knocked it down. Might've been there two weeks or ten years.

She would get it developed but not here. She trusted no one in this town, not even the nameless people who ran the photo service in the pharmacy. In the worst of times she believed that Harford owned everyone.

She sat on the train, gently rocking her way across Pennsylvania. She was cold, she was never able to get warm enough, and all the way home she kept her hand in her coat pocket, clutching that roll of film.

She felt Harford's presence. He seemed to be out in the black landscape, flying along beside her.

But she arrived in Sadler on a wave of trumped-up hope. Her father would be here, alive and well, wondering where the hell she had gone. Or the mailbox would be full of postcards, explaining everything.

In her heart she knew better.

She came up the steps and saw stuff in the mailbox. No postcards. She threw it all on the kitchen table and let it wait while she made a fire. Kept her coat on, still cold as she fed wood to the flames; then sat in her father's chair to look through the mail.

The house payment was seriously overdue. She couldn't let that lapse, it would be paid off in a few years. A letter from the church, wondering where she'd gone.

At the bottom was a letter from you.

Instantly her eyes filled with tears. Tom was dead.

Of course he's dead. Of course.

She remembered thinking when he'd joined the navy: *Now they'll kill him.*

Now they had.

Wonderful letter, Jack. Jesus Christ, couldn't you even give me a return address? Where the hell is Arcadia, California?

The first days of 1942 were like a sieve, irrevocably separating her old life from whatever was to come next. One day she realized that she was putting her mind in order, getting ready for something she had decided to do but only now was coming to understand. Another notice arrived from the bank, darker and more threatening. The house didn't matter, let the goddamn bankers have it. Her father was right, the effing banks were going to own everything in the world anyway. She scribbled a reply—*We have made these payments faithfully since 1915 . . . don't you people have any conscience?*—but then she didn't send it, she burned it in the fireplace. You can't appeal to people on their lack of conscience when they have no conscience to appeal to.

She burned many papers, including the story about March Flack. It didn't matter, she knew it by heart.

In January the phone company took out her telephone. Slowly, like a man dying of very old age, her life in Sadler was shutting down. She stood at the window on a snowy afternoon and thought, *I will never come back here,* but what she would do next was as much a mystery as the disappearance of her father. She sensed an ally in Livia but had never approached her; why, she couldn't say. The closest she could come was that it didn't feel right. *It just didn't feel right, digging around in my dad's affairs that way. And Livia knew nothing. I found that out when I eavesdropped on her and Rue one day in the café.* But she wasn't done with that little town yet, and the town wasn't done with her.

In her kitchen on that snowy afternoon she looked for the hundredth time at the pictures she had gotten out of that roll of film. There wasn't much doubt her father had taken them, but what they proved she didn't know. A series of beach shots, taken at dusk, the Goodfellows group by the light of a bonfire. Becky laughing, Gus looking half amused, Rue and Brinker standing a few feet away, and in the foreground Livia talking with some unknown man. More of the same, focusing on the individuals, Livia still standing close to the camera, talking with the same fellow. Then a series of indoor prints—a radio soundstage, with microphones and lights. Hazel sitting off to one side . . . the Schroeder boys standing at opposite ends. The clock on the wall said 2:03. Another picture, almost the same, at 2:05; another at 2:06. Peter gestured and seemed to be saying something in anger, something important. George listened intently. Hazel looked distracted as if she didn't hear or care or understand what they were saying. None of them seemed aware that they were being photographed. The pictures had been taken through glass, from the dark production room facing the soundstage.

Holly flipped back to the first shot: Livia and the unknown man on the beach. *I wonder who this is. I've never seen him with any of the others.*

That's because he was gone by the time you got here. He was with me then, in California.

Her eyes opened wide. *It's Kendall.*

January 24. The day Harford came to Pennsylvania.

She got off the bus and turned the corner. Froze in her tracks. The Packard was parked in front of her house.

A dozen thoughts raced through her mind. She stood there for a while, then slowly she began to walk up the street.

Darkness came early in the dead of winter. The wartime act hadn't been passed yet and the street was black and deserted. No mistaking that car, though. There were none like it in her town.

She could hear her heartbeat as she passed Emmett's old house. She walked past the hedge and her own house came into view. A car turned into the street a block away and in its headlights she could see that Harford's car was empty. He's out there somewhere, she thought: back in the dark, waiting for me.

Then she saw him. He was sitting on the front porch steps. Wearing those goddamn dark glasses, she saw in the glare from the passing car. Looking like a blind man.

She spoke to him from the sidewalk. "What do you want?"

"I came to tell you something."

His voice trembled: he was nervous. She didn't know what to do next, only that she was vulnerable and afraid.

"Okay," she said. "Come inside."

Her courage bucked her up and gave her more courage, as courage always did. She walked past him and opened her door, facing the dark house. When she turned on the lights he was standing there with his hat in his hand.

The hat reminded me in a strange way of Daddy. For just that instant in the flash of the light the feeling was so strong that it was like a third party in the room. Then I looked up at his face, at those glasses, and there was no warmth about him, no reassurance, and again I was afraid. But I had to hear what he'd come to tell me. I might never get this chance again.

They sat at the kitchen table. She offered nothing, no coffee, nothing. She waited and at last he said, "I've asked everyone about your father. No one knows why he left."

"And you came all this way to tell me this."

He spread his hands, a gesture that said, I'm here, aren't I? He tried to smile but the effort had a chilling effect.

"I'm sorry," he said. "I'm not very good at this sort of thing. But I wanted you to know that I did try."

"Uh-huh." She shook her head slightly, never taking her eyes away from him. "I guess I'm not very good at it either. Right now, for example, I'm having a terrible time believing that you would come here just to tell me this."

He sat perfectly still for a long moment, then shrugged. "You remind me of someone."

She said nothing. He was going to have to do better than that.

"You look nothing like . . . this other person. Maybe it's your voice."

She found this even more incredible. "Sir, you barely let me get two words out of my mouth. If you remember."

"Sometimes that's enough."

"Please," she said. "If this is a game you're playing . . ."

"I assure you it's not. I did everything in my power to find out what you wanted to know."

"What should I do, then, say thank you?"

"I didn't come here for thanks."

"That's good. I'm not in a very gracious mood. My father is missing and you seem to have had something to do with that."

He shook his head. "I didn't."

"How can I believe you? You say you never met him but I know that's not true. I have his word for that against yours. Who would you believe?"

He sighed loudly. "It's exasperating. All I can tell you is, I never met the man."

She wanted to scream at him—*Liar!* But she looked across the room and saw the face of the child peering in through the back-door glass. She gave a small headshake and the child backed away. But a moment later the face appeared over the sill, and in the presence of the child she drew some comfort.

She looked at Harford. "Who told you where I live?"

He said nothing.

"It was that sheriff, wasn't it? That half-assed bumpkin."

Harford pushed back his chair. "I'm sorry. I can see I shouldn't have come." He got up and crossed the room and she followed him to the door, keeping herself half a room away. At the bottom of the front porch steps he turned to her for the last time.

"I don't know what it is. Your voice, your spirit maybe."

Then he was gone.

You know the rest of it. How I came back here. How I became Holly O'Hara that night on a whim at the pier. I won the amateur night, a ten-dollar prize. Not a small thing when you're struggling to stay alive.

At some point I began wondering about those pictures. You don't take pictures like that with a box-style Kodak. So where'd he get the camera? There aren't many places in town that handle cameras like that. I knew he couldn't afford to buy it new. So I stopped at the pawnshop on the south beach and there it was—his gold watch in the glass case. He had hocked his watch for the loan of the camera. The guy had even instructed him on how to use it. Surprising, the guy said, that he never came back for the watch or brought the camera back. So I paid for the watch, and the camera, and then you came to town, and you know the rest.

I thought I'd die when I saw you. All I could think of was . . . well, now they'd have to kill you too.

((•))

SHADOWS
OF AN OLD
WAR

((**1**))

THE hush began a minute before air. Maitland mounted the steps to the booth where Stoner sat tense, his hands on the dials. Zylla, who had written an inspiring score with no notice at all, stood with his baton before thirty musicians. Poindexter spread himself on a chair between two turntables and Livia crouched among the gadgets a few feet away. Stallworth cleared his throat and the noise carried to the back of the room over the heads of two hundred people. The audience watched expectantly. Eastman stood ready with his cue cards. At the microphone to his right, Holly looked calm, ready to go. Kidd stood near the door, with the office staff strung out along the wall to his right. Everyone had come, to find standing room only. There was tension even in the faces of the secretaries. How odd that only Jordan Ten Eyck and Holly O'Hara were calm.

Jordan had had his attack of nerves two hours ago in the dress, but it had all gone so perfectly that suddenly he stopped worrying. Holly was going to be sensational. Maitland had coaxed her into just the right pace for those rousing patriotic numbers and she had come through with spectacular fire, so good that the orchestra had given her an ovation at the end of it. Everything was going to be fine.

"We've got a strong core here," Maitland had told him. "Lots of strength at the heart of it. There are people in radio for whom nothing ever goes wrong. Mrs. Harford was one of those, a creature of the air who never took a false step once the red light was on. Zylla's another, and so is Leland. Rick Gary is nothing short of a commanding presence, and Miss O'Hara is like the rock of Gibraltar. Not to spook you, Jordan, but I think you're like that."

He was so confident by airtime that he lingered through that first long medley before going back to check on his cast.

Holly fused with the orchestra, a perfect bonding, with Zylla leading her like one of his instruments. In the thunderous ovation Jordan slipped away, down the hall to Studio B, where the cast stood on the small stage, quietly giving their lines a final look. A monitor on the wall told them how well it was going, and it was going fine; he could feel the excitement as he came into the room.

Rick Gary was the first to notice his arrival. He looked up from his script and said, "It's sounding good out there," and then everyone raised their eyes, first at Jordan and then at the clock. Pauline and Hazel had been deep in some discussion, which suddenly ceased, and Rue stood alone on the far edge, looking slightly terrified with the moment at hand. Maitland had dismissed her jitters as normal. "She needs that edge to power her performance. I think she'll always have it; no matter how many big roles she plays, she'll always stew in her juices just before air. I've seen a dozen actresses like her and fear never hurt any of them."

Gary had helped her enormously in the dress. He smiled out of his vast network experience and assured her without ever stepping on Maitland's role as director. He was a consummate professional, a short, muscular bundle of dynamite, slightly graying, in his early forties. Rue hung on his every word and gesture and he was charmed by her wit and good looks. He had arrived late in the afternoon and his sudden appearance had galvanized the cast. He had read the script in New York and already knew it well, coming in with a full load of enthusiasm. "This is going to be great," he assured. "I don't care what the networks are carrying in those time slots, we're going to blow them away."

The show had cut upstairs, where Barnet was directing a small group of "ordinary citizens" in a poetic appeal for war bonds. At eight twenty-three the orchestra returned with an overture to the regional medley that Holly would sing going into the drama. "Time to go," Jordan told them. He opened the door and led the cast single-file up the dark hallway. Becky Hart had been stationed at Studio A to make sure everyone got through the doors before she locked them again, and at eight twenty-nine Holly's number ended and the cast came in during the prolonged applause. The timing was tight: even as Zylla brought up the dark theme music, Gary and Rue were still picking their way across the stage. Eastman watched them warily from the center-stage announcer's microphone, and it all looked very ragged as they tiptoed across the cables and stood in the cornfield of mikes, waiting.

But it hit the air in perfect harmony, the lines just right and delivered to the half second, the sound effects cued and brought up without a hitch. Zylla's music flowed over it, potent and inseparable, and in the booth Maitland waved like Toscanini, keeping the mood tense and unbroken with his two-handed direction. The audience sat transfixed, caught by the story even with the trappings so clear. And Jordan had that feeling of life speeding past, of everything going too fast and running out of control. It ended with a question. *So what shall it be for Rudy Adams—this door, or that?* Livia jerked open the door and Zylla's musical sting drove the point home . . . *the lady, or the tiger?* The cast hustled off as Eastman read the epilogue: that never in its history had the United States faced such a threat to its way of life as now; that those fighting boys were depending on the home front to back the attack with war bonds and stamps.

The final thirty minutes took no time at all. Holly sang a magnificent national anthem and it ended in a crushing wall of silence. Maitland had ordered that thirty seconds of dead air before Stoner threw it back to the network. At nine thirty Stoner gave a thumbs-up and the place exploded with ecstatic relief.

Rick Gary embraced Rue and was now shaking hands with everyone. The doors opened and Barnet came in with his little company from upstairs. Hazel stood off to one side, her perfect performance as the scarf woman already forgotten in the hundred and one perfect things that had gone into the show. Pauline crossed the stage to give her compliments to the maestro. Poindexter sat alone where he'd been all night and Livia began packing her things away. Jordan looked up to the balcony and Harford gave him a small wave before vanishing somewhere into the wall.

People milled about, the cast mingling with musicians and audience. The babble spilled into the halls, where Becky Hart began easing people toward the doors. There was still a band show to do later tonight and the room had to be cleared.

At last Kidd called them all together for a talk. Kudos to everyone. "Miss Nicholas, you were exactly right for this part and I never should have thought otherwise. Mr. Brinker, Mr. Stallworth, Mr. Eastman, Miss Kemble, Mrs. Flack . . ." His eyes went around the room. . . . "To Mr. Stoner and our two most capable directors, Mr. Zylla and his incredible musical aggregation, to Mr. Poindexter and Miss Teasdale in sound—our thanks to you all. To Mr. Ten Eyck, whose powerful script came out of the blue only on Tuesday and made us all remember why we do this and what it's all about. To Miss Holly O'Hara, who carried the day with the wonder of her voice. And a special thanks to Mr. Rick Gary, who passed up two network jobs tonight so he could come down here and help us out."

The glow of fellowship and accomplishment was heavy in the room and no one wanted to leave. Suddenly Jordan felt a presence at his right elbow. "Well, Jordan, we pulled it off," Maitland said. "You look as if you never had a doubt."

"I don't know why but I never did."

"The world's your oyster now and you're just starting to know it. In a real way this was your show, not mine. You're going to be one of those people we were talking about. The ones for whom nothing ever goes wrong."

They said hello to Miss O'Hara, who had come up to join them.

"The woman who made us," Maitland said. "You know Jordan, Miss O'Hara?"

Miss O'Hara smiled brilliantly. "Hello, Jordan. Of course we know each other."

((2))

THEY knew each other well. There was no loneliness now, not in the way he had known it before. None of that aching lack, of the empty bed and the empty nights, never a hand to push him away. The word love did no justice to what he felt for her, it was too easy to use on too many things that were temporary and cheap, as if she could be equated to apple pie or a change in the weather. There was nothing about her that he didn't love. It was scary how strong the feeling was and how fast it grew, like nothing he had ever known or imagined. She was even a beautiful drunk.

On a Sunday night in June she surprised him with a private celebration of his birthday. She had never been drunk and it didn't take long for that happy high to arrive. She had bought a cake, elegantly decorated with thirty-three candles, and had a present gift wrapped in a little box. It was her father's watch, gold-plated with a matching fob and the name CARNAHAN engraved on its face. He was touched, almost to tears, but she hushed him with her fingers to his lips. She showed him how it opened, how it had to be set from the inside, and they sat mesmerized by the delicate jeweled workings swinging back and forth in the candlelight. "It belonged to my grandfather," she said. "He was a conductor on the Pennsylvania Railroad, so it's probably a pretty good piece. It's been in my family for fifty years."

There wasn't a hint of self-pity when she said, "Now there's no more family, so I want you to have it."

A keepsake, she said. A remembrance.

Dulaney didn't tell her but of course it was her he wanted, not a remembrance. He knew if he said this the delicate mood she'd been trying to create would turn melancholy and vanish. She said, "Happy birthday, old man," and for one crazy moment they hugged like the old friends they were.

Then she kissed him, and the way she flicked her tongue was not at all old-friendly, nor was the way her smile turned sultry. "I've got another present for you, Dulaney. That one I'll dole out later."

These were the oddest days of his life, forever colored by both her presence and her distance. They were together yet not together, she was his yet she belonged to no one, she had given him the greatest joy and at the same time there was a sorrow upon them that was never far away. This was a truth she never let waver. Their time was short; these days would pass and she'd be gone.

Dulaney knew not to argue when she told him she was cursed. She had on her side the fact that everyone who had loved her had died badly, and if he tried to make her confront it she would get shaky and agitated. The key to everything, he thought, was the drowning of her sister and the crushing guilt she had carried for fifteen years. "You can't imagine the horror," she had told him. "That moment when you know she's gone, and it's your fault. You just can't imagine."

The whiskey loosened her for a time and made her seem happy again. "Now for your second present," she said later. "I'm going to vamp you, Dulaney. Would you like that?" She closed her eyes and put her hands behind her head, bunched up her hair, and gripped it tight. Her underarms were smooth as glass, her breasts pulled tight against the sleeveless top she wore. She made a rosebud with her mouth, like a kiss. Looking at her, he felt a shiver run through him; and she opened her eyes and trembled, and he knew the same ripple had gone through her.

He could taste the whiskey on her tongue, he could see it in her eyes. She smiled, her face all friendly and sad, funny and dreamy and drunk in the same moment. She hiked off her top and wiggled out of her shorts, and her head bobbed. In the distant heights she wavered unsteadily. Her hands groped and joined them together. "Here we are . . . here we are . . . here we are . . ."

They shuddered at the same time and her face went mushy and her nipples got tiny and hard. A long last push, the vamp's postscript.

"Happy birthday, old man."

Later, still wide awake, they dressed and walked to town in the dark. Sat over coffee in the all-night diner and watched the lights blink off along the pier. At some point he had to tell her what he'd been thinking, that she had been wrong about Harford from the beginning. When it came up on its own, as it usually did when they began to talk, he figured the time was now.

She was looking through the plate glass window at the dark world. "He will drive me crazy if I let him. I get the feeling he's out there, watching us. He's always there."

Dulaney let a moment pass. Then he said it. "I don't think it's him. At least, not for the reasons you thought."

He saw the annoyance in her eyes and pushed ahead with his case.

"You've been going on the notion that what your father wrote on that postcard had to be taken literally. If he said he interviewed with Harford, that had to mean the two of them had a face-to-face meeting at some point."

"What else could it mean?"

"That your dad was already caught up in the spirit of the station when he wrote that. When he said, *I went out and interviewed with Harford*, that might mean nothing more than he went there and applied for the job."

"He said he saw Harford."

"But everyone calls the station Harford. It's insider slang. Maybe he thought he'd told you that. *I saw Harford* might only mean that he got a tour of the building."

She hadn't known that, and the news was disheartening.

"Damn. If that's true, I'm right back where I started from."

"No you're not. I won't ever let you go back there again."

At the counter he noticed the headline on the *Times*, which had just been thrown off the truck from New York.

FBI SEIZES 8 SABOTEURS LANDED BY U-BOATS

"Looks like we're in big trouble," she said. "Hitler's coming after us."

"Not with those boys." He looked down the column of newsprint. "Hoover got those bastards almost as soon as they got here."

"It doesn't matter." She closed her eyes. "I'm sure Hitler's got lots more where they came from."

((**3**))

AN air of fate hung over everything they did. Sometimes he'd catch her watching him sadly, as if he had already become part of her past. Then she'd come hug him to her breast and they'd lose themselves in an hour's lovemaking. At noon they talked. About her father and Harford and the station. About Kendall and how he had appeared in Dulaney's life, how he had died in Holly's house, and what this might mean. Only once had she mentioned Dulaney's legal predicament and what might happen if he was caught. She had no illusions about the harshness of the criminal justice system in the year 1942. She knew what he could expect from the people of California. He could do five years. A miner she knew was doing ten years for escape. "His original crime had been something silly, like yours. It started as a fight in a bar. But of course there was a woman in his life to make it worse. He had a frail-looking child bride eight months into a dangerous pregnancy, so he escaped, broke out to be with his wife. They said he used a gun in the breakout."

"A gun always doubles the judgment."

"But at his trial he swore there'd been no gun. I believed him because I knew him. But the deputies were all against him."

"Not surprising," he said. "Deputies never like to admit that you got away easy."

"And they'll do that to you."

"Maybe."

Anyway, there was no use beating it to death. It served no useful purpose to worry about what couldn't be helped. So life went on; he went to work by day and at night she did the same, and for those who pried they stuck to their story: that they had met working together on the war bond show and nature took its course. For now it was enough that they no longer had to hide, that they were together and it was common knowledge. Let them kill us, but if they do they'd better get us both, because the one who's left will burn this place to the ground.

But she kept her word. Never once in those days did she ask him to leave. She wouldn't leave and so he couldn't, and some things went without saying.

Today she was angry. She had overheard some gossip, her own boys talking too much in the club, and she had walked out of the rehearsal and left them hanging. "They were talking about us," she said, and that's all she would tell him. Dulaney could piece it together for himself. The prevailing view was that she had been willing to sacrifice what could have been her own major career for the sake of his minor one, so God bless Jordan Ten Eyck for keeping her here. "Let them talk," he said. "They're only interested because we're such a good beauty-and-the-beast story." She made a face and turned away from him. "If that's true, it's because they haven't figured out yet which of us is the beast."

No, he said, people just liked to talk, and they would always talk about someone whose past was shrouded in mystery. They still didn't know who she was or where she'd come from. Rumor had it that she had turned down at least three offers to go with big-name bands in New York. One was a fabulous deal with a recording contract and a twice-a-week network airshot from Frank Dailey's Meadowbrook. It was the break of a lifetime but the man had told her she had to take it or leave it. "When you need someone, you need her now," she said. "You don't need her a year from now, if she can satisfy herself even then about the matter of her father's death." She looked at Dulaney over a flickering lamp. "The funny part is, I don't seem to care much."

"There'll be time later. You'll still have your voice."

She reached over and took his hand, touching it to her lips. "That's the great thing about you, Jack. You're always on my side and you never ask for anything."

"There's nothing more to want."

"But you've never even asked about the man you saw in my house that morning. Weren't you curious? . . . Didn't you wonder?"

"Sure I did."

"Were you jealous, Dulaney? Did you suffer?"

He told her how terribly he had suffered, how jealous he had been.

"Good." She laughed wickedly. "I should let you wonder about that."

But the night ended happily. The man was an agent, down from New York to twist her arm. He had been there less than an hour.

(((4)))

SOMETIMES she woke him, but just as often he was up and working when she got home in the early morning. He seldom slept more than five hours: four was normal, and he could go for a week on three hours a night without getting fatigued. His best writing time was the three-hour block beginning at 2 or 3 A.M., after four hours of deep sleep. His eyes would open to entire scenes playing across the black universe, concepts that had come so vividly to life after years of stewing in his blood, waiting for him to discover a perfect medium for their use. He would get up at once, pausing only to dress and make coffee; then he'd sit at her kitchen table with the doors wide open and the roar of the surf loud in the room, and he'd write out his vision in longhand, as fast as he could make the words. Later in his cubicle he would put it all into script, and in this typewritten rewrite the thing would come truly to life and take its final form for the air.

In the two weeks following the war bond show he had written a new script every day. Six of these were self-contained plays, stories with no intent to expand or continue. Four were for the colored show, giving him a backlog that would carry them well into August. The other five were the opening chapters of his *Dark Silver* racetracker serial, which he would finish this morning and turn in as a unit.

He knew Kidd was astonished at his versatility and pace, and there were days when he surprised himself. Kidd was stockpiling his scripts, hoarding them for the lean times when the station would separate from the network and need all the muscle it could get. Each morning at ten Becky Hart would drift through the bullpen and almost invariably he'd have something new for her to take down to Kidd. "They're excited that you're doing a serial," she told him. "Those things can be real audience grabbers."

He had now directed three of the Negro shows without help and was beginning to feel at home on the soundstage. The *Times* had taken note of it: twice they had praised the show's writing and courage, in small squibs down in the radio column. Rue had come in for high praise in her dual role as the Grimké sisters, and Ali Marek was taking to radio in quantum leaps. The work itself was invigorating. Except for the specter of Carnahan, these were the days of his life. Kidd was giving him almost unlimited freedom. "Just keep doing what you're doing," Becky had said. "That's the word from the mountain."

He was free of continuity, of time clocks, and the heavy hand of Clay Barnet. Kidd now encouraged him to develop his own projects, certain that what he did would at least be good air, and at best he had written some things that would rattle the timbers of New York radio when they aired next month. But there was always a greater purpose in his life. He walked the halls at odd hours and looked in dark corners.

He wrote in the morning, and in the afternoon he drifted around watching everyone, acquainting himself with all the different pieces that went into a good broadcast. He spent time in the booth with Maitland, watching the old man direct. He sat on the rooftop with Stoner and discussed the pivotal role of the engineer. "I'm your right-hand man, champ," Stoner said, squeaking back in his chair. "Just leave all the technical stuff to me and you worry about the story and the sound and the music."

He got a crash course from Zylla on the uses of music in drama, then spent an afternoon with Livia in the sound room between the first-floor studios. A new door had been added, giving direct access to both soundstages. Dozens of symphonies and miscellaneous recordings, from jazz to classics, from white-hot trumpet solos to lush strings and harps, were being added to the record library, so that a musical background of almost any kind could be created in the absence of a live orchestra. All the sound effects records were being replaced. "Ours were terrible," Livia said. "We hadn't upgraded them in years; they were so scratchy it made me cringe every time I used them."

That night, alone at Holly's kitchen, he thought about it all, and in the morning he awoke with a powerful new story ready to write. He saw Carnahan marching in a group of faceless men under guard, and suddenly he knew that what he had was the first of his prison camp stories.

There before him was a long straight set of railroad tracks, shimmering in the sun. A sign flashed in his face and he had just a glimpse of the word MAYNARD before it changed and became FLORENCE. He was in a small town in upstate South Carolina, where a train packed with ragtag prisoners was being unloaded by men in gray. The prisoners were prodded along at gunpoint, sometime in the autumn of 1864. Sherman was cutting across Georgia and the Rebels had decided to evacuate their prison camp at Andersonville, leaving behind the sick and dying. Among the able-bodied who could walk, there was a lightness of spirit and a feeling of hope. Wherever they were going, it could only be a far better place than the hellhole they'd come from. The war was all but over. *All we've got to do,* Carnahan said as they trudged up the dusty road leading out of

Florence, *is hang on for a little longer.* Dulaney couldn't see the face of the man he spoke to, they were both somewhere far ahead in the column of men, but he knew Carnahan's voice and the profile was clear: the only one wearing a modern-day fedora.

Then their hearts sank as their destination rose from the forest. It was Andersonville all over again, a wicked-looking stockade wide open to the elements with walls at least a dozen feet high and a stream running through it that would soon be like the one in Georgia, reeking of filth and crawling with disease and death. Carnahan sat on the ground with his hat in one hand and the other hand empty, and as night came on he felt the crushing weight of despair in the lost souls around him.

Dulaney took the first step: wrote a sentence that defined his story.

This is a tale of survival in the prison camp at Florence, during a terrible winter in the final year of the war.

Rain washed over Florence as he began to write. All across the compound the fires flickered out, and the ground the men sat on was slick with mud. In the last of the firelight he saw the haggard face of Carnahan's companion and it was Kendall.

((**5**))

HE dreamed that there was no war. There had been a war, but not this war. He had figured out who had killed Carnahan and why, but a thousand years had passed and what he had once known had faded away. His mind opened to the blackness of another summer morning.

His first conscious thought was of that script. The one nobody wanted to talk about. Somehow I've got to read it, he thought.

He rolled out of bed and crept from the room without a sound. Holly found it remarkable that a man his size could do this, get up and be gone and never wake her. "You should've been a burglar, Jack," she told him. "But why don't you nudge me once in a while so I can send you off properly?"

Send me off to the wars, he thought now. To some old war for a cause never quite understood and now long forgotten. Was that what he'd been thinking?

There had been a war, but not this war. His conscious mind had always been slower than the mind of his dreams to understand such things. The mind of his sleep pushed him to write things he never knew he knew, and left it to his conscious mind to haggle over what it all meant.

The script he had just written was different from all the others. It was his first sixty-minute piece, but more than that: it was the first thing he had written for a purpose far greater than the script itself.

Context. But what he really wanted was to see that other script.

A script that had been written the year March Flack disappeared. Accepted and sent up to mimeo, then never produced. Now Kidd wanted it on the air but was leery of the consequences. A radio novice, Jordan Ten Eyck, had given him an answer. Wrap it in context.

His Civil War story was the first piece of the context Kidd needed. Later this week he'd write the tough one, the Japanese family at Tanforan, Americans ripped out of their homes by their own government and put in a prison camp, for the crime of having Japanese faces.

Impossible to do, unthinkable to ignore.

There had been a war, but not this war. But what war and how old? Had he been dreaming of the old World War, of Gettysburg and Bull Run, of the Crimea, the Hundred Years, the Crusades, of Troy?

He thought he had been dreaming of March Flack. He had solved the mystery of Carnahan by linking it to March, not the other way around. You couldn't ask what March had had to do with Carnahan, you could never make it make sense that way—not when you added the Germans and all the stuff about a war that didn't exist when March Flack was here. Instead you had to ask what Carnahan and Kendall could possibly have had to do with March Flack. This seemed to suggest that March had been the only death with a purpose and all the others had been cover-up. That there had been no war at all at the root of it. That the motive might have been anything from a personal grudge to a madman's annoyance with the way March Flack said his lines. That the connection to Hitler might be incidental or imagined, and the Germans were involved by nationality, common interest, or circumstance, take your pick.

He was back where he started. There had been a war, but not this war. March Flack had been in the old World War: so had Harford and Tom Griffin. We were at war with Germany but it was a far different Germany from the one we fight today. And still it makes no sense.

The Germans had to be more than incidental. They had known about the murders of both Kendall and Carnahan and had at least been willing accessories to keep them quiet. One of them, George, had certainly been present when Carnahan died. So I'm back to square one, Dulaney thought. Except for the dream. Except for this new script, and the hunch that something in that old script will lead me somewhere else.

To the old war, he thought, for no particular reason.

((6))

HE had the day free. It was Sunday and there was no Negro show, because this week they were moving to Friday. He gathered his gear for a trip he had been planning in secret. He wasn't carrying much—the two canteens, the gun strapped round his belly, a few fruits and nuts knotted hobo style at the end of a stick. It was four thirty, give or take. Carnahan's watch confirmed this as he clipped the fob to a belt strap and slipped it into his watch pocket.

He wrote her a note—GOING TO CHECK SOMETHING. GONE FOR THE DAY. DON'T WORRY—and left it on the table. She would be furious tonight when she learned where he'd been. He'd be lucky if she didn't banish him to his own bed, in the room downtown that he so seldom used these days.

The sky was overcast as he stepped out onto the deck. There was a rumble in the east and he cursed his luck, that of all the days he had to choose one with weather.

It didn't matter, he was going anyway. Think of those poor bastards at Florence and Andersonville, who slept in the rain for weeks and months, and maybe your own ordeal will seem rather ordinary and small.

He started the car and pulled out quickly. He didn't worry that she would hear him: she was a hard sleeper and it had been a long night at the club. She had only been asleep for an hour and he doubted that the world would see her much before noon.

It would be another hour before the station signed on, so he had to fish for some kind of life on the radio dial. He found a clear all-nighter from somewhere, a guy playing records and trying to stay awake in the three-minute intervals between the music. This was good enough: even the Andrews Sisters at five o'clock in the morning broke his solitude.

He cleared the town and headed west across the bridge as news came on at the top of the hour. The eight Nazis put ashore by submarines were now on trial for their lives in Washington. Two were naturalized Americans, bund activists throughout the thirties; the others had lived in the States, knew their way around, and spoke fluent English. They had given Hoover a full account of Germany's plot to conduct sabotage in America. It had been in the works for years, long before the two countries were actually at war. German Americans had been recruited by the German embassy, and by consulates everywhere, to go back to Germany for training and to get their assignments. Could that be what March Flack had learned? . . . It sounded thin, even to himself, yet he knew they were all somehow linked—March and the Germans, the Schroeders, that crazy Yorkville girl, Kendall, and Carnahan. All dead and linked to the war and to one another.

He looked back over the white marsh, fluttering like ghosts of fireflies in the first gray light from the east. He thought of Carnahan. Turned west toward Pinewood and thought of Holly.

((**7**))

RAIN was falling in the woods near Maynard. In wartime, on a clear day on the beach, dawn would be breaking at six o'clock, but the day was not clear and he had only the sheen on the two steel rails to guide him. The rain was steady and he was thankful for the lightweight slicker he had brought. The gun on his hip swung in time with his step but it didn't weigh him down. It had the opposite effect, able to hearten and keep him.

The dawn went straight from black to gray. There wasn't a sound other than the drip from the trees, and that was a constant.

He had come today for a different purpose but he did stop to check on Carnahan's grave. Five minutes later he reached Holly's road through the woods. He turned east to the sea, drawn by the promise of daylight. The ground was wet, with puddles and stretches of deep slop, but it didn't slow him much. He walked on the grass where the ground was hard.

The woods fell away—he remembered that from the one time he'd walked it—and the land broke into sloughs and stretches of open mudflat. This wasn't like the marsh over by the coast: it was more like an inland swamp, with pools of stagnant water and dead trees sticking up from the bog. The road ran on a backbone of high ground that looked artificial:

probably the remains of an access road to the beach, laid down when Maynard was at its hell-raising best. But there was no place to hide a body here, and that answered one of his questions. The old Maynard town site was the first place with the double attraction: isolation and firm ground.

He came upon pieces of causeway, old planks that kept the road going. He had come well past the point where he'd walked that night in the moonlight, but the country didn't change much. Only once did he look back, and the distance to the woods was equal to the same dark shadow ahead.

He smelled the waterway off to the south; then he saw it, a dull slate color that matched the sky. In time the land began to change; the woods ahead took on a more definite shape, and the small shelf of land flattened and widened. He had come eight miles from Maynard and the world was solid again.

Underbrush reappeared: scrubby stuff, sickly and poor. But it gained strength with every step, a sure sign that he was finished with the swamp. The beach was still some miles away but he had proved his point, that the old Maynard township could be reached by car, on a road that must skirt very near Harford's place. There it was now, the paved state highway running north and south in the distance, with a thick new wall of trees beyond it to the east.

Harford's could only be north of here. He looked back once as he started up the highway. You'd never know that dirt road was there: a hundred cars would pass without one taking notice. Five minutes later he saw another dirt road cutting away to the right: this one well maintained and graded. A row of mailboxes was there at the side. Four of them had names, the fifth only a number. That's my boy, he thought.

Harford's place was a good three miles in from the highway. The road was slippery and he was slowed by the mud, but he reached the gate sometime after nine. Now what? If he went in and got caught, what would he say? There were no easy answers, and he was still standing there contemplating it when he heard a car coming.

It was Kidd's car, he knew it well. He stepped behind a tree as the passenger door opened and Maitland got out to open the gate. Then Maitland got back in the car and they went on up the wooded road. Dulaney stood there for another minute and decided to go in.

The woods deepened, the trees grew thick and tall. The road turned sharply and brought him into a long straightaway. He covered this at the same relentless gait; the road dipped left and the trees began thinning out. He came into the marshlands, and far across the way he saw the flashing red lights of the radio station.

The perspective was different from this side. The marsh was riddled with hard-packed pathways, all the trails old Griffin used when he went back and forth. The road followed the edge for a while, then turned west again into the forest. He looked back across the mile-wide expanse and the billowing rain blotted the tower until only a hint of red flashing in the soup told where it was.

He moved on. Again the trees closed in and the forest looked ancient and enormous. He might have stepped back a thousand years, to the age of Arthur, or half a step to Shakespeare's day. If a man wanted to imagine himself in a forest of ancient Cornwall, or a wood near Stratford, this was a good place to do it.

A small cottage rose out of a dark misty glade, an almost supernatural bit of timing. Stone walls and a thatched roof sharpened the image already in his mind and he went ahead slowly. The windows were shuttered and the path leading through the small front yard was steeped in shadow. He saw other cottages as he came closer, replicas of this one off in the woods. The Elizabethan image deepened: it was part of Mrs. Harford's dream, never used by the theater crowd she had hoped to bring here. Only the cottage at the far end showed any sign of life. The shutters were open and he saw a wagon in a little shed behind the house. So this is where the old man lives, he thought. This is where he practices his craziness.

He gave it a wide berth as he went by. The road came across a small hill and suddenly there was a drastic change in groundskeeping. Fences appeared on both sides and the trees began to thin and he could see green fields like a landscape from the horse country of Florida or Kentucky. He climbed through the fence and struck out across the field, sprinting between the trees till he could walk up to the edge of a barn at the far western edge of the compound.

He could hear horses inside and then, beyond the door, he found himself in a long shedrow with stalls on both sides—a walk-through barn with doors on both ends. He walked past the horses to the far door, cracked it open, and saw the main house only sixty yards away. There was Harford: he had come out to the edge of the porch and looked to be explaining something to the others. Dulaney could see a large building under construction a quarter of a mile away. It was going to be big enough to house an entire network broadcasting operation. Out on the grass was the apparatus for a tower, and steel beams that looked like bones in an elephants' graveyard. He saw trucks, many half loaded with pipes and tools and tarp-covered equipment.

He escaped the way he had come, through the back door and across the field. He melted into the woods and settled again into the dogged gait of a foot soldier. As he came past the cottages he was stopped short by the sound of the old man's coughing. He sees me, Dulaney thought; he's watching even if I can't see him. But there was nothing to do about it and he moved on down the road.

The rest of the day was a gray blur. He stayed on the main roads for the long walk back: it was faster than trying to cross the swamp again and hike back up the slippery railroad tracks. It was two miles to the Pinewood cutoff, then he turned into the long road west. He reached Pinewood late that afternoon and struck out to the south. By the time he got to the old Maynard road the rain was coming down in sheets. He retrieved his car and called it a day. He had come thirty miles.

He tried Holly's number from a phone box in Pinewood but she wasn't in. He prepared himself for a serious ass chewing when he saw her. She still wasn't home when he arrived on the beach, so he stopped at his own place for a shower and some dry clothes. He ate alone, his only real meal of the day, at the fish house not far from the station. Night had fallen as he drove down the beach.

He reached her house at nine and she was there. She jerked open the door and the fear in her face turned at once to anger.

"You bastard! Where the hell have you been?"

But the scolding was brief and his crime forgiven. Pardon arrived in a glass without ice, and she sat quietly and sipped her own as he told her about the day. Later she rubbed his back and kissed the top of his head and he wrapped his arm around her legs and held her close.

((●8●))

HE dreamed that there was no war. Got up at three and exploded into his work, as if the answer to everything lay in some unwritten script still hidden away in his mind. Finished the sixth chapter of *Dark Silver* and immediately began jotting down notes for the most difficult of his prison camp stories. Tried to picture the Doi family at Tanforan but got off on the wrong foot, trying too hard to think like a Japanese. They are Americans, he told himself, and even if they were not it would still be the same. This was his credo in everything he wrote: people are the same all over. Believe that and you can cross any barriers of race and sex.

Now he saw a colored infantry regiment hunkered in the sand in the final moments before a battle. He knew it at once: a nasty little piece of history that romantics liked to dignify with words like glory. There had been nothing glorious about it, just an army of colored men thrown into hell, proving their worthiness to be free by leading the charge themselves. At once he knew his Friday show had to be changed.

They had decided to open with the life of Scott Joplin, a pleasant half hour highlighted by a ragtime collage on Leland's piano—a little too close in proximity and theme to Blind Tom Bethune for his taste, but Waldo wanted a safe

show. He knew Waldo was nervous: they were going to ruffle
some white feathers just by being on in a prime hour, there
was no sense pushing it too far. But this was opening night,
no time to be timid. Kidd hadn't put them there to do "nice"
shows or to entertain white people with nostalgic piano inter-
ludes. This was opening night, for Christ's sake, and in that
predawn vision he knew what he wanted to do.

He started over to the station, went past Mrs. Flack's dark
bungalow, and headed across the dunes. The sand sucked at his
feet, the red light drew him on, and his mind sizzled with all the
creative and tactical problems he faced. The story he had suddenly
seen could not be told in a single half hour. It needed two parts,
the first to get the characters down and make the audience care,
the second to capture some semblance of that desperate charge
into certain death. This meant he'd have to inform Waldo and the
cast, get Zylla involved because now he'd need a mighty score
instead of that piano backdrop, bring in Livia with her bombs and
artillery, and all this had to be done in four days or less so that Friday could be cleared for table readings and rehearsals. All of it fell
on his shoulders but he did not fear it. It made him alive.

((9))

INCREDIBLE Monday. The day he became his own master in
radio. For eight hours he didn't move from his desk, except to
stretch and go to the john.

Waldo called at nine. "Eli said you wanted to talk to me."

"I'd like to change Friday's show."

"Change it to what?"

"Fifty-fourth Massachusetts Regiment at Battery Wagner."

Waldo said, "Jesus." Then, after a moment: "I got no prototype for that."

"I'd like to fictionalize it anyway. Put everything into two colored foot soldiers from the North. All the prejudice that still

exists in our military. I want this story to go beyond what happened and tell what is."

He knew Waldo understood this concept, they had discussed it often enough. Truth is not always accurate. Accuracy can be a shield to hide from the truth. The best fiction is always truer than fact. You learn more about being on the road in the Depression by reading Steinbeck than from any dull compilation of facts. But Waldo had been raised in the shadow of Jim Crow and he was still afraid of his own best material.

"We can stay on the safe path if that's what you really want," Jordan said. "But Kidd has given us his air and I don't think he expects us to soft-soap anyone. We've got an opportunity here to say something that's never been said, and we can be as militant as we dare to be."

"I guess I'd better come down there. I do have some stuff you might could use. I'll be down in the morning."

By ten o'clock he had a script roughed out. Becky Hart came through and he gave her the six chapters of his *Dark Silver* serial.

At noon he called down and told Kidd they were changing the story for Friday. "I've just read your serial," Kidd said. "A wonderful piece of work, Jordan, just outstanding. Can you keep it going with all the other stuff you're doing?"

"The serial's going by itself now. It doesn't feel like work at all."

"All right, if you say so. When can I see the new colored show?"

"I'll have the first part by the end of the day."

He worked through the lunch hour and finished at two. Sent the draft up to mimeo. There would probably be a full rewrite when Waldo arrived but for now he needed three copies that caught his concept.

By four o'clock the word was out: he had delivered a full-blown serial with choice parts soon to be cast. Two of the salesmen had had partial mimeos made for potential sponsors, and Kidd wanted an early start, perhaps as soon as a week from Sunday.

His phone began to ring. Rue called: Becky had just read her the last half of chapter one and she was on fire with the daughter. "I've got to have her, Jordan, she's all I can think about."

Hazel called, wanting the same role. But he had written that for Rue, and he wanted Pauline for the mother. She flew into a rage. "Goddammit, Jordan, this is not fair. You know you're supposed to hold open auditions. You've got no right to play favorites with these continuing roles, they're too important to us all. What is Rue giving you? Is she good in bed? Christ, you're just like everybody else. I know you all hate me, I've always known that."

"Nobody hates you, Hazel," he said, but she had hung up.

This is what a producer does, he thought. Makes a few people happy, breaks a few hearts, makes a few enemies, all in the hopes of coming up with the best mix on the air.

At five o'clock Livia called. "Hey, what are you doing up there? People are talking about you all over the building."

Suddenly it struck him that he was writing his own ticket at Harford.

At quarter to six he retrieved his Fort Wagner mimeos, left one for Kidd and the others for Zylla and Livia, wrote notes to each about the changes that might yet come and what he thought the script would need in music and sound. He went out to eat alone and was back by seven, sitting in his cubicle in the darkening bullpen. The day ended as it had begun, with a vision of the Doi family. He rolled a sheet of newsprint into his typewriter and put down some thoughts, but it was still not working; it somehow lacked the spontaneous combustion of his other stories. This one's got two purposes, he thought. Maybe tomorrow his vision would clear.

Behind him the floor creaked. The Woodsman's ghost, he thought, looking back. The room was black now in all those places where it had just been gray, and the building was virtually empty. His own lamp cast a hazy corona in the middle of the room, and beyond it was the faintest hint of the far hallway. Suddenly he was afraid. He reached over to turn off his lamp—*Then we can both be in the dark,* he thought—but before he did he saw a movement, and the shadow of a man came into the room.

"Hello, Jack," said the shadow.

(((10)))

THE gaunt figure moved toward the light, then stopped at the edge as if waiting to be invited in. As if I'm the boss and he's the hand, Dulaney thought. He nodded his greeting and Harford stepped out of the gloom.

"I had a hunch I'd find you here, Jack. You're always so hard at work, it shames me to think what I'm paying you. How would you like a raise?"

"If you'd like to give me one, sure."

"I would like that. How does a hundred a week sound to you?"

"Like a helluva generous raise."

Harford took the final step into the light and sat on a chair in the opposite cubicle. He took off his glasses and his hand shook . . . as if, perhaps beginning that other morning in the studio, he was forcing himself to do something he had always dreaded. Show his face.

"A man should always make what he's worth, Jack. What you've done this month has amazed us all."

"My name is Jordan. You've forgotten, Jack's just an air name."

"Still, Jack's the name I think of when I think of you. Habits can be hard to break."

"It can't be too much of a habit. We hardly know each other."

"Actually, I know quite a bit about you. I've even read your book."

Dulaney kept his face impassive, giving up nothing.

"What I should really do is leave you alone. Let you do your work under any pretext you want to take on. I'm violating one of my deepest beliefs by coming here tonight."

"What belief is that?"

"Don't mess with the goose that lays the golden eggs."

Dulaney faked a laugh.

"You should never tamper with anything that's going well. But I liked your book, and when you started producing such powerful radio stories . . . well, it became difficult for me not to approach you."

Dulaney sat stone still, watching. Harford reared back into the shadow and said, "You strike me as a man who's uncomfortable with gushing praise, and I'm not normally one who gushes. Maybe we should just leave it at that."

"I'm not sure what it is or where we're leaving it."

"It's whatever you want it to be and we'll leave it back in your own lap, where it belongs. You can be Jordan for whatever reason and for as long as you like. I'll shut up and pay the bills."

An awkward moment passed. Then Harford said, "I had another motive for tracking you down tonight. Would you like to hear it?"

"Sure."

"It has to do with your friend Miss Carnahan."

Dulaney felt a prickly sensation in his scalp and along his spine.

"Perhaps we should call her Miss O'Hara, for consistency's sake."

Cautiously, Dulaney said, "I do know Miss O'Hara."

"Don't get angry when I say this, but I'd hate to have you leave us on her account."

"Why would I do that?"

"She thinks I've harmed her father. Surely you know this. Even if you were not Jack Dulaney you would know it, what with your recent attachment to her. I'm sure she's told you what she suspects about me. I want you to help me convince her she's wrong."

Dulaney said nothing.

"Six months ago she thrust herself into my life. Everywhere I went, she was there. I could have had her arrested, that's how intense she was. But there was something about her . . ."

They looked at each other.

"I still can't put my finger on it. But at times she reminds me . . ."

Harford blinked and shook his head. "Actually there's no resemblance at all between her and anyone I ever knew. Call it a bad case of my own foolishness. And yet . . . something about her touched me. I can't explain it, she just got to me. And one thing led to another."

"What does that mean?"

"Suddenly I wanted to know more about her. Then one morning, I decided that *I* would find her father."

His face was far back in the darkness now. His voice floated across the aisle. "My wife always wanted a daughter. Maybe that explains something."

But if it did, Harford didn't elaborate. He took a deep breath and went on as if he'd never broken his thought. "I figured if I could find her father, she and I could be friends. Nothing lecherous, I assure you. I'm not quite *that* foolish."

He leaned forward into the light. "I thought it would be easy. If you've got money you can find anyone, right? So I hired an agency and took the first step. A preliminary report, a list of his old friends that went back several years. Who he might turn to in a time of trouble. One of the people on that list was you, Jack. They even found me a picture. You were standing with a horse at a Florida racetrack."

Dulaney remembered the picture. He had held the horse for the winner's circle picture, and the next day it was in the *Coral Gables Gazette*.

"So that was the agency's preliminary report," Harford said. "The next step was obvious: send out investigators and talk to the people on the list."

"Is that what you did?"

He shook his head. "Suddenly the idea seemed arrogant, intrusive. As if I were investigating *her*. You can see how she might think that. So I left it alone for the moment, and the moment became weeks. And Miss O'Hara still thinks I'm some kind of monster."

"If that's what she thinks, why would you put her on your air?"

"Are you serious? Of course I put her on, I can't not put her on. Even if there wasn't this . . . *thing* about her, I would put her on. The simple answer is, she's good radio. I'd put Hitler on if he could sing like that."

He made an impatient gesture with his hands. "Come on, Jack, I know you understand this. You've discovered the magic of the air, now you've had a taste of it. Sometimes I think I'd barter my soul in pieces for a few perfect hours. My curse is that I have no talent. When I was young I thought I might write. But I soon discovered how bad I was."

"We're all bad when we're young."

"And some of us will get no better."

"That's hard to say. Sometimes it seems like you're stuck on first base forever. Then you take what the scientists call a quantum jump."

"So Edison was right, is that what you're saying?—genius is all work and no play?"

"I don't think about genius. But there may be something to the notion that a genius is just someone who works harder than the next fellow."

"No, it's more than that. You've got to have vision, and mine was always out to lunch. My role is to provide the playhouse for those like yourself, who have both the talent and the drive."

Dulaney smiled. "It's a great playhouse."

"It was. And will be again."

Abruptly Harford stopped rocking in his chair. "Radio is the greatest invention of the past four centuries. It ranks right up there with Gutenberg's movable type as an earthshaking force. But it's being trivialized in its frenzy to sell deodorant soap and milk of magnesia."

"That's the last thing I'd expect an owner to say."

"Is it? What if I told you I don't care if we make money or not?"

"I'd be surprised again."

"I don't expect to make any money, not if we do it right. Mr. Kidd despairs when I talk like that. He's a programming idealist like myself, but he's still a hard-nosed radio man who thinks we should turn a profit. I know he'll do his best for me, even though he knows I can lose no end of money and still keep us afloat. I've got all the money I'll ever need, and the life span of my family tends to be short."

"I guess that's good, isn't it?"

Harford laughed. "Goddammit, Jack, I like you. Right away I sensed a kindred spirit, though you yourself may not feel that yet. You were a good novelist but you're a born radio man. Do you feel that yet?"

"Yes I do. But my name's not Jack."

Harford smiled indulgently and didn't pursue it. "One of the first things Gutenberg did with his movable type was print a magnificent Bible. The first thing radio did was argue how much selling would be permitted and how ridiculous it would be allowed to get. If it keeps on the way it's going, there won't be anything worth listening to. Right now it's full of sacred cows. The agencies are running everything at the network level and it's getting worse every year. I have this almost morbid fear of the future—not that radio's greatest days will fade away but that its greatest day will never come. Fifty years from now it could be just a medium of hucksters and fools, a whorehouse in the sky. But what if I can be the one who changes that direction?"

He put on his glasses, as if this speech had made him vulnerable in some vital way. "Why do you think I'm here after all these years? Do you think I enjoy haggling with stupid government bureaucrats in order to justify what I do? Does it begin to get a little clearer now, why I put Miss Carnahan on? She is simply the best thing that's been heard on my air in years. Never mind why, reasons don't matter. What Miss Carnahan thinks of me doesn't matter. Her talent is all that counts. It's a thrill to present her, her voice is like a bugle call, a wake-up, every time I hear it. How could I not put her on? I'm honored to put her on, for as long as she'll come sing for me."

He looked at Dulaney over the glasses. "The same goes for you, Jack. I've read your serial. It's marvelous, I'm sure you know damned well how good it is. It's the kind of script I hoped to attract, *if* we're lucky, two or three years from now. I can't imagine anyone not listening to it once they've heard the first chapter."

In the light he flushed self-consciously. "I said I wouldn't gush and here I am gushing. It left me trembling as I read it. Nothing's really happened yet, the story's just beginning, but I found myself quaking in its realism. Then Kidd brought me your Civil War Negro script, and nothing you've done could have prepared me for that. It's the strongest thing I've ever seen for radio. When I read it I knew I had to come see you."

"All that time I was thinking maybe it's too strong."

"Don't ever think that. Don't let the thought ever cross your mind."

"Hell, it's always there. We won't make any friends with that colored show. It's easy to offend people these days."

"Then go ahead and offend them. Anyone who takes offense at a play like that ought to be offended. If they complain we'll offend them again next week. If they challenge my license I'll fight them."

He coughed and sat tall in the chair. "Listen to me, Jack. Someday the networks will try to lure you away from me. *Then* you can start worrying over every word you write. *Then* you can fret about who might be offended if you've got a colored boy being lynched or a good Christian minister cheating on his wife with a teenage girl in the choir. *Then* you can haggle with the men in the booth, who will always represent the sponsor and will win every battle. But not now. Not here."

He stood abruptly. Said, "I've taken up enough of your time." As if I'm the boss and he's the hand, Dulaney thought again. Again Harford became a shadow in the corner of the room. He stood groping with the spirits of the air, a complicated man, wounded and sad. A man who could tremble at a piece of work that would disappear forever the moment it came to life, just as Jack Dulaney had trembled when he'd written it. From the shadows Harford said, "I want to shake the world, Jack," and Dulaney thought, Damn, so do I. In another moment he might have said as much, but by then the shadow man had gone.

((**11**))

HIS sleep that night was deep and unbroken, a stretch of more than seven hours filled with dreams. He knew he had dreamed, he always did, but in the first minutes of the new day he seldom remembered any of it. If he spoke to anyone, or engaged his mind with a piece of work, the dream would be lost forever. But if he allowed himself the luxury of a few quiet moments, it would all come back. Always the last dream first, the one closest to his conscious mind. He closed his eyes and there it was: Carnahan, armed only with his hat, leading a charge of Negroes up the blood-soaked sands of Morris Island. In the dream he himself had been black, one of the doomed men of the Fifty-fourth Massachusetts. Behind him, his buddies were charging around the point, forced hip deep into the bloody surf where the marsh pinched the beach tight. A hurricane of musket fire poured down from the fort and the boys began to drop into the water. What a surprise, he thought: our white officers thought they were all dead in there. How could anything live through the pounding we gave them? An artillery bombardment, incredible to watch, ten hours without letup, almost ten thousand shells lobbed into that little sand fort while our gunboats battered them from the sea. Nothing could live through that, they said, but I knew better. Them Rebs got the power of Satan, they eyes glows in the dark, an' when we come for 'em, they ain't gonna be dead.

Our white officer draws us together for the assault and I say the prayer. Yea, though I walk through the valley of the shadow of death . . .

Carnahan gives a wave of his hat and we start up the beach, crowding around the point as the guns open up in our faces.

Suddenly everything stops, caught like a movie in freeze-frame. A woman's voice cuts across the beach, so quiet now in the absence of gunfire. Livia walks out and stops where two men have just fallen on the wet sand. She looks down at what's left of their faces and raises her own face in despair. *Jesus Christ, I can't reproduce this, there's nothing in my sound room that's big enough. How do you expect me to capture this in a studio?* She is answered by the voice of Maitland, somewhere ahead of her: *Goddammit, Livia, improvise! . . . Isn't that what you're getting paid all this big money to do?* There is an outburst of laughter; Livia looks up at the fort and rolls her eyes, perhaps thinking of last week's puny paycheck, then begins to walk that way. She stops where Carnahan has been frozen, just as he was turning to wave his men on with the hat in his hand. Of course he can't move, but then he does . . . smiles out of his pillar of salt and his eyes cut away to the fort. But now there is no fort: in its place is a director's booth, with Maitland and Stoner sitting behind glass. Suddenly she has the answer. *We'll bring a couple of big speakers right down on the soundstage. Flood the whole place with sound, so the actors hear the same battle noise I'm giving the men in the booth. They'll have to scream to hear their own lines, and maybe that'll give us some sense of the carnage I see here.*

Already Stoner's men are bringing out the biggest speakers ever made: each of them half as big as a house. They must be winched along like a cannon before it's mounted, and it all seems to take forever. It doesn't matter, nobody's going anywhere; even the sun doesn't move until the speakers are mounted and ready to go. One goes on a platform in the marsh, the other on a floating battery out near the ironclads. *Now we can have our battle,* Livia says, and in the same split instant the booth begins to fade, it becomes a fort again, and the men come to life as she starts back down the beach. A shot rings out, and suddenly she's got to run to get off the soundstage before she's killed in the cross fire. She barely makes it, leaping out of the way as the battle heats up. Stoner's men aren't so lucky. The last I see of them they are screaming and clawing at the walls. In that moment, just before they are cut down, I see the faces of George and Peter Schroeder.

His eyes flicked open. The actuality had been superb! In his dream they had almost captured it, caught it as clearly as any catastrophic battle can ever be simulated for the ear alone. He saw Carnahan at the wall, his colored regiment all around him, his Negroes aghast at the magic in his hat. Now at the moment of truth they all wanted to be near him. They would fight from his shadow, where nothing could touch them. He stood on the wall and smacked those Rebs into that great cotton field in the sky.

There had been another dream, and another before that. But he would lose them now. He heard Holly's footsteps in the hall and their first words of the day would dash any memory he might have had. She turned into the bathroom and he had a short vision of the next dream in the chain. They were walking the boardwalk and suddenly the old man, Pauline's friend, had appeared before them. He had come to tell them that it *was* the old war, it was never this war at all.

The door cracked open and she came into the room and sat on the bed. "What's with you, old man? Gonna sleep all day?"

"What time is it?"

"Ten after seven."

"Jesus," he said, his voice thick with sleep. "When did you come in?"

"Usual time. You were dead to the world so I hated to bother you."

"That's what happens when you can't sleep more than four hours a night. One night a month, you die. What about you? Did you sleep?"

"Not yet, but I will. I had stuff on my mind when I got home, so I sat out on the deck for an hour. Then I came in and read a book."

Thirty minutes later they sat on the deck talking and eating. He told her about his dream, what the old man had said about another war, long ago. He couldn't get it out of his head that March Flack was their true starting point. That the others were linked perhaps only by necessity. That the threads went back to the old war, not to this one.

This was new ground to her, something he hadn't shared. "That old man might have the answer to everything," she said. "We've got to talk to him."

"Yeah, but how? He's only coherent half the time. He's shell-shocked and angry and he sees threats behind every tree."

"He's in love with Flack's wife, she told you that herself. That's his weakness."

"That's her interpretation."

"Then it's mine too. I've watched them together since I first got here and I know the signs. The old war's not all that's got him dippy."

They were quiet for a while. "She saw lights back in the marsh," Holly said. "What does that tell you? It was either Harford or the old man. Choose your poison. Somehow we've got to find a way to talk to him. I think it should be me who does it."

"Not alone, you don't."

"He's going to be upset if he gets as much as a glimpse of you. He knows you, he's seen you talking with Mrs. Flack. I can be a new face."

"I don't like it."

"Then you come up with something."

"I can't. All I know is, if you go see him, I'm going to be there."

"We'll see. Now why don't you shut up and put me to bed?"

Tuesday. Another incredible day at Harford. Suddenly he had the last word on everything he wrote. *Dark Silver* was down from mimeo: a thick package of scripts on his desk with a note from Kidd asking for early auditions, cast assignments, and the soonest possible starting date. A note from the sales staff. Could he meet with a prospective sponsor Thursday at noon? . . . a silverware company in Connecticut liked the title and might create a *Dark Silver* table setting if he'd work a men-

tion into his story line every other week. Zylla needed to confer on music as soon as he had the final rewrite for Friday's
show. Livia had some technical questions about the bombardment. And there were at least a dozen telephone slips from
New York, actors in the second tier of radio regulars who had
already heard of him, probably from Rick Gary, and were willing to travel for steady work. Another note from Kidd: the
radio critic for the *Times* was coming down on Friday, would
like to watch the Negro show and perhaps do a short interview,
which would run in the paper sometime next week.

Becky Hart arrived as usual at ten o'clock. "Waldo's waiting for you downstairs. You look like a man under siege this
morning."

"I never knew how much other stuff was involved in writing radio."

"Cheer up, Jordy, the marines have landed. Kidd says you
can have me for four hours a day if you want me. I'll take care
of the busy stuff."

"God *bless* the wisdom of Jethro Kidd."

She laughed. "I've found us a spare room we can use for an
office. That'll get you out of the firing range and buy you
some work time. I'm having a phone put in tomorrow. I
know that's a pest but I guess it's a necessary evil. At least
you'll be out of this bullpen."

They looked at each other for a moment. "What are you
doing tonight?" he said.

"Nothing that can't be changed. What's on your mind?"

"I'd like you to produce *Dark Silver* for me."

It didn't sink in at once, what he was telling her. "You want
me to get some people in for a reading?"

"I want you to produce this serial for the air. The whole
shebang."

She looked stunned. "Are you serious?"

"I can't think of anybody I'd rather have. Who's got better
judgment. Who works harder or is more competent or knows
the business as well."

Only determination saved her from sudden tears. "Jesus,
can you do this on your own?"

"Harford seems to think I can do anything." He shrugged. "Let's find out how much rope they're willing to give me."

"Well, thank you," she said, still fighting tears. "I'll try to do a good job."

"I have no doubt. Now, about tonight. Call Brinker and Rue."

She scrambled for a notepad.

"Tell them I'd like to read them tonight, about eight o'clock. If the time's bad, do what you can, make it tomorrow if that's the best we can do. I need Pauline, too, and both announcers. Tell Brinker he'll be doing the younger son. That still leaves you two key roles to fill before we can schedule the first broadcast."

"Don't forget the villain. That awful man on the racing board."

"I think Eastman may be just right for that. He's certainly got enough natural piss for it." He picked up his notes. "Then I need you to answer these phone calls."

She recognized most of the names. "There are some good actors here."

"That's what we need, a couple of good actors. We want voices for the father and the older son that haven't been heard here a million times over. The father's the family's strength. He's where the daughter gets all her fire. But he's also the fiber, the measured calm of the older son. That's what I need you to do today, right now before you do anything else. Get on the phone and use your best judgment about who might work, then invite those people down for an audition."

"Do you want them tonight?"

"In an ideal world, yes, that would be great. Tell them we'll send a car for them and put them up here in the hotel. Make sure they understand these are leading roles and we're asking them for a long-term commitment. I don't want to change any of those five voices once we're on the air."

"You know who'd be great for the father? Rick Gary."

"Yeah, he would." He thought for a moment. "He sure would."

"If he wasn't so busy on the network."

"Ask him anyway, maybe we'll get lucky, catch him just when he's getting sick of the big-city rat race."

"I think he's got a thing for Rue. That could help us."

"No, that's exactly the wrong reason. He's got to want to play this part. If he comes because of Rue, one of two things will happen, both of them bad. Either the thing with Rue won't pan out and he'll be gone. Or it will and he'll take her away to New York and we'll lose them both."

"Poor Jimmy. He's going to lose her and he knows it."

He thought of Holly and Tom and the way things sometimes happen. But that was life, you couldn't change it and you probably shouldn't try. "Go on, ask him down," he said. "If he comes I'll have a talk with him and we'll decide then if we're buying a load of trouble."

He shuffled through his notes and ticked off the remaining items.

"Would you please handle this? Tell the advertising staff I'll take anybody's money, but all they get is a straight commercial. Make sure the silverware company understands what this story's about. I doubt if most racetrackers have ever seen a formal dinner setting."

"I'll handle it. You shouldn't be bothered with stuff like this."

"Here's another one. A reporter is coming down Friday to watch us do the colored show. Tell Kidd I'm not good with interviews, have him talk to Waldo and the cast. Play up the fact that Waldo was doing this show six years before I got here. Keep me in the background, as far back as possible. I know that's not going to be easy. Do what you can for me."

He shuffled paper. "Touch base with Livia and Zylla. Tell them I'll have the Battery Wagner final first thing in the morning. Both of them need to think big. We need a score with power and sweep. And Livia needs to produce the end of the world by fire and thunder, the biggest sound she can imagine. Tell her we won't know for sure what we've got till the cast gets here on Friday, because I want to try an experiment with speakers on the soundstage. Big ones, placed on the dead sides of the mikes. I want the place flooded with noise, I want the actors to hear it all when the bombardment starts, so they'll have to scream to hear themselves think."

He spiked his notes and she made her own. Occasionally she had a question. Sometimes he had an answer, but often she was left to her own devices.

"Then," he said, "when you get everything else done, I'd like you to tell Kidd I need to see that prison camp script."

She made the note and almost let it pass without comment. But at last she said, "What's going on?" and he gave a little shrug as if to dismiss it.

"I'm trying to give Kidd the context he needs to get that play on the air. Tell him I need to see that original script so I can make the others blend and do what we want them to. Tell him I've already got one written and I'm working on the others. The Japanese script is giving me trouble. It wants to get angrier than how I originally saw it. I keep seeing the faces of those kids at that relocation camp and I'm having trouble getting into their shoes."

"Are you talking about American Japs?" Her eyes opened wide in astonishment. "My gosh, Jordan, what are you *doing*?"

"Just something to go with the script you found. A lightning rod."

"It'll be a lightning rod, all right. Jesus, we'll be attacked by mobs and burned to the ground."

They seemed to be finished. She folded her notes and got up to leave.

"Well, thank you again for the chance."

"My pleasure."

She looked thrilled again, excited. "Suddenly I've got a feeling about this place. I think we're going to do things that may never be done again. The talent's always been here. You were the missing ingredient."

She looked at him through the smoky haze. "Something tells me you'll be needing me a lot more than four hours."

"Then tell Kidd that," he said.

((12))

WALDO had brought him a memoir, written down by one of the battle's survivors, never published, stashed in an archive after the man's death. "I copied it myself by hand, long ago," Waldo said. "Thought it might give you some ideas. I don't think we can use it as it stands, and I'm not sure what copyright law might still be in effect after sixty-five years. But it's got some juice in it."

It was better than that. It reshaped his two lead characters without changing any of the music or sound. An air of excitement had come over Waldo, banishing his fear. He sees it now, Jordan thought: he sees what an opportunity this is. They worked over the noon hour and by two o'clock they had Friday's script marked into oblivion and again ready to be typed for mimeo. "It's different enough now, I don't think we need to worry about the man's great-grandson suing us," Waldo said. But as they finished, the voice of that long-dead black soldier seemed to demand his name, and Jordan typed in a credit line: *Suggested by the unpublished memoir of Private Leroy Stokes, Fifty-fourth Massachusetts Colored Infantry, U.S.A.* "I think we're ready to go," he said.

He skipped lunch and moved on. Alone now, he sat at his desk and in a while the bullpen babble began to fade and the smoky air took on the earthy pungence of a shedrow. Again he saw that Japanese child waving at him through the fence at Tanforan. Saw the worry in her father and the weary despair in her mother as the guard called their names. The father stood and the woman and children came at once to his side. Such quiet people, so disciplined and dignified. So willing, at least on the surface, to make this sacrifice for their country.

Maybe that was their problem as fictional people. They sacrificed too willingly.

His eyes flicked open to the first real glimmer of story.

They were far too orderly and ready to cooperate. Never mind that they had no more choice than a Jew in one of Hitler's camps . . . what they lacked, for the purpose of drama, was that moment-to-moment struggle to survive, the main order of business in Poland and on Bataan and in the Confederate hellholes of 1864. This was a different kind of prison camp. No violent or pestilent death, just a slow, steady sapping of the soul.

If I were Ben Doi I would be angry, he thought. I'd be goddamned angry and I'd do whatever I could to disrupt the harmony of the camp.

What would they do to a Japanese malcontent?

Now his story came in a rush of thoughts and pictures. He'd need to change the hero's name. Doi was too subtle. The listener must know at once what was going on and exactly who the characters were. The name Sakamoto came into his mind and he wrote it down. The father's name is Danny. His wife is named Jill. Jordan had heard that they called themselves Nisei, American citizens born of alien parents. They must speak flawless English: a formidable challenge to the actors who must capture that Japanese touch almost by innuendo, without anything resembling dialect. Danny and Jill Sakamoto. They have two children, Lucy and Leo. For years they have been making monthly payments on a house and a small business in San Francisco. They will lose everything. Danny Sakamoto faces his family's ruin in disbelief, then with growing anger.

In the heat of that moment a streak of rage shot through his eyes and out through his fingers to the paper that suddenly appeared in his machine. The next time he looked up, the day was gone and the bullpen was empty. He heard the footsteps in the hall: Becky Hart, coming to tell him about her efforts of the day.

Rue and Brinker and Pauline were all free for tonight. Stallworth was a maybe; Eastman hadn't been home. Rick Gary didn't answer in New York. "But all the other New York actors are interested and will be here. I've arranged to have them picked up."

"Good. Have you talked to Kidd yet?"

"He's been out of touch all day. Over at the office building sequestered with the man. But your office is ready. If you'd like to see it."

It was a small room across the hall, with a desk and a typewriter and an exit to the roof. She gave him the only key. "If you want to use the roof I can put a table out there. On mild days you can work yourself silly in the fresh air. You can speak directly to God."

She had provided him a shelf of reference books—dictionaries in several languages, a fat one-volume encyclopedia, a world almanac, an atlas, an NBC guide to dialect and pronunciation, and several volumes of military history. There was a globe within arm's reach, and on the wall above him a chart showing the developing theaters of war.

"As your racetrackers would say, we're off and running. My home number's marked on your calendar. Use it if you need anything, day or night. If you get a brainstorm and you want a sounding board, I'm a pretty good one, even at midnight."

She picked up his approval and shrugged modestly. "I'll get your stuff moved over now if you want."

It didn't take them long to move: they made it in one load and he settled in at his desk as the clock bumped its way past six. "I'll bring you something to eat," she said, and he nodded absently as she left the room. Then the muse flooded through him and he knew this was going to be a very good place. He gave the globe a spin and stopped it with his finger. There they were, Carnahan and Kendall, somewhere in the Pacific, torpedoed and cast adrift on a raft, hiding from the Japs in a dense stretch of unpopulated islands. A good straight adventure yarn with no pretensions to be anything else. He leaned over his desk and wrote quickly, raw notes to be filed with his other undeveloped ideas and brought out in their own time.

At some point he began writing script again. He was back at Tanforan with his Nisei and when he looked up Becky had put a sandwich beside him: she had come and gone and he hadn't seen or heard her. And she had left him something else, a folder with a script in mimeo. He read the title page: *A Friday Afternoon,* by Paul Kruger. So this is what it's all about, he thought. All the fuss, all the death. He looked at the clock . . . an hour before rehearsal. And with time on his hands, he read it.

((« **13** »))

FRIDAY was just another day in the labor camp at Germiston. An hour ago two children had died and half a dozen more would be dead by sundown. A day when only six died was a good day, unless one of the six was yours.

The name of the camp hinted at something German. This was especially true today, with news of Nazi concentration camps beginning to come to light. But the play had been written in 1936. The significant year in his own struggle. The year of March Flack; the year Maitland and maybe Kidd had first arrived, however briefly; the year Mrs. Harford died and the station, having just begun work on its new office building, had folded its cards and gone into deep hibernation.

So this was not Germany, not even the Germany of the old war. It nagged at his consciousness but he couldn't place it. He moved on. Now he saw that what he had assumed was a labor camp was something else. It was certainly a prison camp but not a place where labor was enforced. Still, there was death. There was typhoid and measles and malnutrition. There was never enough food and what there was was wormy and poor. One pound of meal a day. No vegetables, no milk, scant meat. Children grew feverish and lay on the hard-baked earth to die.

The heroine was a young woman named Margaret, obviously of some land far away. Her speech should sound foreign yet not be foreign, the writer directed: then, as she speaks, let the stream of English rise out of the elusive context and enhance the mythic undertone. About fifteen seconds in, the original voice should begin to fade as a proxy is potted up to speak for her. This is how the listener would be made to know, by the first voice being absorbed into the second, that it was somewhere far away.

There were no men in the Germiston camp, at least not in Margaret's immediate range of acquaintance. Her world was confined to a dusty earthen street of stinking tents, suffocating, infested with fleas and lice. She shared the tent with two other women, all of them strangers six weeks ago. The younger was named Dort, still a child but soon to bear a child of her own. The likelihood was great that Dort would die, and the child's death was certain. Margaret feared for Dort but also for herself, for she too was in the early stages of pregnancy. She tried not to think of this but it was no use: in the concentration camp at Germiston there was little to do but think, so she filled the hours in the hot tent with her dire thoughts. Only occasionally did she find relief in the pleasanter dreams of a happy childhood.

On Friday the three of them sat as the wind whipped the canvas and the sun turned their inner world orange. At noon the tent had the hue of burnt amber near the roof, retaining its black void on the floor. The three of them sat perfectly still, their faces a hellish mix of orange and black, their arms a deeper red, their bodies disappearing below the waist as if they were half beings rooted in the soupy blackness. The story took hold from the moment of the proxy's arrival and Margaret's first words in English: *If only I could die.*

If only I could die without fear or pain, if I could die peacefully before this bastard child begins to show inside me. If I could die before Poppy comes home from the war and sees me. If I could die I would, but how can I die, God, when I haven't even begun to live yet?

Margaret was sixteen.

She was a year older than Dort and perhaps half the age of Kee, who sat across the tent bobbing her head in half sleep. Kee had a volatile temper and a deep crazy streak, an ugly spirit full of meanness that kept Margaret and Dort always tense and often frightened. They never knew when Kee would open her eyes and strike out at them.

"What are you looking at?"

"Nothing."

"You were staring at me while I slept."

"I wasn't . . . I really wasn't."

"I could kill you, do you know that? I could smother you and no one would look twice at your corpse. They'd just throw you in a hole with all the others who die."

Last week Kee had threatened them with a knife and Dort had reported this to one of the soldiers. Now came the first male voice, with a slender echo-chamber effect to emphasize the flashback.

"Give me the knife, Mother."

"Get away from me . . . get away . . . I got no knife."

"Have I got to come in there and take it from you? You know what'll happen if you make me do that."

Kee had gone mad after her husband had been killed in the early days of the war. So they said, but Poppy had always believed that madness was like red hair and thick bones, in your blood from the start. A wise man, her father. She wondered if he still lived.

In the worst part of the day Margaret dreamed of home. Before the war she had lived on a farm, two thousand acres sprawling across a brown plain with hills in every direction. She lived with her father and mother, two brothers, and a younger sister they had named Cassie in honor of her mother's mother, who had come from abroad. Margaret's twin brother, Jan, had been taught marksmanship by their father from the age of seven and had become a great hunter, and Poppy was also teaching their younger brother, Lar, how to shoot. They planted groundnuts and maize and raised cattle and goats and pigs and chickens. The farm was remote, the sense of isolation acute to a girl growing up there. The village was half a day's drive by wagon and their neighbors across the hills were the Smuts boys, who they saw three or four times a year. Occasionally a traveling parson would pass their way, or a trader in livestock, who'd buy for the market at Cape Town, almost a thousand miles to the south and west.

A few suggestions for sound effects. The jingle and squeak of a harness, the labored breathing of a plow horse. The chickens as she fed them, and at night, in the middle of a July winter, the gentle sound of a fire on the hearth.

A few scenes to bring life to a family. Just enough to make them real. To give them faces. To make a listener care across all that distance and all those years.

We loved one another.

She opened her eyes. If only I could die.

If I could just die and be like all the others.

The music came up. The writer suggested a simple theme on traditional instruments to take it to the twenty-minute station break.

Then, suddenly, a full orchestra to open the second act: a stark change of pace as the protagonist became Margaret's brother Jan and the scope became epic.

The story now followed a single commando unit fighting its way across the veld. A tattered clump of men, always on the run. The war was lost but they had become guerrillas, and they still had bitter lessons to teach these arrogant people who had colonized their country.

They ambushed a column of soldiers at Muller's Pass. Attacked an army on the Klip River, scattering a force so superior to their small numbers that their mettle alone sent the enemy scrambling into the water in panic.

They came at dusk, with the pickets just going out and the officers at mess, sitting on chairs under coal-oil lamps. They killed at random—officers, men, horses—then they were gone.

Hit and run, hit and run: north out of Newcastle and doubling back to hit again. North toward Vriede. Give them hell and then, when they muster up to fight, show them nothing but the wind on the grass and the dead bodies of their brothers.

Out on the veld, far east of what the enemy would call a massacre, Jan sat on the ground and thought of home. They couldn't have a fire so he warmed himself with thoughts of old times. Visions danced in the pitch at his feet and he let them go on much too long. He would often look back on this night, the night of his seventeenth birthday.

His and Margaret's. He wondered how she was, how Lar and Cassie and Mamma were, and how the farm was coming through the war. In the place where the grass grew darkly around his feet he saw his sister's eyes and his heart ached. He loved his mother fiercely but it was always Margaret he thought of, because they had shared the womb and twins are like that.

How many men had he killed in a year? The one tonight: he saw him now. Magnificent mustaches and a full head of bright red hair. Eyes wide open and then nothing: no eyes, no face, gone like a grape crushed between his fingers. Someone's son, someone's brother, someone's dear husband. These were destructive thoughts, the kind of soul-twisting stuff he'd steeled himself so well against. In thoughts of death he again thought of home. He wondered if his mother had yet been told of Poppy's death, and this turned his mind to things that troubled him more. He knew the enemy was scorching the earth, a last-ditch campaign to root out the commandos and crush the resistance. It had begun last fall, in March or April, and from the first he had struggled to put it out of his mind. Poppy had told him on the very day he'd been killed: don't be affected by it, this is still a civilized army we're fighting, they won't dare make war on women and children.

Now they were up, hours before the dawn, trekking toward Standerton. He knew the country well for a farm boy who had never, in his first fifteen years, gone more than twenty miles from home. He knew that the hard-packed road to the left would take him to Johannesburg, the great city on the veld that had once filled his dreams with wonder. He wanted none of it now: he wanted only peace, and a chance to live out his days on the land where he'd been born.

They skirmished with a small party south of Standerton and lost three men. Their ranks had been shredded by their constant marauding, by death and defection. Just before dawn two more men walked away and at sunup only five remained. An angry argument broke out as to direction and tactics, and most went east into Swaziland, a small country, supposedly neutral, where they might regroup and gain time to figure out what to do next.

Jan went alone now. His war was over—never again will I fire a gun in anger, he thought. He followed a dry river bottom toward Nylstroom, a three-day trek. Another half day east to the farm. He felt the queerest mix of excitement and fear as he trekked along the river and crossed, sometime after nightfall, at the wooden bridge. Off in the distance he saw the glow of a burning house. The stench of death was all around him. In the morning he saw, strewn along the road and scattered in the fields, the bloated corpses of many cattle and sheep. Houses and crops burned to the ground. Nothing left standing, nothing left alive. Goats and pigs shot and left to rot where they fell. Chickens scattergunned in whole flocks: whatever couldn't be eaten or carried, destroyed. A barn half burned, doused by yesterday's rain. The scorched bodies of two horses and a mule, and the soggy remains of the hay room sagging like uncut sorghum into the earth. Tack thrown about: what had not been taken, chopped apart with axes or doused with oil and set afire. A dog beheaded, a child's pet, its body riddled by a dozen sabers. All this and not a person anywhere. Not a man, woman, or child, dead or alive.

He had heard about the detention camps, they all had. Much of this talk was said to be the demoralizing tactics of the enemy, but how much of that was countertactic by commandos trying to keep their men from mass defecting? You couldn't know until you came home and saw it yourself.

He was now within that twenty-mile circle of his childhood, a stretch of road he'd seen a hundred times in his sleep. He knew every rise and each blade of grass, but now the land was sucked dry and stripped of everything that had given it life in his heart. He stopped at the crossroads and suddenly he wept. Covered his face with his hands and couldn't move for a long time. He quaked at the thought of climbing that last hill . . . he who had killed a dozen men before his seventeenth birthday . . . he who had been cited for valor. He stood in the road and cringed from the hill until, finally, he forced himself to move.

A blackened cornfield rose to his right. He stepped over the ditch and walked into it and felt the soft give of the ash earth under his boots. Not recent, he knew: not like the stuff he'd seen a few days ago. Torched last summer from the look of it, probably just as the corn was beginning to ripen for the harvest. An entire army must have come through here; he could see the swath they'd cut, the litter they'd left behind. Ration tins. Newspapers bleached white by the sun. Any number of empty cloth tobacco sacks. Soon the whole nation would be black from their fires.

He moved on up the hill and stood at the top of it and felt the breath catch in his throat. Everything was gone—the house, the barn, the outbuildings, all burned flat with the earth. Only part of one kraal left standing where the fire hadn't quite finished with it. A mockery, he thought. An insult. He ran screaming down the hill and kicked it to pieces.

He sat on the ground and waited for the enemy to find him.

This was what it had come to: years of struggle and blood, and for what? England wanted our gold mines. They wanted our diamond fields and now they'd have it all. Annexed, they called it. We've been annexed into their bloody empire, consumed by their greed.

A shadow passed over the boy's head and instinctively he cringed. But the face that looked down at him was gentle and black. Kruin, the weather-etched colored man who had worked for his father forever. Suddenly he was on his feet, sobbing into the old man's arms.

"Young master," said Kruin. His voice was full of shock. This was not done in a land where races were kept in strict separation, but Kruin was overcome by the boy's distress. He patted him gently on the shoulders and said, "Young master," again and again.

His mother was dead. The soldiers had done things to her that could not be talked about, and one of them shot her when she clawed his face trying to keep him from doing it to Margaret.

Kruin struggled with the words. The little master too had been shot. They had found a gun hidden in his coat and had called him a terrorist. He was thirteen years old. But this was no longer a gentleman's war, one of them had said. The Boers with their guerrilla tactics had brought it on themselves.

A renegade unit, the boy thought. A bunch of rogues that made him hate them all no less. But what of Margaret and Cassie?

Kruin knew nothing of Cassie. But Margaret . . . They had done unspeakable things to her, and perhaps they'd have killed her too. But the British regulars had come and they'd rescued Margaret and taken her away somewhere. South and west they'd gone, toward the great city Johannesburg.

A short third act: a mix of orchestra and small instruments. A sudden realization where they had taken Margaret.

If she lives, she must be in the camp for undesirables at Germiston.

The camp for undesirables. Where women and children are starved and thrown into filth. Where rations are doled out according to politics. If you belonged to a man on commando, you got less to eat. Starve the children, surrender the guerrillas: that was the policy and everyone knew it.

For two weeks he was hidden by patriots who warned him not to go there. But he did go, in a British lieutenant's uniform stripped long ago by his comrades from a fellow who wouldn't be needing it anymore.

His friend had warned him. "You're taking your life in your hands. If they look at you twice they'll know you're too young for that uniform. If you say more than ten words your accent will give you away."

But on a Friday afternoon he walked boldly into the camp, a few miles south of Johannesburg, and identified himself as Lieutenant Browning. Told the guard he had to speak with one of the Boer prisoners. Her brother had defected and was giving them intelligence on Boer activity in the north, and they needed her to help establish his reliability.

It was easy: the camp was lax and no one questioned his story. He gave her name to a guard and was led into a street of tents whipped by swirls of dust. They stopped and the guard shook a flap until an older woman stuck her head out and cursed him in Dutch.

"A real loony bird, that one," said the guard, moving on. "I forgot your girl's been moved. She's been infected."

"Infected with what?"

"Don't worry, you won't catch it if you take care. Just keep well back and don't touch them."

They stopped at a barbed-wire pen in the far corner of the camp. "She'd be in here," the guard said. "You know what she looks like?"

"I'll find her."

He took down the wire gate and walked into the kraal. Scores of women and children sat on the bare earth. Gaunt faces, eyes beyond desperation. This was where they were put when they were dying.

"Margaret."

She raised her head. Stared at him but didn't seem to see. The child at her breast was shriveled and splotchy and so was she. Her hair had begun to shed and her arms and face were covered with a rash that anyone who'd been in the army knew on sight. Syphilis.

He had a sudden impulse to snatch the bastard infant and smash its brains out. He kneeled and touched her arm. "Oh my God, Margaret!"

She pulled away. "You mustn't touch me, Jan."

They talked but he was dismayed at how little they had to say. Too much of what they'd shared was gone from their lives: the present was too cruel and to talk of happy times was beyond his endurance. Soon she too would be gone. There was no use denying it, she'd be dead in a week. No use lying, no use living, and yet, in their last moments, he found something to live for. He made her a pledge. "I swear I will kill them for what they've done. I promise I will never stop killing them."

Back to the gate, blinded by tears. To the guard's shack, blinded by hate, and on into the coming South African night.

September 20, 1900. Dusk of another Friday in the Transvaal.

That night he did his first cold murders. Waited for the guards to come off duty and followed them through the streets. In the morning he killed two more: British officers he met on the road back to Johannesburg.

Music up and out. Overture with full orchestra.

Dulaney sat quietly for long minutes, his mind filled with Boers and Germans and long-dead British officers. With Carnahan and Kendall. March Flack as Lord Kitchener, his chest splashed with medals. And Paul Kruger, famous in his day, probably some great South African freedom fighter.

He tried to remember his world history, but his knowledge of South Africa was too spotty and the Boer War had always been slighted in American textbooks. *We* weren't in it, so it couldn't have amounted to much.

Then he remembered something that brought him straight up in his chair and made the hair bristle on his arms. Just a line or two, perhaps a short paragraph read long ago in an encyclopedia. There had been another famous man in South Africa then. The man England had sent to crush the Boers, do whatever it took to bring that damned war to an end.

Kitchener. The man who invented the concentration camp.

((14))

FROM that moment, he never doubted its truth. He read it again, literally now, not as fiction, and suddenly many questions began to clarify.

Why would a killer confess his childhood murders in a radio script? Because he can't help himself. Even after forty years his hatred of England is so intense that he will take any risk to tell what she did to him. He spreads out his case as if the whole world must see it his way—the single-minded intent of the British empire to destroy the women and children of a land they had no right to be in.

Even the Germans make sense. He joins hands with anyone who is England's enemy. Whitemarsh, if it is ever pinned down, will turn out to be just what it sounds like, a German code name. He has probably been spying on British activity in the States since 1939 and maybe much longer, but his motives have nothing to do with politics. He probably cares nothing for the so-called ideals of the Nazi government, they may even sicken him, but still he seeks vengeance for his own personal ghosts. That's why he killed March Flack, an old imperialist who dared throw the spitting image of Kitchener in his face. There is indeed a German angle, but it wraps around a motive much older and deeper.

At some point the German angle takes on a life of its own. The more you do for them, the more they demand. It is so much easier to begin a campaign of spying than to end it, and suddenly the hour is late and even a fool can see that relations between Tokyo and Washington are disintegrating. Any day now there will be war with Japan. Germany and Italy will inevitably follow, and then he will be spying against America, an automatic death sentence in wartime. He knows they must be careful but they are not careful enough. Somehow they are discovered by Carnahan, a handyman with his run of the place, and everything begins to unravel.

Dulaney heard footsteps in the hall and recognized the gait. Becky Hart. She knocked on the door.

"Jordan?"

He looked at the clock. Five past eight.

"Yeah, I'm coming."

"Everyone's here."

"Good. I'll be right down."

He turned over the final page and found a sheet of notes in Becky's hand. Got out his notebook and made his own notes.

In 1936, Paul Kruger had apparently been living in an apartment on New York's West Side, near Ninth Avenue and Fifty-sixth Street. "He did accept our check for the script," she had written. "According to our records it was endorsed P.

Kruger and made payable to a John Riordan, also of that address. So we do seem to own the property, if we want to make something of it now. If we can."

Holly must know this, he thought: she must be told.

Told what? I still don't know who he is. But I know who he was.

((15))

HE came into the studio and Brinker appeared as if he'd been waiting there at the door. "Jordan," he said, "I need to talk to you, now if you can, before we get started." But they were mobbed as the actors came down to meet him and shake his hand. Rue introduced him to half a dozen people at once, and he forgot all the names as they moved into the room and down to the edge of the soundstage. He heard Brinker say his name and he looked up and nodded. Then Becky Hart had him for a short conference at her table.

"Rick Gary's coming. I talked to him about half an hour ago. He's got an early show tonight on NBC so he can't get here till ten. Just a bug in your ear when you start reading the others for the father—the best may be yet to come."

She shuffled her notes. "Stoner and Livia want to sit in, if you don't mind. That's about it. I did tell Kidd what you said. About me producing the show. He laughed, if you can believe that—the man actually laughed at our spunk. I guess I'm yours, sweetheart. Use me well. I look tiny but I'm fast and fearless and I don't break."

Suddenly they hugged each other and he thought, This is how we begin. In an ideal world, sit on a stool at the edge of the stage and begin.

"I apologize for being late and thank you all for coming. I wish I had a part for each of you, but there will be other parts as we go along. Tonight I hope we'll form the core of a standing company, one that can be used on many projects, not just this one."

He talked for a moment about his horse people. How a river of life was what he wanted, a mythic tone wrapped in a hard shell of modern realism. "It's not about horses, it's about people. Here in this studio is where they come to life."

There wasn't a sound in the room as he looked from face to face. Each of them had years in the business, yet he felt a thousand years old in the matters of his story and how it must be told. An actor might not know what osselets were or what a sweatbox was used for, how a horse got on the vet's list and what that meant to people who were not rich and had to keep 'em running. They wouldn't know what a bug boy was, or a bleeder, or when and why a running horse changed its lead. "Don't worry about this tonight. My tendency is to explain nothing in fear of losing the realism. We will try to hold the listener with character and plot and let the background wash over him as it goes along. If I write it right, the listener won't care that he doesn't know these things, and then, suddenly one day, he does."

He waited for questions. There were none, and Becky began assigning them a pecking order. Each would be read alone while the others adjourned to the smaller studio down the hall and waited to be called. Jordan felt a momentary lightheartedness as Stoner made an O-K signal with his finger and thumb. This would be a helluva thrilling night, he thought, if I were Jordan Ten Eyck.

He opened the door to the booth. Stoner had his transcribing equipment ready to cut, with a shiny smooth black disc on the turntable. "I thought you might like some of this recorded," he said. "Then if you've got two actors who are very close, you can listen to them tomorrow before you set it in stone."

"What a great idea, Gus. I owe you one."

"Just look up and nod your head and I'll be recording in here."

He turned, almost bumping into Brinker, who had come up behind him.

"Jordan. I know you're busy but I really need to talk to you. I got my draft notice today."

They didn't say anything for a moment.

"Good-bye, Mamma, I'm off to Yokohama," Brinker said.

"When do you report?"

"Ten days. They don't give you much time. Anyway, I wanted to tell you before you got started. Before you waste any time on me."

"Well," Jordan said lamely. "I appreciate that."

"Rue doesn't know yet, I just found out myself an hour ago. I'd like to tell her now if it won't disrupt your audition."

"Sure. Absolutely."

But they stood there and finally Brinker said, "I guess we'll find out a lot of things now. I hear Rick Gary is coming."

"That's what I hear too."

Brinker laughed but Jordan could see the fear in his eyes. He's dead certain he's not coming back, and if he does, everything will be different.

"He's a great actor," Brinker said. "Don't pass him up on my account if you can get him."

Jordan wanted to say something positive but he'd never been much of a flag waver in the face of bad news. What he finally said was simple: "I've got a good feeling about you, Jimmy. For what that's worth at a time like this."

"You might be surprised what it's worth. I've admired you right from the start. I just wish I could be here to do this damn fine thing you're putting on."

"I wish you could too, Jimmy."

His words felt wooden but Brinker's eyes filled with tears. Abruptly he turned and walked away.

Now we have three to cast, Jordan thought. But that made light of it, and Brinker's departure hit him harder than he could've imagined. He barely knew the kid, but the loss he felt was suddenly deep, almost personal.

He disposed of the announcers quickly. Stallworth would announce and Eastman, after reading a few crucial lines, was made chairman of the Jockey Club. Then Becky began calling the actors, who each came in and read a page or more, pausing occasionally to discuss emphasis and delivery. He called a few back for additional lines and this meant they had passed first muster. They all knew the signs. They were being recorded, the man liked them, they were still in the running.

His direction began modestly and gained strength as the night went on. He sensed at once if a voice was wrong for the character he had created, but he owed them a reading and he cut no one short. He was looking for a certain timbre, and it surprised him when he winnowed the older brother down to three actors who sounded nothing alike. "There's something about that little fella Blake that rings my bell," he told Becky. "I'd like to hear him again and have the others read for the younger son."

"Isn't that Jimmy's role?"

"No," he said, and she looked at him sharply but let it pass.

Rick Gary arrived shortly after ten and went back to the small studio to wait his turn with the others. They all took a break around ten thirty. Becky had ordered hot food and the actors mingled in the lobby, eating and smoking and talking shop. Across the room Rue stood alone, caught in the grim struggles of the real world. Brinker had left the building. Rick Gary had been cornered by his New York colleagues but he pulled away to talk to Rue, who suddenly burst into tears. Gary put his arm around her and led her away to a dimly lit corner of the lobby. Livia watched them from the opposite corner, her face giving no hint what she thought.

Back in the studio Stoner sat behind the glass, in the chair he hadn't left all night long. Jordan felt his first wave of weariness. "It's getting late," he said to Becky. "Let's read Rue next and let her get on home." He could hear the actors shuffling back through the hall behind him, but it was Livia who was close when he turned. She had come to say good night. She had to rescue her sitter. It was going to be a fine show.

"I dreamed about Carnahan last night," she said.

"So did I."

This was probably remarkable, though neither seemed to think so. "He's always saying good-bye," she said. "I'll see you in the morning, if we're all alive then."

They began again, with Rue and Pauline. There was no competition for either part, but he wanted to hear the new man Blake in a scene with both, then bring in Rick Gary as the father and have them all run through the closing lines of chapter one. This took very little time. Even Rue, still pale from the shock of Brinker's news, rose to her part, and in ten minutes they had nailed it.

"The mother's yours," he told Pauline. "You couldn't be more right for it."

"Bless you, Jordan. Now I can get me lights back on."

He told Rue what she already knew: she had the choice daughter's part. "Now why don't you drop Pauline off and go on home yourself."

"I'm not ready to go home yet," she said, a little crossly.

"Don't worry about it," Pauline said. "I can walk over the dunes faster than you can drive me there anyway."

Jordan felt chilled at her words but she didn't seem bothered by the idea of her husband's disappearance on the same walk. He gave Rue a frosty look. "Do me a favor and drive her home."

"Of course. I'll take her home and come back. If that's all right with you."

"Take her home and don't come back," Jordan said. "Go talk to Jimmy."

"What the hell am I supposed to say to him? He thinks I'm glad he's going. So I can go off and be with . . . someone else."

"He doesn't really believe that."

"Then why'd he have to say it? If I wanted to leave him I'd just do it. He doesn't own me. He's got no right making this my fault."

"Right now he's alone and hurting. Go talk to the man, Rue."

"I don't see why I should. Not after what he said to me."

"Then don't go talk to him," said Jordan, suddenly angry. "Be petty and mean instead. When he gets his brains blown out in France you can tell him you're sorry over his gravestone."

She looked as if he'd slapped her. "Jesus Christ, what is it with you men? Why are you all such bastards?"

"I guess it's in the blood," said Jordan in a softer, kinder voice. "You do what you want, but don't come back here tonight. The part's yours if you want it. But if you come back tonight, I'll give it to Hazel."

"Yes*sir*! I shall do exactly as you say, *sir*! Right this goddamn minute, *sir*!" She turned and clicked her heels. "Heil Hitler!"

He closed his eyes until she'd gone.

"What the hell was that all about?" said Stoner through the bitch box.

"That's just our girl Nina," Becky said. "You chose her well for this part, Jordan."

He told them about Brinker, and Becky sighed. "I guess that means we've got one more to cast."

It was now after eleven: he had been here thirteen hours, Becky even longer. He told Blake to go on to the hotel and come back in the morning. In the booth Stoner had finally moved from his chair. He leaned over and spoke into the microphone. "If you crazy people want to work all night, that's fine with me. I've got to get a show ready for midnight. I'll send Joe down to finish you up."

A few minutes later Joe Carella came in and took the chair in the booth. The readings began on the younger brother. They finished at midnight and Becky went home. Jordan went back to Studio B and found Rick Gary sitting alone. "Let's go grab a beer," he said. "I'll meet you downtown at the hotel in fifteen minutes."

(((16)))

"THERE'S a thing about radio," Rick Gary was saying. "It gets in your blood and ruins you for anything else. The only people who ever get out of it are those who can't make it, and even most of them never stop trying. They have a little success and it breaks their hearts that they can't take it farther.

Sometimes it's just bad luck, sometimes a real lack of talent, occasionally a fall from grace. But they keep sniffing out auditions and turning up to compete, and they never get a call. Directors like to work with people they know."

"You can understand that."

"Sure I can. At the same time, some of these people deserve a much better fate. Take your guy Blake. He's been around New York radio for years but all he gets is dog food. I think he's a fine talent and I had a hunch you'd choose him. When Becky told me who was coming tonight, I thought, Ah, Blake! At last he'll get his chance."

They had met in the lobby of the hotel and walked half a block to the bar, where they now sat nursing their beers. Jordan had asked for a table in the back of the room and had seated himself facing the door.

"Speaking of falling from grace," he said. "You probably knew Marty Kendall. I imagine you did a show or two with him."

"Everybody knew Kendall. I did more than a few shows with him. Hell, two or three *hundred* is more like it."

"What'd you think of him?"

"I liked him a lot. We were never bosom buddies or anything, but he was a talent and I respected that. Had an amazing range, was able to make everything sound so *damned* real. How'd you know him?"

"We just met on the road."

Gary nodded as if this had to figure. "He just couldn't leave the sauce alone, could he? That's the biggest tragedy of all. I'll bet his nights were filled with dreams of coming back."

Jordan nodded. "He thought about it all the time."

"Which is what I've been saying. Whenever I start getting cocky I think about Kendall and a few others who have had it all and lost it. Believe me, I know how lucky I am."

This brought them to the point and Gary knew it. "Let's see if I can guess what's on your mind. You want me to play the father but you're uneasy. You're afraid I'll take the part and then get tired of making this god-awful trip every weekend, and at some point, say around the middle of the second month, I'll bail out on you, and there goes your lead character."

"You should be a mind reader."

"It's just common sense, it's what I'd think if I were you. You're probably wondering why I'd take the role in the first place, when I've got everything I can handle in New York."

"So far you're outhitting Ted Williams."

Gary finished his beer and waved for another. "It's simple and complicated at the same time. I'll give you the simple answer. I'm doing it because years ago, when I was a kid trying to break in, I fell in love with an older woman. She opened the door for me. She opened many doors."

"Are you talking about Mrs. Harford?"

"Who else?"

Jordan sipped foam and put a bill on the table.

"Look," Gary said. "You're right, I don't need this job. If you can do it just as well without me, that's fine. I'm here to help you, not cause problems. I'm here because I owe the lady a debt that can't possibly be paid in my time on this earth. It transcends her death, it's always there. As I said, it's simple."

"You also said it's complicated."

"But the simple part is this. I will do whatever I can for Mrs. Harford's radio station."

Jordan drank some beer. "What you're telling me is I can count on you."

"That's what I'm telling you."

Another moment passed. "I'll sign a contract if you want," Gary said. But Jordan was suddenly at ease. He decided the man's word was as good as his own and when he spoke again it was not about contracts or obligations.

"Tell me about her."

Gary shook his head but in the same instant he said, "She was the most incredible woman. It was Jocelyn who got me on *The March of Time* in nineteen thirty-one. I had been in a play of hers five years earlier, just a small part, but we hit it off from the start. We hadn't seen each other in all that time but she never forgot anyone she'd ever worked with. That's how she was.

"Maybe you remember the winter of nineteen thirty-one, Jordan. Those were damn desperate times and I was going nowhere fast. One day I ran into Jocelyn on Fifth Avenue. We went to an Automat and she bought me some coffee and pie and we got caught up with each other. I didn't need to cry on her shoulder; hell, she had eyes, she could see how things were with me. The next day I got a call to audition for *The March of Time*. I was down to my last nickel."

Gary shifted in his chair. "My first big network broadcast."

He coughed. "I was no kid then; hell, I was almost thirty years old. I was one of those guys like Blake, I'd been around but had never gotten that big break. She was my break. The world of network radio is just so *god*damn tight, it can be almost impossible to break into it. But soon I was doing that show almost every week, and everything opened up from that."

He smiled. "So I owe her one. Even now, years after she's gone, she's the lifeblood of that station. There was just nobody who didn't love her. I can feel her in my heart when I walk in there."

"Were you in any of those old Harford shows?"

"Yeah, I did a few. Wish now I'd done a lot more, but I didn't think I could spare the time then. I was too busy getting my career on solid ground; I was hungry for that big-time-network marquee billing. So I missed most of that mid-thirties stuff they did here. But I followed it religiously in the newspapers, and I always thought I should've been here."

"What do you think of Harford?"

"I never met the man, I think he was shy around actors. But he seemed to treat her well and that's what counts. If she wanted something he gave it to her. She didn't care about material things, she wanted a place to work, so he gave her that. Built her a little village across the way for her group. Kidd tells me they're finally going to use that place. They're going to build themselves a rep company, a mix of network and home-grown talent, and that's where they'll stay when they come down. Jocelyn wanted it to be a little colony where ideas could flow and good things happen."

Jordan felt excited by such a thing.

"It's damned exciting," Gary said. "Speaking as a network actor, I can tell you. I look forward to these breaks. Then I can go back and suck the network tit and have the best of both worlds, as Kidd would say."

Gary finished his beer. "So what do you say?—let's sleep on it."

"I don't need to do that. I want you for this show. We need everything you can bring to it."

"Then let's do it. Let's get on the air and kick some ass."

Jordan raised his mug. "For Mrs. Harford."

"For Jocelyn."

((17))

HE was swamped with fatigue but he tried to wait up. Holly would be home in an hour and he had much to tell her. They would talk for an hour, then he would love her and they would sleep till midmorning. He could do this now because he wasn't punching clocks anymore.

He sat at her table, and in the cool breeze coming up from the beach, in the infinite darkness of the eastern sky, he had a vision . . . Carnahan, marching across the veld with a small band of Boers. There was Kendall, dispirited and bringing up the rear, and in a while Carnahan dropped back and tried to help him find his courage again. They stopped at dusk and had no fire. Kendall sat on the ground and looked haggard and spent. Eat something, Carnahan said, but their rations were skimpy and poor. It doesn't matter, Kendall said; we're all dead, can't you see that? . . . we're all dead men. Carnahan smiled and waved his hat over the ration and it became a banquet. Kendall's eyes lit up and he began to eat, and Carnahan rocked back on his heels and watched. His boots squeaked as he rocked and Kendall was amazed that he had found new boots. But they are old boots, Carnahan said . . . see how they're worn through?

Dulaney went to bed and his last waking thought was of that crazy image, almost like a dream. How strange that the boots were new, but they squeaked anyway.

At two o'clock he opened his eyes. He took a shower and then, still bone weary, he lay down on her bed. As an afterthought he left her a note that said WAKE ME WHEN YOU COME IN. Again he fell into a deep sleep, and the next thing he knew it was daylight outside.

He rolled over and looked at the clock. Quarter to nine. The house was dead quiet and he knew in that moment that some basic part of his life had changed.

He got up and came into the kitchen. His note was there on the table, untouched where he'd left it. He went into the front room, feeling the first inkling of fear.

From the front door he looked out at the empty space where she always parked her car. Unease became the beginnings of dread.

Logic said she'd call. She was home by two thirty, almost without exception. She had never been later than three. She would call.

The phone seemed to be working. He dialed the club, expecting no answer, but a tired-sounding man picked it up after two rings.

"Hello?"

"Is this the Magic Carpet?"

"Yeah, but we're closed. Call back after noon."

"Wait a minute. I'm trying to find Holly O'Hara."

"Join the crowd, pal. She didn't come in last night."

His world tilted and spun out of control. He stood in the grip of a terrifying hunch and felt the blood drain from his face.

It was all he could think of. She had gotten it in her head to go see the crazy old man alone. She had said as much and now she was missing.

She had been missing more than twelve hours and he hadn't known it. The enormity of it hit him like the kick of a horse.

For the first time in his life he was truly afraid. Suddenly he was so afraid he felt almost faint in the face of it.

((18))

HE roared into Pauline's yard and left his motor running. Pounded on her door. Heard her moving about. Saw her face at the window and pounded again.

She opened the door. "My God, Jordan! What's the matter, what is it? Jesus, Mary, and Joseph, you look like you've seen a ghost!"

"Where's Griffin?"

"Well, he's certainly not here. He doesn't sleep here, you know."

"When did you see him last?"

"He was here Tuesday. Came over at noon and we walked to the pier."

"What about yesterday?"

She shook her head. "He was supposed to come, but didn't."

It seemed impossible but the level of his fear went up again. For a moment he had to grip the door to keep his legs steady.

"He was supposed to come for a late dinner after the auditions last night but he never showed up. What do you want with him? Has something happened to him?"

He stared numbly at the pulse in her neck.

"Something's wrong," she said. "I knew it last night when he didn't show up. He never stands me up, and this was going to be a special dinner. To celebrate my changing fortune."

"But he never showed up," he said.

She came out in the yellow sunlight and started to say something. But Dulaney didn't hear it. He was gone.

((19))

HIS sense of time and distance blurred to nothing. The bridge, the long stretch across the marsh, the rising mainland . . . he knew these things were there, but they had no substance. Once he looked at his speedometer. He had pushed the old car past seventy-five and left a blanket of blue smoke in his wake.

He reached the Pineville cutoff and Harford's road and the gate and the stone cottages in one long moment. Came to a running stop, leaped over the walk, and burst through the doorway into Griffin's front room.

The door swung back and forth, creaking on its hinges. A dusty beam of sunlight came through the east window and cut the room in half, and he stood peering beyond it. He walked through the sun to the other side of the room. Put his hand on the cookstove and found it cold. Then gave the rest of the place a hurried once-over.

There was a small sleeping room off the front and a bathroom with indoor plumbing and a stand-up shower bath off that. The old man was neat, his place spotless. His bed made, his sink sparkling, his table cleared.

Everything shipshape, everything calm, everything terrifying.

He saw something lying flat on the table. A letter addressed to Pauline. He ripped it open. Felt a new wave of sickness and fear as he read the word *Dearest.*

Aug. 4

Dearest—
  I've always loved you. I have written a true account of what happened on the night of June 19, 1936. This will be found in my papers. Good-bye.

Tom

A suicide note. The son of a bitch had written a suicide note. Sometime yesterday. Yesterday he'd written a suicide note and then gone off God knows where to do whatever he'd set his mind on.

Oh God, Holly.

Oh God.

Oh God.

He jerked open the back door and looked out across the road.

Hurry, he thought. Maybe it's not too late.

He began to run. Five hundred yards into the underbrush he forced himself to stop. Tried to muster his inner strength.

Don't panic, he thought.

Oh Jesus Christ.

Don't panic. Walk, don't run.

He made himself turn back to the cottage. Dabbed away tears of frustration. Thought, Oh God, please. Please let her be okay. Blotted his eyes on his shirtsleeve till he could pick his way back to the road.

God, please let her be okay. Do what you want with me but let her alone. I will spend my life working for the sick and the poor, I'll cut out my eyes, whatever you want, only please, please, please let her be well.

He took a deep breath and a sudden calm came over him, and he walked up through the woods on steady legs. He went to each cottage but all were shuttered and locked. He resisted the urge to kick in the doors . . . he wouldn't find her there and this would only waste more time. The sound of a running motor startled him, but it was only his car, still idling where he had left it. He turned it off and the silence was so oppressive that he had to keep moving or he knew the craziness would start again.

His best chance was to find her car. She had probably driven up to the house, as he had. Parked somewhere here, close to the door, then got out and knocked. He bent to the earth and found the marks, the trace of another car and a few moist oil stains on the ground. Someone had pulled in here and stopped; then, no telling how much later, the car had been driven back out to the road, where the tracks disappeared.

The terrain told him nothing: no flattened grass where the car might have pulled off, no ruts in the higher ground, nothing to tell him whether he should go ahead or walk back toward the gate where the brush was thicker.

He went back for just that reason. The brush was thicker and that meant a better chance that a car might be hidden there. Soon he was in the tunnel of trees where the ground was softer, and here he found traces of cars coming and going. He moved slowly along the shoulder and stopped to look at the grass, to feel the earth with his fingers and rise up and look off in the woods for anything out of place. He found a track where a car had pulled off the road: he could see that spot of fresh oil, then the turning of the wheel as the car went on. He moved faster now. He could clearly see the traces here without having to stop every ten feet to dope them out.

He reckoned he was halfway back to the gate when the trail took a sharp turn left and disappeared. It had veered back to the center of the road, blending into the tracks of other cars going in or out. This gave him a discouraging moment—did it mean that the car had driven on out of the estate, perhaps to the highway and on across the swamp to Maynard? In another moment he picked it up again where it had veered off on the opposite side of the road. Same tread, same car. It had bumped off the shoulder and crossed at a place where the ditch had crumbled and filled. Then it had cut across the country, heading south.

He followed a trail of crushed saplings and broken branches and soon came into a field facing a thicket. Beyond that was a daunting wall of forest. The car had gone straight across to the thicket, leaving a clear track where it had rolled over an anthill. There were better tracks farther along: the grass gave way to lower, wetter ground where streams drained down from the swamp. Soon he saw something glinting and he ran, with his heart going mad, headlong into the thicket.

There. It was her car, baking in the sun. It looked frightful. Both doors were open, the battery was dead, and the keys were still in the ignition. It looked abandoned, lifeless, pallid, gaunt.

It looked like death. His heart sank but there would be no more panic. He was finished with that. Now he undertook the grim, methodical business of finding her. He got out the keys and opened the trunk.

Empty. He breathed his relief and stood looking at the woods. Fingering her key chain, tracing the letters HOLLY on the little steel name charm. At once it conjured up a dozen visions of her face, all her moods. But what it told him was more about the old man, that in the long run he hadn't been worrying about being found. As if there'd be no long run, as if the world ended today. Or yesterday, a scary thing, awful to contemplate. But it meant he'd be easy to follow, if the stalker went slow and saw what was there.

Almost at once he saw a footprint—hers, he knew, and he cursed himself because in his approach to the car he had all but obliterated it. But it was hers—what was left was the mark of a woman's shoe, not the bigger, heavier boots he had seen on the old man. This told him she had come this far alive and well, and it kept his heart thumping hard with fresh hope. She had been driving the car, not riding, and his next thought was obvious. He walked around the car and found the boot mark on the shotgun side.

He followed the old man's track around the hood and it merged with hers about twenty yards away. The ground sloped down, due south into the trees. Here they had crossed a brook. He picked up the trail easily in the moist earth on the other side. They had followed the brook for a short distance, then the old man turned away and . . . and, were his eyes deceiving him, or had she dropped behind him here? The trace seemed clear, with her footprints distinctly imposed *over* the boots as they entered the forest and the way winnowed down to a narrow path. Did this make sense? Would a captor, even one with a gun, turn his back on a prisoner? Holly was strong, the old man had seen better days, and Dulaney liked her chances in any even struggle. Here the path was littered with rocks. Here she could've picked up a stone the size of a man's fist and knocked the old bastard's head off. Why hadn't she? Why follow him off to God knew where? All Dulaney knew was, it had happened, and he didn't know what hope he could take from it.

This new mystery did seem to work in her favor, but it did nothing to lighten his spirits. He had a strong feeling he was about to find her dead, and once this got into his head he found it almost impossible to shake. He dreaded each new crook in the path and he looked warily wherever a body might be hidden. But the path wound on, the tracks telling him he hadn't lost them.

He came to a fence, three strands of barbed wire that cut across the path. It looked like a boundary, probably Harford's property line. He parted the strands and stepped through; then he saw a small patch of blue cloth caught on one of the barbs. A piece of dress, a fragment from the blue dress she had been wearing when he'd last seen her at noon yesterday. He folded it and put it in his pocket and went on.

The tracks on the other side told a new story. The old man had gone on ahead while she struggled with her snared dress and finally ripped it free. The old man had gone on ahead!— you could see his steady gait and then her own hurried prints as she ran to catch up. What on earth, he thought: what the hell can possibly have happened here? He hurried along, at least a dozen hours behind them. The forest deepened and still it went. The ground got harder, the tracks less frequent. He had heard of foot trails that went on forever, paths centuries old that ran hundreds of miles across whole states. He knew one in South Carolina that had always turned him back short. The old folks said it could be walked to the Blue Ridge Mountains in Virginia, though no one they knew had ever done it.

Sometime much later he reached a break, a place where the forest had been clear-cut for power lines. It was a swath fifty yards wide and miles long, running from somewhere inland to the beach towns in the east. Again he picked up their trail in the soft earth: again the tracks told a story. He could see her struggling to keep up. Having trouble with her delicate city shoes. A broken shoe buckle, a popped strap, the entire shoe discarded; then the other one, still whole but awkward; and finally she had thrown it down and hurried across the break in her bare feet. At the edge of the woods the old man had turned to confront her. Dulaney could see the marks of a scuffle where he'd made a quick turnaround and pushed her down. His boot marks digging into the earth as he'd spun on his heels. The place where she'd fallen, the smooth impression of a backside or hip, the clear prints of her hands as she'd shoved herself up to continue her chase. The trail led on into the trees and the path picked up again. Dulaney looked back, a reflex, and that's how he happened to see the ranger tower rising over the trees a quarter mile west.

Even from there he could see it was deserted. On a whim he broke into a run and reached it, out of breath, a few minutes later. There was a sign, U.S. FOREST SERVICE/NO TRESPASSING, but the rickety iron stair was open. He started up, crisscrossing to the top, and as he cleared the trees the tower began to quiver. Suddenly he was wrapped in a heavy droning sound, and as he turned he saw a formation of warplanes coming straight at him out of the south. He pushed up the door and stepped into the small square room as the planes roared over—fifteen, twenty, twenty-five, heading north on some maneuver, so close he could see the faces of the pilots and feel the breath of their engines. The tailgunner waved and gave him a Churchill victory sign, and this gesture lifted his heart; he took it as an omen, his spirit soared, and his trouble seemed swept away in the rush.

He stood with his hands on the rail, looking over the earth. He knew he had come far; it didn't surprise him to see nothing he knew to the north or east. Far away lay the turquoise expanse of the Atlantic. He crossed the room and looked south and the forest stretched on like the sea, empty and vast. But in the vastness he saw a wisp of smoke curling. It looked no more than two or three miles away. He clattered down the stair and started across the break. It was the first sign he'd seen of life on the ground.

((20))

A CHANGE in the air blew the smoke across her face and brought her out of a dream. The old man sat cross-legged in the middle of the clearing, feeding sticks to the fire. He's gone crazy again, she thought. He was like a seesaw, bobbing between clarity and insanity, and a fire in the heat of the day in the middle of summer was a sure sign of madness.

He showed no awareness that she was awake. She suspected he knew, for he missed damn little in that part of his brain that sifted his muddy thoughts and made them clear. He threw his logs on the fire and seemed satisfied; then he unsnapped his canteen from the canvas pouch that held it to his belt and plunged the steel shell deep in the hot coals. She could hear the water sloshing inside it, as if somehow he'd made water appear after she'd watched him drink the last of it yesterday. She herself had had nothing to drink for almost a full day now. The heat had been ruthless, at least in the high nineties even in the shade of the trees. All day yesterday she had defied the sapping effect of it: the water pouring out of her, drenching the dress under her arms, between her breasts, across her back, and down her flat belly to chafe her between her legs. At five o'clock they had crossed that sunny stretch and her skin had gone suddenly dry and was hot even to her own touch. You could fry an egg on me, she would tell Jack. What a crazy tale she would tell Dulaney, if she ever saw him again.

The old man prodded the canteen with a stick, smothering it with coals. She heard him speak—"That's the ticket there"—but this small effort made him cough. He cursed a bellow that made it worse, and for long moments he sat back and struggled for air. A hundred times she had heard that rasping sound he made. He wouldn't live much longer and he knew it, and she knew it and it made her sad even in her own desperate sickness.

She closed her eyes. Oh God, Jesus, was she sick! Maybe she was dying. She knew she had dehydrated; her father had told her the symptoms from his days at hot labor in the sun. The real danger came when the skin got dry, nature's way of telling you you've got no more juice to spare. That's when you've got to lie down in the shade where it's cool, bathe your face and arms with cold water, drink slowly, and suck some salt to get the monkey off your back. But the water was gone and the shade was no relief and there was no salt. Last night had been an agony, a torture filled with dreams of monsters and death, and a shadowy killer who taunted her from some misty place just out of sight.

Dulaney had been in her dreams but he hadn't been able to help her. He would be frantic with worry: she could see him tearing up the world looking for her. Wish I could help you, sweetheart: can't even sit up and ask that nutty old man what he's doing. What a shame it would be to die like this. Almost certainly the old man will die as well, leaving no one to tell what happened to us. Another mystery for Jack to carry, another puzzle to bedevil him.

She felt a shadow on her face and her eyes flicked open. The old man was leaning over her with the canteen in his hands. Jesus, that must burn, she thought; then she saw that the fire was out and she knew time had passed and she had slept through it. The old man said, "Here, drink this," but she couldn't sit up and do it. "Here," he said, gesturing. His face was not the crazy face but the other one, with the kind, decent streak she had seen in him almost from the start. The crazy man had taunted her and drank all the water but the gentleman had returned and brought water for her. The crazy man had shouted and pushed her down in the dirt but the gentleman now hesitated to touch her without permission, even when he could see she needed help. She encouraged him with a weak smile. "If you could just raise me up . . . just a little."

His hand behind her neck was gentle. He lifted her so tenderly and held the canteen with the slightest tremor. The water was awful. She heaved emptily, then clutched his hand

and tried to drink it all. He pushed her away. "Not too much now, I'll give you some more in a while." He did, and she screwed up her face as she drank. "It's creek water," he said. "Flows down from the swamp, so I had to boil it else you'd be sicker'n you are."

The water ran through her. Beads of sweat appeared on her arms and she felt it in her hair. "You're a goddamn crazy woman," he said, and she couldn't not laugh, even though it hurt. "I know what you're thinking," he said. "A pot calling the kettle black." She laughed again and said, "Maybe I was. That makes us a real pair, doesn't it?"

Then she said, "Actually, Tom, I think you're fine," and he drew back as if shocked at her intimate tone of voice. She said his name again. "Tom's a good name. I was gonna marry a boy once, a boy named Tom."

He continued to shy away. She said, "My name's Holly. I think we've earned the right to use first names. And thanks for the water."

He nodded curtly. "You'll be needing some more. I got only the one canteen and it's a fair walk to fetch it, so I'd better get going."

"Don't forget to come back."

She was feeling better now. Time to plan what she should do next. Maybe he'd go off in the trees and kill himself. If that's what he did, it was out of her hands. She had tried hard to save him and had almost killed herself doing it. But it would be hard to take if he killed himself because of her. Maybe this was her payback; by getting sick she had given his life just enough purpose to keep him going.

If he went off now and did it anyway, what could she do? It wasn't her fault: with an old man like that, there was never a single cause. He was pretty well finished, he had said as much last night. His lungs were shot, he couldn't work anymore, he'd never have the woman he loved except as a friend; he got around as well as he did only through tenacity and guts. He was determined not to give in to the ravages of age and the chronic effects of what had been done to him in the war, and on his good days he was still mostly okay. But she knew he had times when his mind slipped away, when he wasn't sure what century he was in, and if he did kill himself it wouldn't be her doing. She told herself this but she knew she had shocked him yesterday, enough to push him off the edge.

She had meant to shock him but the sudden bluntness of her approach had shocked even her. With her first look at his face she knew it was all or nothing. He hadn't heard March Flack's name in six years, and here was this girl young enough to be his daughter, for Christ's sake, demanding answers. She thew questions at him like a cop.

"We know you were out there that night, sir. Mrs. Flack saw you."

His face was pale and she knew she had been right, Mrs. Flack was her ace in the hole. She stood in the doorway, just out of his reach, ready to leap away at any sudden move, or fight him if he managed to grab her.

"Mrs. Flack was there that night."

"No. She had nothing to do with it."

"We talked to her, sir. We know she was there."

He stepped backward and was gone inside the house. The door was open and she came inside, just close enough to see what he was doing. He was standing in the room in a dazed state. His eyes were open but he had a see-nothing look that worried her. I've shocked him crazy, she thought, but suddenly he said, "You've got it all wrong about Pauline. She never did anything." She tried to smile, to encourage him and keep him going, but a sudden movement made her leap back to the doorway. It was nothing: he had gone to the window and was staring out at the forest.

"Sir, would you please just talk to me?"

A slight movement of his head told her he had heard her, but what to do now? . . . what to say? She had seen the power that Mrs. Flack's name had with him but she didn't know how hard to push it. Then he turned from the window and she saw such sadness in his eyes. *Something about him broke my heart,* she would tell Dulaney.

And something told her he wouldn't hurt her, and that's where it began to change. He moved again, across the room to an old rolltop desk. Sat, took out a paper, and began to write. He put what he wrote in an envelope, sealed it, and wrote something on the outside. Came back across the room and put it flat on the table. "You got it wrong," he said. "Pauline never did anything." She felt an almost irrational reassurance in his eyes. He didn't seem at all malicious or mean.

He went into the far room. She heard some rummaging and when he returned he was fastening a wicked-looking knife to his belt. The sight of it brought back her wariness. She said, "What are you doing with that?" but he went on as if she weren't there. At the sink he filled his canteen and now— lying on the ground, waiting for him to return—she couldn't make sense of the canteen. Why would a man bent on killing himself fill up on water when he knows he's not coming back?

Habits die hard. You don't go deep in the woods without water.

Or maybe he just wasn't sure yet.

Suddenly he came toward her. She backed into the yard and around the car. He stopped for a moment and gave her a long plaintive look. "I'd like you to leave now," he said. She shook her head. "I can't do that. Maybe I would, though, if you'd talk to me first." Then, so softly she barely heard it, he said, "There's nothing for you to do here," and that's when the thought of suicide crossed her mind.

She had to say something then, but all that came out was more of the same. This only annoyed him and made him cough, and she waited for that to end and then followed him out to the road.

He went right, toward Harford's house. His gait was ponderous and halfhearted, like a man marking time. He looked back and said, "Miss, you really must leave me alone now," but she stopped where he did and watched him from the distance. He went on and the trees began to thin. Soon she saw buildings and she wondered, What now . . . am I going to follow him up to Harford's front door? I will if I have to. Good afternoon, Mr. Harford, I'm sure you remember me, you killed my father but this isn't about that. Just thought you'd like to know, this man needs help. If you care.

The old man stopped at the edge of the field. He turned and she was standing about thirty yards behind him, and suddenly he lost his temper. "God damn you, have you no decency? Goddammit, can't you go away and let an old man die in peace?" The woods fell into silence. She said, "Is that what you want to do, sir, die?" She knew the answer now, he had actually said it, and those few words had fused them together. If she left him now she might as well kill him herself.

She started to speak but he spoke first. "You've got it wrong about Pauline." She said, "I'm sure I have." He looked at her curiously and she picked up that thought and went on with it. "I'm sure I have it wrong, that's why I need to talk to you about it." He shook his head and waved her off. He started walking, back toward her, and she moved away as he approached. That's a hell of a thing, she thought: try getting a man's confidence and every time he moves show him you're afraid of him. "It doesn't matter," he said as he moved past her. "I've written it all down so it doesn't matter what I say."

Again she fell in behind him and they went back the way they'd just come. She said, "Writing it down is fine, but stuff gets lost. Letters get misplaced. You've got to tend to the important things yourself, Mr. Griffin, you know that's true." He said something to the trees and she heard enough to piece it together. "What do you care?"

But she did care, enough now to take a chance. She stepped up her pace until she was walking by his side. Her right arm brushed against his left and this contact startled him and made him shy away to the far edge of the road.

"I need to see Pauline," he said suddenly. "Is that your car?" She felt a surge of relief. "Yessir, I'd be happy to drive you."

Without another word he went to the car and got in. By the time she got it started he had his eyes closed and looked to be asleep.

She turned into the road. So far, so good. But when she looked at him again his eyes were open. Don't talk, she thought: do nothing to break his revery. Just hope he'll be quiet for the half-hour ride to town.

"Stop here."

She pulled to the side of the road. "We were going to see Mrs. Flack."

"I've got something else to do first. Somewhere to go."

"That's okay, I'll take you there."

This seemed to amuse him. "Hell's a far piece, honey."

She smiled to warm her blood. "I can make it."

"Then drive along the edge here. I'll tell you what to do."

She had a terrible feeling but did what he said. In a while he motioned her off the road. "That's where we're going."

"There's no road."

"Goddammit, my eyes are thirty years older than yours and *I* can see the goddamn road. What's wrong with you?"

She saw it then: more a trail than a road, with a bumpy access across the ditch. She couldn't let him go: if he got out now she'd lose him. "I see the road." She turned a sharp left but stopped short of the ditch. "Sir, I don't think there's anything down there."

"I know what's down there."

She cursed in her mind, a word he'd be shocked to hear from her, then clattered over the ditch and let the single-rut path guide her into the woods. The way thickened and the trees looked impassable. But then it broke up and they came into a field.

"There's nothing here, sir. There's nothing to see."

"Keep going. Into the thicket. Right there."

He opened the door and got out. So did she. He looked at her across the top of the car and his mind seemed to clear. "You're a stubborn one, aren't you? Wish I could say it's been good knowing you."

"I'm not going to leave you."

"Then you'll wish you had. You've got no water and that path doesn't end. You hear what I'm saying, miss?" He took out his canteen and had a drink. "You're probably getting thirsty now, I can see you already starting to soak through that pretty dress. You'd best let it go."

She followed him up to the woods. He turned and gave her a withering look. "You'd best let it go, miss. You need to learn the difference between patience and bullheadedness. If you want to know about March, I've left you all the answers you'll be getting from me. Everything comes out in its own way. In its own time. You can't force an old redwood to move. All you can do is cut it down."

He started off into the woods, and the madness began.

Now it was over and they were sitting on the ground in the late afternoon of the following day. The last of his fires had burned low and the small clearing had filled with shadows. She supposed they were here at least for another night. Poor Jack, she thought. I will have much to atone for.

"So, miss . . . how're you feeling now?"

"Better, thank you."

"I've seen men come right to the edge of death from heat-stroke. It varies from one body to the next, how quickly it claims you." They were quiet for a while, then the old man said, "You've got a lot of spunk. You're crazy as hell but you've got spunk." He coughed and trembled in the effort to control his lungs.

"This is the second time I've dropped out of sight," she said. "People will start thinking I really am crazy."

"You are crazy, I told you that. One day you'll learn, you can't have an answer for everything. You'll be as old as I am and goddamn shocked at how few answers you've finally got. You'll feel your body and mind slipping away and nothing you can do about it. Maybe the end won't seem quite so tragic then."

He sat for a few more minutes, then he began to stir. "I guess I'll be going now."

This shocked her. He had become so clearheaded and now he was talking crazy again. She said, "So all of this is for nothing," and there was a bitter edge to her voice that rankled him.

"Who asked you to come? Who the hell asked you? Now shut up, just listen for once in your life and I'll tell you how to get out of here."

He fidgeted under her eyes, withered in her seething rebuke. Her eyes charged trickery and his voice was a defensive half shout. "Goddammit, do you want to get out of here, or not?" She shouted back: "Oh, you crazy bastard. Jesus Christ, you make me mad! Jesus Christ!"

He stood in the center of the clearing. "Go on, get mad, maybe that'll carry you out of here. Don't try to go back, you hear what I'm saying? It's too far, you'll just be in the same mess all over again. Keep going, push ahead. You'll come to a place about half a mile south and that's where you fork off. The western fork will take you down to a little hamlet."

He coughed. She started to speak but he gestured her down. "Don't try to make it tonight, it's too late now, these woods'll be like pitch once the sun goes down. Go in the morning, you hear what I'm saying? Just bed down right here and sleep as best you can, then at the first sign of light drink the rest of the water and follow the trail. You'll reach the town in a two-hour hike."

He poked at the fire. "I'll build this up for you, it'll give you some light for a while. I'll leave you some wood, not enough to last the night but you'll have the fire for a while."

"I don't care what you do."

"Come on, miss, don't go all spiteful on me here at the last. We may not see each other again."

"That's fine with me. I hate you."

"You seem to've gone to a great deal of trouble for a man you hate."

"It seems I'm not just crazy, I'm also stupid. I wish I'd never come."

"Well, nobody asked you to. Didn't I do everything I could to throw a damper on you? You can't say I didn't."

"If that makes you feel better, do what you want. I can't stop you now. You can go straight to hell if that's what you want."

He stepped away. "That seems to be your last word on it."

"So what are you waiting for?"

"Nothing." He gave a little cough. "Nothing."

He didn't say anything for a moment. Then he sighed. "You really are one hard goddamn woman."

"Oh, stop, would you please just stop! What do you want me to do, beg you to stay? Would it make any difference if I did that?"

"Nothing much makes a difference these days. There's so damn little left in the cup."

She clutched at this. "At least there's something left. That's what you should hang on to. I'll help you if I can."

"What can you do?"

"I don't know, maybe nothing. All I can do is try."

He stared at her.

"I can listen. I can care. I can walk with you on the beach when Pauline's not around."

"I'd be a pain in the ass. You don't want to talk to me, all you want to hear about is what happened to March. Isn't that what you came for?"

"It's not what I found."

He came closer. "Maybe it is."

Suddenly her heart beat faster. "What does that mean?"

He leaned toward her and smiled. "I killed March."

He coughed. "Me alone. I killed him that night on the beach. That's what you wanted, isn't it? Well, you got it. I killed him."

He leaned forward and gave her a crooked smile. "You still want to walk on the beach, darlin'?"

He shook his head. "I didn't think so."

He stood up straight. Said, "I'll be going now," then stiffened and froze where he stood. A few feet away Dulaney had come out of the forest.

((•))

HOLLY

((**1**))

THEY reached the town in the morning. The general store was open at eight and Jack went in to use the telephone, leaving her on the porch with the old man, where he could watch them through the glass.

"Tom . . . why don't you tell me what happened now?"

"I told you. I killed March. He was my friend and I killed him."

"Then you must've killed my father as well."

He smiled cagily as if he sensed a trick. "Sure I did. Damn right."

"What was his name?"

"Whose name?"

"My father's, you fool. Look at you, you don't even know what the hell I'm talking about. If you killed him, tell me his name."

"What difference does it make? I can't remember them all."

"Have there been that many?"

"Oh, I've killed lots of people."

"Then where'd you hide them? Show me one and I'll believe you about the others. What'd you do, snap your fingers and they all disappear?"

"I buried 'em deep."

She shivered at that and a moment later Jack came out and covered her with a blanket. She looked at the old man. "Now he's saying he killed Daddy."

Jack said nothing. She touched his hand. "What are we going to do?"

"Someone will come pick us up."

"That's not what I meant."

"I know. But someone will come pick us up anyway."

An hour later Becky Hart arrived.

((2))

SHE was blissfully warm under the blanket. The hum of the car was almost hypnotic and she fell into a deep hot sleep. When she opened her eyes she saw the dunes and the tower looming above them. The root of all evil, she thought. On the seat behind her the old man coughed, bringing her back to the big question. What are we going to do with him? Turn him loose and he'll be gone again, off in the woods to die alone. Lock him up and there'll be endless new questions to answer. She and Jack would become part of the official record, linked to the old man until his confession could be verified.

Becky seemed to hear her thought. "What's with Mr. Griffin?"

"He's trying to kill himself," Jack said. "I guess for his own good we've got to take him to jail."

"Take me to jail, I don't care. I killed March."

Becky rolled her eyes back in the mirror. Holly shifted and looked back. "I don't know about jail. I think he's putting us on."

"I told you what I did. Take me to jail."

"Let's take him to see Mrs. Flack. Let him look in her eyes and tell her what he just told us."

"No!" the old man shouted. "God damn you, I thought you were a good person! I should've let you die!"

"Pull over," Holly said, and Becky stopped at the edge of the road. Her face was ashen.

"Listen to me, Tom. If you don't want to go see Pauline, tell us what happened."

"I already told you. I killed March."

"Then show us where he is."

"If I do, you've got to promise me. You've got to leave Pauline alone."

"Okay." Holly looked at Becky. "Let's go."

"Where?"

"Tom will tell you."

They came into town. "Here," the old man said, almost at once.

"There's nothing here," Becky said.

They had stopped at the edge of the lot facing Harford's office building. Holly reached back and touched the old man's hand. "Tom?"

"He's there. Under the north wall, where I threw him the night before they poured the foundation. He's down there under a ton of concrete."

"All right," she said softly. "Now tell us why."

"That's between him and me."

"I'd like to know."

"Too bad for you. Why wasn't part of the deal."

"Tom, please. I need to make some sense out of it."

"It doesn't need to make sense. It makes sense to me. You've got to keep your word now. I need to lie down."

She sighed deeply. "I guess that's our answer, Jack. Maybe the only one we'll ever get. I don't know what else to do but take him to jail."

$$(((\textbf{3})))$$

THE sheriff was out of town on personal business until Monday and a deputy booked the old man in. They all gave brief statements. Griffin confessed for the record and told where March Flack was buried; then he signed his statement and was put in a cell.

They walked home along the beach. "What now?" she asked.

"The old man will go before a judge, probably Monday. The confession should be strong enough to hold him until they dig out that foundation and see what's down there."

"And on Monday, then what? We'll have to give a much fuller account. They'll ask how we know what we know and why, and once those questions begin it'll all come out. Who you are. What you did."

"Maybe. But maybe not yet."

"Or maybe already. Harford knows, you told me that yourself. He's probably told Kidd and maybe Maitland, and who knows who they'll tell?"

She was shocked at what he told her next. She had called him Jack, not Jordan, back in the car with Becky. He told her not to worry about it, but she closed her eyes and suffered. God help him, I'll be the death of him yet.

They had reached the house and now he was telling her about an old war and why he believed everything had begun long ago in some South African prison camp. March Flack, Kendall, her father, the Germans—all of it went back to that single motive. One killer driven by vengeance. Rage at an entire nation. The old man's confession had cleared up nothing because the old man hadn't done it. You couldn't separate March Flack from the others, that had always been the problem. The old man hadn't killed anyone unless he had killed everyone, and it was unlikely that he could have killed the Germans and probably impossible that he could have killed Kendall. She let him ask the obvious questions himself. "Why would the old man lie, and who besides Pauline Flack would he lie for?" Her choice was still Harford. But why would Harford allow March Flack to glorify Kitchener on his own radio station and then kill him for doing it?

"He wouldn't," Dulaney said.

They were quiet for a moment. Then Dulaney said, "I'm going up to New York on Saturday. If I can learn who wrote that script I can put it to rest. I've got a name and an address. The house where they sent the check, six years ago, and the name of the guy who cashed it. A fellow named John Riordan."

"Six years. Anybody could be living there now. And you could be in jail by Saturday. It wouldn't take much, you know, for even that deputy to start asking questions about you. Harford found you out easy enough."

"We settled all this two months ago. There's no use beating it to death."

"I don't care what I said then. It's different now." She leaned close. "It's different, Jack."

"How is it different? Are we going to go away together?"

"I don't know."

"Then nothing's different. If you leave here because of me, you'll never have any peace."

She took a deep breath and finally said what she had never let herself think. "Maybe we've taken it as far as we can go."

"Not yet we haven't."

"It's not as if I'll have to wonder about my dad forever. I know where he is now, I know what probably happened to him. Maybe that's got to be enough." She touched his face. "I don't want you in jail, Jack. I don't want you in jail!"

She trembled suddenly. "I should've said that two months ago. What does that say about us? Maybe it's another sign. What I meant when I said we always seem to slip past each other."

"I don't believe that. I've got a killer in my sights, that's what I know. For the first time I've got a real sense of him. I can feel him out there, I can smell him. That's how close he is."

He began gathering his papers and notes.

"What now?" she said. "Back to work as if nothing's happened?"

"That's how it's got to look, hasn't it? The work's there to be done and there's nobody but me to do it."

He looked at her. "Don't think it's easy for me to leave you here."

He told her a little of the terror he'd felt, hunting her in the woods. "Right now I just don't want to let you out of my sight."

"I know that. I know what it feels like."

But she also knew that her premonitions had a way of coming true. "I've got a bad feeling about this. I want you to promise me something. We'll give it till Saturday. Then we cut our losses and get the hell out of here."

She tugged at his sleeve. "Jack?"

"I hear you."

It wasn't much of a promise. Not nearly enough. While he was in the shower she looked through the South African script. Then she read Becky's report and made her own notes about the man named John Riordan and the house on West Fifty-sixth Street.

$$(((4)))$$

WHEN he had gone she soaked in her bathtub. Then, still queasy, she lay at the open window, just under the light ruffling curtains, and slept. She was wakened by the telephone ringing, and she sat up on the bed and let it ring a moment. It was probably Jud wanting to know where the hell she was, and now, this moment, she didn't know what to say.

But it wasn't Jud. A stranger's voice, deep and male, said, "Is this Holly O'Hara?"

"Yes it is."

"This is Knox Butterfield of the *Regina Beachcomber*. I understand Mr. Tom Griffin has confessed to killing March Flack, and that you and a Mr. Ten Eyck had something to do with bringing him in."

She sat up straight and blinked away the sleep. "News does travel fast in this town."

"I keep a close watch on the doings of the sheriff's department," Butterfield said. "This is a big story here and Mr. Griffin's arrest is a matter of public record."

"Well, that may be, but I don't see what I can tell you."

"You could start by telling me how you happened to—"

"I don't think I should talk about this now."

"Please, Miss O'Hara . . . in the interest of accuracy—"

"That's your problem, sir. I don't think I should be talking in a newspaper before . . ."

"Before what, miss?"

She could hear his pencil scribbling, taking down everything she said. And didn't say. Her mind raced ahead, looking for answers.

"Miss O'Hara?"

"Yes. I was going to say, before the sheriff's even had a chance to interview either Mr. Griffin or myself."

"What difference does it make? I don't go to press till Wednesday."

"Then I could ask you the same question. What difference does it make if I talk to you now or Monday?"

"I would just rather—"

"I'm sure you would, sir. But I would rather not."

There was a pause. She was getting her wits about her now. Don't make him mad, she thought. Play to his sympathy. Buy some time, especially for Jack. "Look, Mr. Butterfield," she said in a soft, gentle voice. "Give me some room here, would you do that, please? Wait till Monday and I'll tell you everything you want to know."

"Is that a promise?" His voice hinted of teasing now.

But hers was deadpan, as sincere as she could make it. "Of course."

"What you say indicates that there's a bigger story here than what meets the eye."

"Oh there is, sir. I promise you that."

Suddenly she had another thought. "I will tell you this. Mr. Ten Eyck had nothing to do with it. He was looking for me, that's all. What else there is has only to do with Mr. Griffin and myself."

"Miss O'Hara, can I just—"

"Monday . . . please. I've got to go now. Someone's at the door."

She hung up the phone and parted the curtains slightly, looking out over the beach at the pier. "Good," she said aloud. "Good."

She closed her eyes and had her sharpest memory yet of her sister's funeral. The slate gray sky. The sticky summer heat. The leaves fluttering gently on the graveyard trees. The faces of the people standing around an impossibly small coffin. The

Reverend Clyde Morrison read from the good book, lines that were supposed to give comfort with the untimely passing of a child. Most clearly she remembered her parents: her mother glassy and impenetrable, fragile in her black dress and veil; her father shaken, the only time she had ever seen him quake. *He loved us both more than life. Not like Mamma, who was always partial to Iris.* After her sister drowned it became almost unbearable that she could never fill any of the emptiness in her mother's heart.

The day after the accident her father had taken her for a long walk, out along a dirt road into the woods. She remembered the almost paralyzing fear of his judgment, how badly she wanted to stop but couldn't because he seemed to want to go on and on. At last she fell and lay sobbing in the dirt. He swept her up and she cringed as he buried his face, weeping, against her shoulder. "I can't talk," he cried. Suddenly she remembered that so clearly, his husky voice and the words he said. There were things he had to tell her but he couldn't then, he was still too crushed.

He told her later. This was one of those senseless tragedies that was nobody's fault. She must never blame herself. She must be strong.

She had been raised to be a strong daughter. She had taken many batterings since then, but maybe she could be strong again. She thought of Jack and felt the disaster premonition. Maybe she could be strong enough to save him.

(((**5**)))

At quarter to four she walked to the club and quit her job. Jud was unhappy, but Holly O'Hara had sung her last song.

An hour later she walked across the dunes to the station. She asked for Kidd at the reception desk and a moment later Becky Hart came out to receive her.

"Mr. Kidd isn't here just now, but he shouldn't be long. Would you like to wait for him?"

They went back to Kidd's office. Becky fidgeted, uneasy in her presence. "Can I get you something? The coffee's pretty bad this time of day, but I brought in some lemonade from home. At least that's cold."

"A small cup would be lovely, thank you."

Becky disappeared and returned a few minutes later. "I hope you're feeling better."

"I'm fine now, thank you. Where's Jordan?"

"He's upstairs doing some revisions on tomorrow's show. It's been pretty frantic here yesterday and today. Do you need him now?"

"No. I was just wondering."

Moments passed and the unease grew. At last Becky said, "Why do I get the feeling this is going to be bad news?"

"I've quit the band," Holly said. "I wanted Mr. Kidd to know there won't be any show Saturday night. Unless they find another singer."

"That is bad news. Maybe we can talk you out of it."

"No. This is the right thing for me now, and the right time. But I am sorry for the short notice."

"In radio we thrive on short notice."

Another moment passed. Becky looked up from the desk and said, "So what'll you do? . . . if you don't mind my asking."

"I'm not sure yet. I may just go somewhere quiet."

"Not New York, then."

"I think that's safe to say. Not New York."

"Well, it's our loss. Ours and New York's." Becky smiled and dared ask the big question. "What about Jordan?"

"He plans to stay here."

Becky couldn't hide the relief in her face.

"I guess radio's in his blood," Holly said.

She heard voices in the hall and a moment later Kidd came in. She broke the news quickly and he accepted it with regret, with that same stoic distance he always had. Now it feels final, she thought as she walked out.

At home she gathered her things. A few clothes, not much else. She thought of her car, abandoned in the woods, but it didn't matter.

At the very end, a note for Jack.

Sweetheart,

   This afternoon the newspaper called. I told him the truth. What happened with Griffin was between him and me, you had nothing to do with it, you don't know anything about it, you were only there because you were looking for me, and you have no idea why Griffin would do what he says he did.

   I'll meet you Saturday in New York. Four o'clock outside the old apartment house—you know where. We'll see what happens then.

                                                        Much love

Then she was out of there, walking north into town. She looked back once, at the house and the beach and the sea, and had a brief heartache. Like her old house in Sadler, it was now part of the past. It had not been a good place but like all places some good things had happened in it. She had a one-hour wait, then she was on a bus heading north.

She got to town just before dark. Luck was with her—there was a café on West Fifty-sixth Street where she could sit at a window and watch the house. It was a brownstone tenement, three stories and a street level, with steps in front and another going down on the side. A sign in the window said ROOMS BY THE WEEK OR MONTH. It was a transient's paradise, most likely a dead end.

She was suddenly weak from hunger, and she realized that she hadn't eaten in two days. She ordered dinner and ate it slowly, then sat over coffee and watched the house.

She thought about Dulaney constantly. Flirted with the notion that fate had chosen their meeting place, on the street outside his old apartment house. A replay of sorts, perhaps one final chance to get it right.

Lights were on throughout the house and she could see occasional shadows moving past the windows. A movement on the street caught her eye as four men came up from Ninth Avenue. They turned into the house, skipped up the steps, and went inside. A few minutes later another man came from the opposite direction. A strapping fellow with a thick black beard, who also turned in and went up the steps.

The café was closing. She paid her bill and stood on the sidewalk looking up at the sign in the window. "I'm looking for an apartment," she said softly, and it sounded good, and she crossed the street and went up the steps into a hallway.

She looked at the names on the mailboxes. Quinn. Shaughnessy. Herlihy. Riordan. All Irish. She looked at Riordan and thought, *There he is,* but the box said *Annie Riordan, Manager,* apartment 1.

She thought of everything Irish she had ever heard and on the spot she devised a name for herself. Then she knocked on the door and a moment later stood facing a gray-haired woman in her late fifties.

"Hi, are you Annie Riordan?"

"That's me, Annie Riordan."

"I was wondering about an apartment."

"Come in a minute, I'm on the phone."

She stepped into the room. The woman retreated into a hallway and picked up a telephone. Holly came closer. There was a bulletin board on the far wall filled with thumbtacked clippings, and a moment later she was near enough to read the articles and make out their dates. Some were yellowing, years old; others as recent as last month.

July 1937: KING GEORGE ESCAPES I.R.A. BLAST. Someone had written on it, "And we'll get the bloody bastard next time." November 1939: I.R.A. BOMBS HIT PICCADILLY. One long piece at the bottom seemed to say it all. August 1939: ON THE EVE OF ANOTHER WORLD CONFLICT, THE I.R.A. RENEWS ITS CONTINUING STATE OF WAR WITH ENGLAND.

She turned away as the woman came back through the hall. When Annie Riordan spoke she had a soft Irish accent, unremarkably motherly. "So what's your name, then?"

"Brigit Kelly."

"There's a good name. But what brings you to me?"

"Sign in the window. Saw the names on the mailboxes. Thought it might be a good place . . . you know . . . for someone like me."

Annie Riordan smiled broadly. "It might be at that. I do have one small room left. It's a roof and a bed."

"I can't pay much."

"Can you work?"

"Sure."

At that moment the door opened and the man with the black beard came into the room. "Well, Mamma, whoot've we got here?"

"Miss Brigit Kelly, Johnny."

"Miss Brigit Kelly!" he said as if he'd known her forever. "And what fair wind blew you in here, may I ask?"

Annie Riordan laughed. "You behave yourself. Brigit, this's me son, Johnny Riordan."

"Hello, Johnny," she said, smiling up at him.

"I'm giving her the room, Johnny. She's willing to work."

"Is she now?" He grinned at her: strong, good teeth, flashing through the tangled beard. "The sun must truly be shinin' on us. Come on, Miss Brigit, I'll show you the room meself."

(((6)))

SHE was absorbed at once into the culture of the house. Years from now, if she should live so long, she would remember the hot-blooded gregarious nature of these strangers and how instantly the promise of intimacy became a fact. How easily someone of fair skin and the right kind of Celtic name could become one of them. She took the room at five a week plus chores, and the work began almost from that moment.

She was left alone less than fifteen minutes, then Johnny Riordan was back to flirt and fetch her help with a meeting.

The meeting room was the size of two apartments, on the far end of the third floor. It reeked of old smoke and the stale aroma of last night's traffic, and of a thousand nights before. The furniture was plain and sparse: a long table surrounded by chairs, with more chairs strung out along the walls. The meeting tonight would be crowded: already she could hear raucous laughter through the walls and doors. The meeting room had its own bulletin board with much the same material. I.R.A. KILLS BRITISH CONSTABLE AT BELFAST . . . SIX I.R.A. TEENS WILL FACE THE HANGMAN IN BELFAST MURDER . . . I.R.A. BOMBS EXPLODE IN BIRMINGHAM . . . SIX DEAD IN I.R.A. LAND MINE ATTACK . . .

It was a clan, she could see that at once. It didn't matter what their names were, they were all part of the same dark brotherhood, bound by their hatred of England. Her job was to bring up the eats and beer from Annie Riordan's place two floors down. The old woman did the cooking in her apartment and Holly went up and down the stairs, carrying heavy trays like a waitress in a truckers' diner. A few of the men were addicted to what they called poor man's wop food, and she was sent to the pizza house on Ninth Avenue, where she spent a few precious solitary moments in the fresh air on the sidewalk, watching the pizza man toss his dough to the ceiling before coating it and putting it in to cook. She was bone weary but determined to stick it out.

They were all fund-raisers. Some were from out of town, some from New York, all were involved in the great need of their cause for cash. Skirmish money, she heard it called, and she was amazed at the pile of it on the table, cash and checks in various amounts, which, near the end of the evening, sometime in the early morning, was put in a big bag and taken away by Johnny Riordan to be stashed in a safe place.

The night stretched on. She was allowed to sit and did, in a chair by the wall, while they talked politics. The air was so thick with smoke she could barely see them except as blue shapes. They were loud and happy in their fellowship, and many of them spoke to her flirtingly when she passed; some of them touched her and remarked how she brightened up the room. And she smiled, dead on her feet but still going, and she smiled and smiled and backtalked playfully without going too far.

It ended, mercifully, sometime after one o'clock.

"Leave this stuff till tomorrow," Annie Riordan said. "Let's turn in."

Johnny walked her to her room. "Can we sit awhile and talk?"

She wanted to scream but smiled instead. "Tomorrow. I haven't been well and I got almost no sleep last night."

She was lucky: he was a gentleman, and ten minutes later she was out of her misery, locked in the sleep of her life.

((7))

By the time she got up Friday morning the old woman had the mess cleared away. The apartment door was open when she came down and she could hear a radio playing *The Breakfast Club* somewhere inside. She went in and found Annie washing dishes in the kitchen.

"Well, look who's here."

"I can't believe I slept like that. I'm sorry I—"

"No need to be sorry, darlin'. I could see last night you were dead to the world. I would've chased you off to bed except I was in worse shape than you. I just can't climb those stairs like I once could."

She reached up and snapped off the radio. "Sit over there and I'll give you some breakfast. Are you hungry now?"

"Oh God, yes!"

Annie laughed and soon the place was filled with the smell of cooking food. "So, what're your plans, Brigit? Where do you go from here?"

"Out to find a job."

"Then will you be stickin' around?"

"I'd like to. You seem to have something . . ."

Annie looked at her quizzically.

"You've got something good here," she said.

"It's a sense of purpose, dear. That's what you feel."

"Yes. I guess that's it exactly."

"You can feel it pass from one forsaken soul to another. Some of 'em come from far away, we never see 'em before and may never again, but we try to have room for them when they come." She forked at some bacon and flipped the pancakes. "Without braggin' on meself, I could tell you that this house is known from coast to coast. Among the people who matter to us."

"Do you have meetings like that often?"

"Only all the time. There's always somethin' goin' on. I may not know till tonight what tonight will bring."

"What a way to live."

She said this in an admiring way and Annie Riordan looked at her and smiled. "I wouldn't trade it for anything."

"Have you been doing it long?"

"Almost twenty-five years. Right from the beginning."

"The beginning?"

"Of the cause, of course. Next year it'll be twenty-five years I've been givin' shelter to exiles and patriots. People who've been wronged by the British. I've been collecting money almost that long—not so amazing when you know what I've lost. Me husband and me firstborn son. Johnny's older brother, Daniel. They killed him and the light went out of me life."

"I'm sorry."

"It's what we accept when we take up arms. My Danny was heart and soul for his country."

"What happened to him?"

"He was murdered. They hung him in London after what they called a trial. Did you ever lose anybody like that?"

"Not exactly that way, no."

"It's not a common man's way of sayin' good-bye to the world."

Breakfast was ready. Annie poured coffee and sat with her while she ate.

"Don't get the wrong idea, Brigit. We're not a sub-rosa bunch here, if that's what you're thinkin'. People in the neighborhood know who we are and what we do. It's not illegal. Our boys make no bones of where their hearts are but America guarantees 'em that right, doesn't she?"

Holly nodded. Annie said, "She's a grand old gal, America," and they shared a quiet unfunny laugh.

"I'm glad you'll be staying. Johnny'd be heartbroken if you was to leave us so soon."

"Johnny doesn't even know who I am."

"He knows enough, that one. I haven't seen his eyes and ears light up like that since he was just into his manhood."

She sipped her coffee. "Have you got a regular fellow, Brigit? . . . a beau, or anything like that?"

She laughed. "Nothing like that."

"Which with your good looks is no small miracle. That goes to show you, love. Miracles still happen."

(((8)))

LATER in her room she could see how it must have been. Our boy arrived from South Africa, she thought, more than twenty years ago. The clampdown on immigration hadn't come yet and it was relatively easy to get into the country and start a new life. He landed in New York like so many forgotten millions, and everything opened up from there. He was driven by his hatred of England, so he gravitated to Annie Riordan's boarding house and the Riordans became a kind of surrogate family. This means they know who he is. They may not know everything he's done but they know him like a brother and son. I am one question away from learning his name, but how do I get it without stepping on their trust?

She took a shower. Then, back in her room, she ran every conceivable approach to the question through her mind. She was leery of dropping the Paul Kruger name but nothing seemed to get her around it. She thought she could see the whole story now, beginning with Dulaney's escape from California. An Irishman had been there. An Irishman who had roughed up Kendall, and was with the Schroeder boy when Kendall left the car for Dulaney in the woods. The image in her mind was Johnny Riordan. Maybe not the killer but a bit of muscle when Kendall needed to be kept in line. Just a thug, a mulligan with two faces: tough when he had to be and gentle with her. But she had no illusions about what he'd do to her if she slipped up and he found out her secrets.

"Johnny," she whispered aloud. "How much will you tell me before I push it too far and turn you ugly?"

She had twenty-four hours to find out before Dulaney turned up on the doorstep.

(((9)))

THEY had the afternoon free and he wanted to spend it with her. "You can start lookin' for work on Monday," he said. "Nobody ever found a good joob at the end of the week."

He took her to a tavern he frequented where he could show her off to his Irish cronies. She put up her hair and dressed well and clung to his arm. They sat at a table and drank beer. She drank far less than he wanted her to, for whenever he turned away she poured some back in the pitcher and he drank it himself as the day wore on. He squeezed her arm. "How's my girl?" he said drunkenly. "Is she havin' any foon?"

"Would I be here if I wasn't?"

"Are you me girlie, Brigit? Are you goin' to be me special friend?"

"How special do you want it, Johnny?"

"Ah, you silly sweet thing. You know for sure what 'special' means."

She had never played a whore's game. Would she do that even to get what she wanted?

"Yes," she said. "I do know what it means."

"An' whoot would ye do aboot it?"

She smiled and leaned across the table and kissed him. He came out of it cross-eyed, his guts on fire, trembling with delight. She kissed him again and felt his legs tense as his toenails dug into shoe leather.

"Have another drink, Johnny."

"If I do ye'll be gettin' some help to carry me out of here."

But he did. Drank it down and ordered another pitcher.

He puckered his lips. "Do that again, love."

She kissed him. Let him feel her tongue. Told him he was sweet. A dear, sweet man.

"Let's go someplace," he said.

"In a while. You've still got some beer left."

"Oh Jesus. Why'd ye let me order that refill?"

"Drink it up and we'll go. You can't waste it, it's sinful. My father told me that when I was a little girl."

"You'll have to help me, then. Down th' hatch."

She sipped and he guzzled. They staggered out into the late afternoon sunshine, her arm over his shoulder and her own head suddenly light.

"Gosh, I'm as tipsy as you are," she said, hoping it wasn't true.

"Ah, look at me, I've gone and spiled everything."

"Oh shush that. Nothing's spoiled."

"But I'm too sotted to be yoor special friend, you know."

"There's plenty of time."

But there was no real time at all. They sat on a bench and his head lolled. There was no easy way to get into it, so she took a deep breath and just said it. "I'm a lucky girl, Johnny. When Paul told us about your mother, that was my lucky day."

She wondered if he'd fallen asleep: his eyes had narrowed to slits and his head bobbed slightly. But in time he looked at her and smiled. "Paul, you say?"

She wondered if she could get it out, but she did. "Paul Kruger."

"Ah." He closed his eyes and looked away. Shook his head and smiled at her again. "You say Paul Kruger told you?"

"Well, he told my brother and my brother told me. When he found out I was coming to New York."

"Ah," he said again.

I've blown it, she thought. The sooner I get away from them the better.

But then he seemed okay again; he laughed and his head lolled against her shoulder. "Tell ye what, Brigit, let's get us on back to the house and see whoot Mamma's got cookin' for tonight. Maybe we can finagle a few hours at sooper and I can show you a better time than you've had today."

They walked up the avenue toward West Fifty-sixth. "You go on ahead, Johnny," she said. "I've got to stop at the store and get a few things."

She was surprised that he didn't argue. He leaned over and kissed her neck, then went on to the house alone. She still couldn't shake the feeling that she was in trouble, and her life would be worth much less if she went in there again.

She needed a weapon, something that would give her at least a fighting chance if it got mean. She found it at once, a man's straight razor in the shaving section of the drugstore. It was a wicked-looking thing and it gave her the shivers, but she bought it and carried it out in the pocket of her dress, as if what she would do next was never in doubt. She was very afraid now, but she turned into the street and a moment later went into the house.

(((10)))

THE manager's door was open and the radio was playing something drenched in organ music as she came into the hall. The old woman was sitting in a rocker and looked up from her knitting. "There she is!" she said. "Come in here, Brigit! Come rescue me from this mindless drivel."

They talked for a while and there seemed to be no change in the old woman's attitude. "Johnny came in, fit to be pickled," she said. "He ought to be ashamed of himself, drinkin' like that in the middle of a weekday. What must you be thinkin' of him?"

"I like him."

"Do you really?" Annie said, and something in her tone set the warning bells off again. But then the old woman smiled in that motherly way and it seemed all right. "He certainly likes you. He wants you to be happy here. Worries about the bleakness of that little room."

"It's fine. When I get a job I'll buy me a radio."

"You can use one of mine till you do. Take the little one in the kitchen. I don't use it much."

They talked about tonight. Some people were coming, rather late like last night and from out of town. "I could use your help again, beginnin' around nine."

"Of course."

"What'll you do between now and then?"

A strange question, she thought . . . as if it matters where I'll be. "Maybe I'll rest," she said, "I'm still a little tired. Johnny said we might go out for an early supper."

"Don't be countin' on Johnny. He's dead to the world right now."

Upstairs, she sat on the bed with her heart beating hard and a sinking feeling about what she was doing. She lay on the bed and listened to the radio, her fingers wrapped around the razor in her pocket. She thought about Dulaney but avoided Harford on the dial, as if the walls could hear and know who she was by what she listened to.

In a while the beer had its way with her and she fell asleep. Much later she looked at her watch. Seven thirty and no Johnny.

She came out of her sleep planning her escape. She had put her neck on the block and had learned nothing, but maybe she still had time. How close could she cut it before courage became stupidity? She would stick through Annie's party, and if nothing happened by then, if she hadn't learned what she'd come for, she would disappear in the middle of the night.

But now came a sudden new fear. What if Johnny's suspicion had been aroused and he'd called the real Paul Kruger? . . . Whitemarsh, or whatever he was called down in Jersey. Her life wouldn't be worth a plugged nickel. Whitemarsh might well be on his way right now . . . that creaking floor, those footsteps in the hall . . . any sound or no sound at all might be Whitemarsh, coming to kill her.

The footsteps went past but her heartbeat continued to race.

Did she dare walk out of here now? Just straight down the stairs and make a beeline for the front door. Out in the street she'd be safe. And yet she was so close. Another five minutes with Johnny would tell the tale. Just a name, a hint, some physical characteristic. If they don't know he's a killer, maybe they'll tell me.

It would be a shame to get spooked when another five minutes might tell her everything.

It was almost eight o'clock, time for Jack's radio show. She didn't want to be listening if someone should come to her door, but the temptation was too great. She took the little radio into bed with her and pulled up the blanket, like a child defying her mother's orders. She turned the dial to Harford and found a program of symphony music just ending, a network show coming from Rochester. She felt a sudden new tension and thought, Good luck, sweetheart, as if it mattered. But of course it mattered; she desperately wanted his show to be good. It will be his last program, so let it be something he can remember.

Then it was on and she was caught up in it, hunkered on the sand with those colored troops eighty years ago. The story was vivid even though she could see them doing it, the big studio alive with lights and people and music, Kidd watching from the back wall, Harford from his balcony, and Jack . . . Jordan, for that's who he was now . . . throwing his cues, down on the floor with his cast. How did he get such polish out of those Negroes who just the other day were so inexperienced? How had he had time to blend Livia's bombardment so perfectly with Zylla's score? He is becoming a master, she thought; his show is as smooth and gripping as anything on any network. She listened through the credits and felt a flush of pride. Waited for his name, which trailed the cast, then turned it off and sat in the quiet.

Slowly as she withdrew from it her apprehension returned. The room was dark now, the city's canyons had made the night come early. Downstairs she could hear voices and new movement. Laughter seemed to come out of the walls, far away but clear, a man laughing loudly at something she would never understand. She heard the sound of a door closing; then, a few minutes later, footsteps.

Someone was coming up for her.

((**11**))

TONIGHT the party was smaller: just the two out-of-town men and a few from last night. Johnny appeared suddenly at nine, cold sober with none of the laughing playfulness she had seen in him earlier. The few times he looked at her he seemed angry—not a good sign, she thought, but then Annie had an explanation that made light of it. "It's not you, Brigit, it's just that he never liked those two. It's a personal thing between them. Sometimes it's like that with strong men and opposing ideas about what to do."

"Why have them in your house if he doesn't like them?"

Annie was shocked at such a question. "But they're our boys, love. They might make John Riordan angry but they're still two of ours."

She could hear them swearing through the walls as she came up with the tray. She heard Johnny shout, "That's a fookin' lie, Brennan, carry that fookin' blarney to somebody who'll swallow it!" She knocked on the door and the oaths died away at once. But rancor remained heavy in the room.

"Here's some food for you, Brennan," Johnny said. "You eat hearty and drink up. I won't have you tellin' people you don't get fed at Annie Riordan's."

Brennan, a great bear of a man, said, "Annie always takes care of her people, everybody knows that. It's you that sits over there scowlin'. A man should have a brew at least when people eat under his roof."

"I've had enough beer for one day. But I'll break a bit of that bread to be sociable."

Brennan grinned as she poured his beer. "And who might you be?"

"Her name's Brigit Kelly, and you keep your eyes to yourself."

Brennan liked the sound of it. "So tell us, Brigit Kelly, how did something so fair as you fall into the hands of an oogly bastard like Riordan?"

"Guess I'm just a lucky girl," she said, and everyone laughed.

"There's your answer!" Johnny thundered. Then, to the others, "Next thing you know he'll be lickin' her face."

She looked at Johnny and hoped a playful smile would bring back his spirit. "He hasn't got his hands on me yet," she said without turning to Brennan. This drew a loud laugh all around, which became an uproar when she said, "But he's been so charming, who can tell?"

Johnny laughed with the rest now, pleased as she sashayed out. In the hall she stood for a moment gathering her wits. Then she was downstairs and the hall was empty; for a moment there was nothing between herself and the front door, and freedom. She walked past Annie's door and no one called out or tried to stop her as she opened the outer door and walked into the cool city night.

She stood wavering at the top of the steps. No one was after her, it was all in her mind. And yet her inner voice warned her. Keep going, it said, don't go back in there. But they had let her walk out, proof that her fears were nothing. In his stupor, Johnny Riordan had forgotten what had been said a few hours ago.

And the Paul Kruger business was still there to learn, it was just a question away. The thought made her tremble but she knew she was going to do it because this was what she had come for.

The evening dragged on. Upstairs they haggled and discussed their strategies and the night gave way to the early morning. She came in and picked up the dishes and the trays and she heard some of it. Political rhetoric, skirmish talk, and always the ways and means of getting more money. Brennan had been in Ireland for ten years before the war, and in England off and on. He had done things that had driven him underground, but he was going back as soon as the perilous passage could be arranged. She came in and out and heard fragments, at one point a discussion about explosives and bomb making cut short by her appearance. She picked up the glasses and the pitchers and asked if they wanted any more beer, and soon after that the meeting broke up and they all went off to their different rooms.

Johnny came into the kitchen and sat brooding while she and Annie finished up the chores. "You stop that anger, John," Annie said. "Brennan may be a bellyacher but you know he's a good soldier."

Then it was over, the last mug and plate washed and put away. Annie turned off the lights and went to bed. Johnny took her hand and led her into the hall, toward the stairs that went up to his room. This is it, she thought. How far will I go? How much of me will I let him have?

But he went past his own door. "Let's go up to the roof where it's cool."

"It's cool on the street. We could sit on the steps."

"What's the matter, Brigit, are ye afraid of heights?"

"A little . . ."

"You should be gettin' over that at your age. Come on, I want to show you something."

Up to the third floor and out through a window at the far end. They clattered up an iron staircase to the rooftop.

"I love the city at night," she said, to be saying something.

"It's very pretty. Come over here near the edge. There's a little copin' at the top so it's perfectly safe."

"I don't think I want to get that close, though."

She took heart when he let go of her hand and went on to the edge alone. He sat on the coping and patted the space beside him. "Come sit here."

"Johnny, I—"

"Just for a minute. Then we'll go inside and we'll see what we see."

She sat beside him and he put his arm around her, drawing her tight. "This here's me place," he said. "It's where I come when the world's sittin' heavy on me shoulders."

"Is it doing that now?"

"Aye, I'm a troubled man."

"I'm sorry to hear that. Can I help?"

"Sure, since you're the reason for it."

He tightened his grip. "Tell me aboot Paul Kruger," he said, and his hand tightened again.

"Hey, that hurts . . . dammit, that hurts, Johnny."

"What aboot Paul Kruger? Was I too cockeyed to remember what I heard, or didn't you say that you knew him well?"

"I said my brother knew him."

"And what's your brother's name?"

She was quick and the name Daniel Kelly sprang to her lips.

"What exactly did Paul Kruger tell your brother Daniel Kelly, Brigit? What did he have to say about me and me mother's house?"

"Nothing . . . he was just trying to help me get started in New York."

"I hate to say it, dearie, but that sounds like applesauce."

"I don't understand."

"If you know Paul Kruger, if you know even the first thing aboot him, Brigit, tell me the one thing everybody knows."

She closed her eyes and tried to lean against him but he tightened his hand on her shoulder and held her away.

"What's the one thing everyone knows, Brigit?"

"Johnny, I—"

"What's the one thing everybody knows?"

She took a deep breath. "He's from South Africa."

"Ah! . . . so you do know that much. But what's the other thing, Brigit? The thing you've got to know. The one thing everybody knows."

He waited for a long moment. "What's the one thing, Brigit?"

"I'm not a mind reader, Johnny. I can't tell what you're thinking."

"This has nothin' to do with readin' minds. It's common knowledge, but you don't seem to know it. You get me in me cups and mention a name, but then you know nothing about the man behind it. How can that be?"

His hand tightened. "Shall I tell you? Is that why you came here?"

Again he waited. In the end he told her. "There is no Paul Kruger."

He leaned back and looked down at the street. "The real Paul Kruger died forty years ago. He was a great South African freedom fighter. We still use his name as a badge of honor. It's what we call our South African friends. We say a man is a Kruger the same way you'd call a cousin from Indiana a Hoosier."

He sniffed. "You should've known that, Brigit."

Suddenly he grabbed her with both hands and pushed her over the edge.

(((•)))

Two
O'Clock,
Eastern
Wartime

HIS eyes were closed but he knew they were approaching the city. At some point the thought came over him that he had found the killer and its name was history.

But where was history's instrument? Who was its disciple, its black knight and executioner? He had asked Becky to chase down some facts by telephone and a New York librarian had given her the basics on the South African war. Paul Kruger turned out to be a grand choice for a symbolic name. Still a hero in his homeland, he had been a four-term president of the South African Republic and a voice for Boer rights on a frustrating trip to Europe shortly before his death. He had died in 1904, leaving a two-volume memoir, which Becky had also located and Dulaney would pick up at a bookshop on Fourth Avenue later today. There was much on Kitchener, whose concentration camps had been hotly debated in England. Notable writers had covered the war. Churchill had gone; Conan Doyle had been knighted, not for Sherlock Holmes but for his vigorous defense of England's conduct. Kipling had looked with disdain, saying, in the end, "Those farmers taught us no end of a lesson." The camp at Germiston had been photographed and the pictures of dusty tent streets and the wire kraal were described by the young-sounding librarian, who finally said, "I had no idea."

Becky defined the problem from a broadcaster's view-point. "If we play it straight we're implying a comparison with Hitler, and if we do a disclaimer we water down the impact of the story."

There was no comparison with Hitler, she said: Kitchener was trying to end a war he had inherited and he just didn't care about those people in his camps. You couldn't compare that to what Hitler was doing.

Negligence is not mass murder. But that is small comfort when it's your wife, your child or sister dying on the ground.

To someone who has lost his family, the crime is personal, the comparison inevitable.

They were approaching the Lincoln Tunnel through Union City and he saw the New York skyline flowing past his window. He looked at Waldo and said, "Sorry I haven't been much company."

"I guess you're entitled to be tired after the broadcast last night."

In fact Dulaney had slept little, either last night or the night before. Holly's strange disappearance had rattled him, and her promise to meet him this afternoon was the day's only saving grace.

"I haven't talked much about it," Waldo said, "but it was a real fine thing. We stayed up half the night at Eli's rehashing it."

"They should feel proud."

"That's what I told 'em. They didn't know they could do that."

"And now they'll never have to doubt it."

They turned into the tunnel and a few minutes later they burst into the city. Waldo turned left into Ninth Avenue.

"You can let me off anywhere here," Dulaney said.

They sat idling in a no-parking space. He met Waldo's eyes and Waldo said, "You've done some great things for us, Jordan."

"Not as great as what you've done for me."

"Well, I appreciate that. But the fact is, you can do this show on your own juice now."

"No way, Waldo. If you hadn't been there last night the show would've been a bust. You got that performance out of Eli, and that's what carried the show. Never doubt that, Waldo. You are this program."

He reached over and clutched Waldo's arm, wondering if they'd ever see each other again. A moment later he stood on the corner watching Waldo drive away.

He walked up the avenue, lost in thought. A soft warm rain had begun falling but he barely noticed. I am very close now, he thought as he hurried across West Forty-fifth Street.

It was all mixed up through endless wars and more years than he himself had lived. Radio was simply the conduit, a clear-channel passage of the images and events of one man's tragedy. This is where he's been vulnerable. His old life and the way it ended haunted him, until he couldn't not write it. He put his motive on paper before he even knew he was going to kill March Flack, and that motive is what we needed to know.

He's probably well aware of the risk he took. But he'll always take a risk if he can hurt or embarrass England. The bigger the embarrassment, the bigger the risk he's willing to take. He'd gladly die if he could take England with him.

He knows he shouldn't have used Paul Kruger's name but the temptation to be symbolic was too great, and in that name he left a small trail of paper. Harford's check for the play was a necessary evil—not that the money mattered, it couldn't have been much, but the check had to clear before the station owned the rights and could legally put it on the air. The check was endorsed by Paul Kruger, who might've been anyone, and made over to a John Riordan of that house on West Fifty-sixth Street. The Irishman, probably the same one who roughed up Kendall. Now we'll find out what that's about.

Our Paul Kruger became a spy, that's clear enough. When the first war broke out he was all for Germany, at least until we got into it—late, as usual—in 1917. Whatever he did, it had nothing to do with Uncle Sam: only England was his mad passion. We may never know if he worked for Germany in the first war but I'll bet he did. I think Whitemarsh, if we ever find out what it means, will be a code name, what they knew him by in Berlin. Who knows what he might have done for them over the years? You read about what spies do and some of it seems so harmless. Even if they're not in defense work they can be funnels of information. They pass along the stuff they hear in everyday talk. They put up and hide fellow travelers. They take pictures of British ships docking in New York and pass along the departures and routes when they can get them. Everything counts in wartime, everything adds up.

He wrote this play because somewhere along the way he discovered the power of the air. Without a doubt Mrs.

Harford would play Margaret. But suddenly Mrs. Harford died and it languished in the office until the program director quit and Barnet took over.

Early summer 1936. Maitland and Kidd were here then, but Harford was devastated and the station was slipping into ruin.

This much is certain. At some point March Flack read the script and was infuriated. The old imperialist, whose hero was being slandered. I can almost hear his voice. *It's a goddamn lie. What the hell do you think we are, a race of savages? . . . See here, old boy, let me give you the real life of Lord Kitchener.* Obviously he had some sway with Barnet. But imagine the effect on a certain man when the Boer piece was shelved and Kitchener was glorified in full dress with ribbons and medals . . . it must have been like calling up the devil.

March was killed in a hot rage. The others were all cover-up for the German operation, killed by the same killer for the same personal reason. Somehow Carnahan discovered what they were doing and decided to get some proof. Whatever he got, he sent it to me for safekeeping. But someone found out and we know what happened then.

Kendall was just an actor playing a role he didn't understand. Probably paid with German money, more cash than he'd seen in a month of Sundays. Now I know why he always wanted to pick up the mail. But he never did get it, and the package—whatever it was—is still out there, probably sitting in some dead-letter office.

If I know anything about our boy it is this. He's a deadly shot. He could've killed me three times over that day in Pinewood. He didn't want me dead, that's the only answer. Somehow, perhaps, he still had a watch on my mail. RETURN—DECEASED wouldn't do: God knows where it would end up then, or who would open it, or when.

Dulaney remembered the day his papers arrived at general delivery; the package ripped apart and retied. He remembered the newspaper clipping in the German girl's apartment, telling of Nazi spies in radio, shipping companies, and post offices.

Someone wanted to scare me, stall me long enough that I'd miss my train. So he could get into the city before I did. So he could do what he had to do.

I like this, Dulaney thought. He stopped near West Fifty-third and stood thinking it through again, and he felt certain about almost all of it. Far less certain was how he would approach this Riordan fellow. He was prepared for anything from deception to intimidation. But he was not prepared for what he saw when he walked up the last three blocks.

A police car, parked in front of the house.

He went into the café and took a table near the window and ordered lunch. There wasn't much business on Saturday and it looked like he could sit here as long as he wanted.

For the fiftieth time that morning he thought of Holly, and the question was always there. What if she doesn't show up? She had no blood kin and no ties to any purpose or place. She could disappear forever if that's what she wanted, sink into the vast American woodwork.

What would he do if she decided not to arrive? Of course there was only one answer. Promises be damned, he would find her.

Out on the street nothing was happening. Only that cop car sitting ominously empty. No one on the street going into the building or out. Just the sunlit street and the quiet house and an occasional cab going by.

The waitress brought him some bread and his mind drifted as he waited.

Suddenly he saw the radio career that he would never have, encompassed in last night's broadcast.

Gus?

Just tell me what you need, champ.

Livia?

An enormous explosion shakes the room, a bombshell that makes Stallworth leap away from the speaker with a cry of alarm.

Miss Teasdale seems to be ready.

A wave of uneasy laughter flutters across the soundstage. She drowns it out with a spectacular thirty-second artillery barrage.

Miss Teasdale is definitely ready.

Maitland offers to stick around and Jordan is grateful for the help. For this important opening show they will have two directors—Jordan will work with the cast and sound on the floor while Maitland cues the orchestra and coordinates the entire production with Stoner in the booth. Blake is still here: he stayed over, and will play the white colonel and a few of the smaller colored parts. Potentially a touchy situation, but Blake plays it straight in the first reading and the blacks accept him as one of them. Waldo speaks for all of them from the booth. *He sounds just like my grandfather.*

A few musicians trickle in, and this is how it begins.

The biggest problem as the clock ticks down is Eli. He can't seem to break free of his fear. It has been coming over him as he realizes how far removed this show is from their simple Sunday broadcasts. He will be asked to carry much of it and he knows he's not ready, and the sight of the microphone makes him tremble as it waits for his presence.

Jordan hears Waldo breathing through the open mike from the booth. He looks up and meets the old black eyes through the glass.

Waldo?

Waldo shakes his head. *It's not my place to say this.*

Say it anyway. Do . . . do say it.

Waldo leans close. *He's tense and you're trying to get him to play it calm. Maybe it'd go better if you let him play it tense.*

What a revelation! Turn it into a suspense play! Let him be afraid, even in the quiet passages he writes in his diary to open the show. Make the audience ask themselves, Why is this man so goddamn terrified?

Let's try it that way, Eli. Take it from the top.

Jordan Ten Eyck looks at his script as Eli begins to read. *Diary entry, Ruckus Nation, Fifty-fourth Massachusetts Colored Infantry, Morris Island, South Ca'lina, July 18, 1863.*

Say it with a trembling heart, Eli.

I ought to, my own heart's doing the trembling.

The same lines work both ways. The voice of Ruckus Nation.

I am the doomed.

Good, Jordan thinks. Be as scared as you are, Eli.

We have been thrown down here on this little piece of sand to prove to history and the Confederacy the valor of our race. I must prove this with my life. For three hundred years they've been saying that we are too lazy and ignorant for anything but the very worst kind of work. Only the African is fit for the field in a tropical Southern climate, they say, and their Bible backs them up. Their biblical defense of slavery has been published in all their newspapers. All I've got to show them what a lie that is is that I'm willing to die.

Good, Eli . . . good.

Again Jordan meets Waldo through glass. The old man nods and smiles faintly. He has earned his money this week.

At some point Kidd appears. He stands quietly watching from the back as the table reading continues and cuts are made. Jordan can sense Kidd's anger. A second unexplained absence is grounds for dismissal, but Kidd says nothing and in a while he leaves. Becky has sweet rolls and coffee delivered and they take a break. The blacks are standoffish and reluctant, but they eat hungrily when she hand-delivers it to them.

A flash of white as Harford's face appears briefly on the balcony, leaning out of the darkness to see what they are doing. If it's attention he wants, he must be in hog heaven. No other radio station would air this show. It will swamp them with phone calls and bury them under a ton of mail. Racial injustice in the military is not a thing you do in wartime, and the biblical references will drive the zealots wild.

The time-out is short. The orchestra begins to tune up, and in the lull, he sees now, a stranger has entered the studio.

Becky goes out to greet him and he hears the name. Palmer of the *New York Times*.

Palmer declines her offer of food, of course. The integrity of the great newspaper cannot be compromised for a bit of pastry. He draws her off to the back of the room, and Jordan goes around through the sound room into the hall, coming up close to the door where he can hear them.

Who is that writer-director, Miss Hart? . . . and where did he come from? I've got a pretty good memory for people in radio, but I've never heard that name Ten Eyck before. He seems to've written you a good script.

We think it's a great script. I guess you could call him our homegrown talent.

How long has he been here?

I believe he came in May.

You mean he just walked in here cold, without any prior experience?

We needed a writer and Mr. Kidd liked the way he handled himself.

And now he's not only written this play but is directing it as well. And Kidd tells me he's done others. A serial that's to start soon, and some specials of a fairly sophisticated nature. I can't help thinking that he must have had some kind of apprenticeship on a station of near-network capability.

Not that I know. But he's been a writer most of his life, so it's not as if he'd never touched a typewriter before. As a matter of fact, he published a novel a few years ago.

Jordan cringes, hoping they will move past it. No such luck, of course.

Really? What's the name of it?

Now I'm embarrassed, Mr. Palmer. He never told me.

A quiet moment. Palmer scribbles away in a narrow steno notebook.

I'd like to interview him when the play's over.

Becky doesn't say anything for almost thirty seconds. Then:

He's really not keen on that. Don't get me wrong, it's just that Mr. Brown's been doing this show for years. You can see why Jordan would be uneasy about any appearance that he's taking it over. He would much rather have any publicity concentrate on Waldo and the cast.

I don't do publicity. I'm a newspaperman.

Well, of course. I only meant—

Look, I know the program's history, I've been tuning it in occasionally on Sunday mornings for years. With all due respect to Mr. Brown and what he's accomplished, you've got to admit that this is a far different animal.

Yes, it is.

Silence. Palmer is waiting her out.

He can almost see Becky shrug. *All I can do is ask him.*

Back on the soundstage Jordan takes note of the clock. Behind him Maitland's voice comes through the bitch box. *Do you want to read them again before the dress? We've still got time to go over the rough spots.*

I really think they've got it now. Let's not lose that edge.

The room begins to fill with people: with salesmen and clerks and secretaries and finally the air staff. The show has gained much word-of-mouth notoriety and everyone wants to see it. Pauline and Hazel come in together. Rue arrives alone and sits by herself in a corner. Even old Poindexter is there, standing with Barnet, the two of them watching malignantly. Jordan takes refuge for a moment in the booth, where he shares a last few words with Stoner and Maitland. *I think we're ready,* he says, and thanks them both. Stoner slaps his arm and says, *It's a great show, champ,* but Jordan is only half listening. Through the glass he sees that the local newspaperman has arrived and is talking with Palmer of the *Times*.

Waldo leans back noisily in his chair. *Looks like we got a full house.*

Maitland frowns. *Remind me to get that chair oiled, Waldo. I hate a squeaky chair in a radio station.*

Stoner looks up from his dials as Jordan says the obvious. *Nobody can hear it in here.*

But Maitland is determined. *These things have a way of getting out into the studio unless they're nailed to the floor. Next thing you know it'll be out there, squeaking like hell on the air.*

A cardinal rule in radio . . . let nothing disrupt your sound, even in the smallest way.

Dulaney had been here an hour now and the street was eerily quiet. The waitress brought him a small rice pudding and he ate it, and for the tenth time he read the sign in the window across the way. ROOMS BY THE WEEK OR MONTH. His eyes paused over each letter as the deeper symptoms of boredom set in.

He was working on his third cup of coffee when the door opened and a cop came out, stopping at the top of the steps. A moment later two men in plain suits joined the cop and the three of them talked for a few minutes. Then the uniform got into the police car and drove away. The two suits walked around the house and were gone for ten minutes.

The waitress asked if he wanted anything else.

"What's going on across the street?"

She shrugged. "Some accident is what we hear. Somebody fell from the roof and got killed last night."

(((2)))

IT meant nothing to him then, only that he must stay away from the house and try again another time. He hated to dismiss anyone's life as an annoyance, but this was an annoyance to him now.

He went over to Fourth Avenue and picked up his Paul Kruger books. Walked up toward the library. Sat in the William Cullen Bryant Park, reading and browsing through the dusty pages. Thought it all through again.

When he arrived in the old neighborhood it was well after three. He had plenty of time yet, but something told him even then that she wouldn't be there.

He sat on the steps where they had sat that summer night in 1939, and he watched the faces of people going by. Slowly as the hour came his eyes probed anxiously down the block and beyond, looking, looking for any familiar female shape. A look at the watch told him it was four thirty.

It never occurred to him that something might have happened to stop her from coming. If she didn't show up, that meant only that she had changed her mind, and what could *that* mean? Was she playing some hide-and-seek game, to lure him away from Harford? . . . Or had she actually cast herself to the wind without as much as a final word?

He couldn't believe that, and yet the notion gripped him tighter as five o'clock passed. Her words haunted him. *You don't deserve the grief I'm going to bring you . . . I'm no good for anyone anymore . . . Some of us are just unlucky . . . We bring bad luck to everyone who loves us . . . That's why I'm going to hold you to your promise . . .*

He couldn't say she hadn't warned him.

He began to pace, up to the end of the block to stand on the corner, looking far off at the crossing streets. Back again to sit nervously on the steps. Down the other way. Back again, and back, and back again.

Shadows fell over the sidewalks. Again he had a clear vision of the bleakness of life without her. At six o'clock he knew the worst. She is gone.

Still he waited. By nightfall his last faint hope had trickled away. All that was left was to find her. He had to do that, even if she only said no and walked away again.

He couldn't bear to leave. If he waited just another five minutes she would come, running breathlessly up the street. But half an hour later he was still sitting on the steps.

What is it about despair? he wondered. As a fiction writer it almost always led him to some unrelated insight. If you grieve deeply enough the soul will cry uncle. If you grieve long enough the mind will offer some small sacrifice to quiet the grief.

Suddenly he knew how to trap a killer.

$((\ 3\ ))$

JUST as suddenly she was there on the street, a mirage coming toward him in the dark.

Not a mirage, a miracle. A real woman walking up the block. He forced himself to sit still and wait, but already his heart surged with relief.

She stopped a dozen feet away, still in shadow.

"Holly?"

He got up from the steps and she moved back a few feet, keeping herself in the dark. When she spoke, it was only his name. Just "Jack," but it was enough.

"What's wrong with you?"

"God, what a question. I hardly know where to begin."

"Come over here. Where I can see you."

"No, you come out to me."

He joined her and they walked, two shadows alone on the street. She led him out of the neighborhood toward the park. He sensed trouble and because of this he waited for her to get at it in her own way. Nothing was said for several blocks, until she said, "I knew you'd still be here."

"I was here at four. Like you said."

"I know, I saw you. I watched you for a while, then I left."

"At least you came back."

Again she shied away from the light, turning him into a dark path at the edge of the park.

"What's wrong? . . . Why won't you let me see you?"

"I had an accident."

He was alarmed and it came out in his voice. "What happened?"

"It's okay. But I'm not so pretty anymore."

"I don't care about that."

"Then let's not talk about it. I've got other things to tell you."

They found a bench, quiet and dark. She was a shape beside him, her voice coming up from nowhere, like that first day in the bar.

A moment passed before she spoke again. "Our time is up, Jack."

The seconds ticked away in his head.

"We knew this day would come."

He heard what she said but it had no meaning. Whatever she was thinking, he would talk her out of it. He would tell her how close he was to knowing everything and she would see what they had to do. But when she spoke again he felt this certainty slipping away from him.

"I've reached the end of my rope."

He saw a blurred movement as she touched her face. "When it was just me alone I was fine. I really don't care what they do to me, they can't hurt me at all. But now you're here and they are going to kill you. Don't argue with me, please, I can feel it. It's the one thing I know, and I know it more every day."

Her voice quaked slightly. "I open my eyes and it's there. Today they will kill him. Today he will die. I look at you across my table and I see you dead, under the ground like my father. I see that grave and it's you buried there and I think such awful things. *Don't let it be Jack, let it be Daddy again, not Jack there in the ground.* I hate myself when I think that but I can't stop it, it comes to me a hundred times a day. When I come home and can't sleep, this is why, because I'm full of dark thoughts. I was certain I could get through it but I can't."

"Tell me what to do," he said. "We'll do whatever you want, whatever makes you happy."

"What is 'happy'? I don't know what that means."

"I'll help you find out."

"How can you do that when you're the cause of it? You've made me vulnerable again, I told you you would. Stay with me and you're a marked man, Dulaney."

"Oh, Holly, that is such crap. You're way too smart to believe that."

"Maybe I'm not as smart as you think. All I know is, I need to be somewhere else. A place where I know nobody and nobody knows me. Seattle maybe, or western Canada. I've been thinking I might go to Europe after the war. American swing was a big rage in France before Hitler came. Maybe it will be again. Whatever I do, I need to be away from here. And you, Jack, you may not know it yet, but you need me to be away as well."

"I'll never believe that."

Somehow he had to tell her what he did believe, what he knew. But his words sounded stiff when he said them. "I know how to end this. I can get this guy now. That's where your salvation is. It's not in Canada . . . not in France."

She sighed. "You can't let it go, can you? You're just like I was, you can't let it go."

"I can do anything if I know it's right."

"Then do this. Walk away from it. A year from now you'll see how right it was."

"Damn a year from now. I don't care about a year from now."

"Poor sweetheart. This is such a dirty trick, I know how you hate it. But you'll do it, because I need you to. This is the best gift you could ever give me, Jack. Peace for a couple of words."

His mind picked at straws. How could he buy some time? . . . change her mind? . . . or much more than that, how could he fix her ailing heart in the few seconds before she sent him away from her? How could he tell her that a year or a lifetime of years could not make a dent in his own desolation if she left him now? . . . that he had been a shadow of himself all those years on the road without her? He had no answers: a pact was the best he could hope for. He would agree to anything if she would stay in touch in some minimal way . . . a letter once a year to some cold and distant general delivery. People change in a year, and anything was better than the dreadful void without her. But when he said this he met a wall of silence.

"You still don't understand," she said after a while. "I've got to start over. If there's anything left for me on this earth, I've got to find it in myself. I can't be tied to anyone."

She squeezed his hand. "I don't know, Jack, I can't explain it any better than that."

"Well, I told you . . . whatever you want, that's what we'll do." He sat back against the bench. "I guess I just can't bring myself to say it."

"Oh, sweetheart. Just forgive an old friend and try to think well of her. Disappear into some horse farm. Write your book, do something you love. Only promise me you will never go back to that town again, and never touch this thing after today."

Then she told him what had happened, a shaky narrative of her two days with the Irish Republican Army. Suddenly she was back on the roof with Riordan . . . coaxed there, sweet-talked, gripped in his steely hands, and pushed back over the edge . . . hanging there, her legs still curled around the coping, his face so close she could feel his breath and smell it.

Who sent you here, Brigit? Better tell me now, darlin', before there's a tragic happening.

She tried not to panic. Thought of her father and smiled sweetly.

You're so smart, Johnny, you figure it out.

I am dead, she thought. If he released her now, with a little push, she would fall headfirst into the street. But his hands gripped her tighter and then he was pulling her back over the coping. His face was red with sudden fury.

You *dare* come into my house. Lie to me. Spy on us. And all I ever wanted to do was love you.

He slapped her.

Now you will tell.

He slapped her a dozen times.

God damn you, little bitch hussy! Tell me or I'll break your neck!

He came at her with his fists. She didn't remember going for the razor but saw him recoil in a gush of red. He spun in a tortured little dance and stumbled. She pushed him away and he went screaming over the edge.

"I didn't look down. I knew he was dead. I had an omen just before it happened. When he said he wanted to love me."

((**4**))

AFTER she left he felt a numbness in his spirit, like a sudden paralysis to the body after a fall. He drifted along the streets, walked back into the old neighborhood and back again to sit on the bench, as if she might come along and have a sudden change of heart. But sometime after midnight he had to give it up. He walked across the park and came out on the east end, turned south and drifted, apparently without direction. The city seemed immense. Two people could spend their lives here and never cross paths, and tomorrow she would be gone into the infinite, God knew where.

He sat on benches and stood under the Third Avenue El, watched the lights of trains flicker by, saw bars go dark, and walked endlessly.

A thought kept plaguing him, that if he could find her now she would change her mind and go with him somewhere, to tempt fate one more time. He had never been at such loose ends . . . she had taken not only herself away from him, she had also taken away his purpose.

In the deadest part of the night he found himself in Yorkville. He stood outside the apartment house where the German girl had lived, then he walked around the block to the ramshackle hotel where she and Peter had died. A quick walk, no more than a couple of minutes. How far to the Riordan house? . . . thirty blocks? . . . forty? A different world, yet in the city's universe still just a brisk walk away. Suddenly he saw what might have happened that night, and how. For all his care, Peter had been careless: coming and going for days before settling into this seedy hotel. Plenty of time for him to be picked up and watched by Irish eyes, as a favor to an old Boer friend. Left alone as long as he stayed harmless: never killed if he hadn't been greedy. If he had left the country and never made that phone call he'd be in Germany now, and the German girl would still be practicing her madness a block away. But the man he feared the most knew where he was all along.

Dulaney now walked it himself, as if to confirm what he knew. Well within the hour he stood on West Fifty-sixth Street, and for a time he watched from the doorway of the dark café across from the Riordan house.

Dawn found him walking again, across Times Square, where the only people on a Sunday morning were a few aimless drifters like himself and a whore who stepped from subway darkness and smiled when he walked past her.

As the city came to life he felt ever more isolated and aim-less among the swarming strangers. He stopped at a hash house but had no stomach for breakfast. He sipped his coffee and imagined Holly walking in, defying all odds, and in that moment he knew he had lied to her.

Somehow he would find her, and the gift he would give her was the man who had killed her father.

He called Becky Hart. Two hours later he was back on the beach.

(((5)))

HE slept soundly and was up in the late afternoon, poring over his work at the open kitchen door. The work diminished the emptiness of the house, and soon the Japanese script that had given him such trouble bristled with life. The power of it thrilled him: the story and its people had been there all along but his mind had been too busy with other things to see it. Now there were no other things. The strength of the story had been hidden in the unwritten flashback, and now his characters relived a life they would never know again. Their home had been intimate and warm, filled with laughter and boundless hope. All the promise of America, vanished in the bombs of a Sunday morning. The story took away the carica-ture—the cold icy Jap, the snarling cruel and yellow Jap—and made him a man.

In the end Danny Sakamoto is sent to a real prison. There he will meet a brutal guard who carries a full load of hatred for all Japs everywhere. The outlook is bleak, the implication clear: Danny will not survive to see his family again. His wife faces a shaky future with two small children, everything she thought they owned is gone, and a thousand red-blooded Americans, still seething over Pearl Harbor, will stand and cheer at her fate. But there will be others who will think about it and feel shame, and believe that somehow, even in wartime, we should have been better than this.

So much for the artistic purpose. His real objective was to get the Boers on the air, and these Nisei were just part of the smoke screen that would help him do that. It would be the second show in a series of five, with the Boers coming on the third night. Jordan himself would bring only three of them to air—win or lose, he would be gone on Thursday. But he knew he had to write them all; the package must be complete before Kidd would consider scheduling any of it. This one was now ready for mimeo, lacking only Kidd's approval.

He read it over and for the first time was a little afraid of its power. Kidd might balk if he had gone too far, and then he'd have to count on Harford to stand up for it. This was exactly what Harford said he wanted, it had truth shot all through it. Jordan believed in what he had written: he had focused on the heart, not culture, and the heart was where people were always the same.

Now he had to believe that Harford would veto all caution and run it. It's got to be next week, he thought: it's got to be finished and on the air, and can't be allowed to drag on beyond that. This meant he had to wrap up his piece on Andersonville and write two more full-hour shows in two days, then convince Kidd that all must be produced like a bat out of hell, with the same hurried passion of the writing. The shows must run on consecutive nights . . . a weekly series would push it almost to October before the Boers could get on and give him his chance. But as he thought all these things he realized that scheduling was going to be the least of his problems. Kidd would be heading into his first full week without the network. He would be desperate for something smashing and would pull out all the stops to get it on. And Kidd had enough dramatic sense to know that a weekly schedule would fatally diminish the artistic purpose and water down the impact of the series as a whole.

The timing was perfect. Five shows in five nights, with the main event a week from Wednesday.

★　★　★

At six o'clock he began working on the Hitler show that would open the run. The stories that were coming out of Poland had all the characteristics of a horror show and that's how he would write it, as the kind of raw horror that had never been heard on American radio. Children murdered in present tense, live, on-mike. A young woman brutalized again and again by monsters from some primordial slime. It didn't matter that he had no actual prototype . . . if the Nazis could commit mass murder in one village, they were capable of anything he could imagine . . . if they could gun down children or put them in gas chambers, a humble writer could hardly do them any injustice. But larger questions rose up to confront him—how did the Nazis affect his belief that people are basically the same? . . . Was there something in the German character that compelled them to follow madmen and become worse than animals?— and he sat for a time with his pen held still and his mind clouded with trouble. Then a vision of the Sand Creek Massacre crossed his mind and he shivered.

Suddenly he had an almost uncontrollable need to add a sixth show. He knew this was insane, for where would he put it and how could it help his real purpose and how would it fit the theme as a prison camp story? His writer's mind made its own logic—it was certainly a prison camp if the point could be stretched; those two hundred Indian women and children were supposedly in the custody of the United States Army. In the custody and under the protection, until a band of soldiers led by a bloodthirsty fanatic slaughtered them all, took their scalps, cut out their genitals, and wrote its own day of infamy. Colonel John Chivington, a Methodist minister in civilian life, had given the order. Praise the Lord and take no prisoners.

For an hour he noodled it back and forth and at last he gave it up: nothing could come of it without much more work, and the result would likely be no better than what he had. For Kidd's purpose and his own, he would stick to the plan. By seven thirty he had roughed out a tale so savage that it shook him to imagine it set to sound. His heroine was a young woman named Bela: older than Margaret of the Boer War, much wiser, and with a vastly greater heart. Bela was twenty-three with a husband dead in the war and a small child to somehow protect on her own. He knew at once that she was going to be a magnificent character, one who takes over a story and leaves the writer hurrying to catch up. Her courage should touch every listener, and it should tear at their hearts when she is lost at the end.

This would not be an easy story to hear but it would be almost impossible to turn off. It was a murder story . . . the Nazi kills her tiny son and she finds a surprising way to kill that Nazi and then the Nazis kill her. What it says about the enemy will serve Kidd's purpose, and it will get us off on a grimly patriotic note.

He switched to the portable typewriter and began to write. It was dark outside when he heard the footsteps. Someone had come up from the beach to the deck. Footsteps came across the pine floor.

Pauline Flack peeped around the edge of the open door.

"Jordan . . . I've been looking for you."

"I've been here working."

"I see you have. I tried your apartment downtown. Went out to the station. Called Becky but she wouldn't tell me anything."

"She's become very protective. But I'm always glad to see you."

"I won't bother you long. May I come in?"

"Of course."

He swept up his loose pages and turned them down on the table. "Can I get you something? I think there are some Dopes in the icebox."

"It's good of you to remember a lady's addiction."

He brought the Cokes and sat looking at her over the typewriter. "I can guess why you're here."

"I'm sure you can. I was shocked when I heard about Tom."

"I don't know what more I can tell you. I don't know any more than you do."

"Forgive me, but I doubt that. You must know why Miss O'Hara went out to see Tom in the first place."

He shrugged. "I'd ask her if I could, but she's gone."

"You mean she's left you?"

"It looks that way."

"And you have no idea . . . ?"

She looked suddenly agitated. "But how can you have no idea? How can you not know? This whole thing is preposterous. Tom didn't kill March."

"He says he did."

"I don't care what he says. He's obviously trying to protect me."

"Protect you from what?"

"Somehow he must think I shot March."

"Why would he think that?"

"I was up to here with March and his women. I won't deny I was angry enough. I told you about the screaming row we'd had that day, and there were plenty of witnesses. It was no secret. And what else makes sense?"

"That he killed March himself, for the same reason."

He saw the anger in her eyes. "I didn't say I believe that. But it certainly is the most obvious answer."

She finished her drink and seemed to be on the verge of tears. "Tell me the truth, Jordan. Damn it, man, you know Tom didn't kill March. Why won't you say it?"

"All right. No, I don't believe he did it."

"I knew it. I knew it."

"But what I think isn't evidence. The evidence is in the ground. We'll know more when they dig out that foundation."

"And if they find nothing . . ."

"Then Griffin goes free. It won't matter what he said, if they've still got no body it'll just be the ramblings of a crazy old man. No offense."

She said nothing. Seemed lost in thought.

"Are you worried about what's down there?"

"Of course not." She sniffed. "Yes, a little."

She took a long breath. "March has been missing so long I've come to terms with it. I'm bound to be nervous when they start digging things up."

"I understand," he said softly. "I can imagine how you must feel."

She reached for his hand. "Then go see Tom for me . . . get him to talk to me, please! I can't help him if he won't talk to me."

"I don't think he'll talk to me either, Pauline. I'm not high on his list of drinking buddies. But if they'll let me in, I'll try."

He pushed back his chair. "Come on, I'll buy you some dinner. I just remembered, I haven't eaten all day."

He took her to the Searchlight, the best place in town, where Harford sometimes ate alone at a private table off in a far corner. Over candlelight and wine she told him of her early days on the London stage and nothing more was said about Griffin or Flack. By ten o'clock he was home again. In the full dark of the night Holly was everywhere. He saw her face no matter where he looked and heard her constantly walking as the house creaked in the wind. Only hard work would give him peace, and he plunged again into his Hitler script and had a draft finished at midnight. Rewrote from scratch and got a fine polish on it to end the day. Two done, two to go. His last act of the night renewed his purpose and let him rest. He gathered his *Dark Silver* mimeos and burned them with the originals in the fireplace. Had a sharp twinge of loss and felt especially bad for Becky and for Blake. Then, exhausted, he dropped into the empty bed and fell immediately into a deep hard sleep.

(((6)))

HE stood in the shower the next morning thinking about his dreams. Pushing at the pieces. Searching for meaning, certain it was there.

His breakfast was an orange. It was enough . . . any more and he risked getting sleepy, and this was a morning when his mind needed to be sharp.

He gathered his work together, locked the house, and headed up the beach. Gone were the throngs of people: the sand was white and uncluttered for a Monday morning, the boardwalk strangely deserted, the square and the street beyond it as still as a photograph. He didn't stop at his rooming house: he pushed on into town, past the street of swing and out along the shore road north. The Harford building loomed up on his left: he could see the Packard parked in its place, bright and shiny as it had first caught his attention the day he arrived. This morning Kidd's car was parked beside it, but no sign of any other activity and no one visible on the roof. It was still early, not yet eight o'clock: the staff would begin coming in soon, but for now Harford and Kidd were alone in the big empty building, hatching their plans.

Then as he came past the facade, he saw the sheriff's deputy standing at the north wall. Barricades had been put up, with signs warning people to stay away. It was a crime scene now, and suddenly next Wednesday seemed very far away.

He turned into the dunes. There was nothing to do about it. His only alternative was to cut and run, and where would he go?

"I need to see Kidd," he said to Becky. "When do you expect him?"

"Maybe later this morning. He's over with the man, worrying about opening week."

"It came up on us too fast. Kidd's been busy putting out brush fires."

"Yeah, he knows it, too. He was hoping to have something strong and newsworthy, but that ain't gonna happen."

"Who knows what might happen?"

She looked at him almost breathlessly. She had heard that tone before.

"I think we can go with the prison camp stuff."

She took in the breath, like a plunge into cold water. "I don't know whether I hope you're kidding or serious."

"I've got two finished scripts for you. The Boer script is the third, and I think I can have the fourth finished by the end of the day. That gives me a couple of days to get the fifth worked out. But I want Kidd to read these two and let me know."

He gave her the scripts. "This is going to be a producer's nightmare. Five shows in five days. You'll need lots more voices than we've got here."

"Don't worry, I'll get them." She nodded. "I'll get them."

"Rick Gary can help you. He knows everybody in New York."

"Zylla's the one I worry about. Wait'll I tell him I need five musical scores by next week."

"He'll be fine, he thrives on work. But we'll have to get cracking. Get him into it as soon as Kidd gives us the okay."

He walked up through the quiet building and let himself into his office. For a time he sat still, looking at all the little things she had done for him, thinking of the life he might have had here if things had been different. Then he pushed away the sentiment and was back with his boys in Andersonville.

He had decided to abandon the idea of a split show. That would make it far more difficult and he didn't have time for the finer points of theme. No one but himself would know the difference.

He had already done much of it, and now he needed only to expand it and write the closing scene, then do a quick rewrite. He had been working for an hour when his phone rang. "It's me," said Becky, just above a whisper. "I'm over at the office building. Harford and Kidd are in the other room reading your scripts. I'll tell you this, Jordan, they are bowled over by the concept. You know how Kidd is—he never shows anything. When I told him you'd have five shows in five days I thought he'd faint. I'll be surprised if they don't bow and worship at your lower extremities. Just my opinion, for what it's worth."

At eleven, one of the salesmen from the bullpen knocked on his door. The receptionist was looking for him. He had a visitor down in the lobby.

The sheriff.

((7))

THEY walked out into the parking lot. The sheriff was keen eyed and wilier than he expected, but for the moment there were only a few questions.

"I understand it was Miss O'Hara who followed Griffin into the woods."

"Yes, that's right."

"And you found them there because you were looking for her, not him."

"Yes."

"You were alarmed because she hadn't shown up for work, is that right?"

"Yes, she had been missing all night."

"How'd you know where to look?"

He stopped and put his foot on the running board of the sheriff's car. "Maybe you remember," he said; "she came here looking for her father."

"I do remember that. I didn't place her, though, till you just mentioned it. She looked a lot different then. I believe she even suspected at one point that Mr. Harford had something to do with her old man's disappearance."

"And maybe Mr. Griffin as well."

"Why would she think that?"

"Something her father had written her. I'm not sure exactly what."

"But this—whatever he wrote her—made her think of Griffin?"

"It made her wonder. And when I couldn't find her anywhere, it made me wonder. Then I talked to Mrs. Flack and learned that Griffin was also missing. That's what set me off."

"And you tracked them all that way through the woods. That's damn good tracking, son."

"I was raised in the woods."

"Uh-huh." The sheriff turned and spat a wad of tobacco into the sand. "Where exactly is Miss O'Hara right now?"

"I'm not sure. She left town on Thursday. I don't know where she went."

"Isn't that kinda strange? I hear you two were close."

"It looks like that's over now." He shrugged. "We broke up. That's how it goes, you know. You can't tell about people."

"But you're still living in her house."

"I wouldn't say that. I keep hoping she'll come back. But her rent's due on the fifteenth. If she's not back here by then . . ."

"Then what? . . . You're not planning to leave town too, are you, son?"

"Not hardly. I've got too much going for me here. I only meant that I'll have to let the place go, that's all."

The sheriff nodded. "I guess that makes sense. And if you do happen to hear from her, tell her I want to talk to her."

"Sure."

"And listen, I'd appreciate it if you don't leave town without lettin' me know. I may want to talk to you again when I get that wall dug up."

(((8)))

CALMLY he went back to work. He forced everything else from his mind. There was no sheriff, no Griffin, no Harford or Kidd. Only the job and its payoff a week from Wednesday.

He finished his script. Sat quietly at his desk and thought about the next one.

He thought about Bataan and what must be happening there, and in a while he saw the shape of a story. But at its heart it was the same story he had written about the Nazis. The people were different, but raw brutality as a dramatic device loses its charm quickly.

Becky checked in. He gave her the Andersonville and she left without saying whatever she had come in to say. Always the good producer, ready to protect him when he was working, even when no words were getting written.

No one disturbed him. He knew that somewhere Kidd would be reading his Andersonville, but this was like the other things he knew without thinking, and it didn't matter.

At times he sat half asleep; then he'd open his eyes, to write notes as fast as they'd come. But something was always wrong and he'd cast away what he'd written and again sit quiet, hunting for the random thought or the piece of color . . . anything to get him started in the right direction.

His hero must be an American boy captured on Bataan. He closed his eyes and the kid he saw was Tom, and suddenly he had it, a story wrapped so completely in character that the brutality of the background faded to nothing.

He would write an alternate story of Holly and Tom, the way it should have been. It would unfold in a Japanese concentration camp on Bataan.

Tom would survive. As it should have been.

He and Holly would marry, as they should have done. A whirlwind courtship in the spring of 1941, cut short by the specter of war. Tom had joined the army, not the navy, and was in uniform when they met that day, on a train in New York.

No Jack Dulaney in this alternate world: his own role neatly omitted, the spoiler blipped out, canceled, denied existence.

When they married, in the spring of '41, Tom's best friends were fellow doughboys, standing at attention in uniform. Holly's sister, who hadn't drowned in the lake at all, would be maid of honor.

Three weeks after the wedding, Tom's outfit shipped out for the Philippines, as part of MacArthur's plan to discourage Japanese aggression. We know how well that worked now.

All those boys. What are they going through tonight?

Whatever it was, Tom would survive it. Her face would sustain him, this woman he had known less than a month. It would end on a note of hope, with a promise implied. The war is still there to be won, but the tide is turning, and Tom will live to see her again.

This was enough for now. He would let it simmer overnight and work off the sentimental edges tomorrow in the writing.

He locked his door and Becky Hart appeared, as if she'd been waiting in the hall all afternoon. "How'd it go?"

"It's a little rough," he said. "I think it'll be okay."

"Good. Kidd would like to see you before you leave."

"Well, Jordan. It's a big scary project you've given us."

Kidd motioned him in. There was a tension in the room and it all seemed to come from Kidd's side of the desk. As if suddenly Kidd was afraid of him.

"This puts our beliefs to the test, doesn't it? It's the kind of thing radio must do, but I'm not kidding when I say it's scary. We are going to get incredible heat for that Japanese script."

"I can cut it back if it's too strong."

"No, it's got to be strong if we're going to do it at all. Besides, Harford would boil us in oil if we changed it."

A moment passed. "No, we're in it now," Kidd said.

Kidd looked away, searching his desk for something. He pulled out next week's schedule and Jordan could see that the nine o'clock hour had been cleared for each of the five week-day nights.

"My only second thought has to do with the order of the episodes," Kidd said. "I'd like to move the Boers up to Tuesday and do Andersonville on Wednesday. Bump the American Japs back to Thursday, and maybe that'll give us some quick relief with your Bataan script. If we seem to be Jap lovers on Thursday, we'll kick their asses on Friday. You see what I mean?"

Jordan saw what he meant, and still he felt an irrational sense of loss. Now, as far as his own involvement went, his Nisei would join two others in the trash. But for his purpose— for the Boers—sooner was much better than later, even a day.

Kidd sensed his hesitation. "If you feel strongly about the original order, we can leave it. It's your series."

"No, your changes are fine. Whatever strong feelings I've got, I put 'em in the script."

Kidd asked about the closing script. Jordan promised it by Wednesday.

"We've got a lot of decisions to make," Kidd said. "I'm going to call a special staff meeting Wednesday morning. Get some idea who might be involved with which scripts. Then we'll know who we need."

"I'd like Miss Hart to produce it. The whole series."

"Are you sure? That's a big job you're putting on her."

"I think she's up to it. She's certainly earned a chance."

"All right, if that's what you want. What are your thoughts about directing? I know you'll want to do them all, but I don't see how that's possible. You've still got a colored show on Friday and another next week."

"I can do the first two without any problem. The Boer script will be good experience, directing something that's not mine. How about Maitland for Wednesday and Friday?"

"I'll tell him right away. We'll get the scripts up to mimeo and he can have the Andersonville first thing in the morning."

Jordan got up to leave.

"One last thing," Kidd said. "I can't let you go without saying thanks. Thank you for this wonderful thing."

Kidd smiled uneasily. "You have a brilliant future, Jordan."

"Thank you, sir. That's good to hear."

(((9)))

HE walked alone down the beach. Passed the office building, where the diggers had begun their work. Saw the sheriff standing off to one side, smoking, talking with the man from the *Beachcomber*. As he walked away he felt the pinpricks of surveillance on his back. He climbed to the boardwalk, went past the pier and on past the square to the end. Stood there for a long time, leaning over the rail, staring out to sea. He was still there an hour later when Rue came upon him from somewhere off in the town.

"Hey, stranger. Want some company?"

He said, "Sure," but he wasn't sure at all.

"You look so alone and heartbroken, Jordan. Like a man whose friends have all died on the same day."

He laughed. "Well, you're alive. And still my friend, I hope."

She tried to put an arm over his shoulder but came up short and settled for an arm in an arm. "Once again you are the subject of wild rumors, Jordie. The word's spreading like a fire about your big project next week."

"There'll be some things in it for you, I think."

"That'll be great. But I'm not here to hit you up for work. Honest—I was just out walking and here you were."

"Where's Jimmy?"

"Went home to see his mother before they take him off to war. Someplace exotic called Boise, Idaho. God knows where it is." She sighed. "I guess we're finished. I don't know, I'm sure it's all my fault. I'm such a bitch, as you pointed out."

"But you're a damned pretty bitch, and under it you've got a good heart."

"Don't let that part get around. It'll ruin my reputation."

After a while she said, "We heard you and Miss O'Hara broke up too. This seems to be the month for it."

"People talk way too much in this town," he said gruffly.

"Oh, don't be an old bear. If people gossip about you it can mean only one of two things—they either love you or hate you. We care about you, Jordan. Nobody should be alone. Especially when you don't have to be."

He felt a warning alarm go off in his mind. "Listen, Rue . . ."

She pinched his arm. "At ease, Jordan, I'm not here to pick you up. Not that I'm above it, but right now I can't."

He grinned at her, relieved. "Some sudden disability?"

"Laugh, you bastard, but this is serious. Livia's in love with you."

Now he did laugh.

"I'm not kidding. She is gone, hopeless, beyond crazy."

"Get out of here."

"All right, but don't say I didn't tell you. And please, don't say I did, either. I'm betraying a huge confidence here, but I believe people should know such things."

"Well," he said softly, "your secret is safe with me."

"That doesn't mean you can't *do* something about it, for Christ's sake."

"What do you expect me to do? She's never given me a hint . . ."

"Of course not. That's not her style. But I'm her best friend and she tells me things she'd never broadcast on the radio. You can trust me on this, Jordan. I only hope you've got enough sense to know what to do with it."

He said nothing.

"Just drop in on her. You don't have to fall right into bed with each other, just play it by ear. I happen to know she'll be home tonight."

He shook his head. "It wouldn't be right."

"Why not? Don't you like her?"

"Of course I like her. That's the point."

"What point? Do you still think I'm making this up? I'm sure it's hard to believe, that someone as wonderful as she is could love a moody and unpredictable fool like yourself. So she's got a blind spot . . . so what? She is the best person I know, the absolute best. You'd be the luckiest man alive if you could get her, and look at you, you can't even see your own good luck when it stares you in the face."

Suddenly she was impatient. She scribbled something on a small notepad and shoved the paper in his pocket. "There, goddammit, that's where *I* live. Now you go see Livia, and if she's not totally thrilled, you can come back and see me. You won't get an offer like that every day, Jordan."

She smiled at him sweetly, the living image of the Gibson girl. "So, what's this I hear about five shows in five days? . . . and what's in it for me?"

* * *

He stood at the open door and looked out at the black sea. Strictly speaking, he had not told the truth about Livia. There had always been something between them, hints beginning with that first look at the picnic tables. That and a hundred other looks he had denied. All the days and nights when they had worked together and she had gone beyond the call of duty to enrich his talent with her own. But bringing it out in the open now only had the effect of deepening his sense of isolation, not relieving it.

The first day was done, just a trace of light remaining on the sand. He wondered where Holly was, and he couldn't stop thinking of all these people who had changed his life so much. They came up from the beach and formed a little parade outside the house . . . Livia and Becky and Rue and Gus, Maitland and Harford and Kidd, Eastman and Stallworth and Hazel, even Poindexter and Barnet. And of course, his black players, Eli, Rudo, Emily, Ali. And Waldo, God bless him. He thought of all the things that had to be done by next Tuesday, and it seemed like such a short time and yet so far away. And out of the dark he saw the pages of a script fluttering—not the script yet to be written, for that was now safe, whole and alive inside his head, but the Boer script, and what he must do to it in those crucial minutes just before air.

It was all in the cues. Whatever he did, the cues must remain unchanged.

At eleven o'clock he turned on the light and started the preliminary work on the Bataan script. In two hard hours he had it roughed out, and he thought he might get it down tomorrow, a full day early, and this satisfied him enough that perhaps he could now sleep.

He did sleep, and was up at five.

He went through the morning routine. The shower, the breakfast orange, the gathering of the papers, the trek up the beach.

A harbinger crossed his path as he started through the town. The road north was moonlit and empty, the Harford building rising on his left like a dark fortress. At the north wall piles of sand stood out against the lights. The site looked deserted. But when he came abreast he saw a car parked just off the road, the window rolled down and the shape of a man behind the wheel, smoking.

"Howdy, son. Headin' into work?"

"Morning, Sheriff."

"I've been thinking you might come by."

The sheriff stepped out in the moonlight. "Come on, let's us take a walk."

They went up through the heavy sand to the edge of the building, where a vast pit had been scooped out from the wall. The sheriff stopped and turned, a silhouette against the light.

"I've just been wondering about the old man's confession. You were the first one to hear it—you and Miss O'Hara, and now she's gone. Did you believe it?"

"There wasn't any reason not to."

"Miz Flack doesn't believe it. I hear she's been making a real nuisance out of herself all weekend. She thinks she can get the old man to change his story if he'll only just talk to her."

Jordan shrugged, a gesture useless in the dark.

"She wants me to let you go back and talk to him."

"I told her I'm willing to do that. Not that it'll do much good."

"She let it slip that you don't believe the old man's confession either."

"I did tell her that. But it's just a hunch. I hardly know the old guy."

"I guess it can't hurt, can it? . . . I mean, we want to be fair, don't we? If it gives that poor woman a bit of peace, what harm can that do?" The sheriff dropped his smoke and stepped on it. "But I've got to tell you, son, this looks like an open-and-shut case."

He turned on a flashlight and shined it down into the pit. There at the bottom was a human skull, fused into the concrete foundation. A skeletal face, the remains of an officer's cap jutting out of the powdery cement. Below it, more bones. Ribs, and fragments of the uniform he had worn that night. A row of ribbons representing Kitchener's long, illustrious service to the crown. Below that, more fragments . . . pants, and the sharp, half-uncovered point of a shoe.

The sheriff was staring at him. "What's wrong, boy? Cat got your tongue? Say hello to Mr. Flack."

(((10)))

THE work went badly that morning. His mind kept drifting to that fossil in the concrete, then on to the usual phantoms . . . Holly, the Boers, Carnahan. By eleven o'clock he had put only two scenes in script and it was mediocre stuff, not worthy of sharing the air with the other four. Then the sheriff called and asked him to come in. A car would pick him up at noon.

He went as if he had nothing to fear. Pauline was already at the jail, looking small and pale in a chair near the desk. "They've found March," she said when she saw him. "He was right where Tom said."

He could see that her faith in the old man's innocence had been shaken. The old man's statement—that he had killed March because he couldn't stand seeing him hurt her anymore—was certainly feasible now, and Jordan knew that if this experiment failed she would give it up.

The sheriff led them back through the barred hallways. He touched Pauline's arm and motioned her to be quiet. They stood in the shadows while Jordan went on to the edge of the cell.

"Mr. Griffin."

The eyes flicked open. "What're you doing here?"

"They found Mr. Flack."

"Of course they did. I told you that."

"He was right where you said."

"Of course he was. A man don't get up when he's got a slug in his heart and two tons of concrete poured over his head."

"Is that how it happened?"

"I told you so, didn't I? What do you want? Why are you here?"

Jordan felt a sudden rush of freedom, as if Pauline and the sheriff had gone away. He could say anything, ask any question, and none of it would affect his own plans or how he would do it. "I'm here because Mrs. Flack asked me to come. Because she's very unhappy, and I like her, and she doesn't believe you did this."

"She'll get over it. And in time she'll know why I did what I did."

"She knows it now. That you're trying to protect her."

The old man came up from the cot and stood there trembling. "She must not say that! What's the matter with you, haven't I told you what happened?"

Jordan grew bolder. "You claim to be her friend but you're causing her great pain. If you persist with this story, she will make her own confession."

"No! . . . No! . . . You can't let her do that!"

"I can't stop her. And you can't help her with lies."

"What's wrong with you, are you stupid? You know I did this, I *told* you where the body was."

"They'll say you did it together. Unless you tell the truth now."

The old man quaked with rage. He lunged at Jordan with a roar, his arm flailing wildly through the bars. Then he stopped and stood still and Jordan felt the presence at his right arm as Pauline came up beside him.

"You shouldn't be here," Griffin said. "This isn't right."

"Tom, for *God's* sake tell the truth. I didn't kill March! I've got *nothing* to hide! How can I live with myself if you do this?"

The old man began to cry. Jordan stepped back with the sheriff and left them alone, and in time, after a while, the story came out.

They had had that terrible quarrel on the day of the Kitchener show, and Pauline had lost her temper and thrown a glass of beer in March's face. That night Griffin stayed late on the boardwalk, lingering in the pubs, drinking ale, and playing pinball to work off his rage.

It was late when he started for home. He walked out past the excavation where Harford was building his new office. He didn't think anything special about it then, but it was a cavernous dig and it must have stuck in his mind.

He was somewhere in the dunes when he heard the shots—two muffled pops, but Griffin had been in the war and he knew gunfire when he heard it. The night was cloudy and windy, with gusts blowing in from the sea and carrying the sound into the marsh. He couldn't see much, just the tower's red lights, and he made his way by instinct, having crossed so many times before.

He pushed on toward the station, and at the edge of the yard he found March Flack, shot once in the heart and once in the head. His only thought, from that moment on, was of Pauline.

He dragged the body into the dunes. There was no one to see him at that time of night, but he knew he had to do something before dawn. He thought of Harford's excavation two miles away: a tough go for a sound young man, impossible for an old man with a bum leg. But he began to drag the body with an energy and fire he had not felt in years.

At some point he remembered seeing the handyman put a wheelbarrow in the utility shed. He went to fetch it and in five minutes he had March, as bulky as Kitchener himself, flopped over the wheel, heading east.

He didn't know how long it took: at least two hours of pushing, pulling, and cursing before he reached the hard stuff and dumped March in the hole. He filched a bag of cement from the construction shack and poured it over the body, then added a light coat of sand.

That was the best he could do. If they found him there, he would confess and spare Pauline the anguish.

But he was lucky. The sheriff was slow to investigate, didn't start his search for a full week. By then the foundation had been poured over March Flack's body.

That's why the bloodhound kept going back to that shed. Even then the sheriff might have found blood on that wheelbarrow, but he didn't believe his own dog when it kept howl-ing at the tower. There the case was lost, and in no time at all it passed into local folklore.

((« 11 »))

AFTER that the day was better. He finished his script by five o'clock, and if it was still a sloppy, mediocre job, at least he had it trapped on paper. Again Becky appeared from the woodwork at the end of the day.

"Kidd wanted you to see this before you go. We heard about it this morning and sent someone into the city to get it."

It was the radio column of today's *Times:* half a dozen short squibs under one byline, with the top item getting the bold black headline.

WHO IS JORDAN TEN EYCK?
by Gerald Marshall Palmer

The headline caught the gist of it. A man of mystery, but no mean talent, had arrived at Harford's radio station down on the Jersey coast, to brew a tantalizing audio stew on Friday nights. Ten Eyck had been hired, apparently with no prior experience, and had spent his time writing continuity until his great natural ability with drama was discovered, only in recent weeks. Now, with one spectacular war bond drama and half a dozen Negro plays under his belt, the unsung boy wonder has reportedly delivered even bigger and better things for the immediate future—a serial in the *One Man's Family* tradition, to run weekly in a thirty-minute time slot, and more specials, perhaps as early as next week.

Jordan skimmed to the end. "This fellow is for real, but at this date he refuses to be interviewed. It is said that he once published a novel, but his name is unfamiliar to the *Times* book critic, and nothing was found even in the massive collection of the New York Public Library. Stay tuned."

"That means he's going to dig some more," Becky said with a shrug. "You're not going to be able to hide from him forever."

"No, I can see that now."

"I know you're not thrilled with this, but it couldn't be better for our opening week. Everyone loves a mystery, and Kidd wants to capitalize on it. He'd like to send Palmer mimeos of the prison camp stuff. He thinks we might get a much bigger story this Sunday."

Jordan thought about it as they walked through the halls. Really, what difference did it make? "Let's let Palmer see the opening script, and the piece about the Nisei. That should give him enough to chew on."

"Oh, you're a dear! Maybe this is the time to push my luck . . . what *about* giving him an interview, Jordan? If you get him on our side he can really help us."

He smiled at her, suddenly the soul of patience. "Sure, I'll talk to the man. But not till the series is over. Tell Mr. Palmer I'll be happy to bore him to death a week from Friday."

Now came the difficult hours: a solitude so much deeper than the quiet time Becky protected for him at the station. At work he could be out of the way and alone for as long as he liked, but he always knew that life was a short walk away, down the hall where a room full of people would be glad to see him. Now he must go home to a dead house, and find a way to get through the early evening, get at least a few hours' sleep, and do it all again tomorrow. For seven more days.

In the parking lot he came upon Stoner and Maitland, talking earnestly at the tailgate of Stoner's truck. Maitland had the Andersonville mimeo; he had been telling Stoner how grand it was, what sweep it had, what a privilege it would be to direct it. But Jordan felt detached, as if someone else had written it.

They were hoping to get the group together: another Goodfellows on the beach when the series was over. Stoner thought it would be hard now to find a night when they were all free but Maitland was insistent. They couldn't let it lapse, it was far too important, he had never seen such raw creative energy, everything they were doing now had had its beginning that night. Stoner suggested a Sunday afternoon, maybe in two weeks. Jordan said that sounded excellent. "Two weeks will be fine, Gus. You say when and I'll be there."

((12))

THE special staff meeting convened Wednesday morning at seven o'clock. Everyone on the creative staff had been called, and half a dozen actors had come down from New York at Becky's invitation. She distributed the four finished mimeos and for an hour not a word was said as they sat and read. At eight o'clock Kidd came in and took over the meeting.

"By now you all know what we're up to. There are thirty-seven characters in these four scripts, there's another script yet to come, and each part must be auditioned and cast by Friday. Every role is up for grabs with two exceptions. The leads for next Thursday's Japanese script have been given to Rick Gary and Susan Daniels. Both have extensive experience with the Japanese dialect and they're very excited about it."

Hazel's angry voice arose from the front. "How is it that they saw the script before we did?"

"I read it to them," Becky said. "Last night on the telephone."

"How grand for them. It must be wonderful to be so important. I would have liked to audition for that Japanese wife."

"And I'm sorry you can't," Kidd said. "If we had more time I'd let everyone including the switchboard operator read for it. But I can't ask an actress like Susan Daniels to come down here on speculation. We've already blown her off once. If we do it again we may never be able to get her."

"Why don't you read for the sister in the Boer piece?" Becky said.

"Why don't you hush up, darling? I wasn't speaking to you. I know you're taking that producer's hat you're wearing so very seriously, sweets, but I know what I can do. I don't need anyone telling me what to read."

"I am the producer, Hazel, and I'm telling you we are not auditioning those two parts. If you want to do the Boer piece, I think you'd be wonderful."

"No. I don't want that part."

Across the room Eastman sighed loudly. Stallworth cleared his throat. "Am I the only one who's bothered by this series? That Boer show clearly undermines our war effort, and as for that Jap piece . . . I'm sorry, Jordan, but I think it's a goddamn disgrace. I'm amazed Gary and Daniels will risk their reputations on something as anti-American as that."

Kidd answered from the front of the room. "It's not anti-American, Mr. Stallworth, it's militantly pro-American. These particular Japs are still Americans and only a few of us are standing up for their rights. And one of the most vocal critics of this relocation policy has been Susan Daniels. If you remember, she wrote a letter to the *Times* just last month."

"If she wants to commit professional suicide, that's her business. But I had to say something. I think we're taking a very bad turn here."

"Well, what can I say? Mr. Harford is willing to take that risk. So is Miss Daniels. Anyone who isn't is free to leave with no hard feelings."

But Becky had screened the New York actors well, and Stallworth left alone.

"I've got some more people coming later this morning," Becky said.

"Good," Kidd said. "They can catch up with us when they get here."

He addressed the group. "Auditions on the first script will begin at once. Miss Hart will hear you until Mr. Ten Eyck can finish his final show. When would you like to meet with the cast, Jordan?"

"Tonight."

"Those of you who are selected by Miss Hart, please report back here at seven o'clock tonight. Those interested in the Andersonville show, make arrangements with Mr. Maitland. Miss Hart will hear readings on the Boer script after lunch."

(((13)))

HE rewrote the Bataan script twice before noon. Then he sat quietly at his desk, read through his copy of the Boer War script, thought about every line, and began making notes in the margins.

He had lunch with Livia and Stoner, a short, quick break that took him away for less than an hour. Becky joined them, ate on the run, and left, carrying half a sandwich, for her meeting with the Boer cast. Stoner left a few minutes later. Everyone was in a hurry. Things were rolling now. Livia would be working late on her effects for the Poland show. "I'd like to sit in tonight, if you don't mind."

"I'd be grateful. Your judgment is a national treasure."

She laughed lightly but her cheeks were red. A moment later she said, "I want to talk to you sometime, Jordan. When you come up for air."

"We'll make a point of it."

That was the lie he'd remember. It came back at him at odd moments of the day and would keep coming back, he knew, when he was far away and the time was distant, whenever these people should happen to cross his mind.

He did a final rewrite on the Bataan script, finished up at three, and sent it down to Kidd for a reading. It lacked the power of the opening show but its purpose was different, meant to inspire, not to anger, and it rippled with Tom's character and was haunted by the specter of Holly. He wasn't surprised when

Kidd called up and told him it was his personal favorite of the five shows.

Now it was in mimeo . . . all of them ready to do, with one small exception.

At four o'clock he slipped into the studio and sat watching from the back row. Becky saw him at once but he gave her the hand signal to keep it moving and after a while she forgot he was there. Her direction was astute and she ran her show with confidence and authority. Rue stood at the microphone reading the role of the doomed Boer girl. One of the New York actors had taken the part of her brother, and there were several fresh faces in the group. More actors had arrived from the city: Rick Gary had sent them a tiny girl who looked younger than Rue and was superb in the flashback scene as her mother. Her name was Jane Shoemaker and she had to stand on her tiptoes to reach the mike, but in her voice she was the essence of motherhood. She actually spoke Dutch, giving them a good illusion of the Afrikaans, and Becky was having her double as the proxy voice of Margaret that opened the show.

He was content to sit through another reading, letting Becky handle the order and direction of the cast. That night over dinner she told him what had happened at the morning's Hitler reading. "I had two actresses come down from New York to try for the role of Bela. Then Hazel showed up and I had to read her too, and she read that role so beautifully I couldn't not take her, so she'll be there tonight. I *know* she's terrible to work with, I'm sorry, I couldn't help it, so shoot me or scold me or chase me off with a stick." Jordan laughed and said he would handle Hazel.

Walking back to the station Becky was exhilarated. "Jesus God almighty, I *love* this! I could go all night and all day tomorrow, straight on into the weekend."

"You may have to."

But the casting went incredibly easy. Hazel was on her best behavior and the people from New York were all fine. Jordan watched from the front row and Livia sat beside him, offering an occasional comment and filling her own script with notes. Zylla had already roughed out a score: he sat beside Livia and hummed it as they read, breaking into a full vocal overture at one point and stopping the show with laughter and applause from the cast. And in this spirit of happiness and accomplishment Jordan took them to the Sandbar and bought drinks for everyone.

Where did the hours go? Suddenly it was a new day, full of challenges. He walked past the pit where the remains of March Flack were slowly being extracted with the help of an archaeologist from the university, and thirty minutes later he was immersed in his world. Becky was always there, the last to leave at night and the first to arrive in the morning, and they huddled in her office and went through the minutiae of each script—the cast assignments that were already definite, the actors who would be heard again this morning, a series of new changes as words were added and crossed out on the pages, the sounds the words made and the music that almost seemed part of the little room where they worked. Then came the real sounds: shuffling footsteps as the cast arrived and filed into the big studio down the hall. The day would be cluttered, noisy, nonstop. At eight o'clock they would hear more readings on the German script; at nine the first table reading with the final cast in place; at eleven the same on the Boer script, with readings on the Nisei to begin later this afternoon and tonight. Somewhere in another place Maitland was working with his Andersonville cast and was beginning to think about Bataan. Thus was it getting done. Such was life in radio.

((**14**))

FRIDAY. His busiest day yet. He spent all morning working on the casting for the Nisei. It must seem real, even though he would not be here to see it. Then the readings began and it was real. He cared who would be chosen, it mattered no less than the scripts he would air, and he wanted to hear each reading in its full context, not the piecemeal lines far more common to radio auditions. In the morning Jane Shoemaker had stood in for Susan Daniels, giving him a good effort as the Japanese wife. But she would be leaving at one o'clock for broadcast commitments in the city and they would not see her again until Tuesday, the day of the Boer show.

At noon the Negroes arrived. They stood in the hall, surprised to find the studio crowded with people and ablaze with lights. Jordan waved them in and they sat as a group, off to one side, watching with the rapt attention of gawkers at a fireworks demonstration. He told them he had more actors yet to hear . . . another hour, maybe two . . . but he was not worried about tonight. They would have plenty of time.

Still, it was a loss when Jane Shoemaker left. Becky, who would never make the world forget Sarah Bernhardt, would read those lines in a flat monotone from her table. But as he turned from the soundstage his eyes found the face of the one real actress in the room, Ali Marek, watching him intently ten rows back. Before he could second-guess himself he had stepped to the front and called her name.

She came without question. Whatever he asked, whatever he said: if he told her to slink up onstage like a reptile she would do it. At the microphone she leaned toward him and whispered something, covering the mike with her hand. He shook his head. "Don't think of her as a Japanese. She's just another desperate American. And it pays ten dollars, the same as rehearsal time."

She smiled at that. As she began her reading, Palmer of the *Times* walked in and sat in the back row. She didn't see him: her mind was riveted on the script and her eyes were sight-reading, two lines ahead of her voice. "You're sounding good," Jordan said. "Go ahead and reach for the Japanese inflection when you're ready . . . soft . . . very soft." She did, and she almost nailed it. "That's fine," Jordan said . . . with a little coaching she'd be able to pass on the air. He turned to Becky. "Call the next actor and take it from the top of page six." A thin balding man of forty came in with the mimeo under his arm. He blinked when he saw the coal black woman at the opposite mike: then, calmly, he followed

Becky's direction and went into his lines. The part he was trying for was a guard at the camp and he looked as alien to the scene as she did. But he had what counted, a deep ballsy voice, nothing like the scrawny face that came with it.

All through the scene Palmer was writing furiously in his notebook. Oh, he is onto me now, Jordan thought: he smells blood and will not stop until he has me buck naked in his paper. But Palmer never approached him. Their eyes met only occasionally, and after a while Jordan thought of him as another Harford. A constant presence, a watcher in the distance.

By four o'clock the casting was done on the supporting roles for the Nisei, and the black cast got to work on the *Freedom* show that night. Palmer never moved—the man must have kidneys of steel to sit there that long—and he never seemed to miss a beat. Whenever Jordan worked his magic, if a soft word brought enlightenment to Eli or confidence to Emily, he knew if he looked around Palmer would be writing it down. His own self-confidence was at a peak: he had no doubt about the show tonight and no fears for its outcome. The table reading was easy and quick. Everyone knew the lines, they had been rehearsing all week in the city and could've done it without scripts. Eli was much better tonight, stronger and steadier, even daring to question the script in a few places. Jordan said, "Do it your way and let's see how it sounds," and in the new reading Eli decided, on his own, that the script had been better.

Then came the dress with full orchestra and sound, and an hour later the broadcast. Palmer sat through it all. In that final carnage, as the blacks are slaughtered in their mad dash up the beach, he and Jordan did lock eyes and neither looked away until the music went up and out. Jordan broke the contact as people swarmed around him, and when he looked again Palmer was gone.

Congratulations to the cast for a solid professional job. They are radio actors now. For all the good it'll do them.

In the dark lobby the switchboard was crazy with lights. "Hey, Jordan, want to answer a few phones? . . . see how the calls are running?"

"Very funny, Miss Hart. I've had enough self-abuse for one day."

She offered to buy him a drink but he asked for a rain check. He had one more thing to do tonight. The most important thing of all.

(((**15**)))

So how do you rewrite a script and leave its cues intact? How can you touch so little and still wreak havoc, like chuckholes in a road or a ghost flashing by, so that even the people who bring it to life will deduce only later that what they have read is the opposite of what they rehearsed?

How can you do this and preserve its artistic integrity? Don't destroy it, just twist it—the more realistic it is, the more it will hurt. The one who knows it best, who lived it and knows every word, will go mad. Like that other night six years ago, only this time it's me he'll come for.

He expected a long night but the script answered its own questions. It was Margaret, his twin sister, who could hurt him the most.

He made his first line change on page three.

MARGARET: I loved a British soldier.

A large company of soldiers had camped on the farm for a month. And things happen with people, sometimes the unlikeliest things. This didn't have to withstand the scrutiny of historians, it only needed to sound real.

MARGARET: I betrayed them all . . . Mamma, Poppy, Jan, Lar. I cared about nothing else when he was with me.

Cut the proxy voice at the open. Have her speak English throughout. Then, near the end, cut into the speech of Kruin, the old black man.

Margaret was never raped. There was no renegade British unit. The child she carried came from an act of her own choice.

Her British soldier was an honorable man. He loved her. Promised to come back for her after the war. Never knew of her pregnancy. Her fate.

Done in a few minutes, the easiest rewrite in the history of radio.

What he had added replaced to the line the words he had cut. Everything the same, everything changed: almost all of it left intact. The cues for orchestra, and for sound, would remain the same from rehearsal to air.

He turned off the light and went to bed.

He opened his eyes at dawn and sat for a long time in quiet thought. In a while an image came into his head. It was Carnahan, standing at the post office, in the parking lot, waving good-bye with one hand and holding his hat in the other. He had had a picnic that day with Livia and her boys. He had a package to mail.

Dulaney sat up, fully awake.

Where was the package?

Carnahan stepped out of the car. At that moment he saw the Schroeders, following them into the post office parking lot. A moment later, when he waved good-bye, there was no package in either hand.

He had left it in her car.

(((16)))

LIVIA wore a thin bathrobe at six thirty and her eyes were still heavy from sleep. Her hair was wild and unbrushed, but even at that hour she was happy to see him. That would change quickly.

She went back through the house and closed the door where her boys still slept. She was already wary as she put on the coffee.

"I've got a hunch this isn't a social call."

"No," he said. "I want to talk to you about Carnahan again."

Now she was upset. The pleasure of finding him on her doorstep was waning fast. Anger was not far away.

"What do you want? . . . What more can possibly be said?"

"I was thinking about that package. I was dreaming about it."

She didn't ask what package. She gave him some coffee and sat across the table and looked at him as if they had never met.

"The package he had that day was meant for me."

She said nothing.

"He left it in your car. He saw the Schroeders tailing you and he had only a few seconds to decide. I don't think he knew even then how serious it was. So he left it with you, thinking he'd stall them off and come back for it later that night."

"You're not making much sense, Jordan. I really don't know what you're talking about."

He leaned forward and looked at her evenly. "My name's not Jordan."

She stared at him. Shook her head, angry now.

"Jordan Ten Eyck's a name I made up when I first got to town."

"Oh, that's nice. That's just great. Everything's a lie. Wonderful."

"What I told you about Carnahan and me is true."

"How do I know that? I don't even know who you are."

"I think you do. You know I'm telling the truth and it's starting to dawn on you now what my name is."

"How would I know any of that? Do you think I'm a psychic?"

"I think it was written on the package."

Another moment passed. "So what's your real name?"

"Jack Dulaney."

"So you say. But you've been lying to all of us since you got here. Why should I trust you now?"

Suddenly he knew what to tell her. "Miss O'Hara is Carnahan's daughter. We were all friends together in New York three years ago. They came from Sadler, Pennsylvania. Holly came here looking for her father . . . because she believed he'd been killed."

Her face was pale with shock. "Then he didn't just disappear."

"No."

"Why didn't she talk to me? Why didn't she tell me who she was?"

He shrugged. "She's a complicated lady."

But he told her about that Christmas Eve. "She did talk to you then. You invited her inside. But she wouldn't come. She stood out in the cold, watching while you had your Christmas party."

"My God, that was his daughter? . . . Holly O'Hara is his daughter?"

He nodded.

"I've thought about that woman a hundred times since then. I couldn't even see her face, but there was something between us, I could feel it. And she seemed so god-awful lonely. I couldn't get her out of my mind."

She shivered. "I want to talk to her. Where is she now?"

"I wish I knew."

He let the moment stretch. Then, in a calm, measured voice, he said, "Listen to me, Livia. Listen very carefully and use the sound judgment that I know you have. Whatever's in that package, it's a life-and-death threat to someone. Four people have been killed because of it. As long as you have it, it's a danger to you and maybe to your boys."

"Oh God!" She shivered again and her voice was full of fear and rage. "Who are you? Jesus Christ, who *are* you?"

"I'm just like you. I'm a friend of his who wants some answers."

"Are you a cop?"

He shook his head with a sad little laugh.

She waited a long time.

"He's dead, isn't he? She was right. He's dead."

He nodded.

She cried. So did he, a little.

"Don't ask me any more than that," he said. "I'll try to tell you more later, if I can."

She shook her head and turned away in tears. "Jesus Christ, they killed him! They *killed* him!" She got up, went to the sink, stared out at the dunes.

"Livia, help me. I need that package."

Another moment. She seemed not to have heard. Then she walked away from the window. Poured herself some coffee and left the steaming cup there at the sink. Sat in her chair and said nothing for another minute.

"Livia?"

Her eyes darted up and she looked in his face. "When you talked to me before, I had a bad feeling about this. That night I went home and got it out of the closet. It had been in there unopened for more than six months and suddenly, I don't know why, I wanted it out of my house."

She sniffed. "Maybe I *am* psychic."

She looked away and saw her coffee cup. Went to fetch it and stood there for a moment, not drinking it.

"I didn't know what to do," she said. "I couldn't just throw it away. I sat there for a long time just looking at it. Then I opened it."

She came back to the table and sat. "There wasn't much inside . . . only enough to give me the creeps. A few rolls of undeveloped film. A note. A spool of recording wire."

"What did the note say?"

"He had overheard some people at Harford talking German one night. Not in rehearsal, nothing like that. This was a real conversation, an extended talk. There were three of them. I thought of the Schroeders right away, but who was the third man? He did manage to get that wire recorder going and recorded some of what they said."

"But he didn't say who they were?"

She shook her head. "Develop the film and you'd know. Get someone you could trust, who wouldn't turn *you* in to the FBI, to listen to that wire and translate it for you. Then you'd know."

"Did you do that?"

"No. I did something I'm afraid you're going to find incredibly stupid. I wrapped it all back up and I mailed it."

Her eyes were sad and defiant all at once. "That's what he was going to do with it. So I did it for him."

Dulaney felt the beginnings of a headache. The package was out there for real now, chasing him around the country.

(((17)))

THE thought of it depressed him as he drove down the beach. Then he turned into Harford and the feeling went away. He was no worse off than before: all he had to do was survive until Tuesday.

He had scheduled final readings this morning, a mix of all three shows as he filled in the smaller roles and added finishing touches to each piece. He worked across the noon hour and at two o'clock had a table reading for Monday's opener. What he heard excited him. Hazel was superb. She had an almost flawless Polish dialect and she brought to the character a fire that Jordan Ten Eyck had barely surpassed when he'd written it. She was highly professional, taking his direction without argument and even stopping to help Rue with her Slavic tongue. Rue had a small part, a woman from the ghetto, the beginning of a busy week for her. On Tuesday she would be Margaret, the Boer girl, and Thursday she would play a Japanese child in the internment camp. Maitland was also using her in the closing show on Friday. Jane Shoemaker had won the Holly role and Rue would play the undrowned sister. Would come to the wedding to wish them joy and love and a long life together, just before he shipped out for the Philippines.

They wrapped it up in the late afternoon. He wanted to go on, would've gone through the weekend, but there was nothing left to do. Becky sighed and said, "Damn, we made it." . . . The entire week was ready for air. No more rehearsals until the Hitler dress, Monday at seven.

A sudden quiet fell over the soundstage. Only the five of them remained in the studio—Jordan and Livia, Becky, Stoner, and Rue—picking up stuff, putting things away. Soon even that was done and a vast chasm of time yawned before Monday night. The others felt it too: When Becky asked what they were doing tonight, he was surprised that none of them had plans. The early evening found them still together, walking on the beach, laughing at nothing, killing the hard time, in the grip of the coming week without feeling any need to talk about it. They drank beer on the boardwalk and ate together at the rooftop café, and the word "radio" was never said among them and nothing even hinting of shop talk.

The season was waning, the crowds were gone. They had the roof to themselves and Rue pushed back the tables and fed nickels into the jukebox at the bottom of the stairs. They took turns dancing, overruling Jordan's plea of two left feet, laughing when he stepped on them. The record changed and he shuffled across the floor with Livia while Harry James played "You Made Me Love You" up the stairwell to the evening stars. At one point she said, "I can't figure you out, Jordan or Jack, whatever your name is." But she held him close, as if she'd stopped trying.

"Tell me something," she said. "Are you going to disappear too?"

"What a question," he said. But he answered it. "I might."

"Will you call me? . . . Keep in touch? Don't answer that unless your word is good."

"It used to be. I've had to lie lately, but I don't like it much."

"Then call me. That's all. At some point, if you decide to drop off the earth, give me a call and let me know where you are. And what the hell happened."

At full dark night they were still walking, unwilling to break apart. Rue said, "I love you goddamn people," and everyone laughed. "Don't ask me why, you're all such a pain in the ass, but I do." Becky said, "I think the lady's had one beer too many," and they laughed again. They had reached her house, a small place on the beach not far from Holly's. "Come on in, all of you, I'll fix some coffee and send you safely on your way."

But inside there was still no feeling of hurry and no need to manufacture talk. Stoner had a show to do but that was more than two hours away.

The telephone rang. Becky picked it up and said, "Yessir," then stood speechless as if in shock.

"That was Kidd," she told them. "We made the front page."

It didn't dawn on them what she was saying.

"Palmer's story is on the front page of the Sunday *Times*."

Now it dawned. Stoner whistled through his teeth and said, "Jesus."

"We made the front page," Becky said.

"We're famous," Rue said. "We're famous, boys and girls."

"Kidd said it's full of stuff like 'powerful' and 'groundbreaking.' 'A legendary radio station goes back to its rabblerousing roots.' 'Its opening week certain to spark raging controversy.'"

"Wow, we're famous."

"I guess it means we'll have an audience," Jordan said.

"Are you kidding?" Stoner's voice trembled. "Half the world will be listening to us Monday."

(((18)))

ENDLESS Sunday. He got through it somehow, alone.

He arrived Monday morning at seven thirty and sat in his office with the Boer script, waiting for the staff to arrive. This was where his plan could quickly fall apart. He had never been to the mimeo room but he understood the protocol. It was something like a newspaper, where a reporter's story goes through a system of editors. The reporter never jumps directly to the typesetter, and in radio the writer never goes to mimeo. The script is always seen by programming people, who read it and discuss it and then send it up. He had one advantage: this script had already been approved.

At eight o'clock sharp he took his three rewritten pages across the building to the small room on the northwest corner. A woman he had seen only in passing nodded at him as he came in. She was in her forties and wore a name tag that said she was Harriet Simms.

"Mr. Tenake, I believe. What brings you up to the north woods?"

"I just need a few pages recut. I was told you're the woman to see."

"You bet. You want 'em now?"

He gave her a pleading smile. "Yesterday wouldn't be too soon."

"Grab a seat, hon. Take about half an hour."

He was too nervous to sit. He stood just inside the door while she cut the stencils . . . tapping out the words, he hoped, without thinking what they said.

"How many copies, hon?"

"A dozen should do it."

He heard voices in the hall as people arrived for the day. They faded into the clatter of the mimeo when Harriet ran off his copies.

"There ya go, hon."

"You're a good woman, Harriet. I'd better get the stencils too."

For the first time he saw suspicion in her face. He shrugged and said, "We're making lots of changes and I may have some more yet to come. I need to make sure everything's accounted for. So the pages don't get mixed up."

On the face of it this made no sense, but she handed over the stencils.

"You're sure this is okay?"

"Absolutely."

He thanked her and left.

Home free . . .

Not quite.

As he came out of the room, there was Barnet, talking to one of the office girls in the hall a few feet away.

"Is something wrong?"

"No. Just getting some pages redone."

Barnet cut his eyes down to the stencils in his hand. "If there's a problem, maybe I can help. That's what I'm here for."

"No problem at all."

"Nice piece, by the way," Barnet said to his back as he moved past.

He stopped and turned.

"In the *Times*," Barnet said.

"Yeah, it was. I seem to be having all the luck these days."

A close call.

Now, if his real luck held, Barnet would take it no further. And if Barnet should ask Harriet what had just been done, Jordan had left nothing in the mimeo room that could be compared with the originals.

In his office he cut the stencils into small pieces. He burned them in his wastebasket and crushed the ashes. Then he put the mimeo sheets in a file and locked the cabinet.

Nothing to do now until the Hitler dress tonight. He had lunch with Maitland and they compared notes, and all that afternoon his sense of loss grew. He sat behind his locked door and pretended to write, keeping Becky and the world at bay.

The show went off without a hitch. Dulaney felt the power of it rippling through the air.

Zylla had outdone himself on the score. Hazel was perfect, Livia nothing less than brilliant in sound.

The room was packed with people, all come to watch. At the end of it Harford leaned over the rail and smiled down on him. And in the back of the room he saw the two newspapermen, Butterfield of the *Beachcomber* and Palmer of the *Times*.

Then it was over and the long night began.

Then that was over.

He opened his eyes after two hours' sleep. It was Tuesday.

((19))

HE had scheduled the Boer dress for late afternoon. Unusual for a final dress to be separated from its broadcast by five full hours, but it couldn't be helped. Cumbersome, because it meant assembling the cast and orchestra twice. He had made up a lame excuse for it but no one had questioned him. No one questioned him about anything these days.

He needed that gap in time, to make what he was about to do seem credible to Rue, who would read it. She must suspect nothing until she was on the air with the script in her face and no time to second-guess it. A dirty trick and he would have much to atone for, except for one small detail. He would never see her again after tonight.

He spent the morning shutting down the house and preparing for a hasty escape. He would take with him the effects of their short life here. The scarf she had worn on the beach that day when she had followed him to the beer garden. The picture he had rescued from her house in Sadler. Her father's watch, of course. In the kitchen drawer he found Carnahan's final postcard and it tugged at his heart. It seemed to write a finish to her intentions, as if her own words had somehow failed to make them clear. She was never coming back . . . she was never even looking back.

For the first time he opened her closet. She had left all her evening dresses, and he gathered them and folded them carefully in a box and put it in the trunk of his car. When the house had been stripped of her presence he wrapped his loaded gun in a rag and put it under the front seat. Then he locked up the house and shoved the key under the door.

It was early afternoon when he arrived at the station. Becky had left a note taped to his door, a summary of the press on last night's Hitler show. Raves in every New York newspaper. Tipped off by the *Times*, they had all been listening, and not a naysayer in the bunch. But this first show had been written for patriots and it would have been difficult for a critic to take issue with it.

At three o'clock he went downstairs. The big studio was still empty, and he walked across the soundstage and clapped his hands and made a few adjustments to the drapes.

Blake was the first to arrive. He was playing the lead, the good-hearted farm boy turned into a cold-blooded killer by a three-year war. He came to the empty producer's table, looking for the scripts and suddenly at loose ends when they weren't there. At three thirty Palmer came in and sat in the back row. Becky arrived, her arms full of scripts. The scripts were loose, each in a separate folder . . . easy to read, easy to rig. The cast trickled in and by four o'clock the orchestra was in place. Maitland had come to watch: he sat beside Stoner, out of the way in the booth, knowing that Jordan would direct from the floor. Kidd appeared in the open doorway, then stepped in and pulled the door shut behind him. Harford leaned out of the darkness on the balcony.

Jordan called his cast together. "Okay, let's do this right the first time, straight through without a stop."

He nodded at Zylla and the music began. Becky clicked on her stopwatch and an hour later they were done. A flawless dress, nonstop, just as he had ordered. "Fifty-nine fifteen," Becky said.

"Good. Now, cast, I'd like each of you to write your name on your script and leave it on the table with Miss Hart. I don't want you to read it again, or even think about it, until air-time."

Jordan carried the scripts when he left. In his office, he replaced the three pages and burned the originals. Then he waited.

He sat waiting for almost four hours.

At eight thirty Becky knocked on his door. He sat perfectly still. She knocked again and called his name, urgently now. She rattled the doorknob, and a moment later he heard her hurrying away.

He forced himself to stay where he was. Let it get good and crazy down there as the hour approached and he failed to arrive. Push it to the brink, to that point where they'd have to consider canceling the show. No sooner than that and for God's sake no later.

He could almost see the chaos building. Becky running in and out. Maitland out of the booth, willing to step in and direct it if someone could find the scripts. People swirling about, the orchestra tuning up, Kidd enraged, Harford anxious. All of them helpless in the face of the ticking clock.

He looked at his watch. At quarter to nine he picked up the scripts and walked out of the room.

Not a second to spare now. He clattered down the circular stairwell. Stopped to wedge open the outside fire door with a chair, then hurried on to the studio.

Chaos, as he had imagined.

He cut a swath through it. Becky popped up, yelling furiously over the din. He saw Kidd and Harford, Rue, Maitland, Stoner, Zylla.

Zylla tapped his baton and the orchestra came to attention. Jordan went to center stage and doled out the scripts. It was six minutes to nine.

He called the cast aside. Motioned Becky away and she shrank back, hurt, and sat at her table.

Now the big lie. "We've found a memo from the author with some changes he intended to make."

He looked at Rue. "Most of it's with your character . . . pages three and four. This shouldn't give you any trouble. Just sight-read your way through it and you'll be fine."

She nodded gravely, the good soldier, the old pro at twenty-one.

He told Jane Shoemaker there would be no proxy to open the show. And the New York actor who would play Kruin would also have some changes. "Just read your way through them."

He looked at the clock. "The rest is exactly the same."

They scrambled to their microphones at 1:15, and the studio fell into that deep quiet as the clock ticked its way inside sixty seconds.

Jordan took a long breath. The last face he saw was Livia's. He smiled and gave her a victory sign.

"Ten seconds."

The red light flashed. Jordan cued Eastman and the show was on the air.

He cued Zylla. The music came up.

He cued Rue.

No proxy! . . . a shock to someone, but there was no time to look. Livia brought up the sound . . . the dusty, windy dirt streets at Germiston . . . the flapping of the tents . . . the muffled sounds of the hot, desolate boredom. Rue carried it alone through page two, sight-reading her way, her eyes always two lines ahead of her delivery, sweeping in what was yet to come. She turned the page and saw it at once. In that half second she saw everything. She knew what the change would do to her character, to her brother, to the play, to the point of it. She knew this faster than she could have said it and he could see it in her face. She read the last line of page two and looked to him for help.

She was going to balk. She shook her head and made a tiny gesture of resistance, and Jordan got down in her face and made the hand signal to keep it going. She read the line without a break.

"I loved a British soldier."

Now she trembled and took a long breath that wasn't in the script. She looked at him again, almost pleading, and he coaxed her, the soul of kindness. She looked down at her script and never raised her head again.

"I betrayed them all."

It was in. Let them cut him off the air now, it didn't matter, the damage was done.

He looked toward the door, where the light still flashed red. Back to the soundstage, where the show had settled into its natural rhythm. At the twenty-minute break he scanned the room and saw many shapes, but they were just specters in the heat of the moment.

Another twenty minutes straight from the old script. Then the third shock, in the voice of Kruin. Margaret had never been raped. Her mother, her young sister . . . none of them raped. They had gone away to the north in the custody of the soldiers. The final scenes went skimming by, and the murder of the two British soldiers gave it a hollow feeling at the end.

Music filled the studio and the shapes became people.

There was Becky, too stunned to move. Rue, staring at the floor, taking no glory in her perfect performance. Kidd in the back of the room with his hand over his eyes, and Harford, still at the edge of the balcony, exactly where he'd been standing an hour ago.

Dulaney hurled the script at them and walked out as the pages fluttered to the floor.

Out in the parking lot he fetched his gun from under the seat. He stuck it in his belt and walked around the building, pulled open the fire door, and stepped inside.

The door clicked shut and he stood there in the dark.

((20))

HE felt his way to the crossing hall just below the circular staircase. There he stopped, looking down from the utility room toward the studios and the lobby. The doors to Studio A had been propped open, throwing a bright beam of light into the hall, but no one had yet come out. It was more like a funeral than the end of a big broadcast, as quiet as if a hundred people had just vanished.

Then Kidd appeared in the center of the light. He moved first one way and then the other, like a man who had lost his sense of direction.

"Did you see which way he went?"

Becky's voice was teary. "I believe to his right, sir. Out through the lobby . . ."

Kidd turned and vanished through the lobby doors and Becky came into the light looking tiny and tragic. A soft murmur arose in the distance as people finally began to talk. Now there was coughing and the clatter of musicians packing away their instruments.

Palmer came into the doorway. "Miss Hart . . . could I ask you . . . what just happened in there?"

"Not now, Mr. Palmer. Please."

"The play seemed strangely . . . pointless . . . Compared with the two scripts I read, it seemed to lack cohesion and power."

"Yessir. It did all that."

"You could sense the power in it. And then it seemed to just . . ."

"Trickle away," she said.

"That's it exactly. And that angry outburst by Mr. Ten Eyck at the end of it . . . as if someone tampered with it over his objections."

"If anyone tampered with it, it was Mr. Ten Eyck himself."

"But why?"

"You'll have to ask him that. Excuse me now, I'm not up to this."

Rue came out. She and Becky stared at each other for a moment; then Rue said, "I think I am going to the Sandbar with some of the New York people and we are going to get very drunk together. You want to come?"

"I'd love to come," Becky said. "I'd better see if Kidd needs me. I'll meet you there."

Now came a general exodus. He saw Maitland in the crowd, moving through the clusters of people to stand alone for a moment . . . then, with a last long look back into the studio, Maitland turned and went out.

Dulaney slipped back along the hall to the fire door. Propped it open and went outside. He eased along the edge of the building, keeping in shadow, until he could see the cars in the south parking lot. Maitland came along the path. When he had reached his car, Dulaney called his name.

Maitland came to the corner of the building, his face in the half-light from the parking lot. "Jordan?"

"Yeah, it's me."

Dulaney sensed no rage in the old man, just a sad bewilderment. Maitland put his hand over his eyes. "For Christ's sake, what went wrong in there?"

"What went wrong went wrong a long time ago."

"But God damn it, man! . . . do you know what you've done to yourself?"

"I imagine I know that better than anyone."

"You could have been . . . God knows what you could have been! And you throw it away."

"I guess it wasn't meant to be."

Maitland shook his head. "I don't understand you, Jordan."

"It doesn't matter now. I just wanted to say good-bye. And thanks for all your help."

"Oh, please . . . somehow that makes me part of it, so please don't thank me for anything. I'm too old to be an accomplice in anybody's greater purpose, so kindly keep your thanks to yourself."

He turned and walked away.

The building emptied quickly now, the crowd anxious to distance itself from the thing it had done. In ten minutes the musicians had packed their instruments and gone, the actors had gathered in the parking lot to wait for their last few drinking companions, and Palmer—having caught each of them in turn with nothing to show for it—stood alone under a light in a silver haze of tobacco smoke. The door clicked open and shut as the stragglers came out . . . Livia and Becky, to join the actors and drive away in separate cars . . . Barnet and Poindexter, turning away into the north lot. Palmer started after them and apparently thought better of it. At the edge of the building Poindexter said something and Barnet's high-pitched laugh cut the evening like a knife. No unhappiness there, Dulaney thought. But he had not really expected any.

Palmer stood alone, locked out of the building. A minute later he too was gone.

Only a few cars left in the lot now. His own. Kidd's. Harford's Packard. Stoner's truck. And a car that probably belonged to one of the engineers.

Dulaney went inside, back through the fire door and down the dark hallway to Kidd's office.

He heard their voices and saw the light from the open door.

"I know you're angry, Jethro," Harford said. "But we've got to talk to the man so we can understand what happened."

"Angry doesn't begin to describe what I am now," Kidd said. "I don't care what he says, there's no excuse for what he did to us."

"Excuses don't matter. What I want to know is the reason."

"I'll tell you the reason. He's a loose wire, that's the reason. I never know what he'll do next—if he's not disappearing for days on end, he's pulling some crazy goddamn stunt on the air. I know you love him because he gives you what you want. But what good is he if you can't depend on him?"

"All I'm telling you," Harford said patiently, "is that I believe there's a reason for all this, and I want him to stand in front of me and tell me what that is. Then we can decide."

"I've already decided. I'll never trust him again."

"Don't make things worse than they are. It's only one show."

"I can't believe what I'm hearing from you. That Boer show was the whole reason for this series."

"In your mind, Jethro, not mine. I'll always give up one broadcast to get four good ones . . . or maybe fifty down the road."

"You don't even sound like yourself anymore. That was the one great script in our files that had never been done. From the moment I read it, years ago, I wanted it on the air."

"It's still a great script, that hasn't changed. We can always come back and do it right later on. But it's just one show. Compare that with what Jack Dulaney has given us this past month and, frankly, I get rather ambivalent about the Boers and their war. His Nisei script is just as powerful and it's got far more relevance today."

Nothing was said for a moment.

"I want to go ahead with the series," Harford said. "Just as if nothing had happened. We do Andersonville tomorrow, just as we planned."

"What about Thursday? . . . Maitland will have to direct that, too. I won't work with Dulaney again."

"Don't say that, Jethro." Harford had a sudden edge of warning in his voice. "Don't lay down any ultimatums until we talk to the man."

"If it's going to come down to him or me it might as well come now."

"Oh don't be a fool. We were going to change the face of broadcasting in this country, remember? We're going to take the air away from the hucksters and the sausage makers, challenge the censors, battle the Bible thumpers, as far as our signal will reach. Remember that, Jethro? Where the hell else are you going to go and find excitement like that? If you want to rock the boat, you've got to have people like Jack Dulaney. Wild people, hard to control, you can't do it without 'em. And where are you going to find me another one?"

Kidd said nothing.

"We need to talk to the man," Harford said. "Do you have any idea where he is now?"

"His car's still in the lot."

"Then let's find him and hear what he's got to say."

Dulaney backed away. He quickstepped to the stairs and started up.

Twenty minutes later Kidd emerged out of the shadows, into the bullpen.

"Jordan?"

The floor creaked as he walked down the aisle to Jordan's old desk.

"Jordan? . . . where the hell are you, you bastard?"

He walked up and down, looking in each cubicle.

"You bastard. You son of a bitch, Jordan."

He walked out and Dulaney stepped from the pitch darkness of the interview room. Harford came past in the hall. "He's not in his office. Or in the studio. Maybe he went to town, maybe he left with someone, maybe his car wouldn't start."

"Maybe," Kidd said.

"We'll find him in the morning."

Fifteen minutes later they left the building. Dulaney stood behind the drapes at a window and watched them drive away. He stood still for a long time, looking south across the dunes.

A program of dance music was coming over the intercom as he came back through the building toward the studio. A syndicated show, he knew, music by transcription—not exactly what Kidd would have wanted for a late-night time slot on opening week, but he had holes to fill and only so many warm bodies to help fill them. In the studio Joe Carella sat alone, baby-sitting the transcription discs and talking his way through the station breaks with the continuity sheets before him. The clock over his head said eleven ten.

"Where's Gus?" Dulaney said.

"Hi, Mr. Ten Eyck." Joe looked up at the clock. "He'll be along any minute now. I go off at eleven thirty."

Dulaney went downstairs and stood in the lobby waiting for something, he wasn't sure what. He had a sudden feeling that he had miscalculated—nothing was going to happen—but this lasted only a minute. *Something's going to happen all right, he just hasn't found me yet. And he wants to be alone when he does.*

All that hate couldn't go to waste.

He stepped outside, keeping to the shadows of the building. A heavy cloud bank had covered the sky, like that other night six years ago. A fog was coming in. He was drawn to the dunes, to that same trek March Flack had tried to make, and he opened his shirt as he walked and the gun was cold against his skin. Right about here it must've happened, out at the end of the yard where the dunes began. He looked back. The station was like some outpost in Antarctica, a circle of light with a fine mist billowing around it.

He started across. It was very dark now and the fog was thicker with every step. He reached a point where nothing could be seen, neither the station behind him nor the town ahead. Then it broke and he saw the lights of the hotel where he'd stayed that first night. He stopped there and sat in the dunes watching the road. There was no traffic tonight as mid-night approached. The lights began to go out in the hotel until only the room he had occupied was lit, which gave him the strange sensation of having stepped across time, to sit out-side his body and look back upon himself.

He sat there for a while. Until the car came.

One car, going like a bat out of hell up the shore road north. Somebody in a helluva big hurry, either to get out of town or to get back to the station.

He scrambled to his feet and backtracked across the dunes. Again the fog swallowed him and he went slowly. He had to be careful now . . . someone could be hiding anywhere out here. He picked his way along and ten minutes later he reached the edge of the yard. The building looked empty . . . Carella's car was gone, even Stoner's truck had been moved somewhere, and his own car was the only one left in the south lot. He circled and came in from the north, and there, just as he'd thought, was a car parked in the dark against the building on the north side. He knew he had seen it before but he couldn't place it now. He hugged the building and as he came past it he ran a hand over the hood. It was hot.

This time he used his key to get in. Stoner's voice on the intercom sounded faint and far away as he stalked his way across the lobby. It was five after twelve, and Stoner's show was just getting under way. Dulaney opened the studio door and stood behind it, looking down the dark hall. Nothing there: not a sound, except Stoner's voice, as he moved inside and on down to the circular stair. The staircase creaked under his weight; the floor creaked as he reached the top. He stood up straight and walked against the wall, past his office to the studio.

Nobody there.

At once he had two radically different thoughts: the first, that Stoner was broadcasting from the production room near the open balcony around the corner; the second, that Stoner wasn't broadcasting at all.

The second thought gripped him and held. Stoner wasn't here.

He opened the soundproof door. The studio monitor was turned up loud and he could hear Stoner breathing. He heard the chair creak and he knew then what he should have known long ago.

There was no squeaking chair in this studio.

But there was one downstairs . . . in the control booth in Studio A.

And another in Stoner's shack on the roof of the Harford building.

He took the gun out of his belt and stepped inside. Stoner's voice droned on, his hypnotic resonance filling the room. He was reading a poem, something from Whitman, Dulaney thought. His reading was flawless and brisk. Dulaney moved around the table and looked into the empty slot, where a record was spinning on the deck.

Stoner, by transcription.

A little audio magic. Record the voice part of the show on the rooftop . . . do up several segments ahead of time . . . short pieces, long ones . . . whatever he needed or thought he might need, and he could seem to be here when actually he was somewhere else.

In Pennsylvania, strangling Kendall.

In Yorkville, killing Peter and the girl.

All he needed was an accomplice who was willing to play the records.

Dulaney remembered the night he and Stoner had met. That trip to the dump . . . those barrels of trash . . . old sound records, Stoner had said, sound effects gone scratchy. *We'll be getting some new ones in a couple of days,* Stoner had said. But they weren't sound effects records at all, were they, Gus? . . . it was weeks later, as Livia was showing off the new sound room, when the station finally got around to ordering new sound records from the city. No, those were *your* records, covering at least two full shows while you were away in Pennsylvania.

When killing needs to be done, a man's got to do it himself.

He lifted the needle. Stoner's voice stopped and the room was dreadfully still. He dropped the needle on the record and

Stoner was talking again. He bumped the record with his finger and Stoner skipped a groove. That'll play hell with your sound on the air, Gus, he thought. Maybe the boss is listening.

He thumped the stylus with his finger and it zipped across the grooves. Suddenly Stoner was reading Whitman again. Then he heard another thump, somewhere beyond the studio, and he moved quickly, past the empty chair and around the corner.

A door opened: he could see it through the glass, across the room where the studio rest rooms were. Someone coming . . . the ladies' door swished open and shut.

The ladies' room.

Hazel came into the studio. She stopped for a moment, her eyes wide as if some omen had touched her. Then she shook her head and sat in the slot watching the spinning disc. Waiting for her cue.

Stoner stopped speaking and she potted down the record and brought up some music from the opposite turntable. Dulaney came back around the corner and stood a few feet behind her.

"Very good, Hazel," he said. "You're really an expert."

She jerked around in her chair and fell. The chair clattered against the table and she lay sprawled on the floor.

"Jordan! . . . Christ, you scared the *shit* out of me! What are you doing here?"

She pulled herself up. Took a step back, away from him. She was trembling now, her eyes wide with fright.

"Where's Gus?" he said.

"He's here." A ridiculous lie and she knew it at once. "He had to leave for just a minute. He'll be back."

"That's good. I've got some things to ask him about."

"What things?" She moved unsteadily to the edge of the table and put her hand on it for support. "What things?" she said again.

"For one thing, what he was doing with those Germans late at night."

She clutched at her breast and her knees buckled. She looked around for a chair, didn't seem to see that she had knocked it over. Dulaney picked it up for her and she saw the gun in his belt.

"What're you doing with that?"

He didn't say anything, just moved back away from her. The music transcription had come to an end and the needle was swishing around the spindle. He said, "Record's done, Hazel," and she scrambled for the next talking disc, couldn't find the hole with her trembling fingers, and finally he took it from her and slid it down on the spindle. He picked up the stylus and dropped the needle at random. There was Stoner again, talking out of context, starting with a blip in the middle of a sentence.

"It's the wrong cut!" she screamed. "Goddammit, what's wrong with you, you've put it on the wrong cut!"

"That doesn't matter much now, does it?"

She stared at the transcription and let it run. Her panic seemed to ebb as she thought about what to do next; then, like a vat filling up, it came back again.

"I swear we didn't do it. You've got to believe that, Jordan, we'd never do anything against our country. This was Peter's fault. Peter and George were the ones doing it."

"Doing what?"

"They were spies, of course. We were duping them. Pretending to be their friends so we could get evidence against them."

"Evidence of what?"

"Oh, don't act foolish, I know you're smarter than that. The Nazis were going to land saboteurs here on the coast. Just like in New York and Florida. They were going to come in from a submarine on a rubber raft . . ."

She had lost her breath. She doubled over and breathed into her hands.

"It's all right, Hazel," he said softly. "You don't have to tell me anything."

"Of course I do. How else are you going to tell the police how it was with us? I need you to tell them, Jordan. How it was Peter who was doing it."

"Then tell me about it. What was Peter doing?"

"He was going to talk them ashore and then help them hide their stuff. They would have bombs, poison, nitroglycerin . . . and lots of money. Lots and lots of U.S. cash. We heard they were going to bring in fifty thousand dollars with them. And they'd need a place to hide . . . until they could get inland, where it would be safer."

She looked faint, like the poor dead German girl. He could see the blood pounding in her neck.

"Oh, I can tell you so much. Then you'll know what we've been through. What heroes we are. This was just the first stop. The Nazis have got a whole chain of safe houses all over the country. Once they got ashore, God knows where they'd go. And Peter was going to talk them in."

"What does that mean?"

"It was all in the station breaks. If the coast guard was out he would say, 'Correct eastern wartime is twelve thirty' . . . whatever time it was. If the coast was clear he'd say it the other way. 'It's twelve thirty, eastern wartime.' Vary it from week to week so it wouldn't be obvious."

"And the skipper of a jerry sub could pick up the signal a hundred miles out at sea."

She had begun to cry again. "We were going to report them. I swear to you, Jordan, you've got to believe that."

"Sure," he said. "There's only one thing wrong with that, Hazel. It wasn't Peter who was on the air. It was Gus."

She shook her head.

"It was Gus. He's a killer. He kills anything that moves if it gets in his way. He killed Carnahan and Kendall, Peter and the German girl. And you knew that. You had to have known it. Jesus Christ, Hazel, do you love him that much?"

Anger flared in the fear. "What the hell do you know about love? He's done everything for me, everything. If it weren't for him I'd've died like Margaret, forty years ago."

They looked at each other for a moment as the realization washed over him. "Jesus, you're the sister . . . you're the missing sister."

She leaped at him with the news spike and jammed it into his shoulder. He hurled her away. She banged against the turntable and the needle zipped and jumped and zipped again. Stoner's voice clicked from the monitor.

"It's two o'clock, eastern wartime . . . eastern wartime . . . eastern wartime . . ."

"I hope he kills you! You and that bitch who defiled Margaret on the air!"

Dulaney chilled. His skin was tingly and numb as the second realization hit him. *He's going after Rue.*

He bolted for the door. Behind him he could hear Hazel screaming into the microphone. "Run, Jan, run, he's coming to get you!"

By the time he reached his car she was sobbing on the air, with long stretches of mindless screaming.

(((21)))

HALF a mile from the station he plowed his car into a sandbank. Careening up the long hill he hit some wet sand and spun out, went over the dune, and rolled. The car stopped on its side with a sickening crunch.

He crawled out through the passenger door and ran. Behind him the wheels spun in the air and Hazel shrieked madness on the radio.

He ran. Oh Christ, he ran.

Little Rue. He didn't even know where she lived. All he had to go by was what he'd heard. Two hours ago they were going to the Sandbar.

Past the hotel. Wild thoughts of stopping and using the phone. Calling the sheriff, calling the Sandbar. But he couldn't make himself slow down and the hotel slipped away in the night.

Down the long straightaway into town, his feet making flat clip-clop sounds on the wet empty road. Town socked in in the fog. Like running in a cloud. A faint glow ahead promising an end but never getting any brighter. Past the road where Pauline lived. Not far now.

Forever.

The neon sign floated in the soup. Sandbar. Only a few cars outside. Inside, no one he knew. He stood near the door, quaking with fear and rage, wheezing the wind back into his lungs.

He asked at the bar. The party had broken up forty minutes ago. Forty minutes. He tried calling Becky from the pay phone but her line was busy.

Out on the road, running again. Past the illuminated dig at the Harford building, south across the town to Becky's house.

Her car was there but the house was dark. He walked around it banging on the windows. Nobody home. How could that be? He stood in the soft sand and wondered what to do next.

A voice on the wind. Somebody talking, out in the soup.

Two voices, down on the beach . . . Becky, talking with one of the New York actors. He heard Blake say something and as he came closer he knew they were doing a post-mortem on the Boer show, trying to dope out what went wrong. Figure how Jordan had lost his mind. He heard her say, "It's as if he just . . . snapped."

He put his gun down on the hard sand. No good would come of it if she saw it. There they were, two shapes in the glow of a flashlight.

"Becky . . ."

They stopped talking. He sensed a chill in them.

"I tried to call you. Your line was busy."

"I'm on a party line," she said coldly.

"Where's Rue?"

"What do you want with her? Haven't you done enough to her tonight?"

He said, "Her life's in danger," and that sounded crazy even to him.

He thought if he could just get it said in one clear sentence they'd have to believe him. But there was no such sentence.

"The Boer story was real. The kid in it . . . not a kid anymore . . . still a killer. Been here for years. Worked for

Germany because he hated the British. You read the script, you know why. He killed March Flack. You know why. Killed Carnahan, Kendall, Peter. Now he'll kill Rue."

She said nothing. He tried again. "I changed the script to drive him mad. I thought he'd come after me alone."

He tried to see her in the gloom. "Becky . . . it's Gus."

"No." She backed away. "I don't believe it."

"It's Gus. If I don't find her, he's going to kill her."

"Gus loves Rue. He'd never hurt her."

Dulaney looked at Blake, a shadow in the light. "Will somebody for Christ's sake help me? He's going to kill her."

"She was with us," Blake said. "She just went home a few minutes before you got here. She's probably still on the beach, walking."

"Do you know where she lives?"

Blake nodded. "Some of the actors were supposed to go up there . . . to celebrate . . . if the play had gone well."

"Don't tell him," Becky said. "Don't tell him anything else."

"I've got to," Blake said. "I can't help it. I played that part and I believe him."

"Jesus, you're both crazy."

"Maybe so. But I played that part and it was almost like he'd crawled inside me. Even in the dress I could feel him there, watching me from the booth. Then when we were on the air . . . I'll never forget those eyes. At the break I looked in his eyes and it was all I could do to get through it."

"I'm calling the police."

When she had gone, Blake said, "Do you know where Surfside Road is?"

It was at the edge of town; he had passed it a hundred times and never really seen it. "She's on the upper floor," Blake said. "I don't know the number. I think it's on her mailbox."

Dulaney felt his way back to the gun. He heard Blake's voice, shaky now, off in the dark. "Do you want me to come with you?"

"No. That's okay."

Blake wouldn't be much help if he had to ask.

((22))

HE ran back along the road; then, as the town began to appear, he slowed to a creeping walk. The fog was spotty here, with long half-clear stretches that might help him or hurt. He wasn't sure of anything.

He saw the apartment house a hundred yards ahead, first as a dim shape in the mist, then a new building of steel and whitewashed cinder blocks, two stories with stairs on both ends and long outer walks, like a motor court, on each floor. There were six apartments up and six down—three in a row, then a breaking hall running through the building to the opposite side, then the other three. He stood off at a distance and tried to decide what he should do. He knew he was dealing with a crack shot, one who could pop him with a rifle from almost any distance.

There was no ground cover in the front, and an outside light shone down on the yard and the passing road and the path up from the beach. He couldn't see the back of it without either crossing in the open or circling around and coming up from behind. For a moment he stood still; then he pushed at his indecisiveness and moved along the south side, just within the ring of darkness that reached around the outer edge of the building.

It was better in back: there were trees and scruffy island underbrush and a footpath. He could see most of the front from there, on across the highway to the short sandy hills facing the beach. The lights were out in all the upper-floor apartments—either she had come home and gone straight to bed or she hadn't yet come up from the beach. He moved north along the path and tried to get a better view of the road. Then several things happened at once. A car passed. In the glare of the headlights something shiny caught his eye. And almost in the same instant Rue appeared on the path from the beach.

He moved on north and his worst fear came suddenly true. What he had seen in the woods was Stoner's truck, pulled far off the road and hidden as much as possible between two trees. The hood was cold. He was out here somewhere and he'd been here awhile, waiting.

Dulaney scanned the surroundings and anything was possible, nothing was clear. A new patch of fog had rolled in and Rue looked like a spirit in a bad movie, willowy and fluid, out of focus. She started across the road and Dulaney felt a prickly creepiness as she walked over in full view. He couldn't move, couldn't call out—afraid Stoner would kill her at once if he did—all he could do was hold still and hope she'd make it on into her apartment.

She went under the overhang and stopped, came out leafing through her mail, started up the stairs, stopped, and read something in the glare of the hanging lights. Dulaney shivered and closed his eyes. When he opened them she had not moved, and suddenly a new thought hit him. *He's not out here at all . . . he's inside the apartment.*

Nothing else made sense if his intent was to kill her. And if it's both of us he wants, here we are, why doesn't he shoot? Dulaney had taken a step into the light and now he took another. His heart pounded with fear for both of them, but still no gunshot, no blinding, searing, snuffing finish. He heard her shoes click on the stairs as she started up again, and he ran along the edge of the building, in full view of the sandbank and the road and the trees to the north, but hidden from the landing and the apartment.

Up the back way, creeping, the gun in his hand.

She was on the landing now, coming his way. He took the stairs two at a time and his eyes broke over the top as she walked past the three apartments in the first row. She didn't see him yet, she was still shuffling through her mail as she walked, and he made no noise as he came onto the landing and stood up straight at the end of the walk. He held the gun down at his leg so she wouldn't see it and then her eyes came up and met his and she stopped, startled, and he touched his finger to his lips and motioned her back with his free hand. She stood there a moment, confused, unsure after the events of the evening whether he was a friend or not. She took a breath as if to speak. Again he shushed her, with a wide-eyed frantic movement of his fingers to his lips. She stepped toward him and he waved her back too late: in that jumbled half second he knew he had miscalculated again, that Stoner was not in the apartment but in the darkness of the crossing hall. She passed before it and he was upon her, looping a rope around her neck and jerking her off her feet. Dulaney must have yelled: Stoner whipped around and had her between them, her mail flying and the rope cutting into her neck as Dulaney rushed them. He could see Stoner's gun tucked in his belt—he'd have to let her go to get at it, but no, he was strong, able to wrap the rope around his one hand and hold her up while he went for the gun with the other. Dulaney swung and the gun butt cracked against Stoner's head. His own hands grabbed at the rope and pulled her free, and as she fell he saw Stoner's gun coming up and he fired, twice.

Stoner rolled over and a pool of blood spread out under his head.

Dulaney kicked the gun away. He turned to Rue but she cried out and shrank away from him, terrified.

"It's all right," he said. "It's all right now."

But she wouldn't let him come near.

Up and down the apartment row lights were coming on. Down in the yard he saw the sheriff's car just pulling in.

"The sheriff's here," he said. "It's all right now. I'll go down and get him."

But he went down the back way and disappeared into the trees.

He ran north. In time, and with distance, he walked. He tried to think of other things and shake himself free of the man he had killed.

The town slipped away and the road went on. It was two o'clock by the clock in his head: a perfect night for a landing. The coast was clear, not a mountie in sight, and the beach all gray with the covering fog. Hitler could land an army here this morning, if he'd had a little army to spare. If he hadn't invaded Russia and tried to fight all his wars at once. If his spies hadn't all died.

Hitler was finished, done in by his own evil and arrogance and greed. It was the first time Dulaney had allowed himself to believe it. Hitler's clock was ticking.

He climbed the big dune for the last time and the lights of the tower appeared to his left. He could see shapes moving in the fuzzy glow of the parking lot . . . cars, people, and something flashing like an ambulance. He stood still for a long time and he knew it wasn't safe, but the tug on his heart was powerful and deep. His life had been changed but he was leaving as he had come, uncertain and alone on a foggy night.

His car was just as he'd left it. The motor still ran, the wheels still spun, and on the radio someone had put on an ominous piano interlude.

Clair de Lune.

The piano faded and a voice came over the air. "And now WHAR comes to the end of its broadcast day . . ."

Kidd, doing his own sign-off. And what a day it had been.

Dulaney shut down the engine. Tugged at the trunk and gave it up.

He would leave the dresses and the shoes and all the odds and ends of their short life together. Take only his watch and the postcard, a little money, and the clothes on his back. And the water-stained photograph he had found in Sadler.

The picture was more than a personal treasure. It would help him find her.

Now she must be found. He had defied her curse and had broken it. She must be told.

He would start in Seattle. But he knew she might be anywhere.

It didn't matter. He would find her.

He turned west and started up the long incline to the bridge. There was a moment in the breaking fog when he almost saw the lights of the town. He stopped on the bridge and a new gathering of spirits rose up from the creek . . . Livia and Rue and Harford and Kidd and Maitland and Ali and Eli and Becky and Waldo.

And Stoner . . . Stoner . . . that poor haunted bastard Stoner.

He looked again and the land was gray. The town and the people had vanished, as if in a dream.

((•))

CODA

THE story of Jordan Ten Eyck ends there, on a bridge covered by fog in the third year of the war. His name was never again heard on anyone's air, and with him into the night went the man once known as Jack Dulaney.

Dulaney never wrote another book or answered to any crime. His name was quickly forgotten, except by a few, including, perhaps, an old lady in South Carolina, who died in 1951.

Several attempts were made to write the story of what had happened at Harford's radio station in the summer of 1942. Gerald Marshall Palmer had a story in the *New York Times*, a narrative that finally linked Ten Eyck to Dulaney, that told of his escape from a California road gang and traced him to his roots in Charleston. But Palmer was a critic at heart, far more interested in the creative fountainhead that occasionally, out of nowhere, will produce a Jordan Ten Eyck, than in aspects of the story that might have had more appeal to a police reporter.

In March 1943 the *Beachcomber* ran a piece, blending the facts unearthed by Palmer with startling information that had just come to light. Police in Pennsylvania, acting on a request from New Jersey, had searched the house formerly owned by the well-remembered singer Miss Holly O'Hara, and had found the remains of a missing actor, Marty Kendall, in a crawl space. Because of the origin of the information—a tidbit revealed by a radio actress then confined to the state asylum for the insane—neither Miss O'Hara nor Jack Dulaney was considered a suspect. Said the sheriff: "We still want to talk to them both. Miss O'Hara was apparently living in a New York tenement where a man fell to his death last year, and we'd like to see Dulaney for obvious reasons. But I'm not holding my breath waiting for either of them to come in."

The *Beachcomber* would continue to recap the story every year or two, until economics forced it out of business in 1957.

In 1962 a book was published, telling of Hitler's plans to set up a sabotage ring in the United States during the war. The Stoner affair, as it had come to be known in the press, was given a colorful chapter. But the focus was on the two landings that had actually been accomplished, in Florida and New York, and on the constitutional questions surrounding the extraordinary secret trial of the eight saboteurs—two of them American citizens—and the immediate executions of six. What might have been planned in New Jersey, but was never carried out, was left to speculation.

In 1968 the story was revived again, this time by a magazine with *New Yorker* ambitions: a long article, perhaps twenty thousand words, spread across an entire issue, written in a chic style, variously called metafiction, new journalism, or bullshit, depending on who was asked. The reporter had conducted rambling interviews, sometimes stretching over several days, with most of the principals still alive; then he tried to reconstruct what must have happened, from all the diverse viewpoints. A tricky business, given the vagaries of human nature, but a technique that always reads well in the hands of a skilled wordsmith.

It was effective on several levels, especially in its depiction of radio as a central character rather than mere background. Radio drama had been gone from the national scene for years by then, and this gave it a certain appeal to readers who thought they longed for the simple innocence of those quaint and easy good old days. Old days always look simple and innocent to those who have not lived through them.

Amazing how fast it all went away. How something so big and vital could have been reduced to a theater of babbling deejays and bloated, self-important talk show hosts. In just a few years radio as they knew it was finished. Harford died and his station was sold and sold again. By 1955 it was called WROK, the Big Rock, and a new generation of very different radio people, none of them older than thirty, sat in the upstairs slot, playing rock-and-roll records, talking over their music, saying nothing at great length, filling the air with nonstop noise.

In the end the article tried to follow Harford's people into their lives after radio. A few had kept in touch but eventually they drifted apart. "I can't believe how important we were to each other," said Rue Nicholas, now living in Connecticut. "How can people be that important to each other and then just disappear?"

Perhaps it was only radio that had held them together.

In the early fifties the older ones began dying off, beginning with Maitland and Stallworth. Kidd went into early television. Hazel ended her days in an institution. Rue married a producer at Columbia, retired from the profession, and had three children. Her old boyfriend Jimmy Brinker had gone into the army with no special status, giving up his claim to conscientious objection. He came home with a Purple Heart and had a good acting career in Hollywood. Occasionally he crossed paths with Ali Marek, who got some calls when black faces were needed but was seldom offered anything better.

Waldo died in 1958. Eli marched in Selma and was arrested many times. That same year, 1965, Becky Hart joined the Peace Corps, and was still, at that writing, somewhere in Africa.

Everyone accounted for but Jordan and Livia. Livia had left the island with her two boys in 1946, and no one ever heard from her again.

ON a hot day in 1971, a large truck turned into the drive and pulled up in the north parking lot. The two men wore cowboy hats and the sounds of horses could be heard from the back of the truck. The young man, who might have been thirty or as old as forty, opened the back of the truck to check on the horses. The older man, gray bearded and much larger, walked around the building and went inside. A young receptionist looked up from her switchboard and said, "May I help you, sir?" and he told her he just wanted to look around. "I used to work here."

He left after a few minutes. Not much of it was the same. The picnic area was gone and the big studio downstairs had been ripped out and replaced by meeting rooms. You don't need a studio like that if all you're going to do is play records.

As they drove away the young man said, "Well, how was it?"

The older man shook his head and held his peace.

The changes went far beyond the station. The road into the island was a four-laner now, with houses off in the trees, an occasional gas station, and even an A & P down near the bridge. The bridge itself was a shining thing of steel and cement, and the town had spread, engulfing the radio station and filling the dunes with houses.

They drove south along the coast. The changes were vast, sweeping, total. Forests turned into amusement parks. Chain motels, a new freeway, a never-ending run of townships and suburbs.

"Stop here," the older man said.

He got out and walked, across the railroad tracks and the frontage road. He was standing in the middle of a shopping center parking lot. After a while the younger man came up to join him.

"He's buried here," the old man said. "I can't tell where exactly. But someplace right about here."

He took off his cowboy hat and mopped his brow. "Let's get the hell out of here. I want to get these horses off this truck."

Ringer was the name he went by now. After racing under that name for many years in the West, he had decided to try his luck at the small tracks in West Virginia, Maryland, and Rhode Island. He had done well. His specialty was the bad-legged claimer, breathing new life into the old horse that everyone else thought was finished.

He had made some money but he didn't like the East anymore. Next year he might actually try California. No one was looking for him now.

He had sent most of the horses on with the others. It was a three-day drive, and each night they stopped at a public stable and bedded down, and in the morning they were on the road again.

The radio was full of reports from Vietnam. Three hundred old men and children had been massacred at a place called My Lai. It had been covered up for a year. A man named Calley was taking the blame for it, but there were disturbing reports that the massacre had been ordered by officers who wanted a large body count.

"Nothing ever changes," the older man said. "People are the same all over."

"It's a good thing I was never called up," said the young man. "I swear to God I'd go to Canada before I'd fight in this goddamn war."

"In some ways it's like the Boer War. A powerful, arrogant country goes where it shouldn't. Thinks it can win in a month. Then gets sick of it when the boys come home in bags. We never seem to learn anything."

They drove out of Kansas, into Nebraska. At some point the young man said, "Well, did you get it out of your system?"

The older man laughed.

"I imagine it would've been easier if Mamma had come with you."

"No. She had the good sense not to."

They were pushing it now. They reached the racetrack, Ak-Sar-Ben, just before dark.

"I'll get the horses out," the older man said. "You go on to the apartment and tell your mother we're here."

By nine o'clock his chores were done. He sat alone in the tack room, surrounded by his present, lost in his past. It happened to him a dozen times a week . . . he'd be shoeing a horse or standing on the backstretch rail with a stopwatch in his hand and suddenly his spirit was in another time and place, a cornfield of microphones, a world of soundstages and production rooms and the boundless energy of stories without sight. A thousand creative possibilities crossed his mind. If his new world was steady, his old one was as infinite as the universe.

He heard a noise out in the shedrow: her voice as she stopped to fondle the old saddle pony. He was aware of her in the doorway, saw her shadow as she moved into the light, felt her hands on his shoulders. "You sentimental old bugger," she said, and he laughed and leaned over and kissed her hand.

She joined him there and they sat drinking the beer she'd brought. She said nothing more, left him to his thoughts. She knew where he had gone, and she was still beside him long minutes later, when his mind came back to the here and now. He stared at the picture on the wall, a framed him-and-her shot, taken at the ranch they had bought in Idaho. The camera had caught them at sunset, their faces in silhouette. A gift from their son, who had inscribed it with his favorite lines, from the poet Thomas Hornsby Ferril. *Beyond the sundown is tomorrow's wisdom. Today is going to be long, long ago.*

HISTORICAL NOTES

MORE than twenty-eight thousand Boer women and children died in Kitchener's camps. As many as twenty-two thousand British boys came home in coffins.

One of the central characters was based in part on the early life of Fritz Duquesne, as described by Clement Wood in his 1932 biography, *The Man Who Killed Kitchener.*

Ireland remained neutral throughout Hitler's war. Churchill was outraged when the Irish closed their ports to British convoy escorts. Dublin was sometimes described as a nest of German spies.

Dark Silver was a racehorse in the author's own life.

Jack Dulaney's radio show is obviously inspired by *Destination Freedom,* Richard Durham's groundbreaking series on WMAQ, Chicago. Durham was a black writer of great artistic courage who needed no guiding white hand to produce his powerful scripts.

ABOUT THE AUTHOR

John Dunning, acclaimed writer, bibliophile, radio expert, and passionate student of the mystery novel, is the Nero Wolfe Award–winning author of *Booked to Die* and *The Bookman's Wake* (a *New York Times* Notable Book of 1995), finalist for the Edgar and the Gold Dagger, and winner of the Colorado Book Award. These books have been translated into a half-dozen languages and were bestsellers in Japan.

Dunning, in his own words, "splits his time between hunting books and writing them." He owned the Old Algonquin Bookstore in Denver from 1984 to 1994 and is a well-known figure in the world of antiquarian books. Today he continues to sell rare books on the Internet at http://www.abbooks.com/home/OLDALGON and travels to tradeshows as a member of the Antiquarian Booksellers Association of America.

In preparing *Two O'Clock, Eastern Wartime,* Dunning relied upon his other great passion: old-time radio. A nationally recognized expert, he is the author of the definitive work on the subject. *On the Air: The Encyclopedia of Old-Time Radio* was published in 1998 by Oxford University Press. For many years, Dunning was the host of the weekly Denver radio show "Old-Time Radio," and he has appeared on National Public Radio on the subject of radio, book collecting, and literature. An advocate for the preservation of classic broadcast entertainment, the author has a personal archive of high-quality tapes of some 40,000 shows.

Born in 1942 and educated in the Charleston, South Carolina, public schools, Dunning decided to pursue his writing career early on. By his own admission a "hard knocks story," this career took many turns, each of which provided the author with fantastic material for his fiction. Beginning as a glass cutter in the late 1950s, Dunning soon found himself working as a racetracker in Colorado and California and as a horse trainer in Idaho (the track lifestyle makes an important appearance in *Two O'Clock, Eastern Wartime*). On the strength of his natural writing ability, Dunning became a reporter for the *Denver Post*, a position he held through the late 1960s and early 1970s. During this time he also worked freelance, including a stint as the campaign press secretary for U.S. Representative Pat Schroeder. In the 1980s, Dunning was the book editor of *This Week in Denver*, a biweekly city magazine. Since the publication of *Booked to Die* in 1992, the author has focused upon writing his unique brand of thrillers. He is married to Helen Dunning and is the father of two grown children. Today he lives in Denver, Colorado.

Visit
❖ **Pocket Books** ❖
online at

www.SimonSays.com

Keep up on the latest new
releases from your favorite
authors, as well as author
appearances, news, chats,
special offers and more.

SIMON & SCHUSTER
A VIACOM COMPANY
www.SimonSays.com

Pocket
Books

2381-01